I0604907

ELDRITCH, INC.

A Novel

1st in the <u>Michael Yeager</u> Series

CHRISTOPHER D. OCHS

Anigrafx, LLC
Emmaus, PA

<u>RIGHTS</u>

<u>Eldritch, Inc.</u>
Copyright © 2024 Christopher D. Ochs
All rights reserved.

ISBN-13: 978-0-9981726-3-7
Library of Congress Control Number: 2024922388

Editors: Anigrafx, LLC
Interior Design, Formatting: Anigrafx, LLC
Cover Production: getcovers.com
Published by: Anigrafx, LLC
Printed by: Ingram Spark

No portion of this book may be reproduced, stored in a retrieval system, or transmitted in any form or by any means—electronic, mechanical, photocopy, recording, or any other—except for brief excerpts in printed reviews, without prior permission in writing from the author.

No portion of this book may be used in any manner for the purpose of training artificial intelligence technologies or systems.

This book is a work of fiction. All incidents and dialogue, and all characters with the exception of some well-known historical figures and events, are products of the author's imagination and are not to be construed as real. Where real-life historical figures and events appear, the situations, incidents, and dialogues concerning those persons are entirely fictional and are not intended to depict actual events or to change the entirely fictional nature of the work. In all other respects, any resemblance to actual persons, living or dead, events, or locales is entirely coincidental.

ALSO BY THE AUTHOR

Novels

Pindlebryth of Lenland – The Five Artifacts
Epic Fantasy of Beastly Proportions
My Friend Jackson
A Nightmare of Revenge

Collections

If I Can't Sleep, You Can't Sleep
Bedtime Reading to Inflict on Naughty Children

Anthologies

Meanwhile in the Middle of Eternity
Spellbinding Tales of the Past, Present & Future

Once Upon A Time
Untethered
Fur, Feathers & Scales
Element of Mystery
Season's Readings
Sweet, Funny and Strange Tales

GLVWG Writes Stuff
Write Here, Write Now
The Write Connections
Rewriting the Past
Writing Across America

<u>ACKNOWLEDGMENTS</u>

Many thanks to all the friends and professionals who have assisted me in this project:

<u>Beta Readers</u>

Rachel Arney
Tyler Chapman
Tom Epstein
Charles Kiernan
D. T. Krippene
Karl G. Monroe
Susan K. Monroe
Dianna Sinovic
Laura Trexler

<u>Critique Partners</u>

Charles Kiernan
D. T. Krippene
Bethlehem Writers Group

<u>References</u>

Elinor Gates, Ph.D.
    Lick Observatory, Mount Hamilton, CA
Cora Monroe
    NY Aquarium, Brooklyn, NYC, NY

<u>DEDICATION</u>

To Nix-Nutz, Pochi, and Snickers: the rescues who rescued me.
Thanks for helping me regain and keep my sanity.

ELDRITCH, INC.

CHAPTER 1

My hand slipped into my windbreaker's pocket for the umpteenth time to reassure myself Sindhu's medicine was still there. She had called, concerned that a flareup was building. I could hear her fatigue and wheezing over the phone. Small wonder her lupus hit now, with all the pressure she was under.

I skidded into the parking lot of Lick Observatory a few minutes shy of two o'clock in the morning. With the lot mostly empty, I took pleasure in taking the space reserved for the facility director. Yeah, a real iconoclastic no-holds-barred rebel, that's me.

During the hour-long charge up Mount Hamilton Road, my abused Chrysler K-car threatened to blow a gasket. After I shut off the engine, it dieseled itself into an uneasy dream steeped in burnt motor oil and blue exhaust.

I surveyed the Lick Refractor's dome at the south end of the building. It yawned wide open with wisps of light emanating from within, a sure sign that the crew had hunkered down to serious work.

Unlocking the front security door, I shuffled past the lobby's over-sized digital clock, displaying:

01:55 PST   08:55 GMT   06/16/86

Their reminder of the ungodly hour renewed my sour mood. Any self-respecting biochemistry major who just had his doctoral thesis shredded to bits should be drowning his sorrows in a bottle of cheap tequila before last call. Or ralphing it into the streets of San Jose. Instead, I'm slumming it as a gofer for my fiancée and her astronomer coworkers.

Stomping up the half-story staircase to the observatory floor, I fidgeted with Sindhu's prescription bottle one last time for good measure. I was toying with the idea of handing it over, then leaving to pick up where I left off on my bottle of tequila when she opened the observation dome's entrance.

Wearing her blue and gold UCSC lacrosse sweatshirt hanging loose over hiking shorts, she greeted me with a wan smile and a cough.

I handed Sindhu her bottle of corticosteroids as my eyes probed her face. The telltale lupus butterfly rash across her nose and under her tortoise-shell glasses darkened her mahogany complexion. "Did we catch the flareup in time?"

"I think so." She welcomed me with a peck on the cheek and a mug of coffee. "Here, you'll be needing this."

Accepting the first by returning her perfunctory kiss, I quaffed the second with gusto. Ah, coffee—the life's blood of many a post-grad. And somehow, this band of star-jockeys' java was always top-notch. Tonight, they had my favorite.

"Why's that?" My words puffed out Sumatran steam.

"Tonight's the big night, and it's going to be a long one for all of us."

"If you knew it was crunch time, why'd you forget your meds?"

"What can I say?" she said between wheezes. "I thought I had them with me."

She popped a pill, downing it with a gulp from my mug.

"You sure you're okay?"

"I will be in a minute." Taking me by the hand, she pulled me into the circular telescope room. A blast of mountain air poured down from directly above, and I peered through the open dome at the night sky. Dim operations lights struggled to fill the expansive area of sterile concrete, linoleum, and steel. Even so, the space almost didn't look big enough to house the Lick Refractor, as her coworkers busied themselves around its cylindrical base.

Sindhu must have noticed a frown screwed on my kisser, or something equally petulant. She leaned forward, scrutinizing my face as we walked. Squinting fiercely, she said, "I know that look. What's wrong?"

"I don't understand why I'm on this project. I'm just doing odd jobs and running errands for you guys. I feel like a fifth wheel."

With a sympathetic pout, she said, "I can understand that. I don't think *any* PhD candidate would be too pleased doing teaching-assistant level grunt work." She gave my non-coffee'd hand a squeeze. "But I get the feeling that's only part of it. What's *really* got you down?"

I dreaded this moment. My shoulders slumped, and I tried to coax the stubborn last drop from my mug. "Nothin'."

"Bullshit." We stopped at a cart crammed with coffee supplies, two pounds of whole bean Sumatran, and freshly ground heaven brewing in an espresso machine that someone had smuggled out of Cuba. "Spill it, Michael."

Using that name meant she was serious. I bared my soul, if only to get the thought of her scolding me with "Michael *Avery* Yeager" out of my head.

"My dissertation defense got torpedoed. My doctorate's down the crapper."

"Oh, no..." Sindhu's fingertips flashed to her mouth. "How? What happened?" She shook her head with a vigorous snarl. "Never mind that— who do I kick in the nuts?!"

It was scary how quickly Sindhu could flip on the Mama Bear switch.

I intended to make it quick—a short, sharp, shock; a quick ripping off of the Band-Aid; all that get-it-over-with-quick jazz. I failed miserably. Everything spilled out, in full color and agonizing detail. With each sentence, I became more hot-tempered, more resentful, and maybe a little paranoid. I could almost feel an aneurysm ballooning inside my noggin. Taking a deep breath, I fast-forwarded to the dénouement.

"I was wrapping up my defense of developing a genetic editing technique, all of which is feasible using existing technology, when Dr. Escoffier, the fucking *Chair* of the Biology Department—who hasn't attended a dissertation since Moses—interrupted my closing. He practically ordered the review board to deny my dissertation. A 'wish list of dreams from a Sears Christmas catalog,' he called it!"

My near-screech caught the attention of everyone. Gary Unwin looked up from the scope eyepiece to glower at me. Cheryl Greenbough, the team's computer tech jockey, poked her head out of the scope's base, a Phillips screwdriver in one hand, a gang of wires in the other, and concern on her face. Even team leader Dr. Petrakis managed to tear his concentration away from his digital test bench to gawk through the equipment room's window at me. His momentary surprise reverted to his usual crooked and curious grin.

I had learned to resent that ever-present smile—the type that preceded the punchline of a terrible joke, the type that taunted, "I know something you don't."

Sindhu shooed her coworkers' inquiring looks away with a wave of her hand and an apologetic, "It's okay."

"Ever since getting raked over the coals this afternoon, I've been trying to decide what to do about it. Do I write another conclusion I *know* is wrong, but will get me the stupid degree? Trash the whole thing and spend who-knows-how-long to write up another paper? Pull up stakes and transfer to another—"

"Don't you *dare*!" Sindhu spluttered, jabbing her index finger at the ground. "You're needed right here."

"Am I? Remember what I said about being a fifth wheel? I'm doing nothing constructive here. Everyone is so tight-lipped about this project, I still don't know what you guys are trying to accomplish. I feel like the janitor in a secret laboratory." I shot an angry glance at Sindhu she didn't deserve. She returned a knowing smile more unsettling than Petrakis'. "Wait, you're not doing anything with the CIA, or something gonzo like that?"

"Of course not," she replied with a sardonic grimace that told me I was being ridiculous. "But you *are* needed here. I have a half-hour on the scope while Gary takes a break..." She wrapped my arm in her own and squeezed tight. "...and I need some company that won't talk my ear off with shop."

"In case you haven't picked up my vibe already, I don't think I'll be the best company tonight."

"You let *me* be the judge of that." Sindhu sat in the scope's observation chair, flipped her glasses on top of her head, and snuggled up to the eyepiece. She adjusted the focusing knobs without looking at them, like they were an extension of her body. "And there she is, my queen of the night sky."

I eyed Sindhu up, down, and once more for good measure. I repeated her words to her with heartfelt fondness. And maybe a pinch of lechery, to boot. Who could blame a guy? Between Sindhu's project ramping up to a pitch fever and all my attention focused on my dissertation, we hadn't been together for almost a whole month. Our schedules demanded that both of us sleep with half an empty bed.

"Aw, you're sweet."

"No, I mean it. You always seem so happy—so blissful—when you're stargazing."

She raised her left hand, waving its diamond ring toward the sound of my voice. "Not as much as when I gaze at *this* star." She glanced away from the scope, giving me the once over as well, tinted with her own hint of yearning. "Or at my handsome *Mrgav-yadha*."

My heart melted, just as stupidly and sloppily as the first time she had compared me to the brightest star in the night sky, Sirius.

She returned her attention to her telescope. However, all my thoughts of romance were crowded out by worry. I had spent the last of my money on the deposit for our engagement ring. With my degree in shambles, the jobs I had lined up were on hold—assuming they'd still exist by the time I concocted *Plan B*.

So I did what any red-blooded American boy would do in a crisis like this.

I panicked.

"Sindhu, let's elope."

CHAPTER 2

"What?—*Ow*!" Rubbing her eye after having jammed it against the scope's eyepiece, she scowled at me in disbelief. "What are you talking about? We can't do that. Mom would blow her top."

"To heck with Harini," I said. "I know she's given us the thumbs up—but in word only, it seems. Every time we try to get together with her, she always has an excuse. An important business meeting one week, then her biggest customer has a shit-fit the next week, her ex's family is suing her again the next—"

"That's no surprise. She runs Yakshini Herbal Health all by herself."

I puffed out a chortle, as I did every time I heard that goofy name. "I'll never understand why your family chose that name for an organic supplement company."

"Why not? They're Hindu spirits of nature and prosperity. Why did Nike choose a goddess of victory for their brand? As for *Yakshini*, it's definitely a better choice than naming a car line Saturn, after some Roman god who ate his kids."

"Getting back to the main point, we'll die of old age before we float to the top of your mom's calendar. Either that, or the real reason we can't get her attention is that her approval isn't all that heartfelt."

"Don't be ridiculous. She *loves* you. She's already started planning the—"

"And that's another thing. Neither of us wants a big, traditional, invite-half-of-New-Delhi type wedding." I clasped her hand in both of mine. I knelt again, just like when I proposed. "Once this project is done, how about we skip town for a weekend and make it official?"

The base of the scope rang with a slight tapping sound. Cheryl flashed a sheepish grin at us over the base.

I stood so fast, that my feet nearly lifted off the floor. My face felt redder than Sindhu's sudden butterfly blush.

"Sorry, lovebirds, but we're ready to go," said Cheryl. "As soon as I let Petrakis know I've finished reconnecting things at this end, Gary will want the captain's chair back." She shot us a petite wave, then walked away, leering coquettishly over her shoulder.

"I'm serious," I whispered to Sindhu. "Everything I had planned is shot, and my professional future is in free fall. I need to have something permanent. Something stable." I squeezed her hand tighter. "I need to know we'll be together—*forever*. We can zip to Mexico, Vegas, or get a local Justice, and get married tomorrow."

"Oh, all right," she said with a chuckle and a quick, tight hug. "If only to keep one of us from crying."

"As long as you don't mind being married to a burger-flipper for the next few months. You guys don't need me here anyway."

"Now you cut that talk out," she said with a thin-lipped smile. "I told you, you *are* needed here." Her grin quickly vanished. Grimacing in the direction of the equipment room, her turquoise eyes took on an intro-spective aspect. "I don't see the harm telling you, despite..."

She turned her attention back to me, exhaling a stern huff through pursed lips. "You're here because Dr. Petrakis specifically requested you."

I blinked. "Hunh? That doesn't make sense."

"I don't understand it either. He took a lot of flak from the univer-sity for not selecting the astronomy department's golden boy for the project."

I shot her a playful smirk. "I thought *you* were the astronomy department's top banana."

"I am, GPA-wise. And Gary's number two." Mama Bear was stir-ring again. "But you know how it is. Legacies, fraternities, and all that 'it's not *what* you know, but *who* you know' crap. Fortunately, Petrakis is on loan from some research facility, so he isn't drowning in departmental sub-terfuge."

"Well, I'm stumped. I've never set foot in any of his electrical engi-neering classes, and I can't see how any of this ties into my field of bio-chemistry. Even if he didn't want someone from the Astronomy Department, another student from Computer Science to pair up with Cheryl would be much better suited to your work than me. Not to mention my GPA—granted, it's *cum laude* material, but it ain't a perfect 4.0. Like someone I know..."

I gave her hand a quick kiss. "...who also happens to have a perfect 10.0 body to go with it."

"Down, boy," Sindhu said, returning my playful leer. She withdrew her hand and planted it on her hip, swiveling her chair in the direction of the electronics lab. "If you want to un-stump yourself, why don't you ask Dr. Petrakis himself?"

"I just may do that. I—" The epiphany hit me right between the eyes. I snapped my fingers with a vengeance. "Shit! *That's* why Escoffier nuked my dissertation—the Old Boy network. The Astronomy Chair must've pulled in a favor. That motherf—"

"University politics are a bitch." She planted another kiss, a heavy one that took me by surprise. When we came up for air, she regarded me with those mysterious turquoise eyes. "Whatever Petrakis' reasons were, *I'm* glad you're here, *Brahma bull*," she said with a breathy murmur that could melt candle wax.

I kissed her back. Not like the earlier pecks, nor another steamy osculation unfit for public display—just a somewhere-in-between but heartfelt smooch.

There are countless Hindu goddesses of love and beauty. I selected the one that best fit the moment. "And I'm glad you're here, too, *Rati Devi*." I said with a moon-eyed sigh. "What did I ever do to deserve you?"

"Your taste in fashion." She tweaked the drawstring on my college jacket.

"You know I can't afford Louis Vitton. But one day..."

With a flippant shrug, she continued. "And your self-abuse when you're depressed is so-o-o amusing." Then came her crinkly teasing smile. "Most of all, your heterochromia is so sciency-sexy."

And there went the romantic moment out the window. It's hard to notice from a distance, but up close, most people zero in on my eyes. My right eye is brown, the other a bright moss green. During my formative years, it was the major "*eww*" factor jinxing my social life. It wasn't until high school that it became merely an oddity. Even so, that early emotional scar runs deep, and the mention of it often gets my knee-jerk response of turning into a defensive grouch.

I blew a soft raspberry at my dearest.

Sindhu craned her head, peering into the electronics area. I followed suit. Petrakis hovered near the flip side of a circuit board as he soldered in a series of thumbnail-sized ICs at a fevered pace.

"...mmm, though I wouldn't ask him right now. He's busy replacing a bunch of op-amps that burned out just before you arrived, and we're against the clock." Sindhu chewed her lower lip. "I couldn't say why he chose you, but now that you're here, I might as well let you in on the big secret. Tonight's the night. We're hoping to observe a hexagon on the southern pole of Uranus."

And no, I didn't laugh. Like any dyed-in-the-wool astronomer, Sindhu pronounced the planet's name correctly—"*Your*-ahn-us."

"A hexagon?" I asked, intrigued.

"Yes." Sindhu's knees bounced in front of her in the chair. Her enthusiasm invariably bubbled to the top whenever astronomy was discussed. "Remember the hexagon Voyager photographed on Saturn's south pole in '81? Gary calculated Uranus has the right thermodynamics, atmosphere, and spin to form one, too."

I mouthed that jerk's name with a sneer. We all know the type— the sleaze who thinks he's God's gift to women. Four years ago, he tried to steal Sindhu away, but she turned him down flat. The egotistical lout still thought she somehow carried a torch for him. Not that I was worried. She easily held her own against him, and I certainly wasn't going to step in. That would only piss off Mama Bear at me, and give Gary the satisfaction of having gotten under my skin.

Cheryl returned, dragging a multicolored snake of wires behind her. She nodded a quick greeting before diving into the scope's base again. Behind her, wrapped in a fleece-lined bomber jacket, came Gary.

"She's all yours," said Sindhu. Hopping out of the observation seat, she leaned against my arm.

"What's so special about tonight?" I asked. "Isn't Uranus visible most of the time?"

"About one-half of the year. But unlike the other planets, Uranus spins on its side. For this one week, we have a direct view of its southern pole. A big weather front is moving in tomorrow, so it's tonight or nothing for another forty-two years."

His face welded to the scope's main eyepiece, Gary twiddled the constellation of knobs along with a foot-wide wheel that looked like it was stolen from the bridge of a midget Spanish galleon, he leaned back with a groan.

"We got Uranus on track, but even the Lick's resolution can barely focus on any features. The night air is almost done cooling, so turbulence might ease up later. I can make out the pole now, but not clear enough to see any features." He tilted his head back to apply a few eye drops. "It's a killer on the eyes. One second, I think I can see a hexagon there, then it flashes, and *poof…*"

After a quick rub, he planted his other eye against the eyepiece. "Without Petrakis' digital video rig, we won't be able to make anything out on the pole."

"Digital video?" I asked. "Is that what Petrakis is fixing?"

"Yup." Sindhu lowered her glasses back on and gazed through the dome opening. She clutched her arms close against herself and me as the waterfall of cool air continued pouring down. "It implements a bunch of mathematical operations—Fast Fourier and Hough transforms—"

"Clear as mud," I said with a scoff.

"It analyzes the video, then displays any edges or polygons it finds in real-time. If the hexagon is there, we'll see it on the screen."

From inside the base, Cheryl's voice warbled like an old radio broadcast. "We blew the video amps, driving them too hot." The two of us hopped a step back as Cheryl whipped the cable of wires, straightening them along the floor.

"Hey, Cheryl. When are we going to have the video recorder hooked up?" said Gary.

"Just a minute," groused Cheryl. "More hurry, less speed."

Gary leaned back again. After rubbing his tearing eyes, he beamed a hungry smile at Sindhu. "I need a fresh set of eyes. Maybe you can make it out better." He slid out of the observation chair, proffering it to her with a flourish.

Sindhu glided in. Slipping her glasses over her straight jet-black hair again, she adjusted the scope's focus.

"It's definitely there. But…" Her mouth contorted into a sideways question mark. "There's a weird texture, like it's filled with giant marbles. And… Whoa!" She jerked back, scrunching her eyes shut. Tears squeezed out of both eyes.

Gary inched nearer. His raised eyebrows betrayed that he wished he still was at the con. "You saw it? Like the hexagon brightened for a moment?"

"Yeah."

"That's *great*," he cheered, planting a hand on Sindhu's shoulder and spinning her chair to face him. "That deserves a kiss!"

Luring Gary in with a come-hither smile, she took his hand. Her masquerade flipped to a stern frown, and she bent his wrist back to a painful angle.

It gave a satisfying crack, and Gary whipped his hand away with a yelp. "Dammit, what was that for?"

Ignoring his complaint, Sindhu rose out of the chair. She feigned a coy smile at me and asked, "Mike, would you like to see the wonder of the decade?"

"No thanks, microscopes make me nauseous. Telescopes, too, I'm afraid. I'll wait for the video."

"A biologist who can't use a microscope?" Cheryl remarked, closing the maintenance hatch.

"Bio*chemist*," I corrected. "Not quite the same."

"We're wasting time," Gary grumbled while he nursed his wrist. "The whole night is shot if we don't get this on record."

I chuckled under my breath at the tear dawdling down his cheek. Mister Tough Guy should know better—look but don't touch, Buster.

"Keep your shirt on," quipped Cheryl. "The monitors and recorders are all hooked up. All we need is a signal."

The lot of us turned our heads in the direction of the electronics room. Petrakis was peering through a magnifying lens the size of a 45 RPM record, still slaving away at his soldering. Gary cupped his hands around his mouth and megaphoned his voice at him. "Doc better fix his doohickey quick."

Petrakis ignored him.

"Everyone keep calm," said Sindhu, pulling my arm. "We'll see if we can give him a hand."

We skirted our way around the scope's massive support pylon. I leaned close to Sindhu's ear. "Whaddya mean 'we?' I know zilch about electronics."

Satisfied his wrist wasn't broken, Gary set to swapping out the viewing optics for a boxy apparatus with an empty bay.

We nearly collided with Petrakis, jogging out of his electronics lab's labyrinth of chaos.

"Terribly sorry. I didn't see you." Petrakis timidly glanced at us as he scurried past.

Sindhu craned her neck to glimpse the oblong box in his hands. "Dr. Petrakis, is that your new CCD camera? I wish I had a chance to peek at its insides."

He two-stepped to a halt. "Why, yes—this is my baby. And I'm always changing its *diopters*. Ha!"

Sindhu rolled her eyes and groaned.

Dressed in a white shirt, dark charcoal trousers, and matching vest with an expensive fountain pen clipped in its chest pocket, Petrakis looked like a bank president from *The Great Gatsby*. He held out the device with a sense of humble embarrassment. Scarcely larger than a disposable camera, a square aperture opened on one end, and a wire harness sprang out the opposite. "It wasn't the op-amps that blew. The CCD chipset burned out. That's the way it is with cutting-edge electronics. I am banking this radiation-hardened set will last the night."

"CCD?" I asked whomever might answer.

"Charge Coupled Device," said Sindhu, beating Petrakis to the punch. "Converts images into raw digital data." I was grateful she answered at a level I understood rather than getting an earful of techno-gobbledygook from Petrakis.

"I'm sorry to hear about your dissertation defense, Mr. Yeager. I feel responsible."

I dribbled out a mousy, "Thanks, professor." I bit my tongue before I could snark, "You *were* responsible."

"Not to worry," he said with a wink. "When your name gets accredited in the academic papers that tonight's find will generate, the review board will reverse their decision. They'll do an about-face to *save* face."

I grimaced at his self-congratulatory snicker. Sindhu beamed a toothy grin and squeezed my waist. "His jokes are terrible, but he's not wrong." A sizable tear dribbled down the side of her face.

I wiped the droplet from her cheek. "Are you all right?"

Startled by the dampness, she wiped the glistening trail away. "Some irritation from the scope, I suppose?"

"*Tempus fugit*, Doc," Gary roared from his control seat. "We're blind as a bat until your toy is re-installed."

Petrakis trotted to the scope and deftly slid his gadget into its awaiting empty bay slot. Cheryl unfolded a length of multicolored ribbon cable from the scope's gearbox. She bolted the wire assemblage to the black box, and the first of five LEDs next to the cable beamed a bright red. A second later, the four remaining lights under a Dymo label imprinted with "IVUX" burned vividly green.

Sindhu must have sensed my curiosity. She leaned against my shoulder and whispered, "Infrared, visible, ultraviolet, x-ray."

"Picking up signals across all wavelengths." Petrakis stood, smiling brighter than the LEDs. "Now let's see what shows up on video."

Cheryl bounded up from her squatting position and dashed to the operations room. Everybody trailed after her in single file, with me bringing up the rear. I was anxious to observe as anyone else, but this wasn't my circus—despite feeling like the guy who swept up after the elephants.

I surveyed the operations room, which Gary normally kept off-limits to me. The operations desk and a long table were crammed with a mini electronics lab: oscilloscopes, Tektronix terminals displaying green graphics like the "futuristic" screens on Battlestar Galactica, video monitors and tape machines, stacks of oversized computer printouts organized in metal post binders. However, everybody huddled close around a Commodore Amiga connected to a brand-new Video Toaster—the same equipment with which Todd Rundgren dabbled in the relatively new medium of music video.

She typed at the terminal fast as a journalist trying to beat a deadline. Text flew by the screen until she paused. "Signal is strong," she whispered like she was afraid she might jinx the moment. She eyed the unusually stoic Petrakis. "Shall we?"

"Start recording," said Petrakis.

Gary started up the BetaMax. Though their latest model, it was still large enough to fit snugly into a kid's Radio Flyer wagon.

"Cheryl, if you would do the honors." Petrakis stared at the blank Tektronix screens humming on a shelf above the computer and the video monitor.

She hit the Enter key, and the video monitor popped on with various shades of gray. Within a few heartbeats, its screen filled with an image not unlike a sky-blue custard, with a lighter mottled shape swimming in its center. "So far so good," she breathed. "Now for the real test."

"Try the Hough transforms first," said Petrakis, trying to muster a sense of authority in his voice. Cheryl typed in a command.

"What's Hough again?" I whispered into Sindhu's ear.

"An edge-detection algorithm. It makes underlying images stand out from the background noise."

A haystack of random lines appeared on the screen. They jittered, then suddenly snapped into an identifiable shape.

The prize blazed away on the screen. A perfectly symmetric hexagon, sluggishly turning in the maelstrom of Uranus's polar atmosphere. It shifted and shivered like a giant living thing.

"*Sonovabitch*! There it is," Gary whooped, jumping with both fists raised. He must have been far more excited than he let on—tears coursed down one cheek.

My jaw hung open in wonderment. I slammed it shut before I began drooling myself.

"Wait a minute," interjected Sindhu, rubbing her damp eyes. "At the Lick scope, I could've sworn I saw the hexagon filled with spheres."

Petrakis tore his attention away from the monitor to regard Sindhu with concern. "Oh?"

"Like a plate of marbles."

"Is there something you can adjust, like brightness or contrast?" I ventured.

"Not really," said Cheryl with a dismissive snicker.

"Hey, lady," I said, "it ain't polite for nerds to laugh at geeks."

"The transform uses variables like angle of incidence, and—"

"Yes. Cheryl, give that a try," Petrakis said, tapping his lower lip. "Increase the angle tolerance."

She complied. Like a wish come true, the hexagon filled with a myriad of circles, roughly akin to a fly's compound eye. An audible gasp from everyone told me that the team hit the cosmological equivalent of pay dirt.

"Ho- Lee- *Shit*," Gary breathed. He leaned on the long table for a closer look. "Ladies and gentlemen, it is officially time to break out the champagne."

I took Sindhu by the shoulder and pulled her close. She responded with a bear hug. I didn't dare breathe. The entire crew burst out in a cacophony of simultaneous exclamations that mirrored my own confusion.

"What are those small circles?"

"Are those mini-cyclones?"

"Are we sure Uranus is just hydrogen, methane, and ammonia?"

"Saturn has *nothing* like this."

"How can such a structure be stable?"

I felt like I was watching a documentary of a historic moment in science, except all the players were people I knew. Despite everyone's giddiness, I couldn't shake the feeling that something cosmically wrong was about to happen—like we had arrived at the point in the film where Alderaan explodes, the Terminator plops out of an electrified hole in time, or the Xenomorph bursts out of John Hurt's chest.

Petrakis wasn't helping my anxiety. He stared at me with an enigmatic raised eyebrow and his damned smile. I finally found my tongue. "How wide is that thing?"

"About one-half Earth's diameter," Sindhu answered, bouncing on the balls of her feet.

Petrakis humphed at the screen. "That's just visible light. The CCDs are more sensitive to ultraviolet. We might find more detail at those wavelengths." He tapped Cheryl's shoulder, snapping her out of an apparent mild shock. "Try infrared first, in case I'm wrong, please."

She did so, pecking the keyboard like a child fingering a typewriter for the first time. The screen reacted, displaying the scene with deeper contrasts.

"Nothing helpful," said Gary. "Let's see what ultraviolet does." Cheryl hit the U key.

The hexagon's border shone bright as burning magnesium. The circles thickened, their dark centers moved. More circles appeared and jostled for place, then disappeared, like bubbles in a rolling boil. The room went silent as a library when the roiling sea froze. All the spheres flashed in unison with searing light.

"Didja see that?" Gary blurted out with vindication. He rubbed his eyes before squinting at the screen again. "That's what I saw at the scope— Sindhu too, I'll bet. The whole inner area flashed gray a couple of times an hour while I watched."

"What could cause that?" Sindhu turned to me with a tear-stained face. The mood was heady with excitement, but I didn't think she would get *that* worked up. "You're the biochem wiz, Mike. What do you think?"

"Haven't a clue," I replied with a shrug. "Chemical reactions don't happen that fast over that large an area, especially in supercooled environments. Maybe something from the core released a pulse of energy, and the marbles fluoresced?"

"Dare we enter the realm of X-rays?" Petrakis leaned over Cheryl and tapped X. The room went silent, save for the sound of equipment fans and chattering disk drives. My heartbeat pounded in my ears. All eyes were plastered on the video screen.

A strange new image built up, line by line, pixel by pixel. The Video Toaster stank of overheated microchips.

Like before, the circles packing the hexagon thickened, their centers filled with inky voids. But now, something dimly stirred within each of them.

"Are those... *eyes*?" Cheryl whispered.

My skin bristled, every hair standing on end. Sindhu's arm squeezed me close. She was taut as a sitar string.

Like soldiers responding to a command, the irises in the host of alien eyes constricted and twitched, aligning to some common focal point. I swore they could see us through the video screen. A flash of white pulsed on the screen, then it went dead black.

"That's what burned out the last set of CCDs," Petrakis exclaimed.

"What the *fuck*?" said Gary, ending with a shout. He was no longer staring at the screen. He held the back of his hand, drizzled with blood, up to his face. Turning toward us, his face tensed with abject fear.

Blood mixed with his tears coursed down one side of Gary's face. What was once an eye was replaced by an orb of pure white—not sclera with its fine network of blood vessels, but seemingly solid alabaster stone.

"I can't see!"

CHAPTER 3

Startled by Gary's scream, we all jumped a step away.

Cheryl's shriek of "Holy *shit*!" drowned out my cry of surprise.

Gary's hand clawed at his bleeding eye socket. His other eye rolled up into his forehead, and he toppled sideways. His body slammed onto the desk, smearing lines of blood on the video screen and printouts on his way down to the floor.

Gathering my wits, I broke away from Sindhu and grabbed Gary's limp body.

I had scarcely laid him prone, preventing his head from smacking the hard floor, when the sound I half dreaded struck me from the side.

Sindhu had collapsed on the floor next to me, her face streaked with blood as well.

If my heart had a voice, it would have howled. Like Gary, her right eye had turned white as polished marble.

"What's happening?" Cheryl dropped to kneel close to Gary.

I swiveled to cradle Sindhu, raising her to a sitting position against me. Removing her glasses and sweeping away strands of her black hair, I shuddered at her contorted face. The right half was the visage of sleeping serenity I had mooned over many a night. Her left side wrenched in a crazy quilt of spasmed muscles. The stone eye sheened like wet eggshell. The color drained from the surrounding flesh in a widening circle as I watched with horror. I checked her pulse at her neck—a pitiful attempt to stop the pall of helplessness overwhelming me.

"Where's the first aid kit?" Petrakis demanded. When Cheryl didn't respond, he clapped his hands in front of her nose. "*Where?*"

Her head snapped back like she had been slapped. "Downstairs, by the machine shop."

"Get it." Petrakis slid a printout binder under Gary's head. He shoved another in my direction. "Lay Sindhu flat until Cheryl arrives with first aid. And don't touch the affected area. It might be infectious."

I scowled at Petrakis with a swirl of horror and confusion. What the hell happened to Sindhu? And who replaced the whimsical Petrakis with a take-charge army sergeant?

After settling Sindhu on her makeshift paper pillow with care, I dashed for the wall phone next to a fire extinguisher on the far wall. I dialed 911. The receiver squawked at me. I cracked a knuckle punching nine for an outside line. Another jarring tone of denial.

"Dammit, I can't call out for an ambulance."

Petrakis pulled out his pen, its side enameled with an Oriental dragon coiled about a cloud. "Just as well. What could an ambulance do? They'd have no idea how to deal with this."

"And *you* do?"

Pointing his pen's cap at his mouth, he addressed it with a tone as he might a butler. "Namiki, if you'd be so kind, call in the Eldridge airborne containment team standing by. Inform them we have Patients Zero and One, requiring immediate pick-up. We also need a containment perimeter—no Mundanes in or out."

"No *what*?"

Ignoring me, he held his pen close to Gary's face. "Transmit to all other observatory operatives that an intrusion is confirmed at Lick. Positive identification of the Euryale. All operatives are to prevent other observatories from viewing Uranus." He turned in place, holding his pen over Sindhu's tortured, silent scream. "Send these pictures to Eldridge."

I let the receiver fall and wedged myself between Sindhu and Petrakis. "What the hell? Are you insane? You *are* with the CIA!"

He stood, calmly returning his pen to his pocket. "You mean the FBI. CIA operates exclusively outside the US—at least, they're supposed to. Who knows, these days? The answer to all three of your outbursts is 'No.'"

"Then who's Namiki?"

He patted the pocket holding his pen. Its dragon eyes pointed straight at me. "She is my scribe."

"Your what?"

"Namiki is my secretary, recorder, librarian, researcher… She can find out most anything—except who she was before she died."

"*Died?*"

"Died," he repeated with a firm nod. "Just like all scribes."

"Now I know you can't be from the CIA. They couldn't be this loopy."

"Actually, I'm on loan to the university from an insurance firm named Eldridge & S.Q.Amos."

"Never heard of it."

"Good. That means we're doing our job." He scanned me up and down, leaving me with the impression I was being evaluated. And failing.

"We don't have time for this crap." I surveyed Sindhu's face. The skin between her scalp and mouth had hardened and lost all color. Distended veins of white branched out over her jaw.

"Quite right, quite right. We must slow the infection." He knelt and finagled Gary's jacket off halfway. "Oh dear. It's far faster than any-thing we expected. Where the blazes is Cheryl?"

I crouched closer to Sindhu, rocking on my knees. Taking Sindhu's wrist, her thready pulse alarmed me. Whitish veins crept down her neck, disappearing under her sweatshirt. A creeping void sucked at my heart, eager to tear it out. "This isn't an infection. It's spreading more like venom."

"What I don't understand," said Petrakis, scrutinizing both Gary's and Sindhu's faces, "is why Sindhu is infected as strongly as Gary. She had far less time at the scope."

"Her immune system is messed up. She takes steroids for lupus. Wait…" I said, shaking my head in disbelief. "They caught an infection from the telescope?"

"No. From what they observed *through* the scope."

"How is that possible?"

He stood suddenly and smacked the rewind button on the Beta-Max. Watching its tape counter, he pressed the play and pause buttons simultaneously.

The video screen brightened with the clouds of Uranus, superim-posed with Video Toaster graphics. The player marched the tape step by step, displaying a new still frame with each chiff sound from the video player's head.

Petrakis examined the graph that flashed on the first of the four

Tektronix scopes. Advancing from screen to screen, he tapped his pen on each display as it lit up. "It's not an infection or venom. It's radiation."

I couldn't make sense of the smooth curves interspersed with serrated peaks. "How do you know? I've never seen radiation do anything like this to tissue."

His shoulders sagged, not unlike when I explained polymerization to a freshman for the umpteenth time. "Not only were the CCDs enhancing the images, they also separated the spectra the Lick telescope collected. Infrared, visible, ultraviolet—"

"X-ray. Sindhu told me."

The video frame flashed with the honeycomb of angry eyes. I flinched, shielding my face with one hand. "Whoa—don't expose me, too!"

"Don't be thick, Mr. Yeager. It doesn't spread through video. You must be exposed to the Euryale radiation directly, lenses and mirrors notwithstanding." Petrakis crowed, rapping his pen on the last display when it flashed a new graph. "Ah, just as I thought."

The pen emitted a tiny squeak.

"Apologies, Namiki," he muttered. "See here, Mr. Yeager? The X-ray frequency distributions are non-Boltzmann."

"In English?"

"They are not natural."

My legs had fallen asleep. Either that, or the floor of sanity was dissolving underneath me. How do I deal with a mad scientist *cum* secret agent, radiation from outer space, and an unknown disease attacking the one person in this world I truly cared about?

Cheryl pounded through the doorway, puffing like she sprinted up Mt. Hamilton. "Found the kit. Wasn't where it should've been. I got ice packs, too." She skidded to a halt between the two victims and positioned one bag of blue slush over the bloodless spiderwebs spreading from Gary's eye socket. I placed the other over Sindhu's eye.

"What do you mean by 'not natural'?" I scowled as I plowed through the first aid kit.

"There's an intelligence behind it. These peaks occur at specific frequencies. I wouldn't be surprised if they continue into gamma rays. If only we had CCDs that could measure that high."

I disgorged the medical kit, pulling out any liquids I could find. Astringents. I had to find astringents. Along with the ice packs, they might slow the spread.

I tossed a plastic bottle of peroxide and tubes of antiseptic to the side. I wondered if there might be iodine in the kit, in case it was radiation. After a moment of indecision, I handed cotton and a bottle of calamine lotion to Cheryl. She eyed Petrakis warily, as if he were speaking a foreign language. I set to crushing aspirin into a container of witch hazel.

Petrakis skittered between screens, giddy as a kid who discovered a second batch of presents under the Christmas tree. He jammed his pen in his vest pocket and pointed with an index finger. "See these peaks in X-ray? And in the infrared? Do you understand what the Euryale have done?"

"Kinda busy here, doc." Lifting the ice pack, I tested with a dab, then plastered the aspirin paste around her eye. Her flesh was hard and unyielding. I might as well have been polishing a statue for all the good I seemed to be doing.

Cheryl made dubious progress with the calamine on Gary. No way I was sure any of this might work, but I was desperate to clutch at any straw.

Petrakis paced the length of the operations room, drumming his temple with his fingers, talking to no one in particular. "The X- and gamma rays break the sugar-phosphate bonds in the DNA backbone. The infrared frequencies could manipulate the separated nucleotides." He turned toward me with an urgent stare. "You see what they're doing?"

"Who is doing what?" I shouted. I threw a roll of gauze tape at Petrakis. "What nuthouse did you escape from?"

Petrakis caught it and tossed it on the table. He mumbled out the side of his mouth, "What do you think, Namiki? He's here because I asked him. He's a Yeager and could be a legacy—an Unaware. We need his help."

His pen issued a quick piping like a muffled bosun's whistle.

"I'm willing to take that chance. He *must* be made to understand."

The pen shifted itself from one side of its pocket to the other.

"Glad you agree. Mr. Yeager... *Michael*. I need you to pay attention for a few seconds."

That grin returned to his face. I wanted to punch it.

Petrakis pulled out a wallet-sized packet from his vest and shoved it in front of Cheryl's nose.

"You're with the police?" she said, thunderstruck.

"Read the badge aloud, exactly as you see it, Ms. Greenbough," said Petrakis. "I want there to be no doubt in Mr. Yeager's mind."

"San Jose Detective, badge number 021." Cheryl spoke in crisp bites, as if she had received an order.

He swiveled the badge at me, precisely as a robotic arm. "Now, *you* read it aloud."

His words were oddly compelling, his voice irresistible. As commanded, I spoke like I was trapped in a dream. "Assessor Anton Petrakis, Eldridge & S.Q.Amos Insurance, Inc."

He slipped the badge into his back pocket. "I knew it," he exploded, knocking me out of my fog. "You see through the badge's illusion! You're not a Mundane. I *knew* the Yeager family had one more Potential in it. You might be Chuck's second cousin twice removed, but you've definitely got his talent." His grin grew to a size that screamed "manic obsessive."

My jaw dropped and I sucked air. "How the hell do you know about my family?"

I almost said, "adopted family." A warning bell inside my head told me he already knew too much for comfort.

"Chuck Yeager's an employee of Eldridge, retired. You think he went up in the Bell X-1 merely to break the sound barrier? His real mission was to deal with the things waiting up there." Petrakis spoke with authority, as if the truth of what he said was unimpeachable. "He drove the X-1 straight through the heart of the djinn guarding the realm of the supersonic. You *do* know that your name means 'hunter,' don't you?"

I exhaled a breath that I held seemingly for ages.

"What the hell you talking about, you psycho?" shrieked Cheryl. "Get down here and help us." She peeled off the ice pack and gasped. Gary's face had succumbed entirely to the grip of stone. Veins of white marble snaked down his neck as we watched.

Petrakis pointed at the expanding stone. "I *was* talking about radiation. The upper frequencies transmitted by the Euryale rip apart DNA, just as cosmic rays have done over millions of years. But at this intensity and these specific frequencies, it operates with surgical speed and precision, unlike ham-handed evolution. Then, the infrared frequencies move the separated ACGT bases to new locations. Just like those plastic players on a child's electric football field. Though with far more accuracy."

"For what purpose?" I wailed.

"Colonization."

I blinked when the word hit me. I glanced between Gary and Sindhu and despaired at their creeping doom. Nothing sane made sense. God help me, I was beginning to believe him.

"But that's the 'why.' We have to figure out 'how' to have any chance to combat this."

A sudden realization chilled me. "You *expected* this. You knew this was going to happen." Acid poured out of my heart. I wanted to tear out Petrakis' throat.

"No, we only suspected. Our Actuarial Department is good at predicting intrusions, but even the Oracle of Delphi was not infallible. We only knew the attack would start tonight, and it would involve 'Uranus in retrograde,' or however our oracles say it. We weren't sure the intrusions would be the Euryale, or if observatories would be the first to be affected."

"But you *knew*," I growled.

"Tonight's data is the first confirmation that we face the Euryale. We knew for centuries they turned creatures to stone, but we didn't know their method was genetic. And we never dreamed it could be done this quickly from such a distance."

He tapped his forehead again in thought. "There must be something special about how the retina reacts to Euryale radiation."

"Turn to stone? Like Medusa? Is that what these Euryale are, that you keep spouting off about?" I could barely wrap my mind around the concept, even with what I had witnessed.

"Not precisely. In my people's mythology, Medusa was a single person. In reality, they are an entire race. And remember, Medusa had two sisters—Stheno, 'The mighty one,' and Euryale, 'She who strikes from afar.'" Petrakis massaged his chin as he surveyed the room. "What the Greek myth-makers failed to grasp was that those three sisters were in fact sibling civilizations, each in competition to claim Earth for their own. The Greeks also thought they were demigods using magic. They couldn't comprehend it was an alien technology."

"How do you know all this?" I asked.

Sindhu's pulse became irregular. I cradled her head. My eyes pleaded with Petrakis.

He clamped one hand over his forehead and scanned the room. "Since it's DNA-based, you had the right idea to slow the exposure with cold, Cheryl. Now, what we need is something to cool our poor friends down even further until help arrives. Ah-*hah*!" He snapped his fingers and pointed at the far end of the room.

"Enough of this crap," said Cheryl. "You're no detective, you freak. Where's the ambulance?"

"I couldn't get an outside line," I muttered. "Petrakis radioed for an extraction team."

"Containment team," he corrected absently before unlatching the fire extinguisher from its harness on the wall.

"You *bastards*," Cheryl shouted. "Wasting all this time while they're *dying*?" I dodged the bottle of calamine she hurled.

Gary's jaw spasmed open, and his arms shot up. His half-stone hands clamped on either side of Cheryl's skull, dragging her back down. He wrenched her head over his own.

She scrabbled futilely against the smooth floor, shouting every word in her four-letter vocabulary in a single breath.

The network of thickening alabaster veins that entwined Gary's body glowed a blistering argent. A column of baleful gray light shot out from his stony sockets straight into Cheryl's face. The air around the light sizzled with tiny arcs of electricity.

Cheryl screamed.

CHAPTER 4

The stench of burning hair and flesh tore at my throat. I fought the urge to retch. My reflexes got the better of me, gagging when bile burned the back of my sinuses. I dropped Sindhu's arm and stumbled back against the desk. Zeroing in on the nearest wastebasket, I heaved out a mouthful of coffee-flavored puke.

Gary sat up stiffly, his legs still flat on the floor. He hurled Cheryl away from him. Her body rolled away like a mannequin, her stiffening limbs flailing against linoleum. Her face had been blasted white, frozen in a rictus of wide-eyed terror. White webs of stone invaded her flesh around it, growing in length and width.

The thing that had been Gary rose with unexpected speed. Its limbs jerked like coil springs unaccustomed to anthropoid motion. Lifeless veins, bright as polished china, sprang down its hands. Its mouth opened and emitted a howl that reverberated like some monster emerging from a cave. The thing clawed at Petrakis, its frantic rakes reaching for a limb, a torso, a head.

Petrakis blocked a few strikes with the fire extinguisher. The deflected blows ripped the sleeves of his otherwise immaculate shirt.

The human/alien chimera clamped onto Petrakis' left wrist. It drove him against the long table. The computer and video equipment jounced, and volumes of printouts fell on the floor. Tearing the extinguisher out of Petrakis' grasp, it flung it to the ground with a thump strong enough to dent the linoleum.

"Namiki, we could really use that assistance now, please," Petrakis' voice boomed like he intended to wake up the back row of a lecture hall.

The crooked lines of stone in the chimera's hands flashed. Their ashen light coursed up its forearms, disappearing under Gary's shirt. The ghastly light reemerged at its neck, filling its entire head of living stone with glowing unearthly hatred.

The dreaded moment came, and that hideous column of sizzling gray light blasted at Petrakis' face.

Warned by the gathering light, Petrakis turned his head away. The monster's hardened fingers tore parallel gouges across his cheek. Petrakis grabbed a bound set of printouts and shielded his eyes. Spirals of smoke sprayed from the manila cover where the deadly ray struck.

The creature pressed Petrakis hard against the table. The prof's back bent as if it might snap in two. They grappled for control over the printouts, wrenching them from side to side. The monster's stony hands glowed again with increasing brightness.

I snatched up the fire extinguisher that lolled at my feet and charged. Cocking the extinguisher like an ungainly baseball bat, I put every ounce of my being behind my swing.

The cylinder smashed against its head. The marrow of my bones shivered from the impact. I jumped back as the thing's head shattered into pieces. Razor-sharp shards of stone and tissue that looked like it suffered a year's freezer burn tumbled across half the room. The chimera's body crashed to the floor, shattering. Broken rubble shot out from every opening of his clothing. A coarse slurry like sand in pus oozed from the thing's jagged flesh.

My legs wobbled, and my keister landed on the edge of the desk. Shaking hands refused to let go of the extinguisher. My chest heaved in microbursts.

Petrakis straightened his back from its tortured angle. His vertebrae grated audibly back into place. He reached one arm behind himself, rubbing his lumbar with his knuckles. The other arm furiously stabbed at my feet. "Don't look now..."

Inches away, Sindhu crawled toward me on all fours, flat on the ground like an iguana. White webs of alabaster spread down the nape of her neck, snaked along her dusky arms down to her hands, and poked out from under her hiking shorts along her hamstrings.

She grabbed for my ankle. I nearly jumped out of my shoes. Sindhu's head ratcheted upwards. The vision of beauty that once stole my heart was gone, perverted into a roaring scowl of pure malice.

I raised the extinguisher again. My arms quaked above my shoulders, balking at the order to strike my brain shouted. I sobbed, pleaded, screamed her name.

"I said '*Don't look!*'" Petrakis cried. He grabbed another set of bound printouts, opening the binder like a book. Diving on top of the clutching Sindhu, he plowed her head into the floor under the splayed stack of paper. He hitched a leg over her back and forced her down with his weight.

She struggled, lifting her torso off the floor a few inches before Petrakis wrestled her down again. Sindhu was a supple minx to begin with, I could only guess at what new strength the touch of stone afforded her.

"Cool Cheryl down," Petrakis barked, "before she can expose us, too."

My arms unfroze and dropped. The extinguisher almost socked me in the gut. Stepping past the desk corner, slivers of Gary crunched under my shoes.

Cheryl raised her body like a four-legged spider, her joints bending at impossible angles. Her bleached stone maw thundered a roar that no human could give voice to.

I squeezed the trigger, drenching her face with foam. Jumping to the side, I avoided her blast of fatal light. I wielded a printout stack from the long table like a shield and charged. Tackling Cheryl, I smothered her tacky face with the oversized papers. She struggled to wriggle out of my hold.

"Great," I shouted over my shoulder. "Now what do we do?"

The creature's arms and legs turreted in place, clamping over my torso and legs. The printout slipped from one hand, exposing her mouth. It screamed like a demon from the pit. Its body flashed white, accumulating power. A beam of bright energy hit the printouts with so much force, I swear I felt a recoil. Burnt paper filled my nostrils. I prayed that the thick stack of paper the binder held was good shielding from plain old hard radiation.

One granite arm released its grip on my back and twisted one-eighty degrees. It flipped us over like a turtle. The white veined limb crunched back into place. It tore the smoking printouts from its face. The thing's extremities fired up again, sending their energies toward its head.

I scrunched my face so tight, the hairs of my eyebrows rubbed against my cheeks. Stony fingers pried my eyes open again.

I cried for help, though Petrakis had his hands full as well.

A *chuff* and something whizzed past my ear. A ting of metal, and a silver blur ricocheted off the side of the monster's head. Two more *chuffs*, in rapid succession. I gawped at two bright red tails of hypodermic darts protruding from fleshy patches in the thing's neck.

The white brilliance in its head faded. The chimera mix of Cheryl and Euryale collapsed. Its deadweight whooshed the air out of my lungs like a bellows.

I scrambled from under the creature's stony embrace. A hand clasped my wrist and hoisted me to my feet. I was stunned into silence by a tall, powerfully built woman in fatigues and combat armor.

She raised her mirrored visor, revealing a battle-hardened face slathered in blue paint. Affixed to the center of her forehead lay a ruby the size of a quarter. That thing could inflict serious hurt on whomever was on the receiving end of a headbutt.

Slinging her air rifle over one shoulder, she wordlessly handed me over to Petrakis.

"Come along, Mr. Yeager. The *coupe poudre* and diluted *aqua regia* have done their work. We need to give the containment team elbow room." He laughed out loud. "*Elbow* room! Get it?"

"No."

"You will," he said, with an odd chortle.

"Wait a minute—*Aqua regia*?" I shouted at Petrakis. "That's nitric and sulfuric acid, for God's sake. Are you trying to kill them? And what the hell is coop *pooder*?"

"Not to worry, Michael. The *aqua regia* is buffered to weaken the Euryale without harming human tissue. As for the *coup poudre*, it's Eldridge's special blend of zombification powder. I was exposed to it once. A most unique experience."

Stumbling over my feet, I offered little resistance to the surprisingly strong arms hauling me out of the room. Petrakis on my left and GI Josephine's two blue left hands holding my right—

Two?

I gawked at the skin of the ten digits poking out of her open-fingered gloves. Dark cyan in her knuckle wrinkles gradually lightened to teal under her nails. No camouflage paint could do that.

The soldier tilted her head forward, facing me. The gem on her forehead flashed a brilliant crimson. "Assessor Petrakis, why are we taking this

Mundane? I see no Euryale in him," she said, flavored with an Indian accent stronger than Sindhu's.

"Assessor..." I muttered. My disbelief took another solid gut punch. "It's true?"

"He's not a Mundane, Lieutenant Yadavi. He's an Unaware, possibly a Potential." He beamed like a prospector who hit the motherlode. "From the Yeager bloodline no less."

The blue soldier regarded me, eyes wide. Then she grinned, her deep indigo lips stretched thin over triangular teeth. One right hand gave a thumbs up, the other waggled like she hadn't decided. My addled brain was ready to cry 'Uncle' when I caught the embroidered patch on her topmost shoulder—Durga Regiment.

"Durga?" I spluttered, recalling a terrible Bollywood film that Sindhu had forced me to watch. I searched out Petrakis, pleading for a scrap of sanity. "The fucking Hindu warrior goddess?"

Petrakis shrugged, still smiling with abandon. My knees buckled again, and I went limp.

The azure Amazon lost her smile and swung me over her shoulders in a four-handed fireman's carry as easily as I might tote a five-pound bag of potatoes. She growled, "You're talking about my Great-great-grandmama, so watch your mouth, Unaware."

Lugging me out of the ops room, she and Petrakis stood by the doorway as two more blue multi-armed troops hupped through. The first one tended to the transmogrified Cheryl and my poor Sindhu, starting by extracting the hypos from their necks. From a first aid kit marked with a caduceus—a winged scepter with two snakes twined around it—she produced a *real* one. She peeled one serpent off the rod and whapped it around Sindhu's forearm. It wound around her limb like a metal slapband, its mouth clamping down on its tail.

The second trooper unslung her sizable backpack and pulled out two helmets. They looked like welder's hoods, except without the visor. She clapped them over the subdued chimeras' heads.

With the click of the padlock on Sindhu's metal hood, something snapped inside me.

I struggled against Four Arms' forearms without success. "Let me go. I've got to see her," I shouted. With a nod from Petrakis, she deposited me on the floor.

I scrambled through the door and knelt by Sindhu's abused and mutated body. As I cautiously arranged her limbs to more customary human positions, the third soldier handed two orange emergency stretcher boards to her compadre. She then set to the grisly task of shoving Gary's larger chunks and his clothes into a body bag.

After gingerly helping my fiancée onto a stretcher, three pairs of hands dragged me away. My pleas to remain with her fell on deaf ears.

"I'm afraid we must insist this time, Michael," urged Petrakis. "We must let the containment team… *contain* this intrusion." One blue trooper unwound a thick hose from a canister on her back.

Manhandled out of the room, I spied three drop lines. Their lengths spooled through the dome's opening, hanging miraculously from the silent night sky.

That silence was sliced by the whine of a powerful impeller motor whirring away in the operations room. The commando with the canister vacuumed up the smaller pieces of Gary. His shards clattered in the tank, like lug nuts in a blender.

The two uniformed demigoddesses shuffled out of the operations room, hefting Sindhu's and Cheryl's stretchers between them. I hurried by Sindhu's side, holding her hand despite half of it changed to unyielding stone. We reached the dome's center, and I was buffeted by a nonstop column of air blasting down.

"What the hell?" I yelled at the new insanity above. The stars in the night sky strobed, winking out and glinting again rapidly.

"That's a company helicopter," said Petrakis, his straight black hair whipping back and forth.

"What are you talking about? I don't hear anything."

"It wouldn't do to attract attention. For night operations, our field division cast a Silence over the engine and rotor blades. Any nearby campers will attribute our passing as a rush of fickle mountain winds."

"Cast?" I scoffed emptily. My last wisps of skepticism and reserves of bravado were fading fast. "Next you'll tell me it's magic."

Namiki's cap spun around. She peeped out something akin to laughter. Petrakis flashed a momentary expression of exasperation. "Is that so hard to believe, Mr. Yeager? After all you've witnessed tonight?"

A fourth rope lowered a rescue basket through the dome opening.

One of the Durga triplets lay Cheryl's rigid form in it. The basket zipped skyward, fading into the darkness.

"Where are you taking her?" My heart shivered, knowing that

Sindhu was next.

"The Bracers of Asclepius will halt the advance of the Euryale effect for only a short time," said Petrakis. "We must get both patients into stasis chambers as quickly as possible."

"Which hospital?"

Petrakis faced me, serious as a pallbearer. "No hospital can help them, my boy. Not even our own facilities, I'm afraid. At least not yet. The best we can do is put them in cold storage until we find a remedy."

The basket lowered again. Yadavi towered over Sindhu and me.

"Cryogenics?" I said, pulling Sindhu close. "Like Walt Disney's head? That's a crock. Cryo doesn't work for anything more complex than bacteria."

"Disney does not employ Frost Giants for technicians." His wily grin reappeared for a curtain call.

Petrakis pulled his CCD apparatus out of the scope and tucked it into one the squad's backpacks. The whir of the vacuum cleaner in the operations room ceased. Sindhu and I were soon surrounded by all three blue Durga. The one with the canister leveled her vacuum brush in my direction. The others were poised with tense readiness. I felt like a quarterback about to be sacked by a thousand pounds of linebackers.

I caressed Sindhu's shoulder. Even though I was powerless to stop them, my gut told me that Petrakis was right. Her best chance of survival was with them.

"What will you do with me?" Trying to ignore the Hindu version of the Valkyries, I faced Petrakis. "Before tonight, I never heard of any operation like... Eldritch or whatever your company is called. My guess is no one else has either, and you prefer it that way. Are you going to put me in cold storage as well, to keep me silent?"

Petrakis shook with a belly laugh. "Heavens, no, Mr. Yeager. We want you to work with us."

"Work for you?"

His shoulders sagged again with disappointment at my lack of comprehension. "Work *with* us."

Petrakis nodded at the lieutenant. "Send your squad and Ms. Mehra up. You wait here."

Yadavi sliced the air with hand signals at her squad. Sindhu's basket whisked away into the night. The medic and janitor Durga troopers grabbed two ropes and yanked them like Victorian butler's bell-pulls. Up they went, hanging on with half of their hands, one boot in sling harnesses at the ends of their ropes.

Under hair buffeted about like windshield wipers gone insane, Petrakis regarded me with an avuncular expression. "It is your choice, Michael. But I hope you will join us at Eldridge. You have the potential, just like your distant relative. You are merely unaware of it. We can help you develop it. And you can help us."

"Help you? Why?"

"To protect Earth, of course," he replied. "This world is under constant assault from beings and forces trying to intrude into our planet, our dimension, our reality—many using tools from magic to super-science."

He straightened his hair, which was immediately blown into chaos again. "The Euryale, the Stheno, the Medusa? They are just one class of intrusion. But we two mortals stood against the Euryale—and you without any training. You've proven your value to Eldridge."

His shoulders relaxed again, not with disappointment, but with an empathy reflected in his eyes. "Consider this—you'll not only be helping Eldridge. You'll be helping your beloved Sindhu as well. I've grown fond of her, too." His face screwed up into an embarrassed grimace, and he rubbed his fingers together. "That didn't... come out quite right. Anyone can see you two belong together."

"Help her how?"

"I've read your dissertation. Your conclusions are absolutely correct. Gene editing is possible. We've seen the reality of it tonight with our own eyes. Perhaps you can help develop the technology for Earth to catch up to the Euryale. Eldridge has magnificent research facilities, but I can promise you nothing... except the chance to save her. The chance to reverse her mutation."

Save Sindhu?

God, I wanted to go. My mind's eye morphed Sindhu's tortured chimera grimace back to the delicate visage of my betrothed. But my feet stayed welded to the floor. My mouth refused to speak.

"The alternative is not too bright, Michael. And I'm not talking about your academic future. If you choose to stay, you'll be left here alone to explain all this." Petrakis gestured grandly, his arm pointing toward the operations room. "All of your friends missing. Signs of violence. Blood stains. And you, weaving a yarn of mythological creatures from space, your friends turned into monsters, leaving you as the sole survivor, saved by a mysterious firm whose name you can't remember. What will the Mundane authorities think?"

Namiki shifted in his pocket and clicked her cap. Petrakis stepped into the sling at the end of one of the two remaining ropes. "I am sorry to put you in this bind, but you must decide *now*, my boy. The police and other Mundane authorities are on their way. And Sindhu's and Cheryl's bracers will not last the trip if we delay departure."

I tried to move. I tried to talk. I could only whimper at the fading vision of my beautiful Sindhu.

"Besides, we'll need your experience in forty-two years, when Uranus's northern pole is aimed at Earth."

"We must leave, assessor—" Yadavi wrapped a portion of the unused rope around both her right forearms. "—*now*." She offered its harness in my direction.

"Join us, Michael," Petrakis pleaded. "See for yourself that there is still wonder in this world. Maybe use your abilities, logic, and some humor to return your fiancée to the human race."

"Humor?" I croaked, fighting the dizzying wind. I took a step to one side to maintain my balance.

"You must learn to lighten up, my boy. If you take yourself too seriously, you won't survive in this business."

Namiki clicked her cap open then shut, finally sinking into his vest pocket. I think she was sulking.

"Corporeally, that is," he said with a shrug.

I surveyed the dome and the wreckage of the operations room and slipped the harness under my arms. I nodded my head once with determination, and I ascended into the silent whirlwind above.

Hold on, Sindhu.

CHAPTER 5

My legs dangled hundreds of feet above the observatory. Yadavi pulled me out of my drop harness, and my eyes wanted to pop out of their sockets.

"Don't let go," I screamed. Except that nothing came out. Wind whipped downward from silent helicopter blades whipping silently above my ears.

Around the far edge of the mountain, I spotted a pair of spinning red lights of police cars zooming up Mt. Hamilton Road toward the observatory. Petrakis was right. I'd be in a world of hurt if I had remained down there. Except... who called the police? Namiki?

With all four of her arms, Yadavi slammed me into one of two pairs of empty flight seats facing astern.

Petrakis plopped himself into one of the four seats opposite me, facing forward. He busied himself strapping himself in. After pulling the last restraint diagonally across his shoulder, he donned a headset.

I tried asking him questions along the lines of "How'd the police get here so fast?" and "Where the hell are we going?" My breath rushed past moving lips, but no words came out. The silence was deafening.

He pointed at me, then at the various portions of his own flight gear.

I fumbled around my seat, searching for my restraints. Not easy to do in near pitch black, the only lights being two red exit panels, one each above the open side hatches, and scant illumination from the cockpit.

Yadavi must have seen me flailing. Either that, or she elected herself as Mother Hen. With one hand, she pushed me back deep into my cushioned seat and held me there. Her other three arms fastened my waist and shoulder restraints, then shoved some headgear down on my head, nearly ripping my ears off. She patted my cheek before giving it a hearty slap, followed by a sardonic wink.

She spun around to face the opening leading into the aft compartment. All four of her arms started gesturing, the upper and lower pairs each performing an orchestrated choreography of their own.

Hell of a time for her to perform a Hindu *mudra* hand dance, I thought. That was, until Petrakis responded with his own set of signals. One of her blue-skinned subordinates astern replied with three thumbs up.

Before Yadavi closed the port hatchway, I caught my last glimpse of the emergency vehicles as they pulled into the Lick Observatory parking lot, skidding to a halt next to my heap. The air whipping furiously around the cabin settled.

She reached above my head and pounded the wall separating us from the cockpit three times. The helicopter leaned forward and accelerated. My restraints squashed the wind out of me as we rushed to our unknown destination.

Petrakis continued signing to Yadavi at a furious pace. She responded with a single motion that made Petrakis stop dead in his tracks. He stared at her with a look that made my skin tingle.

For every Bollywood production that Sindhu made me watch on VHS tapes that made it to America via the international friend-of-a-relative-of-a-friend network, I returned the favor by setting her down with a good-ol' American schlock B-movie or a few episodes of the *Twilight Zone*. That's what Petrakis' expression reminded me of—the look a *Zone*'s protagonist had when they realized their situation was far worse than what they bargained for.

With a final nod, Yadavi vanished into the helicopter's rear compartment to assist her squad. Her subordinates opened two body-length steel chambers. Wisps of cold mist flowed over their edges, dissipating into nothingness. They lowered Sindhu and Cheryl, still strapped onto their transfer boards, into the containers. A final cloud of mist puffed out as they closed the lids.

A deafening rush of sound imploded my eardrums—the roar of the helicopter engines, the shriek of air whipping past the cabin, the whir of the blades above. I clamped my hands uselessly over my headphones. I inadvertently shouted into my mic, and Petrakis winced.

"What happened?" I shouted into my headset. "Where'd the silence spell go?"

Petrakis pointed to his right. In the corner seat opposite me sat a hooded figure. Her dark robe, the low lighting, and Yadavi in the way most of the time kept me from noticing her until now.

Though unrestrained, she nevertheless remained glued to her seat. She held out one delicate hand inches below her chin, its palm curved and facing upright. In front of her floated a green crystal, beaming an emerald chiaroscuro that danced across her sienna face recessed within her hood. A dim sphere of gray streaked with curlicues of jade surrounded her head and neck. Her emotionless face remained unperturbed by the scream of machinery, despite her not wearing any cumbersome headgear.

"Don't bother saying hello to Elrameshe," said Petrakis with one eyebrow raised. "She would not acknowledge you, even if she could hear you." He must have seen my look of bewilderment, then clicked his tongue at her vaporous sphere. "She's the one who cast Silence around this helicopter. It seems she didn't dispel it—only shrank it around herself, probably so she can ignore us."

I leaned over, peering beneath her cowl. Her slender, angular features were stunning and bespoke of an unearthly grace.

"It's not polite to stare, my boy. She is *Koire-kwente*, a Forest Elf. Not only that, but a highborn mage and seer. She would sooner cut out her tongue than talk to a human unless absolutely necessary."

"Then why is she helping us?"

"It is required of her." Petrakis rubbed his nose. Something about that must have amused him. "She is part of a cultural exchange program between Eldridge and the *Koire-kwente*. One of Eldridge's mages lives with their kind for a year, while one of theirs serves with our company. I think this is the third go-round for her. Or is it her fourth...?"

Aliens of living stone, offspring from Hindu goddesses, and now Elves? I twisted in my seat to take a gander at the flight crew. My jitters dropped a notch once I confirmed they were both human.

As I settled back into my backward-facing seat, the top of my head began to itch fiercely. It usually does that when snow is in the forecast. It's done so since as early as I can remember, even as a kid. However, the front windscreen was clear as were the skies themselves. Maybe it was the sudden change in altitude that made my skull tetchy.

Elrameshe's hood jerked up.

Framed by her cowl, flowing dark cinnamon hair interwoven with strands of spun copper tumbled out. She looked straight at me. Her almond-shaped green eyes burned with astonishment.

She spoke soundless words into her crystal, which pulsed with each syllable. After the uttering of her last word, she raised her other palm to her chin. Pursing her lips, Elrameshe blew over the crystal toward me.

Elven butterfly kisses? The invisible touch of perfumed lips landed on my own. My vision became tinted with streaks of gray and jade. The roar of the helicopter faded.

"*Caun Anor Cuithas*! You... are *here*?" echoed her voice—not from my headphones, but from where she sat, as clearly as if we were alone in a soundproofed room.

I sat up so straight, that my restraints bit into my hips and shoulders. Elrameshe's urgency matched the surprise in her eyes.

"You have arrived far earlier than anyone had allowed for. I and the other Sisters are not prepared. I do not even possess the means to free you."

I glanced over my shoulder. The men in the cockpit continued their duties unperturbed. I turned back to face her and shrugged my shoulders, upturning my palms. It became apparent Forest Elves didn't understand the human expression for *I dunno*.

Petrakis stared at me, sparing a glance at Elrameshe, then began speaking rapidly into his headset. Nothing came over my gear.

Elrameshe's surprise turned to consternation. She spoke again into her crystal. "Did you not hear me? Someone beyond our sight brought you to Eldridge before we are ready. I and my two Sisters are not able to protect you yet."

Yadavi emerged from the rear compartment, something dark in one of her hands. She glanced at Petrakis, who nodded in my direction.

Elrameshe grasped her crystal. With a wave of her hand, the whorls of gray and green were swept away from my vision. The scream of the engines rushed back, peppered with the pilots' chatter in my headset.

The next thing I knew, the blue trooper tore off my headset with one hand, held me still with another, and *fwipped* down a black hood over my head with her upper set of arms.

Black silence.

CHAPTER 6

And just like that, the blackness was gone.

I squinted against the harsh brightness of a rather cramped room. Irrational images of having been being spirited away to *Area 51* danced to the tune of my hyperactive paranoia.

Facing me stood Yadavi, her lower pair of hands clamping my arms firmly against my sides. In her upper right hand was the hood. She unceremoniously dropped me into a sitting position on a twin bed. The scent of fresh linen and pine oil surrounded me.

She folded the hood smartly and stashed it to hang from her belt. She looked directly at me. "Good luck, recruit," she said with a knowing smirk before exiting the room and closing the door behind her.

Petrakis sat facing me on a matching twin bed with his legs crossed. He wore a new change of clothes—a hideous khaki uniform with all the panache of a plain brown paper bag.

I hastily scanned the rest of the room. It was cramped and sterile, like a college dorm room before anyone had moved in. Two beds, two desks and chairs, two lamps, two shelves, two chests of drawers, two alarm clocks, one window, one door. Next to my bed's pillow lay a stack of clothing, all in the same khaki material as Petrakis' new duds. Even the combat boots had the same blasé color.

"What the hell happened?"

"I am afraid I must apologize again, my boy. I neglected to tell you that we could not let you monitor our travel route."

Following my first inclination, I wobbled to my feet and looked out the window. The bright sun beat down on a sparse coniferous forest.

"It was night just a second ago," I said. "Where are we? The other side of the world?"

"No," he answered. "Though it might have felt quick as a snap of your fingers, it is actually tomorrow morning—courtesy of Yadavi's bag of tricks."

He chuckled at his jest, tapping the point of his nose with a finger. "Standard issue with any Intrusion Containment Team. It keeps the wearer pliable yet unaware of the passage of time. Yadavi and the other Durga call it a 'Bag of Holding,' which is some inside joke I suspect. One that I don't quite get," he said with a shrug.

I tore my sight away from the window. "Fine, but where are we?"

"An Eldridge training facility is all you need know." Petrakis stood. Placing his hands on his hips, he arched his back and stretched with a slight grunt. He smiled a wistful smile. "I have fond memories of my own training. A rather eye-opening four months."

"*Months*?" I sputtered out, slapping my hand against my forehead. "I have to wait that long until I can help Sindhu?"

Petrakis stood. "Not to worry, my boy. While we brought you here, Cheryl and Sindhu were conveyed to the nearest Eldridge medical lab. They're being tended to by Eldridge's best."

He wagged a finger at me while stepping toward the door. "As for you, you are on the accelerated program. Your training shall last only four weeks."

"Good."

"Don't thank us yet. There are pros and cons to that, I suppose. Much shorter, but much more intense, I'm afraid." He put his hand on the doorknob, then paused. "Oh, I almost forgot. The elven sorceress who spoke to you before we escorted you here..."

"Elrameshe?"

"Ah, yes." He snapped his fingers. "That was her name. Do you recall what she said to you? It slips my mind for the moment."

I squinted at him. So much for my poker face. Her words were still fresh in my mind.

"*I and my sisters are not able to protect you.*"

But Petrakis couldn't have heard that. Elrameshe was in my head.

His ham-handed feint made me rethink my reply. "I... don't remember clearly. Something about me being especially grubby, even for a human."

Petrakis issued a small *humph* as he evaluated my fib. "I shouldn't be surprised. Like I said, Elves are discriminating. Though it is surprising she spoke to you at all."

He opened the door behind him, revealing a bare hallway of painted masonry block.

"Your training begins this very morning. I'll be dropping in twice a week to see how you are progressing. In the meantime, allow me to introduce your dormitory lieutenant and personal instructor, Caltrop."

Into the room clomped a beastly red half-man, half-bird. Tall enough that he needed to duck through the doorway, the critter placed his hands on his hips and wore a sneer of disgust as he eyed me up and down. Wearing wooden sandals on clawed feet, he puffed out his chest under a khaki short-sleeved shirt. His feathered arms bristled, ruffling larger in a show of dominance.

"Caltrop, may I present Mr. Michael Avery Yeager."

The giant bird-man pointed a half-hand, half-claw at me. He furrowed his brow, his bushy black eyebrows knotted into a threatening arch. "*He's* a Yeager?" he snarled with the gentle tones of an angry crow's caw.

I couldn't stop staring at his ridiculously long nose. Or was it a beak? "About that, Dr. Petrakis," I stammered. "You really should know that I—"

"I'll let you two get acquainted. See you in a few days, my boy," said Petrakis, before disappearing down the hall with a wave.

"Welcome to Eldridge & S.Q.Amos Insurance, apprentice," the creature growled, towering over me. "Now, drop and gimme twenty."

CHAPTER 7

I changed into the fashion nightmare that fit scarcely better than a khaki Hefty bag. Despite my biological clock insisting it was around four o'clock in the morning, Caltrop threaded me through a maze of alternating physical and academic obstacle courses for a full day, riding my tail worse than an Army drill sergeant.

One hour, I'm tossed into *Survival 140: Riddle Contests and Creatures Who Use Them*, the next I'm fast-stepping it through zig-zagging lines of tires with a gaggle of students, half of whom were only slightly more agile than I.

The other students—that is, "apprentices" or "scum," depending on the instructor addressing us—came from various nationalities and age groups. I felt pity for the apprentices fifteen or so years older than the rest as they lugged themselves through the physical challenges. I had extra empathy on the side for the whole bunch, too, seeing we all wore the same humiliating beige uniform.

By the time I had my last scholarly class of the day, *Cosmics 110: A Necronomicon Primer*, I had picked up on the rhythm of my new existence, along with a few other observations. Normally, each course was one or two weeks long and intensive. Since I was on an accelerated schedule, the powers-that-be sat me down in just one class of each course. Which meant I would always be playing catch-up, with the instructor dropping their syllabus and reams of reading material in my lap before giving me the bum's rush into my next hour of physical torment. By the end of the first day, I had already amassed enough paper to fill two ring binders and enough bruises that would put a Dalmatian's spots to shame.

Caltrop corralled me as I limped across the campus quad to my dorm room.

"Not so fast, apprentice," he chirped. "You got one more stop before mess, study, and rack time." He wrapped his feathered claw around my arm and yanked me in a new direction so hard, I almost dropped my binders.

He escorted me to a white Quonset hut at the farthest corner of the quad. Once inside, my senses were assailed with bright white lights and the nip of disinfectant. Walking up to the reception desk, Caltrop handed me off to a physician's assistant conversing with a staffer typing at the desk's word processor. "Apprentice M. Yeager, reporting for initial PQ assessment," said Big Bird's meaner, redder cousin.

"What's a 'PQ assessment'?" I asked. "Can't this wait until after I eat? I haven't had—"

"You'll *do* what the nice lady tells you to do," said Caltrop, his caw rasping like two cinder blocks rubbing against one another. "Report to my office after you finish here and had mess."

"May I ask why?"

"I'm your study buddy." Trust me when I say there is nothing quite as disturbing as a giant bird-man-thing forcing a smile through his beak. "Some things taught here are dangerous to study the first time alone."

The woman nodded at me with compassion. "He's right, you know." After Caltrop marched away, she added, "He is a *Tengu*, after all."

"A what?"

Shaking my hand, she said, "You'll learn soon enough. I'm P.A. Kovalenko. If you would follow me, we'll set you up for evaluation." Her blond hair, tied back in a bun, exposed a pair of circular cloisonné earrings inscribed with a weird glyph—a warped pentagram that looked like it was trying to do the Twist. The eye in the contorted star's center seemed to stare straight at me no matter how the earrings dangled.

She guided me down a straight hall into a spartan room with a single chair and a metal table in the center. "Now, relax here just a minute. I'll return with the *Lapidibus Habilitas*, and we can begin your PQ assessment."

"Not to sound like a total idiot, Ms. Kovalenko," I said, "but this is literally my first day at Eldridge. I have no idea what you just told me."

"Oh, I'm sorry." A blush peeked out from under her cheekbones. "PQ is your paranormal quotient. That is, how strong a psychic or magic ability you have. The *Lapidibus Habilitas*, or the 'Aptitude Stones,' are the tools we use to measure it."

"Stones." I shrugged it off with a roll of my eyes. "Of course. How else would one measure PQ?"

"Back in a flash," she said, closing the door behind her.

Her "flash" didn't last an eternity, but it was long enough. Meanwhile, I was left to worry about what the stones might reveal. I still hadn't corrected Petrakis' misapprehension about the Yeager bloodline, but rather that my stepmother gave me her maiden name. By the time Kovalenko returned, the questions of my lineage versus the apparent ability I had demonstrated back at Lick devolved into a heated argument. Namely, was I a legitimate apprentice or a *mundane* Mundane and a fraud?

She strode in, wearing a stethoscope curled into the pocket of a fresh white lab jacket. Its borders were edged with glittering scarlet and embroidered astrological and alchemical symbols. The lapels displayed the same unnerving star sigil that graced her earrings. Holding a black lacquered box with brass corner braces in both hands, she closed the door behind her with a push of her heel.

Her attention remained on the box as she placed it on the table. Mumbling a phrase in Latin, she opened the lid and produced a pair of fist-sized pieces of stone, smooth hemispherical mounds of ordinary granite one might find at the base of a rocky waterfall. "Rest your arms on the chair and turn your hands palms up, please," she said with a clinical expression. "Hold the *Lapidibus* as steady as you can."

Time *lub-dubbed* by as Kovalenko listened to my heartbeat over my chest and back. After she passed her hands over the stones with another quick passage of Latin, the granite warmed in my hands. The top of each stone glowed with a neon-green ring the size of a dime.

"Now let's see what the *Lapidibus* tells us." She lowered one ear to the stone in my right hand. Puffing out a noncommittal "Uh-huh," she cocked her head to listen to the other. An expression of concern wrinkled her thin blond eyebrows. Stepping to the side, she regarded me with pursed lips—like she had to inform me that I had herpes.

"Most unusual, Apprentice Yeager. According to the stones, you only have a PQ of—"

Kovalenko stared at me, like a movie's freeze-frame.

I ventured a tentative, "... a PQ of what?"

A voice behind me replied, "Of *one*, Master Yeager."

I jumped to my feet, the stones still clenched in my fists, ready to use them as bludgeoning weapons. I relaxed my defensive stance once I realized who spoke.

"Elrameshe," I peeped.

She stood before me in a dazzling gown of emerald and jade. Around her brow and copper-streaked hair wrapped a wreath of silver, but that was a trick of the eye. A chain of intertwined salamanders, each forged to devour the tail of the next, formed the ornate circlet. Dangling from her neck hung a pendant jewel, glowing with an unearthly green that my eyes refused to bring into focus clearly.

I glanced at the immobilized Kovalenko. "What did you do to her?" I weighed the stones in my hands, about to place them back into their container.

"*No,*" Elrameshe commanded. "Keep the stones in your hands, Master Yeager."

The sorceress drifted to my side with a grace so subtle it seemed she floated. "Be at peace. She is not harmed. I must speak with you."

I looked at her sideways. "About what?"

She placed her hands on the stones, her index fingers atop each of their glowing green circlets. "I must speak with the *real* you."

The stones went ice-cold, and I, like Kovalenko, became frozen. Aware, but unable to move.

Elrameshe chanted several sentences in a language I had never heard before. Her words washed through me like ocean waves, vanishing into a point inside my skull. Between each breath, her eyes fluttered. She swayed gently, never letting go of the stones. Her sentences repeated caches of words over and over, leaving me with the impression they comprised a name, an honorific, or perhaps both?

Tawar, Anor, Cuan, Cuithas. I think... were those her same words from before?

Her eyes snapped open, and her hands recoiled from the stones. I collapsed back into my chair, gasping for air.

"I do not understand. You are there. I can *feel* you," Elrameshe said, her eyes pleading with mine. "I see your crest on the Silver Door. But it will not yield to me or the stones. The Red Watcher refuses us." Her hand flashed to her mouth. She looked like she was about to weep.

Her pendant gem popped with a blinding pulse of green, then dimmed like a dying ember until it was black as onyx.

"No!" she cried. Cradling the dead crystal in her hand, she spoke to it in breathless spasms. "I must not return. Not yet... Yes, I have found him. He is *here*... Yes, I have completed my task, but the vessel is utterly defenseless. Anor needs the Gems of Binding. I must bring it here and free him from—"

Her form wavered, the very substance of her body losing its material existence. Though her hands passed through mine, she held me fast with her eyes. "Master Yeager, you are not ready, and help may be too late in coming." Her body became transparent, like stained glass. Urgency filled her voice. "Tell no one of what passed between us, or of what abides in you. You are not yet able to discern the Foe."

And then, she was gone.

"—one," pronounced Kovalenko, accompanied by a pout. "I hope you're not disappointed with a PQ that barely registers, apprentice."

I coughed, blinked, and shook my head, blathering a Ralph Kram-den *hamana-hamana* for effect. It seemed appropriate at the time.

"Are you quite all right?" She pulled a retinoscope from her jacket's hip pocket and blasted its light into my eyes.

"I... I'm fine," I stammered. My legs jounced, waiting for the signal to dash out the door. "Are we finished?"

"Yes," she said, almost as a question. "We'll add your result of PQ-1 to your admission records. I'll also recommend an additional regimen of PQ calisthenics to your orientation plan..."

I skedaddled out the door before she finished her sentence.

CHAPTER 8

I'd been called all sorts of names this day. Apprentice, plebe, newbie, not to mention *scum* by one over-the-top half-orc instructor. This evening, I added *vessel* to that list, whatever Elrameshe meant by that.

With the guilt of not straightening out my adoption with Petrakis, I was already burdened with a super-sized impostor syndrome. Add a twenty-four-hour dose of aliens, magic, technology straight out of Buck Rogers, calisthenics with a bridge troll phys ed instructor named Goatsbane, topped off with an elven sorceress talking to someone supposedly *inside* of me—was it any wonder the underpinnings of what I had considered reality since age six were kicked out from underneath me?

My after-hours study session with Caltrop was a blur. Elrameshe's dire warnings bounced around my head so hard, I couldn't concentrate on my studies, no matter how sternly Caltrop lectured me. I was on caffeine-deprived autopilot, except for the parts where he told fantastic tales of how his people, the *Tengu*, taught mankind how to make steel and the fine art of swordsmanship. The next thing I knew, my alarm clock blasted its battleship klaxon next to my pillow at five o'clock in the morning.

The next four weeks were the most intense schooling I've ever endured. Each day began with breakfast in the mess hall. But you didn't dare sit and chow down until the entire hall finished reciting the Oath of Service, a rather grim soliloquy of duties and obligations to Eldridge & S.Q.Amos Insurance and its officers, followed by an even darker list of punishments. I felt like a first-grader learning the Pledge of Allegiance while the teacher held a gallows noose.

And don't get me started on the mess hall coffee. After a semester of being spoiled by the Lick Observatory crew's smorgasbord of java from every continent, the brew served at the commissary tasted like blackstrap molasses drained from a spittoon. Which meant Caltrop drank it smooth as mother's milk.

Nevertheless, the three-squares-a-day at the mess was a welcome respite from the daily ordeal of six classes and four physical training sessions. Also welcome, because the other apprentices left me alone during meals.

I figured they avoided me because: as the new-kid-on-the-block, my social ranking hovered around pond scum; or my accelerated schedule prevented making any personal connections with ever-changing classmates; or because Caltrop sat across from me at every meal.

I chose the last reason, as my personal trainer from hell was terrible company—boisterous, overbearing, and critical about everything, down to my refusal to drink the mess hall coffee.

"It'll put feathers on your chest," he would crow every other morning.

By the end of the second week, it dawned on me that my classes and the mess hall were less crowded, which didn't help my company networking efforts either.

"Where is everybody?" I asked Caltrop.

"Flunked out of the academia. Scared away by the Oath. Couldn't cut the mustard in physical training. Whatever the reason, they're not your concern, apprentice."

"Were they sent back home to their previous lives? I'm kinda curious, as there might be a delicate situation waiting for me back—"

"Petrakis gave me the lowdown on the Euryale Intrusion. The adjuster sent to clean up that snafu is having a devil of a time *adjusting* Petrakis' name and yours out of the remaining observatory staff's memories and the police records. Why're you asking me this anyway, plebe? I'm here to make sure you *don't* wash out. So, relax—that's an order."

"So what happened to the dropouts?"

Caltrop banged his feathered fist on the table, and a dozen heads snapped in our direction. Coffee lava blupped a molten ring around his mug. "*Emperor's diapers*, apprentice! I said, *drop* it."

I remained silent and pouting, staring at him while he downed the last swig. To my surprise, he fidgeted in his seat several times between bites of his suet. Without a warning, he blurted out, "Knock that off, apprentice. Your two-colored eyes are *fuan'na kimoi*. Worse than a serpent's stare." He jumped up, jostling the table. He quickly returned with a fresh mug of the commissary's mud.

"If they're lucky, they were mindwiped and returned to their former lives," he groused.

"Is 'mindwiped' what I think it is?"

"Every minute of their time here, every contact and event in the world of the Mundanes that led them to Eldridge, all of it's erased from their memory. Where and when we can, adjusters insert them back into their old existence, with some reality adjustment to explain their absence. If not..." Caltrop shrugged his shoulders and took a swig.

"Adjust... *reality*? Holy crap."

Caltrop flipped his table knife, catching the handle in a fist. He jammed the blade into the table between two of my fingers.

"*Samurai's blood*, apprentice," he spat. "Where was your head on day one? No cursing on Eldridge premises. You're relatively safe here, but a curse like that in a proper Eldridge office building is playing Russian roulette."

"Sorry, I must've had a caffeine withdrawal headache that day." I shook my head, trying to recall what we were talking about. "So the dropouts, if they can't get adjusted back... then what?"

"Ever wonder where the really whacked-out homeless people come from? The ones who walk around wearing a board saying 'The end is near' or other end-of-the-world stuff?"

Memories from the various cities I'd lived in flashed by. A shiver raced up between my shoulder blades. "Man, that's unfortunate."

"No," he growled. "Unfortunate would be if they broke the Oath. Then, they'd be *redacted*."

"What does that entail?"

"You don't wanna know, apprentice." Caltrop's shoulders shook, and the feathers on his crest and back of his neck ruffled to attention before he calmed down by meditating over his coffee. "Now stow it. I've said too much, and you're gonna be late for your next class. Which is...?"

"*Aliens 201: Sol's Neighbors—Empires and Rogue Civilizations*."

"Correct. Now move your butt. Double time!"

CHAPTER 9

After two weeks of intensive training, my classes began to blur together. I was forgetting what I had been taught a few days prior. The worst case was *Cryptids 220: Elves*. The monotonous adjunct professor had the lightning speed of a sloth on barbiturates and a voice that would put Tolkien to sleep. Small wonder that little old me conked out halfway through the process by which elves may seek asylum on Earth from their parallel world.

I kept falling further and further behind, until *Aliens 201*.

That class was a rarity, as my schedule dropped me into the first session of its two-week program. I also hoped it might give me insight into the Euryale and the other Gorgon races—something I might use to return Sindhu to normal.

As soon as I entered the classroom, I could tell the professor had prepared for me. The center front-row desk had a pair of binders labeled with my name. I picked up the materials and surveyed the room, looking for a less conspicuous seat while the other khaki-clad students filed in.

"No, Mr. Yeager," said a gravelly voice. Through a door separating the classroom's whiteboards the instructor emerged, carrying an overhead projector, depositing it on a wide counter. After hastily writing his name, "Prof. Algernon," on the closest board, he pointed to the center desk. "Please take your assigned seat."

Dressed in relaxed-fit pants, a blindingly white short-sleeve shirt, and a thin black tie, Algernon's outfit matched my impression of a 1950s aerospace engineer to a *T*. That plain vanilla wrapper was undone by what his clothes did not cover. His skin had the texture of a leper with a bad case of plaque psoriasis and patches of scattershot acne scars thrown in, topped with a bald head stamped with a face run over by a dump truck overflowing with Ugly. His gait was stiff, making me think he had arthritic hip joints on top of whatever else his lousy roll of the genetic dice had dumped on him.

Last week, *Cryptids 230: Demi-humans—Half-elfs, Half-orcs, etc.* taught that some interspecies mismatches may result in spectacularly beautiful or abysmal creations. I could only wonder what kind of unfortunate pairing produced Algernon.

I expected the professor's course would be an exhaustive and dreary rendition of *The Rise and Fall of the Roman Empire… i-i-i-in Spa-a-a-ce.* Instead, I was pleasantly surprised at the course's nuts-and-bolts introduction to the aliens we'd most likely bump into.

"If we are to understand an interstellar neighbor's civilization, we must first be familiar with both their physiology and physiognomy," began Algernon. My biologist's brain was more than ready to dive headfirst into the new playground opening up in front of me.

First there were the Epsalians. Thin and spindly bodies topped with bulbous heads featuring large black lidless eyes made them a perfect fit for the "little gray men" portrayed in so many beloved B-grade creature features.

I guess the crackpots surrounding Roswell every so often weren't so insane after all.

Eldridge apparently has a binding contract with them, requiring they leave our star Sol and its planets alone. Whether or not that treaty is honored is another story. The Epsalians are so incredibly technologically advanced, in addition to setting themselves on an ethically and culturally superior pedestal, that they consider existing interstellar laws inconvenient. Which usually results in a half dozen mauled cow carcasses every so often before Eldridge chases them off Earth again.

I raised my hand. "Why do they have such interest in cows?"

"They don't," Algernon replied. "It's their way of insulting humans, their message being cattle are far more interesting."

Then, the professor discussed the second of our next-door neighbors, the Valdaan. I must have been the very picture of a kid in the candy store, wide-eyed with a stupid grin on my kisser, when he displayed a multi-layered diagram detailing the exterior of a Valdaan specimen. Flipping overlays back and forth, the exoskeleton was replaced with layered diagrams of internal structures, organs, vessels, and even a secondary endoskeleton. The creature was both beautiful and hideous—an insectoid centaur, with a back half built like a giant cockroach tank, and its vertical front torso similar to the thorax and head of a giant praying mantis.

Algernon swept the diagram off the projector, stating, "If you see a Valdaan in full battle armor and a weapon, run. If you see a Valdaan without them, run faster."

There was something strange about the creature's forelimbs that I couldn't catch before the slide was replaced with the next transparency. I hoped to satisfy my curiosity later, during that night's study session with Caltrop.

I raised my hand again when a troubling question popped into my head. "You didn't mention if we have a treaty with the Valdaan."

"That's a topic far too complicated to cover in today's session. Suffice to say they have not abrogated any agreements for several centuries."

The remainder of the period dealt with the two other races that lurked around our celestial neighborhood: the Horde and the Karne. Again, the scientist in me was fiercely interested in the Horde's semi-amphibious biology, marginally intrigued by the mystery of their declining population in the past decades, but totally uninterested in their dealings with the other races. Then there were the Karne—some mysterious hyper-intelligent *über*-race that saw itself as the lawgiver over the local squabbling interstellar children. They were a giant question mark that no one dared mess with.

Algernon signaled the end of the class by turning off the projector. Something felt wrong. I raised my hand a third time. "What about the Gorgon races—the Euryale, Medusa and Stheno?" Algernon showed no emotion. "They're *here* in our solar system, but you didn't cover them. Why?"

"They are not native to our region of the Orion-Cygnus Arm in the Milky Way."

"They're local *now*. Why not cover them? Eldridge has to know something about them."

"We do. They were contained thousands of years ago, imprisoned deep in the cores of the outer gas giants."

This guy's elusiveness raised my hackles. "Yes, but—"

"Your questions will have to wait for another day, Mr. Yeager," said Algernon before collecting his materials and exiting the door between the whiteboards.

I kicked my chair down the row and stormed out the room's main exit.

No help for Sindhu, *again*.

CHAPTER 10

My anger at Professor Algernon soured the rest of my day. A basic mistake nearly got me drowned during *Phys Ed 220: SCUBA*, and I had zilch ability to concentrate during *Psychics 110: Aura Detection*. Even if I was on the ball, it wouldn't have helped that class in the slightest. My attitude toward ESP was one of sky-high cynicism.

As far as the existence of aliens was concerned, I didn't need further convincing. On the subject of so-called mythical creatures, any cynic would have a hard argument against the living, breathing examples of Caltrop, Elrameshe, Goatsbane, Yadavi, and the rest of her Durga squad. And I've experienced enough magic to make even me an ardent believer.

With apologies to Arthur C. Clarke, I couldn't see how 'magic is indistinguishable from sufficiently advanced science,' when I had examples of magic and super-science staring me in the face at the same time. It would be like saying I couldn't distinguish between oil and sufficiently advanced water.

As far as *espers* were concerned? They didn't wash with me. It didn't help that every PQ instructor struck me as an escapee from a bad William Castle film, and that their shtick had all the hallmarks of a carnival sideshow.

The worst were the ones who claimed clairvoyant powers. *Psychics 215: The Future of the Future* was forty-five minutes of sheer torture. It should have been a full hour, but the 'expert medium' was late due to 'unforeseen circumstances.' I couldn't put my finger on it, but something about creepy oracles who claimed the ability to draw back the curtain and peer into the future rubbed me the wrong way.

At least the food, starting the third week of training, was improving.

"Fewer apprentices, better grub," said Caltrop, between gulps of steaming suet loaded with fresh berries and a side of mealworms.

"Grub!" said a familiar voice, with a chuckle mixed in. "Why, my dear Caltrop, you have a sense of humor, after all."

Petrakis' graying hair and clothes were more disheveled than usual. He seemed to be experimenting with growing a mustache, though the rest of his stubble refused to become a beard. He sat beside me with two mugs of steaming coffee.

I drooled and snatched away one of the mugs the second the aroma of Jamaican Blue Mountain hit my nostrils. Sweet steam rose from my mouth when I said, "Doc, you're a godsend."

"Apologies for not checking in sooner, my boy," said Petrakis. "I've been busy with some DNA research."

"Right up my alley." I sat up straight, beaming. "What kind of research?"

"I'd rather not say until I reach my conclusions."

I plunked down my half-empty mug. "Can't I get a straight answer from anyone in this company? First, Caltrop refused to tell me what redaction is all about. Then you dangle a research carrot in front of my nose, only to suddenly get tight-lipped about it." I glanced between the two of them, seeing if I got a rise out of them. Nothing. "The worst was this morning when Professor Alger-*none-of-the-above* wouldn't give me the time of day about the Euryale. I swear, if I wouldn't get redacted—whatever that means—I'd love to put him in a fun-house of mirrors, just to see which one makes him look normal. That is, if they all don't shatter at first glance."

I stared at the curious expression on Caltrop's face. He attempted to fold his beak into a smile again. Petrakis snickered quietly, his index finger against his nostril.

My shoulders drooped, and my voice slouched. "He's behind me, isn't he?"

Caltrop's smile vanished. "You will apologize to both the *perfesser* and your sponsor, plebe."

I bit my lip and did so. One does not disobey an upset *Tengu*.

"Apology accepted." Algernon took a seat between Petrakis and Caltrop. Leaning forward with his crusty elbows on the table, he placed one scabrous hand over the other. "The reason I didn't answer your question about the Gorgons is that nobody in Eldridge knows the answer. Our best theory is that an alchemist in Ancient Greece banished them from Earth. We have no records of their origin star system nor the method by which they were imprisoned." He spread his fingers and rubbed their tips, one hand against the other, sounding like sandpaper against wood.

"An ancient Greek wizard? Where was Eldridge?"

Caltrop cuffed the side of my head. "*Shinjuku's demons*, apprentice! We covered that in the first week, *History 101*."

"We did?"

Petrakis sighed, his patronizing smile an even worse punishment than a second clop from Caltrop. "This organization has had many faces over the centuries, my boy. The legal entity of Eldridge & S.Q.Amos Insurance is only the most recent. Our company assumed its current façade around the same time Lloyd's of London was incorporated."

"Even so, Eldridge has gaps in its history," mused Algernon, still focusing on his fingers. "So much was lost when a pair of Efreeti set fire to the Great Library of Alexandria."

"Efreeti," I mused.

"Fire demons from Persia," growled Caltrop.

Algernon stopped to focus again on me. "Which is why I thought I'd join you here today—to ask your help filling in those gaps. I would very much like to hear whatever you can tell me about your experience against the Euryale. Although I've read Dr. Petrakis' report, I'm sure it pales against hearing the actual experience told firsthand."

"We'd be happy to," said Petrakis.

"I don't understand your interest in the Euryale." I said. "What makes a historian so curious about aliens in the first place?"

Algernon grasped his right index finger, snapped it off, and tossed it to me. "My credentials, Apprentice Yeager."

With a mouse-peep of a yelp, I skidded back in my chair, spilling the last of my precious Blue Mountain. Caltrop's arm flashed out, catching Algernon's finger. Grabbing my shoulder, he righted my chair, dragged me back to the table, and jammed the professor's errant digit into my own hand.

"Go ahead, I don't bite," said the professor. "And neither will that. But I would like it back when you're finished examining it."

I did so feverishly. The edges of the finger changed as I watched, losing its detail. The skin changed color, and the fingernails became as coarse as the rest of the tissue. I rubbed the outer coating of the finger with my own. Its surface felt like moss-covered coral. Up close, it carried a faint odor of fresh kelp.

In a flash, the answer clicked, and I returned the finger. "It's like equal parts algae, coral, lichen, and... tendon? You're not a single organism. You're a... I'm not sure what to call you... a symbiote colony?"

"Close enough," said Algernon. He stuck the finger back onto its waiting knuckle. A few seconds later, he flexed his hand, then formed a fist. "Good as new," he said, pleased with himself.

"This is amazing," I mumbled with a low chortle. "But whatever you are—"

"An Oovlid," said Algernon.

"Why weren't you listed in your own lecture?"

"I am sorry to interrupt this impromptu biology class," said Petrakis, standing. "But I have some business with Apprentice Yeager. I'll happily give you an interview and discuss the Euryale Intrusion in detail. I'd prefer Mr. Yeager concentrate on his backlogged studies for now. And Caltrop, I'll be sure to have your apprentice back in time for his next class. Which is...?"

"*Cryptids 203: Monsters by Continent*," I said. "But I'll need my notes from my previous cryptid class first. My room's along the way."

Saying our goodbyes, Petrakis and I headed across the quad at a hasty clip. Overcast and chilly, the walkways were almost deserted. I was summarizing my recent classes and my gripes about them when Petrakis slowed his pace to a stroll.

"No time for small talk, my boy. Have you seen Elrameshe during your training?"

I avoided stumbling over a pavement divider, and her warning rang anew in my ears. "*Tell no one of what passed between us, or of what abides in you.*" I concentrated on my feet. "That elven sorceress from the helicopter? No, I haven't. Why?"

"She is obligated to serve Eldridge for several more months, but has been AWOL for the past two weeks." He clasped his hands behind his back, chewing on his thoughts for several paces before speaking again. "Normally, I wouldn't have given it too much thought. Forest Elves, by nature, can be simultaneously inscrutable and flighty. But *Koire-kwente* take their obligations seriously, which leaves me a mite concerned."

"Who last saw her?" As if I didn't know.

"That's one of the items I am investigating—without much success, I'm sad to say." Another pause of silence, another dozen footsteps. "If Elrameshe's disappearance weren't enough, Lieutenant Yadavi has been behaving strangely as well."

"How so?" *That* was new.

"Her intrusion event report was uncharacteristically brief. When I asked her to clarify some details, she gave me a bit of a runaround. What's more, she's been closely following Sindhu's progress."

My ears—and my spirits—perked up. "Really? I would think that was a good thing."

"Oh my, yes. There's nothing inherently wrong with that. It's just uncommon for a Durga to follow up on a previous assignment so diligently." Petrakis stopped suddenly, staring off into the distance. "There is something amiss here, my boy. I can smell it." He tapped his nose. "While I'm pleased as punch I brought you into the Eldridge fold, you are beginning to attract attention—at upper management levels I had not expected. Now, with Elrameshe gone, I am concerned."

"How can I help?"

"Just keep a low profile. Attract no further attention. Don't even ask questions during class. Have you made any friends among your classmates?"

"No, I really haven't had much of a chance."

"Good. Keep it that way," he said.

If Elrameshe's warning about hidden foes wasn't enough to spike my paranoia, Petrakis finished the job.

"And if you experience anything unusual—"

I spluttered out a derisive laugh. "*Unusual*, he says."

"—or distressing, discuss it only with Caltrop or myself." He turned to face me. "I'm deadly serious, Michael. There's an eddy of unanswered questions swirling around us, and I don't know who or what is stirring the waters. Now, get about your business. I shall see you when your training is complete."

"If I don't wash out, that is," I rasped.

"Have faith, my boy," he said with a wink. "You're a Yeager." He was out of sight when I remembered I still hadn't told him I *wasn't*. All the while, Elrameshe's voice kept nattering away at me.

"*You are not yet able to discern the Foe.*"

CHAPTER 11

The company song blared over the quad over our graduating class. I never thought I would miss Grieg's *Pomp and Circumstance*, but Eldridge & S.Q. Amos Insurance never missed an opportunity to put its stamp on anything. A faculty barbershop quartet—with the Gestapo half-orc supplying the high-flying countertenor—accompanied the canned orchestra. They sang the company's Alma Mater, which was essentially a subtle rewording of the Oath. After a century or two, I would've thought they'd have come up with better rhymes for "death."

Surveying the ongoing spectacle around our pared-down twenty-odd graduates, I gauged my fellow graduates. I had only seen most of them once or twice during my time here at *Eldritch Academy*—their nickname for the place. A few of the people, who persevered through the full four-month regimen, gave me a thinly disguised sneer that shouted, "Who the *fuck* is this clown?"

I sighed with gratitude there were no fawning relatives in the audience. That always reminded me that I had none. I felt marginally better when I spotted Petrakis and Caltrop in the crowd, barely twice the size of the graduating class. Petrakis' shirt was ready to burst with pride, but Caltrop's beak was set into a definite frown. I did a double-take when I spotted Algernon and Lt. Yadavi in the back row.

My brain and body ached during the entire ceremony. My legs cramped when ascending the steps to receive my certificate. Small wonder, given the double-dose of orientation-on-steroids I endured the previous day. My last classes in alien super-science, magic indoctrinations, and psychic defense exercises were crammed with every tidbit of last-minute information the instructors could shove into my head. Goatsbane was no better, throwing everything, *including* the kitchen sink, into his final obstacle course. As a *bon voyage* present, he administered a "healing" massage that broke at least three statutes of the Geneva Convention.

With the ceremonies complete, I was itching to slip back into my Mundane street clothes. Back in my room, I came to the pleasant realization that my clothes were looser and tighter in the right places. Not only that, my favorite jeans had transformed into high-waters that rode up tight on my calves when I sat. Somehow, I grew a whole inch taller in four weeks. Was it something in the water?

I chuckled at the uninvited thought of whether Sindhu might notice, only to sniff away a sudden wet, stuffy nose.

Like all silver linings, this minor miracle hid an undercoating of lead balloon. I was forced to change back into a fresh set of the only thing that fit—my khaki apprentice duds. I was about to put on my boots when Caltrop burst into the room and snatched them away.

"Graduates don't wear combat boots."

"Oh, good," I said, genuinely pleased. "I know just the footwear that goes with khaki cargo shorts. Can I request a pair of Crockett & Jones chukka boots? They're pricey but worth every penny."

"Here," he cawed. Tossing me a floppy pair of black footwear with Neoprene soles, he added, "put these on."

Holding them up, they unrolled. My hopeful smile vanished. "Ninja *tabi* shoes?" I said. "You expect me to wear these split-toed monstrosities in public?"

Yadavi, in full-dress Durga uniform, turned the corner. "You got a problem with that, Mr. Yeager?" she said.

I looked down. She wore the same footgear.

"On *you*, they look good." Alas, sarcasm is wasted on demigods and their offspring.

Caltrop stepped aside, allowing the warrior to advance into the room. I couldn't interpret the expression on Yadavi's face. It seemed like her pride, worry, happiness, and pity were rolled into one ball of blue Silly Putty.

"How is Sindhu doing?"

"No progress." She averted her eyes for a moment. "But she made it to stasis in time. The Euryale infection is arrested."

"Given everything I've been taught the past four weeks, I expected something more positive by now. Who's her doctor—or mage, as the case may be? What's their prognosis?"

Stonewalled by Yadavi's silence, I searched Caltrop's stoic expression. Behind him stood Petrakis, whose only reply was a shrug.

Placing one pair of hands on my shoulders, she said, "Courage, *Mrgav-yadha*. You shall see her again."

I gasped at her use of Sindhu's pet name for me. "*What* did you just call me?"

Her second pair of arms were blue lightning. Before I could say another word, Yadavi snatched that diabolical black hood from her belt and whipped it over my head.

CHAPTER 12

Off came the hood.

I found myself in a seated position again, my elbows resting on the contoured arms of a medical examination chair. Only this time, I fumed at Yadavi, standing before me with an unapologetic frown.

"*Never* do that again," I snarled.

"I won't have to," she said as she smartly folded the hood over her belt. "You are at your newly assigned location, the North America-California Eldridge facility, in Sacramento."

"That's not what I mean," I spat. "Who told you that name?"

She ignored my question, instead looking to one side.

Disturbingly similar to the Quonset hut room where I had been subjected to my PQ test, the only difference being a picture window and doorway into an observation room and exit beyond.

In the outer room stood Caltrop, his feathered arms crossed over his chest. They clamped a clipboard against his chest. He glowered at Yadavi and me. After four weeks, I still couldn't tell if he was ticked off at the whole world, or just me. He nodded at the blue Durga with a simple, "Dismissed, Lieutenant."

Yadavi leaned in and whispered, "A mutual friend told me. I am not your foe, Yeager."

My jaw drooped as she gave Caltrop a cursory salute and exited the room. Elrameshe's warning screamed in my head.

Into the observation room sauntered Petrakis, dressed in two-thirds of a pinstriped three-piece suit, replete with a pair of green arm garters. Add a visor, and he'd be the very picture of a card sharp from a

Roaring Twenties gin joint. Since my rushed orientation began, Petrakis had let his salt and pepper hair grow. Today, he had tied it into the beginnings of a ponytail.

Grabbing a pen from a shirt pocket, Caltrop signed the clipboard with a flourish. He handed them both to Petrakis, who obliged with his countersignature.

Once Caltrop and his paperwork left the room, Petrakis grinned like a fool. Not at me, but at the anteroom's sparkling new Compaq computer. The tabletop model—a *laptop* they called it—had been obtained from the latest upstart startup trying to horn in on IBM's dominance in personal computers. From the raw covetousness in his eyes, it must have taken every mote of discipline to keep his techno-geek hands off it.

With Petrakis distracted for the moment, I tried to reorganize my thoughts into some semblance of sanity. After all, Yadavi's little name-dropping blasted my world even more out of kilter.

Since my arrival at Eldridge's boot camp, Caltrop had been my teacher, den mother, drill sergeant, and shadow during my orientation. Petrakis, on the other hand, served as good cop to Caltrop's bad cop. At least, he *should* have, but some hush-hush mystery had kept him away much of the time.

By his own report, Yadavi had already been acting strangely, keeping a close eye on my fiancée. Petrakis reported no change in Sindhu, caught between the worlds of flesh and stone. But then, Yadavi dropped my pet name, that only Sindhu and I knew.

Then there was Algernon. Out of the score of instructors force-feeding me a dozen two-inch binders' worth of information about the workings of Eldridge into my head, only he had taken an interest in my situation.

All the while, Elrameshe's dire warnings played in my head like a skipping phonograph.

Sindhu, what have we fallen into? And how do we get out?

I shook my head, stupefied at the fact it had been only four measly weeks since she was taken from me at the Lick Observatory Intrusion.

Intrusion—I hated that word. Such a disgusting, *professional* term. So official, so sanitized. So despicably respectable. A vile euphemism that reduced untold pain, suffering, and death to a rubber stamp as socially acceptable as "Paid in Full."

It was an intrusion that thrust me into this new existence that lurked the curtain of reality. It was an intrusion that took my Sindhu from me. And that goddamned intrusion left her on the precipice between existence and oblivion. If I helped find her cure, not only did I hope to be the one to deliver it to her, but also be the one to push the button that would destroy the entire fucking Euryale race.

Petrakis leaned against the far wall with his arms folded severely. The impatient taps of his foot echoed off the open door.

"So, Doc, where is Sindhu?"

"Same place we are, the Sacramento regional office building."

"Really? Don't get me wrong—I'm glad Sindhu's with us, but why Sacramento?"

"It was the closest Eldridge location."

"So, I'm here to work on getting Sindhu back?" Things were looking up.

"No, that is a happy coincidence. You are here to fill one of many open personnel requisitions. Our department's top manager, Director Ventnor, had several openings. As a matter of fact, half of your graduating class is here as well. New York, London, Prague, and Nairobi are most upset."

Petrakis' hungry eyes never left the screen of the open laptop. His fingers drummed his elbow while his stiff upper lip tamped down his giddy impatience.

My mind turned to speculating which position they might assign me. With my biochemistry background, they could assign me to study alien physiology; or space viruses—one orientation class indicated that they filter down to Earth remarkably often, to which our response is to sneak them into the yearly flu shots to prevent an epidemic; or maybe they'd let me continue along the lines I had worked back at UC Santa Cruz, researching genetics to combat the HIV responsible for the recently discovered AIDS scourge. Now, wouldn't *that* be a kick in the pants, if it turned out HIV was of alien origin?

Let's face it, I would much prefer to discover the cure for Sindhu's infection. I would work like a slave to have her back in my arms again.

"Okay, let's get to work, then," I said. "Why am I cooling my jets here in detention?"

"Patience, my boy. One last set of tests. Your initial PQ was surprisingly low. Especially for a Yeager."

"Yeah, doc. About that—"

A woman wearing a white medical jacket strolled between Petrakis and the window. His eyes followed her as she entered the examination room. "Good morning," she said without looking at me. Her previous jacket embroidery of red had been replaced with silver thread versions of the strange glyphs. The central eye of her dancing star earrings still followed me, regardless of how Kovalenko stood.

"Hello again, Dr. Kovalenko." My eyes did a quizzical dance around the room. "Wait a minute, I was told we were in Sacramento."

"We are. And it's still just Physician's Assistant Kovalenko," she said, somewhat annoyed. Her expression was quickly replaced with one of recognition. "I was wondering if you were the same Mr. Yeager from before."

"I'm glad you remember me."

"An ability of PQ-1 is a bit of a rarity at Eldridge."

I slouched in my chair. "Ouch."

"It's only four weeks since I last tested you. It's unusual to re-test so soon."

Petrakis leaned over the outside table and clicked a button next to the window. Over the room's ceiling speaker crackled a tinny version of his voice. "Mr. Yeager's orientation was a rush job. We crammed the usual four months into as many weeks."

Taking a step back, she eyed me like she was giving the once-over to a used car with a sizable dent in one fender. "What was the hurry?"

"I've asked that very question several times."

"If you can get an answer out of Director Ventnor, be sure to let me know." Petrakis resumed his stance, leaning against the wall with his arms crossed and his fingers drumming his forearm. His intense stare and grin of anticipation resumed their sentry duty.

"That kinda explains why *I'm* here," I said. "Why are you in Sacramento?"

"I completed my duties as an adept. I now serve as a prioress of the Banduri."

"The what?"

"A sacred order of female Druids," she replied, as matter-of-factly as reciting her telephone number. Just as she had done before, she placed the granite stones in my hands and uttered a mystical phrase. The top of each stone glowed again with a brightly colored ring.

"Blue? They were green last time."

"Different spirit energy in the stones, different color." She strode toward the door. "The High Priestess will see you in a minute, Mr. Yeager. Now, relax and remember—keep those stones steady until she gets here."

"You mean the doctor?"

"Yes. That, too," trailed her voice as she exited the examination and outer rooms.

Petrakis was a statue, save for his eyes that followed Kovalenko. The stones in my hands grew heavier with each passing minute. My wrists were beginning to ache when she returned, ushering the doctor into the examination room.

She was a Rubenesque raven dressed in a lab coat. Her garb had the same mystical borders as Kovalenko's, except her embroidered sigils seemed spun out of gold. Her black hair spread across the shoulders of her medical jacket like squid ink. Around her neck hung a silver necklace adorned with an enameled disc matching her assistant's earrings—that same unsettling all-seeing-eye. Like Kovalenko, she too, brought in a black lacquered case, but with gold hasps instead of brass. From its inner black velvet resting place, she raised a smooth ring of curiously speckled granite slightly smaller than a pie tin.

"That's new," I quipped.

Kovalenko closed the door between the rooms, shooed Petrakis away from the desk, and sat down. Her eyes were rectangular beads of reflected computer screen.

"I'm Dr. Fleischer. I've been assigned as your psychological and paranormal evaluator. How are we feeling today, Mr. Yeager?" Her doctor's smile was infectious. I could feel my cheeks bunching up despite my best efforts to maintain my wariness and an outward expression of apathy. Even Petrakis's tight-lipped anticipation had been replaced with a hearty smile.

"Just dandy, your priestliness," I said with unexpected perkiness. "What's this new toy? Do I trade in these paperweights for it, whatever it is?"

"No. This is part of the *Habilitas* as well. The hand stones measure only your current PQ. With this ring, the spirit's power is expanded, and it can predict what PQ you might achieve in the future. Now, I have to warn you, Mr. Yeager. This may hurt unbearably."

"That's nice," I cooed, beaming with serenity.

Something in my head clicked, and I recalled a defense instruction from my first week of orientation. I narrowed my eyes with new insight, forcing the puppy dog grin off my mug. "You've beguiled me to relax. With an aura of some type."

"Excellent, Mr. Yeager."

"You're not serious about the pain, then?"

"Piffle," she said with a lighthearted scoff. "The *Habilitas* is as painless as the Happiness dweomer I cast over these rooms. If you hadn't noticed it before we finished, however, I would have no choice but to flunk you."

My abdomen clenched when I recalled what that might entail. For starters, I'd be subjected to a memory wipe—including forgetting everything about Eldridge.

Including Sindhu.

I couldn't decide which would be worse: implanting false memories of an irrevocable breakup with my fiancée; or that she died by some freak accident like getting hit by a bus; or that every nuance of her existence would be purged, replaced by a desolate fiction that we had never met at all.

Then there was the possibility the wipe failed, and I would be redacted. After Caltrop first enlightened me that such a thing existed, I couldn't wheedle more out of him or Petrakis. He'd deflect my questions along those lines with something akin to "Tut-tut, my boy. I'm sure it will never come to that. You're a Yeager, from an excellent bloodline. Remember, your name means 'hunter,' after all."

I had tried several times to disabuse Petrakis of his mistake since Lick Observatory, but the opportunity to raise the issue never seemed to pop up. In any event, the revelation would crush him now. That, and probably get me into a bubbling cauldron of trouble worse than a simple memory wipe.

It troubled me that no one at Eldridge had discovered my adoption yet. Maybe their much-vaunted records system had some holes in it, after all.

With her eyes closed, Priestess/Dr. Fleischer held the polished granite torus in front of her with both hands, muttering a sibilant string of arcane phrases.

All three stone objects began to hum soft and low at the limits of my hearing. The ring rose from her hands. Once it attained the doctor's height, glyphs glowing the hue of a Bermuda lagoon lit up, wrapping around the ring. The device floated to hover a foot above my head.

Fleischer opened her eyes, flattened her hands, and the stone ring descended. It stopped level with my eyebrows and began to turn. Slowly at first, accelerating until the symbols were a blur.

Had this happened my first week at Eldridge orientation, I would have blurted out, "Is that supposed to happen?" I have since learned Eldridge employees usually know what they're doing.

Unless one hears "Uh-oh," that is. Then hit the deck.

"Relax, Mr. Yeager," said Fleischer. Her siren voice could coax a foaming rabid dog to wag its tail and roll over. The blue circles on the hand stones tilted toward me. I had the uncanny sensation the stones were actually looking at me... or *inside* of me. They had an unsettling accusatory quality about them.

The doctor pulled a folder from underneath the lacquered box and an ivory scrimshaw pen from her lab coat pocket. "Well, Fibula, let us see what we can find."

Fibula? My mistake—it wasn't ivory. Its name would also explain the unusual shape. At least it wasn't a human bone.

While I understood employees could name their pen whatever they wanted—as the spirit of the scribe inside cannot remember their name before they passed on—it struck me as a terribly demeaning act to rename the poor soul after the item in which they were housed.

"Mr. Yeager, I see here you failed to receive your doctoral degree. Bummer." She regarded me with a slight pout, while her eyes invited a response.

"Yes." I squirmed a tiny bit. The ring whined as it moved to reposition itself, centering itself again around my head just above eye level. "College politics, doctor. The astrophysics department convinced the committee to trash my dissertation. Payback for Dr. Petrakis choosing me as his assistant instead of the astrophysics wunderkind."

"Try not to move, Apprentice. The three pieces of the *Habilitas* may be stone, but they are delicate instruments." She alternately eyed the ring, spinning at a constant rate, and listened to the hand stones. Satisfied they still operated properly, she flipped to her next sheet. "Don't worry about your scholastic record. If you pass today's tests, we can have a company adjuster change that. Depending on the quality of today's results, maybe we'll even add a *summa cum laude* notation to your new PhD."

"That would be nice."

Dr. Fleischer pointed her index finger at the stones and whirled it about, stirring the air. The blue ringlet eyes swiveled on their granite surface to face her, and she bent at the waist to peer into them. "Oh my," she fretted. Her eyebrows twisted as tortuously as her mouth. "That is unusual."

With my head straight, I strained my eyes, perchance to catch whatever she saw in the Aptitude Stones. No such luck. "Anything wrong?"

"Your record shows Ms. Kovalenko recommended a course of PQ calisthenics. You *did* practice, no?"

"Yes." I did them all right. I followed them to the letter, and Caltrop made sure I did my daily exercises. Never mind I had zero confidence in the whole ESP business. "But heart wasn't into it."

"Then you must have eaten your Wheaties, Mr. Yeager. A defeatist attitude like that usually nullifies any attempts to improve one's paranormal quotient. That and only four weeks' time? Nevertheless, the *Habilitas* indicates you now have a PQ-2." She scratched her head briefly, then dove into her sheaf of papers. "Most unexpected, even for the Yeager bloodline. Let me double-check the stats on your parents. Erwin and Esther Pritchard, correct? They seemed like fine people," said Fleischer with an approving nod.

"My *adoptive* parents," I said flatly with a shrug. "They were all right."

The stone ring whined. "Keep still," Fleischer admonished again, a few decibels higher.

A coffee mug full of pencils clattered on the floor in the anteroom. Petrakis had jumped from his leaning wall to plant his open palms on the computer desk. He gawked at me through the window, looking like he swallowed a goldfish. Kovalenko tried without success to shove him away from her computer.

Oh, crud. Sorry, Petrakis.

Dr. Fleischer scoffed with a dismissive chuckle. "Adopted? Don't be silly."

"I'm serious. I was adopted when I was six years old. The Pritchards never told me who my birth mother was, and by law, the state of Alaska can't." A glance at Petrakis was followed by a guilty shrug in his direction.

The ring wobbled, almost screaming at me. Fleischer didn't—she instead flashed an instant of confusion at me. "That's..." She paged through several sheets in the folder before she hammered a finger on the exposed page. "...impossible. You *are* a Yeager, from your mother's side."

"No disrespect, doctor, but if this is some psycho-analysis test, or another aura trick, it's in catastrophically poor taste."

"No, no, Michael." Fleischer held the folder up to my face, avoiding the spinning ring of stone around my noggin. "See here? Your DNA has the same markers as Mr. Pritchard and Mrs. Pritchard née Yeager. They *were* your biological parents." The urgency in her voice barely overcame the rising pitch of the whirring ring.

The snow-detecting scar on the top of my head itched.

The spinning glyphs' color shifted subtly from a solid icy blue to include thin streaks of red. The stones' eyes duplicated the unsettling change.

She flipped the pages to another DNA test. "And here as well. This scan confirms you're related to Adjuster Emeritus Chuck Yeager."

Having scoured through a few hundred genetic chromatographs with my advisor's HIV/AIDS research, I handily spotted the matching patterns in the high-tech scramble of white, gray, and black rectangles. Evidence notwithstanding, there was a flaw in Fleischer's reasoning.

"Now I *know* you're BS-ing me, doctor. DNA testing only became available last year in '85. Erwin and Esther died six years ago, buried under burning ash when Mt. St. Helens blew its stack."

The itch on my scalp burned. The spinning ring screamed to a halt.

I screamed louder.

CHAPTER 13

The inside of my skull felt like it was being scraped out by a citrus juicer. Through my tear-filled eyes, the glyphs blazed brightly, their colors shifting back and forth from cobalt to carmine and every hue in between.

The ring lowered, blocking my vision. Without warning, it shrank, squeezing against my eyes, ears, and the back of my skull. The thing twisted, grinding against my hair and skin in a vise-like grip. I felt like my head was being yanked out by an oil filter wrench.

I spilled out of my chair onto my knees, pulled by the granite ring imbued with a will of its own. Through my eyelids pressed shut tight, my vision was still bathed with burning blue swaths darkened by red light made darker with my blood.

Kovalenko yelled, "Priestess? What is the *Habilitas* doing?" Her voice distorted as the overhead speaker strained past its peak volume.

Fleischer made a reply, but what wasn't drowned out by my own wails of agony, she said in a tongue I didn't recognize. The only thing I caught between both her and my cries was her shouts of a strange word, "*Alberich*," over and over.

My fingers found small gaps between the stone and my head, but I couldn't get any leverage to pull it off. A searing red flash momentarily blinded me. If someone told me two miniature volcanoes had erupted behind my eyes, I wouldn't argue with them.

Both hands vibrated with the cracking of stone and an explosion of sapphire blue, loud as a pistol shattering my eardrums. The pressure crushing my skull vanished.

A blood-curdling scream was cut short with a sickening gurgle, followed by the rat-a-tats of dozens of stones striking the walls and dribbling onto the surrounding floor. Granite dust filled my nostrils.

Wiping blood and grit from my eyes, I gawped as the two remaining pieces of the ring in my fists crumbled into pebbles. Fleischer lay on her stomach with her face turned toward me. Her expression of shock was marred by eruptions of blood from a dozen punctures and lacerations. On the two hand stones lay her folder's remains, blazing with cold blue fire.

Holes like bullet strikes pockmarked the observation window. Kovalenko and Petrakis peeked over its sill with wary eyes. An ear-splitting klaxon sounded. The examination room flooded with red light. A second of silence, and the alarm repeated.

I scrambled on all fours over to Fleischer, puffing with exertion as I rolled her bulk onto her back. Acid jumped up my esophagus when I spotted several shards of the shattered ring plunged deep into her throat. The bloodied spikes of granite stabbed around her larynx—in a near-perfect circle. My hands were poised to remove the projectiles, but I stopped myself. If they were removed, she might drown in her own blood.

Her eyes fluttered and turned toward me. They didn't burn with hatred, fear, or accusation. They flew wide with wonder. She opened her fist, her trembling fingers curling again to beckon me closer. I turned my head to lower an ear close to her face. Her mouth slick with crimson spittle, she gurgled, "You poor, wonderful thing..." She attempted a piteous smile, only to be interrupted with a red cough. "Two houses seek the traitorous third... both the High and the Gray... the soul of the son is forfeit. He remains hidden within. You must protect Alber—"

In unison, the spikes pulsed blue and dug deeper into her flesh, as though pushed in by some invisible hand. Fleischer's mouth filled with liquid, and she sputtered red foam. Her lips and face turned pale.

The alarm blasted my eardrums once more. The door behind me whammed open, and Kovalenko and Petrakis circled us.

Kovalenko checked Fleischer's pulse, whipped open her priestess's silver embroidered jacket, and began the steady rhythm of CPR. "Turn her head and ventilate her."

"Her airway's blocked. We can't remove that shrapnel," I said.

"Do– as– I– *say*," she barked, her syllables in time with every thrust applied to Fleischer's chest. "Any air is better than none."

Petrakis slammed a first aid kit on the floor and slapped its largest gauze pads on Fleischer's worst bleeders. The oversized bandage near her jugular and another over her femoral artery soon flooded with bright crimson. The three of us continued our dance of futility until the emergency medical staff arrived.

The bullhorns ceased the moment the two men crossed the threshold of the examination room. I goggled at how their gurney floated with no visible means of support other than four beams of unworldly violet light vibrating down from each corner. On the side of one rail, someone had slapped cockeyed stickers with the logos of Pegasus Air, TWA, and Pan Am.

The medicos whisked Fleischer away on the silent gurney. A third EMT with the nameplate "Alvarez" hovered around me, inspecting the ring of abrasions and bruises around my cranium. Kovalenko leapt to her feet to follow her priestess, but I grabbed her wrist and held fast. "Let me go," she wailed.

"Fleischer kept repeating some word over and over." I swallowed. "Then she said something about houses seeking a traitor. What did she mean?"

Her thin wrist, slick with bloody sweat slipped out of my grasp. "I must be with my priestess if she passes!"

Alvarez assisted me back into the examination chair. Regarding Petrakis with a sardonic eye, I asked the forbidden question. "Was that *supposed* to happen?"

"Most assuredly not. But let's double-check with an authority." He pulled his pen out of his vest pocket. "What say you, Namiki? If you please, can you find any other instance of a *Habilitas* test that ended so... unexpectedly?"

I half expected the enameled dragon spiraling up the length of the high-quality pen to move. After a pause, the pen cap clicked itself once. Petrakis returned Namiki deep in his vest pocket. The pen raised itself until the dragon's eyes peeked over the seam.

"She says no."

"I get the feeling my assessment is a colossal flop. First, Dr. Fleischer confirms my PQ is near the bottom of the barrel, then I find out you screwed up my birth records. While I'm wondering if you guys are going to mindwipe me, her magic toy tries to kill me. When do I get redacted?"

"My boy, try not to count your eggs until they're broken." Petrakis sidled over, planting his feet in front of me. He folded his arms and glowered at me.

It really wasn't a glower, but the absence of his insipid know-it-all grin made it feel almost as bad.

I winced as Alvarez wiped cold rubbing alcohol above the tender lumps blossoming above my ears and on the back of my skull. She then dabbed a salve around the same areas. My eyes watered when I caught the whiff of a stench like broiled skunk—with the fur still on. It was worth it. The pain vanished, and I could sense the swelling going down.

"When were you going to tell me you were adopted? I stuck my neck out for you, based mostly on my supposition you had the Yeager bloodline."

I tried not to look sheepish. "Don't dump this on me—they're *your* records. I tried to tell you several times, but I never had the chance. You, everybody, and every *thing* at Eldridge have been giving me non-stop crash courses on every topic between the Sun and the Tenth Planet—from etiquette, protocols, and regulations in that encyclopedia you call a company primer; from magic to aliens; from angels to demons; from Old Ones to Elder Gods... Then there's the screwball courses like '*Cryptids 305: Housebreaking a Cryptid*' and '*Psychic Defense 210: How to Die Less Horribly.*' I haven't been able to think about much else. Just surviving each day filled every waking moment." I kicked one of the ring fragments across the room to make my point.

Petrakis unfolded his arms and grunted. "We *have* been pushing you. But honestly, until the matter of your lineage is settled, I cannot foresee what consequences might fall out from this oversight... for either of us."

"You don't believe the Eldridge DNA tests, either?"

"Call it a healthy skepticism. It's still a fledgling science. Or it could just be a bureaucratic mix-up—these things happen in any corporation. Another possibility is that your parents were lying to you."

"Why in the world would they lie about *that*?"

He shrugged. "I try not to presuppose, I merely follow the evidence. That's the making of a good scientist, as well as a good assessor." Petrakis paced a few yards around the room but gave up when pebbles of the shattered *Habilitas* crunched under almost every step. "So let's dive into the available evidence. What do you remember before age six? Anything about your supposed birth parents?"

"I have no memories before I was adopted. I barely remember moving from Anchorage, Alaska to Lubbock, Texas with the Pritchards age six."

"Unusual… Most children begin to form memories by age four or five."

"Erwin attributed it to a concussion I received during the Good Friday Earthquake. They told me I was the only survivor from my first foster home, rescued from some cubbyhole after it collapsed. Esther believed my mind chose to erase the trauma of my experience in one of the worst quakes in America."

"You don't refer to them as 'Mom and Dad'?"

I turned my gaze at my shoes, suddenly filled with an awkward unease. "It never felt right somehow. They didn't seem to mind."

"How soon after the earthquake did your family relocate?"

"I'm not sure. I think it was the day after. Esther wanted me to be far away from anything that might stir up the memory, and as quickly as possible."

"Curious… traveling so soon after such an injury." Petrakis shuffled over to Fleischer's pile of paperwork reduced to ashes, tiptoeing around the bits of stone shrapnel with care.

"I think Erwin was concerned about aftershocks."

Petrakis inspected the remains of the report, holding his open palm over leaves of gray ash. "Not even warm," he said with a scoff. Brushing off the cinders, he lifted out the stones, turning them about in his hands. Their accusing blue rings had vanished. He mused to himself, "Well, Petrakis. What do you make of this?"

Without looking at her medical tote the size of a king-sized gym bag, Alvarez deftly extracted a hand mirror. Holding it between my head and hers, she said something I hadn't heard since I was a kid watching Miss Nancy in *Romper Room* on the boob-tube. "Romper, bomper, stomper boo. Tell me, tell me, tell me, do."

The mirror's surface dissolved into crystal transparency.

Ignoring me, Alvarez continued, "Magic Mirror, tell me true. Does Yeager's head have a boo-boo?"

That corny TV shtick was for *real*? I dove into the disorderly file cabinet of my memories, frantically trying to recall if I did something rude when Miss Nancy called my name through the television screen.

The mirror darkened, and a ghostly image of the Alvarez's skull, brain, and vertebrae filled the portal. Her bony jaw moved as she spoke.

"Silly me," she said with a *tsk*. "I can never tell which side is which until it's working." She spun the hand mirror about, and I could see her face while she fluoroscoped my noggin. She instructed me to sit still as she circled about, her gaze fixated on my skull through the magical medical apparatus.

"Will I live?"

"Of course," she said with a titter. "Though there's a network of unusual fused cracks at the juncture of the sagittal and coronal sutures."

"You mean the top of my skull?"

"Yes. I've never seen a break quite like it. It's shaped somewhat like a yin-yang, except with *three* teardrop shapes."

I cracked a sardonic grin. "Might explain why it itches when it's about to snow."

"What's more troubling though, is a large mass underneath that area. It's not a hematoma, but the tissue is three times as dense as the surrounding gray matter."

Every muscle along my spinal column twitched. The specter of brain cancer pinched me in the ass.

"Did you have an accident as a baby, before the anterior fontanelle had a chance to fuse?"

"No idea." I was relieved Alvarez didn't ask about the big C. Or maybe her bedside manner kicked in just in time. "Weren't you here when I told Dr. Petrakis I have no memory before age six?"

"Were you abused as a child?"

That got my hackles up. "No."

"Did the *Habilitas* attack you there as well?"

"No, that stupid thing buzz-sawed around my whole noggin."

"That matches up with the hairline cracks on both your temporal bones." She slipped the mirror back into its fitted pocket deep inside her tote. "Nothing life-threatening, but what I found is serious enough to mend them right away. And maybe check that brain mass. Let's get you to the ER."

Petrakis and I tried to relax after Alvarez called for transport. Both of us failed.

Unable to sort out which question to ask first, I burbled out small talk instead. "Thank goodness that alarm stopped. I was afraid it would finish the job the ring started and split my skull."

"Yes, it *was* obnoxious," said Alvarez. "But at least be thankful you were in the medical wing. They don't use the corporate emergency system."

Petrakis must have caught my perplexed expression. "You covered that on day four. I suppose you can be forgiven for not recalling that under the circumstances."

Further explanation would have to wait. A new orderly rolled an ordinary earth-bound wheelchair into the examination room. He handed it off to Alvarez, who guided me into the chair.

"I don't rate a UFO taxi?" I said, accompanied by a mock pout.

"Ignore him," said Petrakis.

The three of us cruised through mostly empty hallways. Occasionally someone we passed would gag behind us, once they caught my trail of burning skunk. One of the questions I had been harboring finally climbed to the surface.

"Will Dr. Fleischer be all right?" Though I fretted about her condition, my underlying motive for asking was pure self-interest. Only Fleischer could explain her bizarre warnings.

"She's getting the best care on the planet." Alvarez navigated me around a tight corner. "But right now, I'm more concerned about you."

"Fine," I grunted. I should have expected a noncommittal answer. "What happened to me back there, Petrakis? Namiki says exploding killer rings aren't a common occurrence. So, what *was* that?"

"Not my field of expertise. You'll have to ask Dr. Fleischer," he said between huffs. His face took on a harder edge. "Or Kovalenko, if the worst..."

"What about videotape? Is there a security recording?"

"We are not in the habit of having cameras in medical observation rooms," said Alvarez, in a tone that indicated she took some slight umbrage.

"What about the new computer? Was it recording anything that might give us a clue?"

"Not that I saw. Just Kovalenko's notes and observations," said Petrakis. "It is quite difficult to coax Old Magic to talk to new technology." He flicked my shoulder. "Day ten. If you keep asking questions for which you should already know the answers, Mr. Yeager, I might recommend the medical department take the cost of the *Habilitas* out of your pay."

"Then I hope Fleischer makes it. Kovalenko couldn't tell me what she meant."

"Oh? What did the doctor say?" he asked with an intensive note.

"I only got bits and pieces. She repeated some word—*Alberich*—

several times. Then she mentioned... that houses are hunting... for the soul of a traitor? Or his son? I'm not sure, it all happened so fast."

"Soul?" he said with an incredulous tuck of his chin. "That's far outside the purview of the *Lapidibus Habilitas*."

We rolled over a floor transition strip between medical sections. My temples pounded with fresh railroad spikes. "Then what—"

"Enough questions for now," said Alvarez. "Dr. Petrakis, you'll have to wait outside."

Another sharp turn, and she trundled me into the rightmost of three bays in what I assumed was the ER treatment room. In the leftmost bay, I spied a trio of medical personnel huddled over Fleischer. Her blood-soaked white and silver robe hung over the edges of the levitating gurney. Unlike her attire, she seemed to be in a vastly improved state. Her minor wounds were treated, and the gauze panels triaged over her gaping wounds had been replaced with new bandages, free of fresh blood.

A glowing globe of yellow hovered over Fleischer's throat. The medicos' distorted shadows splayed onto the privacy curtains separating the bays. Their angular lines had a sinister aspect, reminiscent of the nightmarish *The Cabinet of Dr. Caligari*. While examining her throat, the attending personnel asked questions in hushed voices. The globe pulsed in rhythm with softly spoken responses in Fleischer's untrammeled voice.

To the doctor waiting in my bay, Alvarez perfunctorily said, "minor fracture along both sphenoid-temporal fissures." She held up the Magic Mirror, showing a snapshot of my skull with all its fractures.

The doctor's brow flashed annoyance. He sighed, followed by his shoulders sagging with resignation. After wiping clean the skunk salve from my temples, he turned to a tall cabinet on casters behind him. He selected one of its drawers and pulled out a rod of dark indigo crystal, crazed with hundreds of tiny fractures filled with sulfurous rust. At its thinner end were two spherical nodules. He clicked a plastic switch on the rod's thick end.

Two needles of yellow light jutted out of the crystal protuberances and began to cross and recross each other in a pattern resembling knitting needles in action. Holding the apparatus near my temple, the doctor ran it down the sides of my skull, uncomfortably close to my eyes.

With a satisfied grin, the doctor stepped back and shut off the device. He placed the electro-magic wand back into the waiting drawer. With an expression more snarl than smirk, the doctor ambled out, adding,

"Do notify me if there's another emergency. Like if the patient stubs his toe."

Only after I unclenched my teeth, did I notice the stabbing pain had vanished. I looked at Alvarez expectantly. "Can I go?"

"Not quite yet." From a smaller cabinet she produced a humdrum EKG monitor and pasted its terminals on my chest and limbs. "Just relax. We'll need to keep you under observation for a bit, while we line up some tests for that brain mass."

I tried as best I could to settle myself into the unforgiving hospital bed. My racing thoughts revolved around the events of the past hour. Questions to which I couldn't even assign words were pursued by fears that laughed diabolically. They all stumbled to a stop when the conversation spilled over from two bays over.

"What seems to be the problem here, ladies and gentlemen?" said a haughty velvet voice that sliced through the hushed medical and magical palaver.

"Glad you're here, Director," said a man's voice, constricted with anxiety. "As you can see, we've closed her multiple lacerations. We bypassed the throat blockage with a tracheotomy, so the patient is no longer critical. However, we can't seem to extract these stone fragments near Dr. Fleischer's larynx."

Kovalenko's voice chimed in, shivering with apprehension. "We've tried forceps, a Nepalese *hataa-una* spell, even the torque-tractor ray."

"The new tool reverse-engineered from the crashed Epsalian vessel?" asked Mr. Velvet Voice.

"Yes," answered the male. "But when we pull on one needle of shrapnel, all the others flash blue and drill further down. If we had two extra pairs of hands, we might try to extract all of them simultaneously."

I wriggled off the bed as quietly as I could manage. Corralling the EKG wires in one hand, I slowly rolled my monitor close. Through pursed lips, I silently exhaled as I bent over and peeked through the foot-wide gap between the privacy curtain and floor.

Around the gurney's violet levitation rays circled three pairs of powder blue sneakers and a pair of patent leather Oxfords. Oxford Man hummed for a moment. "What is that material? Obviously not ordinary stone."

"They're remnants from the *Annulus Habilitas*," said Kovalenko.

"Remnants you say," said the director. "*That* is why you're running into resistance. You cannot just yank them out. You must reason with it."

"Reason?" said the first man.

"With the spirit that inhabited the *Habilitas*. It's spread over all these remaining pieces." The sneakers shuffled around each other, making way for the Oxfords as they moved to the other side of the gurney. "Good Heavens, what caused the *Annulus* to do this?"

"Priestess Fleischer was re-evaluating a new graduate," said Kovalenko. "One with PQ-2."

"Only two?" It was the Oxford man's turn to sound apprehensive. "Who was the interviewee?"

"Michael Avery Yeager."

The director sucked in a sudden draught of air. "Oh, yes. Adjuster Emeritus Charles Yeager's relation. He advised me on our new graduate's situation."

I cocked my head at the unexpected intimation. Something was not adding up. Everyone at Eldridge thinks I'm related to this legendary big-wig, and now I find out this big shot I don't know from Adam has been keeping tabs on me?

"After my call with the elder Yeager, I read Apprentice Yeager's file. That lad has a lot to live up to. With such a low PQ, that will be a tall order." After a long filling of his lungs, he blasted out a whistling sigh. "Well, let's at least get an eyewitness account of what happened."

My body tensed, ready to jump back on the bed. I gradually relaxed, except for my ears, which stood at attention to catch the stream of mumbles from Director Oxford Shoes. I was beginning to regret not paying closer attention to Latin in school—

"We greet thee, *Turia Feir*, Watcher of Mortals; *Luin Turith*, Blue Watcher amongst your own kind," said the Director.

—and even less attention during *Cryptids 400: Elven Language*.

A sliver of a whisper fluttered under the privacy curtain. I tilted my head and held my breath, but could not make out any of the Elven words which glistened like silver run along the edge of Damascus steel.

"Tell me, Watcher. How did this sad fate befall you?"

A long stream of argent syllables shimmered like a placid river.

"I understand. You have my word your secret shall be kept." The director took another barrelful of a breath. "In return, please spare your servant Fleischer and return her to us. She has learned her error and shall keep her silence as well. I shall see to it."

The Oxfords took a step back, and the blue sneakers shuffled forward. Soon clinks of stone in a metallic pan chimed in rapid succession. Kovalenko sighed in relief.

"You have my thanks. Rest now, *Turia Feir*. Your long task is done. Return to your brethren and rest in the homelands of *Band Cevan*." A nervous silence filled the air until a delicate exhale fluttered the curtains. Mr. Velvet and his Oxfords faced the sneakers. "Where is Apprentice Yeager now?"

"He's here in ER, two bays over," said Alvarez.

"*What!*" spluttered the director, his refined baritone marred by gritty anger. He spat out another phrase of Latin, and all fell silent.

CHAPTER 14

The beeps from Fleischer's heart monitor ceased.

I kissed the floor, trying to see if she had flat-lined.

A forceps clattered on the floor—except there was no clatter. Three pairs of sneakers jumped away. They should have squeaked like a squad of basketball players. I heard nothing of the sort, only silence.

Just like the helicopter that pulled me out of Lick Observatory.

Time to play possum. I clambered back onto the bed as stealthily as anyone could, only after I realized the spell didn't extend to my bay. Laying ramrod straight, I shut my eyes. The pair of Oxfords' heels clacked on the floor at the foot of my bed.

"Good evening, Mr. Yeager. If you're going to attempt deception, you should have better control of your autonomic system. I don't need an EKG monitor to see your pulse is well-nigh jumping off your wrist. Besides, it is not a good idea to attempt to fool your director."

I snapped open my eyes, focusing immediately on a paunchy balding gent sporting a white mustache not quite grown into a handlebar. In his charcoal three-piece business suit, he was a ringer for the Monopoly man. He took a pair of pince-nez glasses from his jacket pocket and unhooked my medical chart from the foot of my gurney. His pen of gold and jasper peeked its cap out in front of a smartly cornered handkerchief.

"My director? I passed?" I almost blurted out the question of whether memory wipe and redaction were off the table, but my common sense kicked in and told me not to give him any ideas.

"It is not written in stone yet, but my fellow directors have fewer personnel requests in the HR queue." With a laconic blink of his eyes, he replaced the chart. "Their requests are lodged predominantly with Non-Human Resources."

Swinging my legs over the bed's edge, I sat up to face him. I searched for a badge on his lapel and jacket pocket.

"My apologies. I'm Director Ventnor—Departments of Assessments, Adjustments, and Accounting, North America West Coast." His hands stiffly at his side, he gave a curt nod and snapped his legs together. I half expected a click of heels.

I slid off the bed and did the same. Not that ninja split-toe shoes would click. "Might I ask a question, Director?"

"By all means." His smile seemed confused, like his mustache fought his mouth to hide his impulses. I could only guess if his similarly bushy eyebrows hid nervousness, impatience, annoyance, or cruelty.

I wanted to ask, "What's the big secret," but the direct approach would surely hit a brick wall. "Actually, two questions. Will Dr. Fleischer pull through, and who is... was *Turia Feir*?"

"The priestess's prognosis is good. Though I doubt she will be able to speak, let alone cast any spells, for a long time. One unfortunate proviso of her particular brand of thaumaturgy requires her healing to proceed at its own pace. A curative spell would return her voice but render her useless as a Banduri. As far as the dear departed spirit of the *Habilitas*, I'm afraid you'll have to wait for an explanation until after your Oath of Service ceremony."

"Oath? I've already signed two trees' worth of nondisclosure agreements."

Ventnor chuckled. "Mere paper containing simple legal devices. You'll find at Eldridge & S.Q. Amos Insurance, there are things more concrete than Man's law. And far more binding."

"Can you at least tell me why *Turia Feir* attacked the both of us?"

His pen inched up between his handkerchief and pocket lining, then clicked its cap twice.

"Yes, Hadrian?" Ventnor uncapped the pen and pulled out a pocket notebook from under the opposite lapel. I caught the pen's brand embossed on its gold clip.

First, there was Petrakis' Namiki Dragonne Special, then Fleischer's creepy eponymous bone pen Fibula, and now Ventnor's Hadrian Unlimited. Did everyone name their pens after the material or manufacturer? It's not like the dear-departed spirits inhabiting them would mind as they couldn't remember their previous names. Still, I would hate it if my boss called me something utilitarian like "UC Santa Clara" or "Biochemist." For a place with the *unusual* oozing out of every corner, I found it disappointing that Eldridge's senior employees demonstrated so little imagination.

The pen slid out of Ventnor's hand and danced a little jig on his notebook. It jotted the period at the end of a sentence with proud finality before slipping itself back neatly into his waiting hand.

Ventnor raised a bushy white eyebrow before gnawing on his mustache. He slipped the pen into his jacket. "I see. Please inform Vice President Hibara that the three of us shall be there momentarily. Also, clear my calendar for the rest of the evening."

Hadrian clicked twice and sank into its pocket.

The levitation gurney carrying Fleischer glided behind Ventnor, guided by a masked ER orderly and Kovalenko. Their sneakers fluoresced powder blue iridescence next to the unearthly columns of violet light. Alvarez followed, entering my bay with her best nurse's smile.

"Remove his monitor," said Ventnor, clasping his hands behind his back.

Alvarez's eyes darted between me and the equipment displaying my vitals. "He's still under observation and waiting for tests."

"Release him under my authority," he shot back with the decisiveness of a hanging judge.

After a flustered acknowledgment, she removed the EKG pads. I yipped when she peeled off the last one over my heart.

"Walk with me, Mr. Yeager," said Ventnor. He strutted out of the ER at a pace that belied his portliness.

Petrakis sat alone on a sofa in the waiting room, lost in thought. His fingertips bounced off each other, like five-legged spiders doing jumping jacks. He bolted to his feet when he spotted us.

Ventnor quick-stepped past him without a glance, only saying, "We *three* are required." Petrakis fell into order behind us without a word. His face went quite pale. I gave him a noncommittal "*I dunno*" shrug.

Our little trio walked a Byzantine path past several departments, many of which would be found in any insurance company in the Mundane world: marketing, records, accounting, sales, and other snooze-worthy departments. However, I'd be willing to bet they didn't have anything like the Remote Viewing or Astral Clientele units we passed.

As we marched through each section, we left a wave of hushed whispers and raised eyebrows in our wake. I was sure I heard a few snickers and snorts in the mix. With the combination of a resolute director wearing a snarl that would stop a clock with a nervous plebe in tow, it could be forgiven if any observer inferred the poor newbie was going to get his butt reamed out. My ears and cheeks burned from the undesired attention and my rampant imagination.

Ventnor halted in front of an elevator, its doors inlaid with the corporate logo in mother-of-pearl and onyx. He placed his palm on a darkened glass panel to his right, which flashed a verdant green.

Having to wait in silence for the elevator was sandpaper on my frazzled nerves. I noisily inhaled between my teeth, about to ask a question, but Petrakis picked up on it. His whole face became a frown, and he shook his head to quash the question before I could ask. I fretted if I would ever get an explanation as to what Dr. Fleischer's warnings might mean.

The doors whispered open. Once inside, I scanned for the elevator buttons. There were none. The sealed car did not budge.

"With whom is your appointment, Director Ventnor?" The woman's voice vibrated from the floor through the soles of my feet at the same time they registered in my ears. I searched high and low for a speaker. It must have been tossed into the same trashcan as the buttons.

Inspecting his manicured nails, he said, "Vice President Hibara, please."

The doors opened a split-second after the words left his lips.

Led by Ventnor, we ambled into a lobby befitting a grand hotel. On our left, a mural in the style of Hokusai's *Great Wave* depicted Mt. Fuji beset on all sides by catastrophes. To the east, a cresting tsunami threatened to grapple with the mountain's base. To the west, a fire-breathing squid *kaiju* that would dwarf King Kong attacked the snow-capped peaks of the slumbering volcano. Behind the holy mountain, a menacing stormfront approached. Within the dark clouds spitting great arcs of lightning lurked a pair of sinister red eyes.

On our right was an array of plush office chairs, one-quarter of them filled with an assortment of people dressed in immaculate business attire, each with an attaché case. Interspersed between them sat various humanoids from the world's mythologies, wriggling in chairs designed for human comfort. In their hands—and claws—some clutched scrolls sealed with ribbons, others held red envelopes.

I inched closer to Ventnor as we walked along a red carpet runner leading to a desk, behind which sat a young Japanese woman. Racing stripes of vivid emerald flowed down her polished jet-black hair past her temples. She stood with a polite smile, circled to the front of her desk, and bowed to Ventnor. Her demure smile and nails were painted with the same brilliant green. She extended an arm, pointing toward a pair of doors embossed with the depiction of a young but fierce warrior, wielding a spear in one hand and a sword in the other. His helmet bore a golden symbol—three broad leaves of ginkgo enclosed by a circle. He rode astride a ferocious beast, an awe-inspiring combination of unicorn and dragon, snorting out steam from flared nostrils. A fox with multiple tails ran alongside his chimera mount. I hoped the bas-relief was not an accurate representation of our VP.

The receptionist pressed an unlabeled button, one of a dozen on a small console on her desk. From the device's speaker issued a woman's voice, quite different from the previous flat emotionless elevator announcer. She projected confident sultriness that could entice Odysseus away from the Sirens. "Vice President Hibara will see you immediately. If you would follow the receptionist."

A rumble of indignant gasps, growls, and snarls emanated from the peanut gallery behind us.

The double doors swung open toward us, only wide enough for us to enter single file. My mounting case of butterflies delivering nasty-grams to my stomach was interrupted by an aroma that made time stop. Notes of camphor, cinnamon, and conifer calmed my jitters.

The room was dominated by an enormous square Oriental wool area rug, the corners of which were posted with four alabaster urns. Around it, warm wooden floors reflected the ceiling lighting. Cypress and camellia bonsai stood guard at the ends of two Chesterfield couches of coffee-black leather facing each other. A long coffee table separated the opposing sides. On walls several feet behind each couch hung floor-to-ceiling scrolls of rice paper inscribed with two-foot-tall *kanji* characters. I tried to memorize them, hoping to decipher them later.

At the far end of the square was a similarly overstuffed chair, behind which brooded a series of sliding wall panels. Their mural depicted a pastoral scene in pastels, painted with highlights of gold. It was pleasant enough, if not for the center panels, where two ogres in samurai battle regalia clashed swords, their blades crossing at the center doors' seam.

Standing with hands folded in front of herself, Ms. Emerald Accents faced the panels. They presently opened, and through them ambled a slight twig of an elderly man. Short and bespectacled, in a formal suit befitting a prime minister, he shuffled into the room. I tried not to think how foolish my apprentice's garb appeared by comparison.

A split second after I saw him, I *sensed* him.

If I, as a low-grade paranormal misfit, could pick up the tingle from Dr. Fleischer's beguiling aura, then even a Mundane could perceive that VP Hibara radiated serious juice. Enough to blow every light bulb in the building.

His smile hinted at an inner serenity, like he had solved the riddle from some cosmic Sphinx. Three steps behind him followed a woman carrying a black ceramic tea service dotted with cherry blossoms dancing on a delicate breeze. She was the spitting image of our stunning receptionist, except her nails, lips, and racing stripe blazed a radiant sapphire. Her hair's colorful accent shimmered with brilliance and tinkled like a myriad of tiny bells, suggesting that each strand might be spun from actual gemstone.

The sliding panels closed, their ogres' swords meeting to strike each other again. But not before the swish of silk caught my ear. The hem of an ornate black and white kimono flashed behind the gap, and a confusing mix of musk and cherry blossoms tickled my nose.

Our receptionist bowed deeply, as did Ventnor and Petrakis. I did as well, though Petrakis had to snap me out of my gaping stupefaction by pressing firmly on the back of my neck. Hibara sat in his chair, descending into its plushness with aristocratic grace. Selecting one couch, Ventnor followed suit, as did Petrakis and I in the other facing him.

The sapphire attendant served us in order by rank, silent as a forest fawn. I swear I could hear myself sweat. The green tea, with its hint of jasmine, flooded my being with much-needed calm, washing away the enervation from today's events as an appreciated bonus.

The moment I placed my black cup back in its saucer, the vice president closed his dark brown eyes and spoke.

Though I could order food in San Jose's Japantown restaurants without embarrassing myself, Hibara's speech was utterly unintelligible to my ear. After a few sentences addressed to Ventnor, I got the impression his words, whatever language it might have been, came out backward, like a recording in reverse.

Ventnor hung on every word, until he replied, "Yes."

Hibara peppered him with a series of short interrogatives. At least, that's what they sounded like. Ventnor swallowed with an audible gulp, like he was getting grilled on the witness stand. He said, "I did not witness the incident, nor have I had time to assess the situation fully. But I believe your assessment is correct."

Toward Petrakis Hibara turned, his eyes still closed and his saintly smile unperturbed. Another stream of backwards babble flowed out of his mouth.

Petrakis glanced in my direction and swallowed. "The *Annulus Habilitas* first attacked Mr. Yeager, trying to crush his skull. Dr. Fleischer then shouted several strings of words. I could not infer if she was issuing a command, warning, or prophecy. The *Annulus* shattered. Shrapnel hit the doctor, stopping her in mid-sentence."

Then Hibara turned to me. His eyelids opened, slow as a curtain rising, revealing pupils like glowing embers.

"What did Priestess Fleischer say to you?" he said in plain English.

My reply was unusually calm, the tea having dissolved the jangling anxiety that had my adrenals jumping all afternoon. "She repeated the word '*Alberich*' several times. She said she felt sorry for me, then tried to warn me that two houses were hunting for the soul of a traitor's son."

I desperately wanted to ask Hibara what all that meant, but I couldn't have forced the question past my lips without a sledgehammer.

Hibara blinked, and the searing amber vanished from his pupils. After a pause long enough for a bead of sweat to run down the nape of my neck, he stated, "I see."

I wanted to jump out of my seat and ask, "What do you see? Do you know what Fleischer meant?" My legs and my jaw refused to budge.

He stood, his aged body rising effortlessly as though gravity were an annoyance that could be ignored. He nodded once to us all, saying with firm politeness, "You will excuse me."

My superiors also stood, facing him as he walked behind my couch. No one had to tell me I had best do the same.

My jaw finally unclenched, only to hang open. One of the rice paper hangings behind me had vanished, replaced with another pair of double doors. Their mahogany panels were inlaid with a stained-glass mosaic of a pagoda castle illuminated by the rays of a glorious sunrise.

Mss. Emerald and Sapphire met Hibara at the doors' center. Grasping their recessed handles, they slid the ponderous pocket doors open.

Hibara ambled into the darkness beyond. As he crossed the threshold, his body disappeared into liquid blackness that rippled like he belly-flopped into molasses. The blackness enveloped him with an audible *gloop*.

The "Gem" twins walked the doors closed without a word. No sooner had the ponderous halves of the glass pagoda joined than the two women opened them again.

From a dimly lit cavernous room beyond the doorway came the faint sound of splashing water. From the murkiness emerged Hibara, holding between gloved hands a lacquered wooden tray, on which lay a silver platter, a sheet of vellum, and a pen in a cheap plastic box. Like my apprentice duds, the pen was out-of-place and embarrassingly utilitarian considering the surroundings.

Hibara pressed latches on the tray's underside, and delicate wooden legs swung down and locked in place. Standing the folding table down, he regarded me again with his hands at his side and a patient smile. "Mr. Yeager, if you would, please?"

I circled around the couch to face Hibara from across the tray.

"Who will stand with him?" The request struck me as an order, instead of a question.

"I shall." Petrakis moved to my side. His eyes had a dangerous look.

"Read and sign, Mr. Yeager," commanded Hibara.

Whatever's in that tea should be patented. Otherwise, I'd be jumping out of my ninja footwear.

In front of me was the Oath of Service.

I scanned it quickly, as I knew it by heart—I should, since I started every day for the past month with its recitation. However, I stopped myself mid-paragraph and reread it from the beginning, this time more deliberately, ensuring every word written down matched exactly what I had memorized.

Much of the Oath could pass for the Boy Scout pledge, except its provisos about evaluations, appeals, judgment, and punishments, punishments, punishments. Even though I have no firm belief in a Final Judgment at the End of Days, reciting those clauses always sent a shiver up my neck.

Once I satisfied myself that the document was kosher, so to speak, I took up the dime-a-dozen pen and signed my name. I raised an eyebrow at my cursive squiggles drying into the parchment of actual sheepskin.

My signature was in red.

I placed the Pilot-brand pen back on the tray. My index finger tingled with sleep numbness. From the fleshy tip welled up a pinprick of blood.

"Oh, no, Mr. Yeager," said Hibara, his smile constant. "She is *your* scribe now. Welcome to Eldridge & S.Q. Amos Insurance."

CHAPTER 15

"She?"

"Congratulations. Take it, my boy," Petrakis whispered. His severe eyes stared at Hibara, unblinking. "Put Pilot in your shirt pocket for now."

After a moment of thought, I took up the pen in both hands with a bow of the head, as one would formally accept a business card from a Japanese citizen. "Thank you, Hibara-*sama*. If you please, I think I shall name her *Amelia*. Though only her spirit rests here, she was once human and deserves a modicum of respect, and therefore, a name." And since my scribe could never remember her name, I figured what better name to give a female Pilot?

Amelia clicked her cap twice. I guess she approved.

From the broadening of Hibara's gentle smile, I surmised he was either impressed or amused. Probably the latter, and not in the best way.

"Accompany me, Mr. Yeager." Hibara turned on his heel and strolled into the darkened room beyond.

It struck me that he didn't call me "apprentice." I took that as a good sign.

Until I felt the point of something sharp between my ribs behind my heart. I rotated my head ever so slightly to my left. Petrakis was so close, he could gnaw on my shoulder.

"I'm sorry, my boy," he said. "As your sponsor, I am required to do this."

"What the fu— *heck* are you doing?" Caltrop's words of wisdom stopped me from saying something much more colorful—no cursing inside any Eldridge building. Add that to the list of things nobody's explained to my satisfaction. "I signed the Oath. Is this necessary?"

"Just follow Vice President Hibara," said Petrakis. Ms. Sapphire suddenly appeared to my right. She leaned forward with a grin, somehow polite yet unmistakably deadly, and one arm bidding me onward.

Petrakis' dagger point dug into my skin at unpredictable intervals as we walked with unsynchronized steps. I said out the side of my mouth, "Is this how you initiate all new employees?"

"Certainly *not*, my boy. Special circumstances."

The burble of splashing water grew louder. The carpeted floor gave way to thick grass, two steps after which we trod upon crumbling limestone. Faint wisps of aromas reminiscent of rare orchids tickled my nostrils. The air became heavy with humidity.

With every step, the stone became less riddled with defects. Their irregular edges became smooth cuts and blossomed with a rainbow of stains and colors. Mortar gaps speckled with moss were replaced by solid concrete.

Light beamed down onto the source of the babbling splashes. Out of a simple well encircled by knee-high white marble, danced a jet of diamond-clear water. Upon the rim at regular spacing were placed twelve goblets of various materials: gold, silver, cast iron, pewter, cobalt glass, and others I could only guess at.

The whole arrangement was surrounded by a mosaic of the colored stone blocks. My curiosity burned to untangle what the stone around the well might depict, but I couldn't—not from this angle.

From the shadows around the well emerged eleven figures. I half expected the group to be shrouded in hooded garb and golden masks. Instead, they all wore business attire of the highest caliber—men and women of every nationality wearing an assortment of top-drawer business suits, fine Italian leisure wear, and Gucci power suits with knee-length skirts. Even the occasional outfit boasting regional flair made an appearance, like a stylized monk's saffron robe or a sari of fine silk. My tastes favored the smart ensemble worn by the gent leaning on a stylish umbrella. His suit had the unmistakable lines of a custom creation from London's Savile Row.

Except for Hibara, they all stared at me. Half of them regarded me with surprise; the others spanned the whole emotional gamut from amusement to scoffing derision. I prayed my stupid apprentice's khakis weren't riddled with perspiration stains.

"Welcome, friends. My sincere apologies for calling this *ad hoc* meeting." Hibara bowed to the group, and they responded with slight nods. Raising his arm in my direction, his hand waving me forward, he continued, "Allow me to introduce our newest employee, Mr. Michael Avery Yeager. While he is related to Adjuster Emeritus Yeager, with whom I am sure you are well acquainted..."

I hoped he was right. Otherwise, it was "Redaction, here I come."

"...there is another reason I have asked him to join us in Florida."

Florida? I tried to whisper to Petrakis over my shoulder, but the jab of steel in my back was a good persuader to drop it.

"In this place," Petrakis hissed an inch from my ear, "it is best not to speak unless spoken to."

Ms. Sapphire turreted her head toward Petrakis. She raised a finger to shush us.

"I must protest in the strongest terms, Hibara. This is most improper," said the gent at the well's ten o'clock position. He bristled with short-cropped hair, strong Russian features and accent to match. His double-breasted suit was made with good material, though it did not fit him well, like his tailor drew inspiration from a Lego figure.

The woman directly across from him nodded in stern agreement, then tossed her sari's tangerine sash over her shoulder with a flourish. "I concur. Taking the liberty of admitting anyone lower than director, let alone a new employee, into this sanctuary is unprecedented."

My heart crimped. Her dress, voice, and accent reminded me why I was putting up with all this horse manure. God, I missed Sindhu.

A third voice muttered, "Insulting."

Hibara remained as unperturbed as a mountain lake. "If you will permit me to enlighten you?" When no new objections arose, he continued, imparting a rather lengthy explanation in his unsettling reverse speech code.

I kept an eagle eye on the expressions of the other eleven. I wasn't sure what to make of the tableau of suspicious glances and piercing stares of shock, wonder, or disdain. The Russian fellow went paler than I thought a living human was capable.

After gently clearing his throat, Hibara asked, "Are we all in agreement?"

Eleven heads nodded—including the three quibblers, albeit

begrudgingly.

Hibara took the chalice nearest him on the well's marble wall, a porcelain goblet that had once been broken and reassembled, the cracks and joints filled with gold. Embossed on one side glittered the same trio of ginkgo leaves that graced his office door.

Ms. Sapphire stepped forward, handing her boss a smaller chalice of alabaster china finer than anything Limoges ever produced.

Hibara dipped both receptacles into the water, rippling with sparkling waves. The eleven approached the fountain and scooped up water in their unique chalices waiting for them.

Facing me, Hibara held both vessels in front of himself. He then uttered in an uncustomarily loud voice, "Michael Avery Yeager." He pronounced each name separated by a formal pause, like a pastor at a wedding —or funeral.

"In recognition of your sacrifice, we offer you this boon."

"What sacrifice?" my brain shouted. One I had made, or one I was about to make? Possibly involuntarily? Every muscle in my limbs tensed, and my toes tried to curl around the hard limestone. Petrakis' dagger in my back pricked sharp as ever. Whatever it was in the tea that once calmed me fizzled away, and my ears burned with fresh adrenaline. Hibara's countenance, in stark contrast, was wholly unreadable.

"Whereas this body recognizes the tragic situation of your betrothed, Sindhu Mehra; whereas we acknowledge with somber gravity the solemn promise you both had made each other; we sympathize with your loss, hoping she soon may be released from stasis and returned to the fold of humankind. Therefore, looking forward to that day when we might rid her of the Euryale's curse; or that day you choose to no longer wait for her restoration; we, the Circle of Ageless Waters, admit you into our fellowship and offer you the boon of the *Fuenze deLeon*." He extended the alabaster chalice toward me.

DeLeon? Holy crud, they were offering me the Fountain of Youth.

I thought of pinching myself to rouse myself from this dream. I didn't need to—Petrakis' knife did it for me. Everything remained stubbornly real. My hands stayed glued at my sides.

"Be at peace, Mr. Yeager," said Hibara, soft as silk. "I can guess your suspicions and apprehensions. Strangely enough, these waters *are* poisoned. But their unique amalgam of chemical, magical, and spiritual components combine to make a remarkable elixir. Sir deLeon named this his

'Fountain of Youth,' but that is a misnomer." Hibara swept his gold-veined *kintsugi* chalice in the direction of his circled comrades. "If only that were true. We all would much prefer to be our younger selves again. Sadly, such is not to be. Had deLeon inquired of the native Timucuan shaman before slaying him, deLeon would have more properly named this miraculous creation a 'Fountain of the Ageless.'"

He faced me again, his benevolent smile replaced with an unsettling neutrality. He raised my milky white chalice higher. "If you partake, you shall not age. But be advised you must return every year to maintain your current state." He leveled his forehead at me, and his eyes flashed a momentary golden flicker. "One last proviso, Mr. Yeager. You must *never* speak of this boon, nor your acceptance into the Circle, outside this room. Do you accept?"

A parade of scenarios tumbled past my imagination. What would happen if I did? What must I do when outsiders figure out I don't age? What about my mistaken lineage? What—

Then a memory of my dear Sindhu's face pushed my worries aside, with her smile that could melt a glacier. I could almost feel her arms embracing me, and every inch of my body and soul ached to be with her again.

A deep breath, and I clasped the goblet in a shaky hand.

We thirteen partook. The water was refreshing, but I felt no different.

The knifepoint drilling into my back relented, and Ms. Sapphire took a spot between me and Hibara. I was beginning to intensely dislike her pleasant smile. Hands flat on her thighs, she bowed, then took both our vessels and placed them on the well's edge.

"Welcome to the Circle of Ageless Waters, Mr. Yeager. You have been granted a singular honor, and are now a member of an exclusive fellowship, one that until today was made available only to the upper echelon of senior management. We all trust you shall use this to the benefit of Eldridge & S.Q.Amos."

I nearly choked on a gulp. "I shall."

The Russian added, "We shall be watching."

Before turning toward the well, Hibara addressed Sapphire. "Please escort these gentlemen back to my reception parlor. I have one final item of business to discuss with my fellow regional vice presidents."

Sapphire held out her hand to Petrakis, who returned her knife which looked more like a foreshortened *katana*. It disappeared into a fold of Sapphire's skirt. She walked ahead of us into the murkiness, her torso twisted somewhat unnaturally to watch both us and the path ahead.

Fevered splashes of conjectures wouldn't stop appearing out of nothingness and bounce around my head. What's behind the aptitude Fleischer found in me? Who was *Turia Feir*, and why did he attack the two of us? What were these mysterious "houses" hunting for a soul? What if Fleischer was trying to warn me that this soul was, as she said, 'hidden within?' Like Judgment Day, there are a lot of things that I scoffed at before I joined Eldridge. Reincarnation, despite Sindhu's belief, was one of those spiritual mumbo-jumbos I had never bought into. Over the past month, however, so many of my sacred cows had been slaughtered, that I wasn't sure of much of anything anymore.

What were Petrakis, Ventnor, and that menagerie of VPs keeping from me? Are they all hiding some conspiracy, or are they protecting me from something? Was Sindhu's situation indeed the reason I was admitted to the Circle?

On an entirely different tack, what happens when I stop drinking from the fountain—do I revert to my actual age, or do I shrivel up and die on the spot, my dust vacuumed up by some nameless Eldridge janitor? And why did I have to be forced at knifepoint?

The dance of questions jarred to a halt focusing on the central riddle —Could all the events in today's chaos prove I truly *am* a Yeager? Even if it were so, I couldn't easily disregard my stepparents and a lifetime of experience.

It was enough to make me want to indulge in impromptu primal scream therapy. Instead, I rubbed my temples to stop my head from spinning. I hissed a sharp inhale when I discovered my skull's bones might be healed, but the skin and muscle were still tender.

Out of the gloom surfaced the familiar double doors and Ms. Emerald. I squinted against the sudden inrush of light as Sapphire and Emerald slid open the doors.

I paused, regarding both of them with an inquisitive eye. "Do either of you ever speak?"

The Gem twins shook their heads, and their shoulders bounced from silent giggles.

I stifled the desire to ask if they were human when I caught Petrakis' aghast expression at my impropriety. The women must have read my mind, as they shook their heads a second time. Their courteous yet lethal smiles positively beamed.

I pushed it aside, as I had a more important question to ask Petrakis.

"Was it necessary for you to hold me at knifepoint? I signed the company Oath in blood. Wasn't that enough?" I wanted to add several juicy expletives, but in this room, that surely would have rained down a bolt of lightning on my noggin. Red-faced anger would have to suffice.

Petrakis rubbed his hands together. "Some time ago, this sanctuary had been penetrated by a malignant spirit, lurking within the body of a newly-promoted VP. During the admission ceremony, the combination of the Oath and the waters brought the intrusion to the surface. Because of that precedent, your life was potentially forfeit until you drank, and your sanctity confirmed."

"Until? Wouldn't a dagger in my heart after I drank be kinda... *pointless*?"

Petrakis might have beamed his mock painful smile and put an index finger against one nostril—his usual acknowledgment of a pun. Nope, not this time. He was serious as a tax audit.

"Oh, you're still mortal, my boy. You might never age and possibly heal rapidly, but you are otherwise subject to the whims of the Grim Reaper, just as every other human." He wiped his sweaty palms on his pants' thighs. "Now let us leave this room, and quickly. We are tempting too many Fates talking here."

In the middle of Hibara's spacious parlor stood Ventnor, holding his pocket notebook. His scribe Hadrian was dancing a jig of jots and tittles. As the four of us crossed the threshold, Ventnor looked up. His eyes locked on me with burning accusation. I could practically hear him screaming, "You little shit. How do *you* rate?"

His mustache hid the *scritch* of teeth grinding. Clearing his throat, he put away his pen and notebook, then straightened his vest. "Mr. Yeager, you might be interested to know Dr. Fleischer is out of immediate danger. However, due to the severity of her injuries, she has been placed in a medically induced coma."

"Most unfortunate," mused Petrakis.

"But," I stammered, "I saw her injuries. They weren't that bad."

"Well, *Doctor* Yeager," Ventnor coughed again, loud enough to make his jowls bounce, "apparently, there were complications. In addition,

I advised her physicians to take this measure to preserve her vocal cords. You see, *any* speech at this time might end her spell-casting ability."

"I see." What I really saw was another roadblock to answering the riddle of my lineage, that *Alberich* nonsense, and those who might be hunting me.

"In the meantime, PA Kovalenko has gleaned the data from your abortive aptitude evaluation, along with her observations and recommendations. Vice President Hibara has also reviewed them and issued a directive for your initial placement. I wholeheartedly agree with his decision."

Assuming redaction was not the verdict, where would I be assigned? Would I be sent to medical research to combat any number of new viruses and bacteria? Or find new medicinal agents to incapacitate alien hostiles? More probably, they'd start me out as a basic R&D tech, like any biochem major without a full doctorate. Regardless, did I dare hope to work on the cure for my dearest Sindhu?

"Tomorrow morning, you shall report to the Actuarial department, in the accounting division. Dismissed, Mr. Yeager."

Accounting?!

Are you fuc— flippin' kidding me?

CHAPTER 16

Petrakis and I rode the elevator with Emerald. I attempted to make some small talk with her, but I couldn't think of a single yes-or-no question in the space of one second before the doors opened again. Extending her arm, she nodded, inviting me to exit.

"This is where we part ways for a while, my boy. I must get back to my research." He swiped his nose at me as he stepped back from the doors. Smiling at Emerald, he said, "To the library, if you please, my dear."

In the hallway stood a red-haired woman dressed in no-nonsense business attire. At her side, she held a folder and a small zippered valise. "Good afternoon, Mr. Yeager. I'm Ms. Fillmore from Human Resources. I'll be taking you to your new assignment."

She nodded at Emerald and Petrakis with a quick word of thanks, and the steel and onyx doors closed behind me. "But first, we have a few minor details to take care of."

I was puzzled by our hallway, empty except for us. "You were expecting me?"

"Of course. Now, if you would come with me?"

I followed Fillmore past arrays of windowed offices on both sides. Turning a corner, I squinted against bright golden rays of sunlight beaming horizontally through the west windows over a forest of cubicles. The sun was about to set, and I was overwhelmed by a sudden desire to murder a steak dinner.

"We seldom get a new employee still in apprentice uniform, but we appreciate your situation was a special case. Nevertheless, HR is fully stocked to deal with such circumstances." She stopped at a set of double doors and opened them. "We can't have you leaving our building dressed in such a fashion."

I blinked at a Texas-sized dressing room, replete with racks of jackets, trousers, white shirts, ties, socks, and shoes. In one corner stood a full-length tri-fold mirror.

"Go right ahead, Mr. Yeager. Select your size. I'll be outside when you've finished changing."

Once inside, I shed my khakis and *tabi* at a speed that would impress a TV quick-change artist. Rifling through the jackets, I paused with one in either hand—one a snug fit for a Munchkin, the other with room to spare for Andre the Giant. I pouted, sad that only a single style in deep navy blue was available. Not my best color. At least the shirt was cotton, not a polyester blend.

I quickly picked out my size. Then I had to find my *new* size, when I rediscovered that my old waist size hung loose, my old shirt size stressed the chest buttons, the collar was too tight, and my sleeves and inseams needed another inch.

Finally satisfied at my outfit in the mirrors, I was about to exit when a moment of panic hit. I rescued my scribe from its khaki pocket, slipping Amelia in my jacket's inside pocket. But something still didn't quite feel right.

Director Ventnor's final instructions in Hibara's office crawled back into my head. "Take care, Mr. Yeager. Normally, company policy allots scribes only to assessors, adjusters, and upper management. Therefore, Pilot's abilities must never be used in the presence of others."

"My pen's name is Amelia, sir."

"Yes-s-s," Ventnor said, drawing out the last consonant under his white mustache. "Neither let anyone other than Hibara, Petrakis, or me know you are in possession of a scribe. It would raise indelicate questions that would..." His pause could frighten a king cobra. "...*inconvenience* Vice President Hibara."

Substitute "royally piss off" for "inconvenience."

I hid Amelia inside my jacket and opened the door.

"My, looking quite sharp, Mr. Yeager," said Fillmore. She pointed back the way we came. "Follow me, please?"

Back at the elevators, I placed my hand on the palm reader. It remained dark.

Fillmore blanched. "Gracious, no, Mr. Yeager. That's for upper management floors only." She pointed to the three elevators on the facing wall. The center elevator deposited us—where else?—the thirteenth floor.

"If you could hurry, it's already past the end of regular business hours, and you need to meet your new supervisor."

Walking briskly beside her, I asked, "Is this my new Eldridge regulation uniform?"

"Goodness, no. That's just to tide you over 'til you get home. Which brings me to the many things prepared for your new existence."

She zipped open her valise and one by one, handed me a series of wallet-sized cards. "Here's your company ID, which you will need to enter any Eldridge property, your driver's license, updated with your new Sacramento residence's address, voter registration with the same, Social Security card, company healthcare card, two major credit cards each with a limit equal to six months' salary, and an ATM card attached to your new savings and checking accounts. You'll find your signing bonus has already been deposited there."

"A new residence..." I muttered to myself.

"Yes," she said. Handing me a set of keys, she babbled away. "A nice two-bedroom, two-bath townhouse. All your belongings from your previous residence have been transported there. Those are for your residence and your car. Eldridge took the liberty of giving it a full tune-up and maintenance. Did you know your inspection was overdue?"

I inspected my Social Security card. It had the same number and was laminated. Everything else showed no sign of my previous life in San Jose. "...*and* a signing bonus?"

She regarded me with incredulity. "You signed the Oath, did you not?"

"Yes."

"The standard is three months' salary."

Money. The thought almost made me stumble. Filthy lucre was the farthest thing from my mind over the past four weeks. But it was as good a place as any to start my re-introduction back into the real world. Or Mundane world, whichever term fitted best.

Fillmore glanced at my hands, fumbling with my new pile of cards. "Where's your wallet?"

"I didn't think to look for one in the changing room."

She *tsk*-ed her impatience. "Not to worry." She extracted a new plain men's billfold from her valise, handing it to me. The price tag still hung from the inner liner.

Turning a corner down another branch in this floor's rats' maze of cubicles, I lost my bearings. Fillmore steamed ahead. "Now, about your new position..."

Ever since Ventnor doomed me to accounting, I pictured the drudgery that came along with the term "actuarial"—dull numbers and statistics, all meant to reduce the grand plan of creation, existence, and the meaning of life down to two simple numbers: a time of death and how much to pay out. The sea of cubicles did nothing to dissuade me from my drab preconception.

"Accounting here at Eldridge & S.Q.Amos is quite different from what you would find in other insurance companies. You shall be working in an Advance Threat Prediction Group—ATPG for short."

"Prediction?"

"With a supervisor and five other staff, your group's function is to predict and evaluate when, where, and how the next intrusion—be it alien, spirit, demonic, or other-dimensional—might occur."

"So, no balancing books of profit and loss?"

"Gracious, no. Our Mundane employees do *that* on the third floor." Fillmore peeped out a fingernails-on-chalkboard giggle. "Though most of your work will take place on this floor, ATP group members occasionally get to stretch their corporate legs, coordinating with the Assessment department. Once in a blue moon, a member might be selected to accompany an assessor on a field assignment. Since you know Dr. Petrakis, you're already familiar with that." She squeezed her valise to her chest. "That must have been so exciting!"

"That's one way to put it."

"If you're extremely fortunate, you may even have an assessor temporarily assigned to the group from time to time. But I'm getting ahead of myself." Fillmore turned again down a skinnier walkway lined with cubicles on either side. I was totally disoriented, but at least I neared the end of the labyrinth. This last long row of cubicles terminated in an office door.

It was closed, and the vertical shades along the floor-to-ceiling window were angled almost completely shut. "Ready to meet your supervisor?"

Fillmore didn't wait for an answer. Knocking at the door, she ushered me in once we heard a muffled approval from within.

A wall of humidity and the odor of an aquarium about to go sour hit me full in the face. Bubbling in the nearest corner sat the offending item, its cover light shining down upon an aquarium opaque with algae. A ladle hung over the side.

A man, his back angled toward us, sat in the nook of an L-shaped desk. His immediate workspace held a Sun workstation surrounded by stacks of papers and folders in disarray. The rest of the desk was loaded down with half-unpacked boxes.

He tapped away at his computer, its screen displaying a series of overlaying windows filled with a Supervisor's Hell of reports and Gantt charts. The second-ugliest person I'd ever seen stood and turned, extending his hand toward me.

"Mr. Yeager," said Fillmore, "allow me to introduce to you the supervisor of ATP Group 217, Mr.—"

"Algernon?"

CHAPTER 17

As before, his wretched skin was horribly mottled. But his face had shifted, like he had transformed into his brother. He must have caught the consternation sliding across my face.

With an understanding grin, he said, "Hello again, Mr. Yeager. You'll have to forgive the mess. I haven't had much chance to unpack. You'll have to pardon my appearance as well, as it changes with every sleep cycle. My growth and rebuild modifications are subtle. I try to correct them to maintain my humanoid guise, but the differences accumulate over time, and it's been... almost two weeks since we met last?"

I shook his hand. At the initial touch of living and moving coral, I quailed, pulling back my arm as though I touched a live wire.

"I'm sorry, Professor— Mr. Algernon," I said, tripping over my words. "I guess the memory of my run-in with the Euryale is stronger than I expected." I took his hand again, firmly this time.

"Just Algernon. And I understand your reaction. My interview with Dr. Petrakis revealed much. I'd still like to discuss your own experience when you feel ready."

"Well, I see you're off to a wonderful start," interjected Fillmore, while she and her overly saccharine voice inched toward the door. "When you're finished here, Mr. Yeager, you will find a courtesy car waiting at the front door, ready to take you to your new residence."

Algernon thanked her and closed the door, inviting me to sit. Picking up a coffee mug in one hand, he snapped up the ladle from the aquarium in the other and scooped a heaping helping of the algae bloom into his mug.

Resuming his seat, he took a sip and exhaled with satisfaction. "Can I offer you anything? I have a few bottled waters around here, someplace…"

"Without sounding too forward, Algernon, you can offer me some answers."

I thought it was a coincidence when Kovalenko showed up at my new work location. The reappearance of a second person I barely knew made my nerves twitchy. Elrameshe's warnings became as persistent and vexing as the proverbial angel on my shoulder.

"Why are you here in Sacramento?" I asked.

"This past semester teaching at the Orientation Centers was my last, and I wanted to broaden my experience. An ATP group seemed to be a good place to start. They placed me in this group, as the previous supervisor was recently transferred."

"Anyone I know?"

"I don't believe so. Someone named Merrill."

The name didn't ring any bells. "Okay… Why are you so interested in the Euryale?" I wanted to add, "What can you tell me to help me cure Sindhu," but I kept my peace.

"Because they are a bit of an enigma. One which has intrigued me for quite a while, and has troubled Eldridge for quite a long time. Millennia ago, the Euryale spearheaded the Gorgon Wars against several interstellar species, leaving behind an entire spiral arm of destruction. First, the Epsalian, who they subjugated quite handily, despite their superior technology. Then they set their sights on the Valdaan."

"I recall from your class that those are Earth's nearest neighboring interstellar species."

"Correct." He took another slurp. "The Euryale drove both of them almost to extinction."

"How did Eldridge stop them?"

He pointed a finger straight up. "*That* is the puzzle. The method by which the Ancient Greeks imprisoned all three Gorgon races is lost."

"Oh yes, you said before. The Library of Alexandria?"

"Such a pity." Algernon nodded, a frown making his pug-ugly kisser even worse. "Eldridge—that is, you and Dr. Petrakis—were able to staunch their latest intrusion attempt. They have been trying to escape their prison ever since Herschel re-discovered Uranus in 1871. We never had to worry about them between then and now, as earthbound telescopes were not powerful enough to bring the Euryale ray into sufficient focus.

With Dr. Petrakis' measurements, we at least now know how their weapon works. But we are left with a series of dire questions: Do they have a similar weapon on Uranus' North Pole? Will it be stronger next time—perhaps strong enough to not require a telescope looking down the barrel of their transmogrifier? Will Eldridge be ready to protect Earth during the northern Uranian solstice in forty-two years?"

Playing the innocent, I said, "Who knows if I'll even be around in 2028?"

I nearly jumped out of my skin when Amelia shifted inside my pocket. I smiled nervously at Algernon, who didn't seem to notice.

"Your expertise may be required even sooner, depending on when Earth sends manned missions near the hexagons of Jupiter or Saturn."

Algernon set aside his mug. "But enough of worrying about the far-flung future. It is late, and we should focus on the here-and-now at Eldridge & S.Q.Amos. If you follow me, I will introduce you to the team."

Following him out into the cooler, drier air, we ambled past empty cubicles.

Each desk had its desktop computer adorned with their owner's personal knick-knacks—plastic Garfields and Snoopys standing next to happy-go-lucky plushy Cthulhus and the like—but no photographs of friends or family. Of course, there was my cubicle, with my nameplate already hung, and my mostly empty desk piled with twelve orientation binders.

In the other halls we strolled past, cubicles' clothbound and metal walls were dotted with the usual office paraphernalia of calendars and charts. Many were accompanied by something unusual and unique: a *Kolchak: The Night Stalker* movie poster used as a dartboard; a doomsday bingo card, one "Cryptid Pathogen" away from winning (or losing, depending on how you look at it); Eldridge's official wall-sized quick-reference glossary of commonly encountered mystical symbols; and a set of numerical flip-cards keeping tally of "Days Since Last Accident."

It displayed "014," with a Post-It note attached, declaring, "Thanks a *lot*, Merrill."

Somewhere near the middle of a neighboring corridor, Algernon paused. "Yeager, may I introduce Natalie Adelman. Her field of expertise is cosmology and astrophysics. She assesses cosmic threats, and by that, I mean much more than supernovae, gamma-ray bursts, and the ilk."

"He means 'when the stars are right,' and all that cosmic abomination horse-hockey," she said with a lopsided grin.

A petite brunette, she wore jeans, with a light red gingham shirt under a leather vest. I checked if she wore cowboy boots to complete the ensemble. Her tan canvas high tops with the state of Nebraska embroidered on the ankle were close enough to fit the bill.

"Natalie was the group's interim supervisor until I arrived," said Algernon. "She'll be your mentor while you get settled in. Seek her for guidance on company policies and regulations, where the coffee machine and break room are, and so forth." He turned on his heel and moseyed back toward the main hallway.

Natalie grabbed her coffee mug and shooshed me along. "Get a move on. It's way past quitting time. Time to meet the rest of the crew."

We reached a small conference room, its door slightly ajar and vertical blinds louvered to thin slits allowing shoelace-wide views of the handful of occupants inside. Their voices hushed the moment we entered.

Despite Natalie's get-up, I somehow expected the rest of the group to fit my picture of garden-variety business folk. I was not prepared for the hodge-podge of college fraternity comedy film escapees.

"Good evening, everybody." Algernon attempted to be cheery, but it fell flat this late in the day. "This is our new group member, Mr. Michael Yeager. You may have heard of him. He is the gentleman who helped thwart the recent Euryale Intrusion."

Around the room's oblong table, a few heads nodded. Reading the faces of my new coworkers, they were evenly split between impressed, surprised, and apathetic.

I responded with a weak grin and a wet fish of a wave hello.

"His background is biochemistry, so his focus will be biological intrusions—leading micro-biotic events like extra-terrestrial germs, and consulting me on macro-biotic alien or novel cryptid situations. Now, introductions all around." Algernon pointed to the person to my immediate left. "Hector Castellanos is our resident computer specialist. He's our main contact with the IT department and monitors computer networks across the globe for rogue AI and alien computer viruses in the Mundane world. Once you're settled in your cubicle, he'll acquaint you with our computer network's operating system and programming language."

"What computer languages do you already know?" said Hector.

"Not much. It really wasn't called for in my line of work. Enough BASIC and FORTRAN to be dangerous, I suppose?"

Hector gave me a nod. His spectacles enlarged his inquisitive eyes. My heart went out to him. Nothing says "nerd" more than a decade-out-of-style plaid shirt and a pocket protector. "No worries. The *Plan-10* operating system and tools are easy to learn."

"Plan... *10*?" I sputtered. About a year ago, Sindhu had dragged me to the theater for a loopy Bollywood extravaganza. I returned the favor by introducing her to an equally terrible American piece of schlock. Visions of *Plan 9 From Outer Space*'s bloated Tor Johnson and wasp-waisted Vampira shambled in my head. If the memory of sharing laughter with Sindhu wasn't so painful now, I might have guffawed at Eldridge's ill-named OS.

"What?" he mumbled at the Asian woman next to him. "Did I say something wrong?"

"Dai Jiā-lì is our math wiz," said Algernon, "and a specialist in statistics and databases. She scans academic journals for breakthroughs in higher math that might lead to unfortunate events like inadvertent space folding, dimension leakage, or consciousness modification. She also excels at spotting alien-influenced mathematics in business and academic circles."

"Call me Jolly," she said with a temptress's smile. Her attire was a few notches more revealing than the most eye-catching work casual. Like Hector, I struggled not to ogle her barely loose tunic over hip-hugging spandex pants.

"Barandir is next. He is our liaison to the Faerie folk. His duties mainly consist of keeping tabs on current events in the anthropomorphic species outside of Humankind. What you humans might call 'Middle Earthers?'"

Tall, lanky, and attired in a rendition of renaissance fair kitsch fashioned out of blue denim, Barandir looked up from his earthen mug of green tea. He bristled at Algernon's use of the term, with his auburn ponytail flicking like the tail of an annoyed cat. "Inhabitants of *Tawar Cevan*," he muttered.

"Completing our team is Sofia Urdsen, this ATP group's oracle. She is our guide to future events, and alerts us to developments beyond the Mundane's horizon. We frequently re-prioritize our work according to her visions."

That would explain her clothing. The plus-sized woman sat motionless, hugging herself tight in a multicolored crazy-quilt of a cloak. Her black bangs hung ready to stab her hazel eyes staring in rapture at the ceiling.

I suddenly felt overdressed in my pants with leg creases that could cut paper, white business shirt, and gold power tie.

Sofia passed her hand over her face. "We've met."

"We have?"

"Yes, in the cards," she replied as she fanned out a Tarot deck. Hector sneered into his notebook in front of him. I shot my new supervisor a sidelong glance, one he did not return.

Algernon clasped his hands together. A small sifting of calcified dust fluttered down through his palms. "All right. Thanks for staying a little late. I'll see everyone bright and early tomorrow morning?" As everyone filed out, Jolly took the long way around the table and squeezed herself between me and a nearby chair, swishing her perfect behind against me.

If Sindhu were here, Mama Bear would make quick work of her.

"I suspect you've had a very busy day, Yeager," said Algernon. "I'll escort you to the front entrance."

We remained silent as a smattering of employees joined us on various floors. A tan sedan awaited us at the base of the company sidewalk, and Algernon and I said our matter-of-fact goodbyes.

I stared through the rear passenger seat window as we rolled out of the business section of Sacramento, through center city streets toward the suburbs. The driver tried chatting me up about the local sports teams, but he gave up quickly. The rest was a blur until he stopped at a city block of condos.

"Here we are, sir—address 4F."

4F? Oh, the irony just kept piling on. "I wonder what Eldridge's numerology department would say," I mumbled as my ride drove away. I struggled to identify which cookie-cutter townhouse was my new residence when I spotted—*her*.

She hadn't been much to look at in San Jose, but whatever the Eldridge grease monkeys did, my Chrysler K-car looked like it had just rolled off the assembly line. From that vantage point, finding my condo was easy.

Not knowing what to expect, my hand trembled as I unlocked the front door.

Even before I switched on the light, I was overcome with a barrage of odors. New wood and fresh paint mingled with old carpet infused with years of cooking aromas and incense.

I shuffled through the front room into the dining room, past our second-hand oaken table bearing the four lotus mandalas Sindhu had painted in each corner. The kitchen, though outfit with new appliances, was redolent with the scent of jasmine basmati rice, cumin, and turmeric. Glass-faced cabinets revealed our trove of curries and chutneys concocted from her family's recipes.

Meandering into the bedroom, I chuckled at the freshly made bed, every crisp fold ending in hospital corners. I wanted to fling off the covers and crumple the sheets into disarray to restore their usual state. Opening the two closets—*two!*—I was shocked at how much spare room there was in my closet, and how little there was in Sindhu's. At the end of one rod hung Sindhu's favorite indigo and turquoise *sari*.

I took it off the rack, admired its gold embroidery for I don't know how long, then shambled over to the oval mirror in her corner of the bedroom. I held it up at my side, staring at its reflection alongside mine, imagining her in it.

Put a boutonnière in my jacket's lapel, and the scene could have been a wedding photograph.

"Sindhu, let's elope."

I collapsed onto the corner of the bed and crushed her beloved dress against my face.

Perfume and her scent filled my nostrils, and I wept.

CHAPTER 18

During the next month, I immersed myself into my new occupation. Doubly so after quitting time. Anything to push aside the searing memory of Sindhu's face half-transformed into stone.

I spent most every evening slaving on the department's backlog of predictions, sometimes poking around the slush pile of cold cases languishing in the weekly Assessor's Bullpen. At least once a week, I found leads that would either close the case as a false prediction or breathe new life into the investigation. On at least one occasion my digging caught up with an actual intrusion. In any event, I let Algernon deal with taking the credit.

Why did I lay low? After the interdepartmental shit-show at UCSC, I had no stomach for company politics. Stepping on an assessor's toes by showing them up or stomping on an oracle's reputation seemed a lightning-quick way to get blackballed.

Take for instance, the assessor from the St. Petersburg branch who threw a royal fit after I determined Russia's version of the Yeti was responsible for the unsolved murders at Dyatlov Pass in 1959. A case he inherited from his mentor, it was his meal ticket with which he milked Eldridge for every company perk he could sleaze. He had to be restrained before he could cast a curse from Baba Yaga's cookbook directed at Algernon's head. The scuttlebutt was that he ended up redacted.

My nightly ritual ended with an hour devoted to one or more pet projects: locate any hints about Sindhu's medical status, try to track down Dr. Fleischer, play detective on why an Elven Watcher literally wanted my head, or find out who Amelia had been in her previous life.

Tackling my stacks of two-inch binders crammed with handouts from orientation never seemed to make it to the top of my to-do list. Occasionally, I would crack them open, then get a headache from reading piles of info peppered with policies and procedures. By comparison, my master's degree paper on *DNA Matrices and Facilitation of Gene Expression* was an easy read.

To sum it all up, I figured keeping myself busy in an empty office was better than rattling around my empty condo or crying myself to sleep in an empty bed.

The fifth Monday began the same as the previous four—a nine o'clock meeting to review the previous week's progress. Predictable as the sunrise, Algernon reviewed everybody's status. He began every question with, "Where are we on..." followed by our various projects, previously determined by predictions made by Sofia or other groups' seers: a potential rise in demonic activity in Scotland; reports of novel cryptid activity in the vicinity of Tippecanoe; An "unexpected" coronal mass ejection sometime next year; Pure sulfuric acid rain over the location of the 1908 Tunguska Event during its next total solar eclipse—

"Speaking of clouds," Natalie interjected—by which I mean, she said unhurriedly between Algernon's long sips of his algae concoction— "How's Merrill doing?"

"Who's this Merrill I keep hearing about?" I whispered to Barandir on my right.

"The descendant of Merlin, and our last supervisor. He transferred to another group."

I still couldn't place Barandir's accent, which had the texture of a babbling brook. He sipped what I had learned was not tea, but some concoction of herbs and other homeopathic ingredients of questionable value to medical science. I was never sure if the fragrant aroma invariably surrounding him was the tea or himself. Whatever it was, it drowned out the odors of my bland coffee and Algernon's hideous algae brew.

"*Was* transferred, you mean," said Hector.

"Merlin who?"

"*The* Merlin."

"Oh..." I blinked, embarrassed by my ignorance. "Did he get promoted?"

Barandir *pff*-ed through a dainty smirk. "Hardly."

"Merrill's doing quite well for himself," said Algernon. "He has finally found a home, as an actuary in the Long-Term Threat Assessment group." His news was followed by a drizzle of snickers around the table.

I leaned over to my other side. "Natalie, what am I missing?"

"LTTA is where dim bulbs go to die," she replied under her breath. "After the mess he caused last month, it's a wonder he wasn't *redacted*."

"Everyone knows why he wasn't," hissed Hector in my direction. "Legacy hire."

"Got that right," Natalie said after a quiet scoff. "Merrill may come from an honored family line, but fence posts on dear-departed Daddy's ranch could beat him at checkers."

"If we may continue," said Algernon. He rounded out the meeting with his own update. "Sofia's prediction last week concerning Epsalian and Valdaan skirmishes outside the Kuiper Belt has been handed off to ATPG Omega for investigation."

"There's ATP groups that aren't numbered?" I asked Natalie. "What do they do?"

Her left hand batted my question away. "Later."

It was only then I realized Sofia had not yet joined our meeting. No sooner did the observation pop into my head, than Sofia burst into the meeting room.

Her brow was drenched in sweat. She must have run quite a distance, probably from her soundproofed oracle room on the floor below us. Her bedazzled cloak flourished behind her like she forded headfirst into a tempest. She collapsed into the nearest open seat with the flowing movements of a silent-movie drama queen, her forearm coming to rest draped over her eyes. She sighed dramatically, her voluminous abdomen heaving under her cloak that had somehow wrapped itself around her.

"Gaea, clear my vision," she implored the heavens. Snatching Barandir's tea, she gulped it down without a moment's hesitation.

Barandir lunged halfway out of his seat, attempting to pluck the mug out her grasp, but even his lightning reflexes missed the mark. "*Ii naúan a firen*! That's not meant for human—"

Sofia's face snapped to energized attention, a strange light glowing in her eyes. She leaped to the whiteboard hanging on the wall behind Algernon. All eyes were on Sofia as she frantically scribbled on the board. Necks craned left and right as everyone, myself included, tried to view the drawing obscured by her flowing cloak. Her sentences were broken by her wheezing. "The hunter from the darkness... searches for his foe... the new stranger…"

She said the magic word—*foe*. Elrameshe's final scream echoed once again in my ears.

Sofia stepped to one side to show us her work. In coarse black lines, she had drawn a thin humanoid figure. With a bald head, pointed ears, and spindly limbs ending in fearsome claws, she had filled the creature's image with dozens of specks and stars, like mosquitoes skimming on the surface of water.

"The Tarot foresaw it… through the Tower card…"

"That doesn't tell us much," said Hector to himself, though loud enough for all to hear. He frowned sternly as he cleaned his glasses. "Every prediction you bring us ends with the Tower Card, the 'Harbinger of Disasters.'"

Sofia calmed herself with a deep breath, and the ethereal light behind her irises dimmed. "The reversed Magician paired with the Three of Swords portend great suffering. The Crystal of Khandbari confirmed it… showed me its terrible form… The hidden one is *here*… in Eldridge."

"Here?" said Algernon, swiveling to face her.

She stumbled to the nearest open chair, sank into it, and promptly passed out.

"Oh, brother," said Hector with a roll of his eyes.

"I tried to warn her," sighed Barandir.

"Yeager," said Algernon, regarding me strangely. "Your name means *hunter*, does it not?"

I couldn't tell what emotion, as a colony creature, he tried to show. It could have been suspicion, for all I knew. I wondered if he was even capable of emotion. I took a sip from my mug. "The only thing I'm hunting for in this company is a decent cup of coffee. Besides, I'm pretty sure I don't look anything like *that*."

"All right, ideas?"

"If anything, it might be hunting for *me*," I added, ending it like a question, and probably with a pinch too much drama.

"Actually," said Algernon, "anyone in your graduating class might be the target. Seers do not necessarily predict events in their own group."

Jolly, wearing tight-fitting one-piece activewear under an oversized basketball jersey of China's Olympic *Team Dragon*, leaned forward. Her elbows stabbed the tabletop with a thrum as she rubbed her palms together, and her bosom squished against the table's edge. "Then who is the hunter?"

"Most probably a shapeshifter of some type," said Barandir. "I doubt a creature with such an appearance would be among the ranks of Eldridge employees. As Sofia indicated, it is hidden, and a creature such as that would need to hide."

Algernon nodded his agreement, then pointed at the drawing. "Do you know of anything that would resemble our friend here?"

Barandir shook his head.

"Nor do I know of an alien race with these characteristics." Algernon turned to face the table again. "Natalie, you've been rather quiet. Your thoughts?"

Sofia shot up in her seat, her eyes bursting bright through her black bangs. "He lurks among us, but others lie in wait. If they fail their dark deed, the earth shall rise, the waters shall flood, the sky shall fall." She gasped for air, then fainted back into her chair again.

"Can we trade our oracle for one who isn't bucking for Hollywood?" said Hector between lips drawn tight.

Natalie cleared her throat loudly. "Since we don't have a leg up on aliens or mystical critters, all we got left is the time aspect. Jolly, I think this would be your bailiwick."

"My bail...?" Jolly sat back, twirling her pen around her index finger —an eye-catching trick almost every Asian employee could perform like second nature—one I could never seem to get the hang of.

"Your area of expertise. After Sofia wakes up and files her Oracle's Report, request clearance from HR to search the employee databases."

"I got access right after Merrill's incident, remember?" Jolly shot back.

"Oh, right. Look for anyone, like Michael here, who has recently joined the company. Like Algernon said, start with the latest graduating class. Heck, I'd even broaden the search to include anyone who's had a status change during the same time. Promotions, transfers, firings, mindwipes, redactions..."

While she spoke, I pulled Amelia out of my pocket and copied down the curious diagram—badly. Leonardo da Vinci I ain't. Scribbling out my first attempt, I scolded my lack of artistic talent, muttering, "Oh, please."

As I made a second attempt, Amelia started to pull. An instant later, she was the one drawing, and my hand was just along for the ride. My eyes darted from face to face, checking to see if anyone took notice.

"Define *recently*," said Jolly. "How far back do I go?"

"The date of the Euryale Intrusion. When was that, Michael?"

I suddenly found it difficult to swallow. Amelia kept drawing, dragging my forearm along, as I replied, "June 16th."

"Start your search a month before that, just to be on the safe side," added Natalie.

"Hardly a challenge," said a disappointed Jolly.

"We have a plan," said Algernon, picking up his empty green-stained mug. "Let's get to it."

Sofia's eyes snapped open. "They strike today!" Just as quickly, they closed again.

"Great," said Hector. "Another rush job."

While almost everybody filed out of the room, I remained seated, contemplating Amelia's copy of Sofia's drawing. Barandir waved his tea underneath Sofia's nose.

"I'm up," she blurted out before pitching to her feet and allowing him to escort her into the hallway.

Jolly walked behind my chair and ran her hand along its back, the tips of her fingers grazing the width of my shoulders. My spine jerked straight with electricity.

Once everyone else filed out of the room Natalie swiveled to face me. "What's on your mind, Michael? I can tell when you're troubled. Anyone could, as a matter of fact. Your eyebrows were going fast enough to knit a sweater."

"Am I that transparent? I'll have to work on that." I set Amelia down on my notepad.

"Your two-tone eyes draw attention to it. Anyway, work on it *after* I stop being your mentor." She kicked the door closed, leaned back, and propped her sneakers on the table. "So, spill."

I closed my eyes for a moment and my fingers squeezed the tension draped across the bridge of my nose. "What's up with Hector and Sofia? I don't think he's said one kind thing about her all month."

Natalie scoffed and stuck a thumb in the door's direction. "Oh, that? He wanted company permission to pursue a relationship with someone outside of Eldridge. Sofia and her crystals gave it the thumbs down."

If any coffee was left in my mug, I would have done a spit take. "Wait—we need company permission to *date*?"

"You still an *Untrained*, Michael? Read the corporate regs, if not the non-disclosure agreements you signed on day one. Falling back on the excuse of 'my employee orientation was rushed' is getting old."

Seeing the consternation on my face, she scoffed again, this time with exaggerated annoyance, and began a recitation. "'*Rule 1*: Absolutely no personal relationships between Eldridge employees. *Rule 2*: All personal relationships with persons outside of Eldridge must be pre-approved by director level or higher. *Rule 3*: All personal relationships between human and non-human sentient beings must be pre-approved by vice president level or higher.' There's a fourth rule about the critters in long-term storage facilities, but I don't think even Hector is *that* hard up."

I shook my head in disbelief. Where did these relationship rules leave me and my fiancée, Sindhu? We definitely broke the second rule the moment I signed the Oath, and possibly the third and fourth, whatever it was.

It infuriated me that neither my previous mentor, Petrakis, nor Director Ventnor mentioned this. Then again, Vice President Hibara *did* use Sindhu's relationship as my fiancée as the reason to admit me to their Circle. He *had* to be aware of the infractions. Something inside me *still* didn't accept his justification at face value.

"What about pre-existing relationships?" I tried spinning my pen around my index finger, Jolly-style. Amelia bounced off my knuckle, rolling back onto the drawing.

"No such thing. Any personal attachments coming in, and you wouldn't even be offered employment."

"That explains why no one has photos of friends and families in their cubicles," I said with a sour note.

My confusion and frustration spun around my head like tops. I almost blurted out the obvious contradiction that Sindhu and I presented, but Hibara's warnings for total silence regarding the Circle rang between my temples. I slammed my jaw shut with my teeth clamping hard, producing a click that echoed off the walls.

"Any other newbie questions, Alaska?"

"Okay, I get it. Next fucking topic."

"Whoa there, Tex!" Natalie went pale. Pushing with her legs, she zoomed her chair away from the table. She scrunched her knees against her chest, like she dodged a bucketful of spilled water. "Didn't anyone tell you not to curse here in Eldridge?"

"Sorry—my tutor Caltrop warned me during orientation. I still don't get what the big fuss is."

"Loose lips can have the dangest consequences inside company walls. Just the other month, a supervisor let an 'F-bomb you' slip when his Director told him his budget was cut in half. The sad thing was, some noodle-head of a wizard cast a *Command* spell improperly in the room on the next floor above. Three guesses who."

"Merrill?"

"Bingo. His botched casting generated a bunch of mystical energy overflow. It dribbled down into their meeting room, and... I'm sure I don't have to paint you a picture. One Director against five supervisors? *Whoof*! The poor guy couldn't walk for a week. That's how we got Ventnor."

I held back a snicker of *schadenfreude*. "No wonder Merrill got the heave-ho. Getting back to these 'Rules,' this has been bothering me for quite a while. What the heck is up with Jolly? Why is she always such a pricktea— a *tease*? She's constantly trying to get a rise out me, Barandir, or Hector."

"Barandir?" She soughed out another scoff. "Hardly. She knows he's unreachable."

"How's that?"

"He may be a half-elf, but he sure has the snooty attitude of a full Forest Elf. Kinda like their version of *Mr. Spock*. Barandir would sooner slice off his lips rather than kiss a human."

Natalie goggled at me. She covered her mouth and nose to hide a giggle that ended in a snort. "You didn't *know*? You never noticed the pointed ears under that mop? Oh, brother, Michael. What turnip truck did you fall off of?"

I pursed my lips and bit them shut, while she released the laugh dying to get out. Once she caught her breath, I asked, "Let me guess—half elf, half human. How is that even allowed, given Rule 3?"

"If you can get him to open up about it, you'll be the first. Though I have a hunch he's an outcast in *Tawar Cevan*, the Forest Elves's world."

"And here I thought Elves were so noble."

"As for why Jolly acts the way she does around any male with a pulse?" She shrugged between snickers. "The rumor mill is clogged with theories about her—even before that vixen transferred here from the Beijing branch."

She flipped her palms face up, one hand then the other, as she enumerated and weighed each bit of gossip. "Some say she was originally fat and ugly until she out-riddled a djinn in Nepal and wished for a perfect 'ten' body; others think she drank a botched love potion; the goofiest one I heard to date is she's possessed by a succubus. That one's too ridiculous to give a second thought. She'd be slammed into long-term storage or strapped down for an exorcism before she could say 'boo.' Me personally? I think she's watched too much American TV and convinced herself she's got to behave like a sex-bomb to be successful."

"So what do you recommend I do?"

"Just ignore her."

"Easier said than done." I folded my arms across my chest.

Natalie rose from her chair. "You gonna be okay?"

"Yeah, though I think I need to talk to Algernon."

"Good. I need a break from mentoring. You ask more questions than a hoot owl." She gave a quick wave and sauntered away. Her off-key whistling of *Always on My Mind* got cut short, interrupted when she bumped into a custodian trundling his cleaning station out of my row of cubicles.

CHAPTER 19

The whiff of Algernon's aquarium algae farm had gone from sour to rancid, though he seemed oblivious to the stench. Once again, he was glued to his computer terminal. Two prominent windows on his screen were filled with forms with portions blotted out with horizontal black bars. His printer buzzed as it scrolled out copies.

"Michael," he rasped. "Just the person I wanted to see. Please close the door." He grimaced for a second, then shook with a ragged cough. "I hoped to interview you about the Euryale Intrusion, but Sofia's prediction takes precedence. While we wait for Jolly to finish her database search, I accessed employee records, yours and your fellow graduates."

Algernon slipped the first printer page across the desk to me. "Can you explain why much of your personal information has been redacted on your employee record?" His raspy voice became increasingly coarse, like tires running over gravel. "Ah—From the look on your face, I can see you were unaware of that."

Did my eyebrows give me away again? I measured my words. "Not easily."

After another hoarse cough, Algernon said, "Not to worry, Michael. As your superior, I am duty-bound to keep your information privileged. Anything you divulge will not leave this room. Can you at least enlighten me why your birthplace and date, along with your parents' identities, were expunged?"

"I don't know my birthdate, or my real parents. The records were lost in an earthquake before I was adopted."

"What about everything else? Your stepparents, prior residences...

Everything before your stint at university is blacked out."

The barbershop quartet of Hibara, Ventnor, Petrakis and Elrameshe advised me to clam up. "I'm surprised as you are. I don't know what to say."

"I take Sofia's warning seriously. So should you."

"Believe me, I do. Her vision has me worried."

"So, is there anything else—"

His body shook with a hellacious cough. I feared his body might crack and fall apart at the joints. After the spasms ceased, he held up his hand, signaling me to wait. He reached into a bottom desk drawer and pulled out a water bottle.

He guzzled the entire pint in short order. Exhaling a deep sigh, he calmly opened another drawer and produced a plastic and metal pyramid with a triangular base. Holding it flat in his palm, he tapped its topmost rounded corner and set it on his desk. The four triangular points of the tetrahedron glowed an intense hue of blue.

Algernon relaxed in his chair and spoke. His voice wasn't even remotely human. It sounded like a conch gargling deep within its shell.

The pyramid brightened and spoke with a woman's voice. "I'm terribly sorry, Michael. Human speech is taxing and dehydrates me quickly."

"Natalie?"

Algernon chuckled before gurgling a reply. "Oh, yes. Natalie was kind enough to lend her voice to my *trans-lex*. I preferred her voice over the device's generic, distressingly mechanical voice."

I marveled at the device. "A trans-lex, you say?"

"Standard issue for new non-human employees, while we learn the native language. I kept mine for those occasions when I need to rehydrate."

"Then what's the aquarium for?"

"Lunch," he gurgled. "Now, where was I? Is there *anything* else you can tell me, to help find this 'hunter?'"

I shook my head.

"Maybe this will help you be more forthcoming." Algernon pulled the second sheet from his printer and handed it to me.

"What's this?"

"My own personnel record," said Natalie's voice as he blupped away.

It, too, had been heavily redacted, revealing little more than his name, employment start date, current status, and a photograph that looked like his cousin once removed—and every bit as ugly as a walking scar.

"Like you, Michael, there are reasons my data is restricted." He looked to the side. I could see his gears turning as he wrestled with a decision. He must have reached one, as he leaned forward and rested his elbows on the table with his pebbled fingers interlocked.

"I told you at orientation that your people's name for my species is the Oovlid. As you correctly observed at the time, my body is a community of several symbiotic species. The closest comparable lifeforms would be lichen, but that would be a gross oversimplification—and one that I find a little insulting. You could say I am equal parts coral, plankton, cuttlefish, and jellyfish."

"Where do you come from? You couldn't have evolved on Earth without us discovering you by now."

"There is that infamous Earther ego." Even though it was Natalie's voice, I could hear a note of rebuke in Algernon's burbling. "But you are correct. My people inhabited a system beyond the Valdaan Empire."

It took a second for an inconsistency to connect for me. "Then why didn't you cover the Oovlid during *Aliens 201*?"

After downing a second bottle of water, he glubbed, "Because my people are no more."

"Was it the Gorgons?"

"No. In fact, we are immune to their weapon. The organism in our bodies' collective that manipulates the coral zoophytes neutralizes the harmful effects of their ray."

His words jolted my heart. "Can your Oovlid physiology be used to help—"

Don't say Sindhu, Yeager. Remember Rule 3.

"—the two Euryale victims?"

"When we learned there were infected casualties from the Euryale Intrusion, ATPG Omega requested a tissue sample from me. I gave them a second sample two weeks ago as well. I expect they will request another sample once the latest one is used up. Only time will tell when they have a breakthrough."

"Thanks," I whispered. Empathy squeezed my lungs tight. "If it wasn't the Euryale or the other Gorgons, what happened to your people?"

"I don't know. *No one* does. I was piloting a vessel, shipping desperately needed supplies to the Epsalian-Gorgon war front, when a Valdaan cruiser attacked. I crash-landed in the Arctic ice fields—three thousand years ago, I am told. Eldridge had discovered my craft a decade ago, then revived me from my Void stasis chamber once they reverse-engineered the device five years later. I offered to be an envoy between my people and Eldridge."

"But Eldridge is not a political entity."

"In the strictest sense, no. Not as far as any Earth nation is aware. In the larger scheme of things, Eldridge is Earth's *de facto* representative to alien races, regardless of whether they have made proper diplomatic contact, or intruded into Earth's space. It is rather difficult to explain further than that."

Algernon took our printouts and tossed them into a shredder under his desk. "Under Eldridge's supervision, I tried contacting my people for another full year, while learning anything Eldridge had about Epsalians, the Valdaan, the Horde, and the Karne. The truth was unavoidable—one day the Oovlid were there, fighting the Gorgons, the next day they *weren't*. I am..." Algernon shrugged with a sigh. "...the last of my kind. The investigation closed, and Eldridge offered me a position. I decided it was better than returning to Void stasis."

He swallowed heavily and put away the trans-lex.

"I'm sorry." I shook my head from his fire hose of information. Hopefully I could sort it out later.

"Why do humans always apologize for events they had no hand in?" he asked in his own voice.

It was my turn to shrug. "It means we sympathize. But how does all that explain why your information is redacted?"

"Epsalians regularly scan Earth computers when they trespass—even Eldridge's, despite our best efforts. And those are the intrusions we know about. We have little idea what the Karne are capable of. There may be another alien intelligence at work of which Eldridge is unaware. Until Eldridge can determine the cause of the Oovlid disappearance, it was deemed best to withhold my true nature from any computer databases."

Every muscle in my back clenched when the realization hit. Did Amelia, listening to our conversation, put Algernon at risk? I didn't dare tell him of our eavesdropper. Vice President Hibara would have my hide.

A wave of guilt cast a shadow over my heart. Algernon had helped Sindhu, a total stranger. Now, I may have endangered him. And I came in here to ask him for help.

I owed him. It was time to put some skin in the game.

"Sofia's vision has me worried." Which was the understatement of the year.

"You already said that." Algernon sat back and waited.

"Until I joined Eldridge, I believed I had been adopted. My stepparents, Erwin and Esther, had told me so, until the day they died. It wasn't until my assessment at the end of company orientation, that I discovered that my stepparents *might* be my actual parents. Initial DNA check says I am, but I'll have a tough time accepting that until I see reliable confirmation. Even so, I don't understand why that might be a reason to black out my info."

I gritted my teeth as I debated about how much more to divulge.

"Indeed... Why would your parents mislead you about such a thing?"

"You'll have to ask them."

"That would involve a mountain of paperwork and approval from Eldridge's CEO. Tell me about your family life. Maybe there's something there that can help."

Algernon's request was the snowball that started the avalanche of me spilling my guts.

"Erwin was in the US Forest Service, stationed in Girdwood, Alaska. Esther worked in the Anchorage county clerk office. I was six years old when they adopted me. Erwin's work moved him to a different location every couple of years, it seemed. Esther and I were just along for the ride. Fortunately, as a civil servant, she could find work anywhere. They never set down roots, which meant I couldn't either."

"The forests of this world *are* spectacular." Algernon had a momentary faraway stare. "A gem in any solar system. In what other cities did your family live?"

"San Fernando, Rapid City, Fort Collins, and Mt. Adams. That's where they died, in 1980."

He looked at the ceiling, his eyes reading the soundproof tiles. I thought only humans searched their memory in that manner. "Ah, the Mt. St. Helens Intrusion?"

"Wait... the eruption that killed my parents was an *intrusion*?"

"Yes." Algernon rubbed his chin in thought. He had mimicking human mannerisms down pat. "A skirmish between the Forest Elves and other creatures from *Tawar Cevan* spilled into this reality and escalated to disastrous proportions. It almost wrecked the Human-Færie Armistice."

"There's an armistice?"

"I don't understand, Michael. That is the most basic topic covered the first day of orientation, *History 101: Origins of Eldridge*."

"Don't forget my orientation was a rush job. Why it was pushed through is a question no one has answered. I had so much information crammed into my head, I barely remembered my name after four weeks."

"Very well, the Human-Færie Armistice," he said with a heavy sigh. "Soon after Mundanes conceived of writing, let alone recording their history, the Empyrean Triumvirate, forerunner of what has evolved into Eldridge today, had forged the Human-Færie Armistice. It is the mystically binding legal device which has kept an uneasy peace between Humans and Middle-Earthers for millennia."

Algernon crossed his arms over his chest. If he was attempting to emulate annoyance, it came across loud and clear. "If I had taught your class, I would have ensured you remembered at least that much."

I stared at my knees while sorting out how these things applied to me. The Elven spirit, Blue Watcher, contained for who-knows-how-long in the *Habilitas*, wanted me dead. Yet Elrameshe, a Forest Elf, acted like an ally. Then again, she was officially contracted to work with Eldridge.

Come to think of it, why were there elves in Eldridge? Was their service part of the armistice? The last thought ringing in my head concerned Barandir and his half-elf lineage. Was he indentured or a regular employee? Whose side would he fall on—Forest Elf, human, or neither?

Algernon's scratchy voice pushed me out of my spinning head. "Were there any events in your previous family life, that seemed strange at the time? Perhaps involving elves?"

Shaking my head again, I added, "I'm sure if I had seen elves before Eldridge, I'd remember it."

I stopped there. There were a few events in my life that were way beyond unusual, but they were not paranormal and certainly not elvish. However, I was in no mood to talk about how Esther had slipped into dementia late in life. Hers was a mental illness so deep, that it sucked the life out of Elmer as well, turning him into a shadow of his former self. She had suffered some insanity so dark, that my stepmother—my mother?—tried to kill me.

"I think I need to talk to Barandir," I said.

"Why is that?"

I wanted to come up with something more substantial than, "Just a hunch," but that was all I could manage.

"Thank you, Michael." The hint of a smile on Algernon's face seemed earnest. "I appreciate your trust in me."

"Likewise." Opening the door, my curiosity got the better of me. "By the way, how did you get the name Algernon?"

He walked to his aquarium and refilled his lunch mug with his over-ripe green concoction. He lifted the ladle with his answer. "Of all the sym-biotes that comprise my constituent macro-cells, none are algae."

"Let me guess, Petrakis suggested that name?"

"Yes, he did." He cocked his head at me. "How did you know?"

CHAPTER 20

Barandir was rarely in his office cube, but it was my best shot.

Halfway down my hall in the cubicle farm, Jolly waylaid me.

Couching a ream of manila folders in one arm, she pulled one from its center. Leaning forward, she gave me a clean line of sight down her loose-hanging *Team Dragon* jersey. She foisted the folder at me. Doing so, her loaded arm pressed her cleavage into a bountiful curve. "Here you are, *tiánxīn*."

I rolled my eyes at the overly familiar term. It was embarrassing how she called every male "sweetie"—even the untouchable Barandir. I ruffled through the pages inside. "What's this?"

"I made spreadsheets of all the new and reassigned employees that Algernon requested." Two-thirds of the way through, she pointed at one entry. "See? Here's your entry, *qíngrén*." She placed her hand on my right shoulder and planted her breasts squarely on either side of my left shoulder blade. Magnolia and earthy tones of sandalwood surrounded me.

I took a sobering breath, wondering what her latest term of endearment meant.

"I expanded my search to include company awards and honors... oh, and deaths as well."

"Deaths?" I said with a cough. "How can an intrusion hurt someone who's already dead?"

"With this company, one never knows. If you look on the last few pages, I added objects and material Eldridge acquired over the past two months, as well."

"Material? Hopefully, not ordinary things like business supplies."

"No, silly. Unusual items from archaeological digs, estates, that sort of thing—Oh!" Jolly snatched the handout back from me, replacing it with a thinner one. "Sorry about that, *tiánxīn*. That was Algernon's copy. As a supervisor, he's got a higher clearance and is allowed to see more of employees' personal info."

"All right, I'll look this over as soon as I talk with Barandir. You wouldn't happen to know—"

Algernon's office door swung open wildly, rebounding off its doorstop. Stumbling out came Algernon, rivulets of green streaming out of his mouth, spreading across his shirt. His hands grasped at his torso, one over where a human heart would rest, the other where his ersatz appendix would be. Jolly and I stood agape as he took one last lurching step before pitching headfirst onto the floor.

His body broke into chunks.

The thin carpeting was hardly a cushion against the reinforced concrete flooring underneath. Algernon's head snapped off, rolling to the side. Its mouth still operated, expelling dregs of algae scum. One arm broke inside his shirt. Its sleeve acquired a new zigzag where a straight upper arm should have been. His knees shattered, leaving one leg's lower half behind, and the other leg bent at a gut-wrenching angle.

I dashed forward, shouting to Jolly or anyone within earshot. "Get medical down here. Make sure they know it's Algernon and can treat an Oovlid."

Jolly's stacks of folders tumbled out of my cubicle, followed by the blips of my speakerphone being dialed. Kneeling by Algernon, I met his stony eyes. His face and his hands smoothed out, slowly losing their rough texture. His mouth moved, but no sound came out. A rush of air from his neck sputtered out noxious green goop.

My moment of panicked indecision was shoved aside by a flash of memory from the mess hall at orientation. I shoved Algernon's head back onto his torso, pressing and twisting it until it roughly fitted the ragged contours of his broken neck line. I figured if it worked for a finger, maybe...?

I repositioned my hands to avoid touching the oozing green vomit. His algae concoction mixed with digestive juices fizzed as they bleached the carpet. I had no urge to discover what it might do to human flesh. A few seconds, and some of his jagged corners knit together.

"Good," wheezed Algernon before he passed out. At least, his facial features ceased melting. The rejoining stopped halfway done. It left me afraid to let go of his head, fearing it might tear apart again.

Jolly emerged from my office. "The medics are coming."

I grabbed her wrist and pulled her down to Algernon's side. "Choose a limb," I said, "and reconnect it. Press them together until the EMTs arrive. ...and don't touch the green stuff!"

She unbuttoned his sleeve, shoving the cuff past the break, up to his elbow. She pressed the separated wrist and hand to the forearm. It wouldn't knit.

"They better get here fast." I snarled at our corridor, filling with gawkers. I was about to shout bloody hel— *heck* at them, when Natalie shoved them aside, leading a paramedic team of three. I wanted to release Algernon's head into the gloved hands of one of the medicos, but he stopped me.

"You're holding it just fine. Keep it in place just a little longer." He popped a plastic tube from his yellow EMT vest and dabbed a clear fluid along the joint line.

My nostrils twitched at a pungent odor. "What is that?"

"Ethyl cyanoacrylate."

"*Krazy* Glue? You're kidding."

"It's what Monterey Bay Aquarium uses to repair coral," he said with a shrug. "Okay, you can let him go." He crawled over to Jolly and, with her help, re-aligned Algernon's broken arm.

"I think he was poisoned," I said to the team leader, pointing toward the steaming carpet blotch. "His food source is the aquarium in his office. It stank like all get out today. Couldn't he smell that?"

The medic didn't answer me. As he applied glue to the arm, he barked at one of his staff, "ET Vial 23, just below the sternum." The second paramedic jumped into action, cutting the front of his shirt along its buttons. Taking out a cordless drill from his EMT carryall, he snapped on a core borer bit. He pressed the tool down in the center of Algernon's torso. The carbide teeth tore into him, spewing a cloud of coral dust in every direction. With the hole bored out, he popped the cap off a hypodermic big enough to be a turkey baster, injected a reddish fluid, and sealed the coral plug back into Algernon's chest.

I assisted the team, sliding the rescue board underneath him. It took all four of us to load Algernon's rocky weight onto the gurney. Jolly placed the calf that fell out of Algernon's trousers alongside, handling it like it was covered with poison ivy. The moment they glued the limb back on, two of the medics dashed off with him to the elevators, while the third remained behind with an oversized Dirt Devil, vacuuming up stray chunks of Algernon.

My stomach flounced when his work reminded me of the Durga squad collecting the last bits of Gary back at Lick Observatory. "Where are you guys taking him?"

"The Medical Spa."

"Spa?" I stabbed a finger at his apparatus. "Our boss is still missing a few chunks. What can you possibly do there?"

"They have salt-water sensory deprivation tanks there. Wrap him in a boatload of kelp, and it's the best place for an Oovlid to reassemble itself."

I stood aghast, but I couldn't think of a better solution. "You're the expert."

He snapped off the vacuum's power and dashed away.

Jolly held her hands in front of herself with revulsion. They were covered in Algernon dust. She hurried past me with a frowning grimace and an abrupt, "Excuse me."

After taking a moment to calm myself, I collected the strewn folders and loose papers Jolly had tossed into my cubicle. It took a few minutes to find my handout.

Like the previous work I'd seen from her, it was organized logically. The first table was sorted by last name. A second table had the same info, this time ordered by their situation: I quickly spotted my name among the others in my graduating class in the new employee table; Algernon and Merrill figured prominently in the section listing promotions, transfers, and demotions; and a small table at the end gathered together those unfortunates who were mindwiped. I supposed that no redactions was a good thing, although I was a little puzzled that no retirements were listed. In a company with sixteen locations worldwide, statistically speaking, at least one person should have retired *somewhere* during the past two to three months. Maybe Jolly or Natalie could enlighten me on that little mystery when we had a spare moment.

I jumped to the last table labeled "New Acquisitions." Much of it was dreck I expected—the Crystal of *Whatsits*, the Spheres of *Whoozat*, the Tome of *One-Vowel-Followed-by-Nine-Consonants*, and a few other unpronounceables.

What, no Atavachron or Interocitor?

My heart jumped halfway up my aorta when I spotted a pair of entries in the middle of the list: Euryale A and Euryale B.

That had to be Cheryl and Sindhu. Their inventory dates matched up perfectly with the Euryale Intrusion. But listed as mere acquisitions, no better than antique salt and pepper shakers in an auction bargain bin? I followed my finger across the wide table of data, making sure I didn't shift a row while determining their whereabouts.

Their locations were listed as ILTS-CA-2E718 and 2E719, wherever *that* was. It certainly wasn't Sacramento's medical section or any laboratory I ever heard about.

My temper flared, and I wanted to shout. If Algernon were still here, I would be haranguing him 'til the cows were abducted. But that would be pointless—the real people to grill would be either Director Ventnor or Vice President Hibara. Yeah, like *that* was gonna happen.

I slammed the report and its folder on my desk. Then I grimaced at the name on the folder. I had been reading from Algernon's report, not mine. I dove into the small tower of folders I had stacked, feverishly searching for my version. Once I located it, I did a quick comparison.

My copy had neither Sindhu nor Cheryl listed. Now I was *really* pissed.

I switched the copies, inserting my version back into his folder. Just in time, too, as Jolly returned mere moments later. Her face and hands were still damp, and she looked relieved.

"Where's Natalie?" She must have been really shook up, as she didn't call me *qíngrén* or *tiánxīn*.

I scoped around over the cubicle's edges. No sign of my mentor. "I guess she went with the EMTs? Here's the stack of papers you were carrying. I didn't have a chance to put it in any order."

With a simple word of thanks, she scooped them up and hurried to her next destination. The second she was out of sight, I copied down the info related to Sindhu and Cheryl, in case Jolly noticed the switch.

I sat down to my computer and started poking around for any corporate information that could clue me into what an ILTS was. I frowned at my screen's reflection, when my hand knocked the mouse on the floor. A quick survey of my desk, and it quickly became apparent almost everything on my desk was not where I had left it. A whiff of cleaning solution itched the top of my nose.

I was wondering what business cleaning staff had here this time of day, when my mental to-do list flagged me down. "Oh right, I wanted to talk to Barandir."

I left my cubicle and planted my face into the chest of a burly brick wall of a man dressed like a funeral director.

CHAPTER 21

There are tried-and-true techniques detectives use during interrogations to entice their suspect to talk.

ATPG Alpha was using all of them on me.

The cramped room had its temperature set high enough to be uncomfortable. My metal chair wobbled. Two padded metal chairs across the table from me bore sagging lines of wear. They frowned at me with grave disappointment. One of the overhead fluorescent lights flickered occasionally. The observation mirror several feet beyond the anchored metal table in the room ensured that its annoying blinking was always in sight. My interviewers—or interrogators, depending on how you look at it—were undoubtedly on the other side of the glass, discussing their plan of attack.

Of course, there were the additional Eldridge touches. The room's walls and ceiling were painted flat black. The floor molding was tinted with a dull orange, as though glowing from fires stoked below. The base of an empty wastebasket beside the door bore the same pumpkin hue. My guess was that the color scheme was a psych trick to help the person interviewed contemplate their future if the session did not go well.

A stenography machine waited next to the two empty chairs. A high-end video camera the size of an oversized shoebox sat on its tripod, ready to record what anyone in the room said or did.

Last but not least, a cube of gray marble the size of a soccer ball sat on the table near my right hand. The kisser carved into the side facing me would give Algernon fierce competition for an ugly contest. The irises of its eyes were simple circular holes above a flat aquiline nose. Its wide oval mouth was bored deep, as were the smaller boreholes for nostrils. The face was framed by carved locks of granite hair, including a mustache and beard. It scowled at me like a child after their first bite of Brussels sprouts.

I wondered how many of my coworkers from ATPG 217 were sweating it out in a room exactly like this one.

Before today, I had never heard of ATPG Alpha. After a moment of reflection, it stood to reason that if an ATPG Omega existed to handle threats directed at Eldridge from outer space, there had to be an Alpha handling skullduggery from within the company—the corporate equivalent of Internal Affairs.

I spent the remaining time slowly fuming about how Alpha appeared on the scene with all the finesse of a wrecking ball. Mere minutes after Algernon was whisked away to medical, a troupe of burly men-in-black types corralled me and my coworkers into an out-of-the-way conference room. Similar goons, except dressed in white coveralls and hardhats, tossed our cubicles as we were led away. I snorted back a snicker, watching one of them in a hazmat suit, siphoning Algernon's aquarium into a bio-hazard container.

I managed to say, "I'm pretty sure it's not airborne. Check his bottled water, too," before my beefy escort told me to shut my yap.

Herded down the corridors, Natalie objected like a bucking bronco at them rifling through her stuff. Hector quietly scribbled down their badge numbers. Sofia huffed and puffed at anyone who would pay her any heed. Jolly strutted her stuff under their noses and dark glasses, while Barandir contemplated at them.

We were herded into a surgically white conference room with a gleaming white oblong table and chairs. I was shoved down into my seat. "A guy could go snow blind in here," I grumbled.

One of the Eldridge *mafiosi* louvered the vertical cloth blinds flat along the glass wall. Once we were all seated, another black-suited linebacker placed a trans-lex in front of each of us. Perplexed expressions surrounded the table.

Before any of us could think to ask a question, the beefiest of the lumberjacks in worsted wool said, "Do not touch." No sooner had he issued the command than his fellows stood by each of our seats and tapped the tops of the trans-lexes. My curiosity was piqued when the corners of the devices glowed red, rather than the neon blue the time Algernon used his. A second later, they tumbled over, balancing themselves on one of their points, and began to slowly rotate. The men stood solemn as palace guards, their hands clasped in front of themselves, and their lantern jaws set in dour expressions that would give a charging bull second thoughts.

I wondered aloud, "What language are we going to speak now, trans-lex?" I scanned the faces of my coworkers, but they were either concentrating on the glowing whirligigs in front of them or scowling at their guard. "Hey Natalie, what's the deal?"

She didn't react, still frowning at her spinning device. Barandir looked at me and mouthed something.

"What?"

The head Alpha goon responded, "Your coworker said, 'We cannot hear you, and you cannot hear us.' So, you might as well clam up, Sunshine, until we turn off your *halt-lex*."

Talk about a nifty way to ensure your witnesses don't have a chance to compare their stories.

I stewed. Natalie stewed. We all stewed.

Except for maybe Barandir. Who could tell what thoughts hatched between those elvish ears? It unnerved me that every so often, he stared at me with his trademark unflappable deadpan expression.

After watching the clock's minute hand crawl for a quarter of an hour, a silhouette behind the vertical blinds sauntered up to the door. A woman's voice, slick as axle grease, said, "Bring Ms. Adelman to the first interview room. Report back to me the others' room numbers once they're separated." The diminutive shadow turned on its heels and marched away.

One of the intimidation squad tapped Natalie's halt-lex off. He then indicated she stand and guided her to the door.

"Buck up, Michael. You're in for a rough ride," Natalie said over her shoulder as her assigned tough guy escorted her to what I hoped would be a simple debriefing.

Yeah, right.

Since they nabbed my mentor first, I thought they might be going one by one and by seniority. No such luck. As soon as Natalie's Alpha gorilla whisked her out the doorway, the bouncer assigned to my chair turned off my halt-lex and hefted me out of my seat like I was a GI Joe doll. He then escorted me to an underground level, lower than any I had ever visited in our building. The elevator didn't even indicate a level name when its bell rang our arrival.

After cooling my heels alone in the overheated interview/interrogation room, a sheen of perspiration covered my whole body. I leaned over and smiled at my image in the dingy mirror.

"Hello, is anyone there?"

In response, the camera started recording, its red light blinking a steady rhythm. The stenography machine tapped out my syllables, falling silent as it waited for my next words. I assumed they both might be scribes, not unlike my pen Amelia.

A stray thought crossed my mind—could scribes have a hierarchy similar to that used among the living? Whatever the answer, it meant I couldn't talk to Amelia while under their scrutiny.

Two people in black ties and business suits entered through the door. First in marched a pale woman whose build matched the silhouette I spied outside our meeting room upstairs. Smartly dressed, her light gray pantsuit contrasted with her black crew cut, dark rouge dusting her cheeks, and deep maroon lipstick. With eyes the color of a twilight storm, she struck me as a cross between Annie Lennox and Wednesday Addams.

In her shadow walked a slight man wearing mirrored aviator frames. His suit was styled identically to the goon squad upstairs, though cut from a superior material. He tried to hide a large bald spot with a comb-over of strawberry blond hair. From one wrist hung a Polaroid 1000 instant camera.

The pair stopped two paces from the table. The woman stated in a polite but commanding voice. "Please stand for a moment, Mr. Yeager." The video camera and stenography machine jumped back to life.

I accommodated her, and the gentleman aimed the camera and shot. The camera mechanically purred as its undeveloped photo rolled out. He handed the square of film to his partner.

They took their places across the table from me, sitting with an accuracy rivaling that of Olympic-class synchronized swimmers. In likewise lockstep, the two placed pairs of thin manila folders in front of themselves and opened their topmost ones. They contained exact replicas of a dossier crammed with pink, yellow, and white papers. Identical photographs of my face were paper-clipped to the folders' inside jackets.

The snapshot wasn't my official Eldridge corporate ID photo, nor was it very complimentary. Even upside down, I could surmise it had been taken on the sly during one of my less photogenic days at UC Santa Clara. While the lady slipped the Polaroid over it, I glanced nervously at the black rectangles of my redacted personal on her topmost sheet.

The woman folded her perfectly manicured hands on the table between herself and the folder. "Good morning, Mr. Yeager. I'm Assessor Lenoir, ATPG Alpha," she said in a breathy contralto. "My assistant here is Mr. Pellagati."

He didn't nod. I wasn't sure he was even breathing. The telltale stench of old cigarette smoke permeating his clothes quickly surrounded me. What a horrible way to ruin a fine suit.

"Let us begin by getting the formalities out of the way," said Lenoir. For the benefit of the scribe machines, she stated the date and a string of digits I assumed to be an investigation number. "State your name for the record."

Which I did. I also succinctly answered the rest of her list of basic questions: my employee number, date of employment at Eldridge & S.Q.Amos Insurance, my current position at Eldridge, my current address, et cetera, et cetera, blah, blah, blah...

"Et cetera, et cetera, blah, blah, blah." I twitched in my seat. Did I say that out loud? Lenoir and Pellagati didn't seem to pay any heed.

She paged through the sheets in her folder. "You only have two-and-a-half months with us at Eldridge. Goodness, all you've been through in such a short time, and now, today's events as well? Your company record either foreshadows a promising future or an ignominious end."

Probably both.

"Probably both."

I jerked, pivoting around in my seat, searching for the source of what sounded like my own voice. Was it piped in from behind the two-way mirror? My eyes settled on the frowning stone block with wary suspicion. I was pretty sure its oval mouth hadn't moved.

Meanwhile, Lenoir's lips curled slyly, hiding a secret.

She ran a finger down the edge of the freshly developed Polaroid. The contours of my body stood out from a stark black background. My outline, composed of a thousand tiny lightning bolts, registered with a dark umber, with small patches of raw sienna coloring my heart and most of my brain. Small strokes of brown spread from my hands and head. A dollop of brick red hovered just under the top of my skull.

In the photo's corner sat a numbered legend—Rating 1 matched my umber traces, Rating 20 ended in a blazing blue-white. "Let the record show Mr. Yeager rates as PQ-3."

It dawned on me that Dr. Fleischer never had the chance to write down my result of a PQ-2. I had the strangest urge to correct Lenoir, but something inside told me to keep quiet. I hoped my eyebrows wouldn't ruin it for me.

"That's not right," I blurted out loud. My cheeks burned with consternation. "What the—?"

"*What*'s not right, Mr. Yeager?" Lenoir's grin curled into a snarl.

I focused on Pellagati's sunglasses. If he was throwing some sort of aura at me, it didn't feel like the one from Dr. Fleischer. I stared at the ugly marble block again, trying to discern any change in its severe features, wondering if it was the reason I couldn't keep my mouth shut.

"My last measurement was PQ-2." There was no point in hiding it anymore. The psychic cat was out of the astral bag. "I guess that information got lost when Dr. Fleischer's *Lapidibus Habilitas* attacked us."

The top of my head tickled, which struck me as out of place. There certainly was no chance of snow in this sauna bath of an interrogation room.

"You'll have to forgive Mr. Pellagati," Lenoir said, accompanied by a dangerous chuckle. "He has this talent to convince people to say whatever is on their mind."

Pellagati continued his imitation of a corpse. I took a quieting breath and tried to sense him out. The old scar itched again. Sure enough, I could feel the tendrils of his aura trying to wheedle their way into my conscious thoughts.

"Revealer empaths like Mr. Pellagati are PQ-8 or higher. As a PQ-3, resisting him would be pointless—although you are welcome to try."

In the presence of these two characters, I suppose I should have been properly cowed. For better or worse, the wisenheimer in me decided to test the waters. "So what is that picture—surely not Kirlian photography?" I added an overly loud snort for good measure. "Did you run out of Aptitude Stones?"

"The *Lapidibus Habilitas* are used only by Druids and a few others who cling to the old ways. As for this..." Lenoir *fwipped* the Polaroid with her index finger. "You're not far off. Mrs. Kirlian was employed in the Remove Viewing department. She tried to steal this process fifty years ago. ATPG Alpha suspected she was going to defect. So we strung her along, performing a mindwipe and a phony process when she betrayed Eldridge. What Mundanes call 'Kirlian photography' is a colorful but meaningless stunt." Her eyes flared, taunting me. "However, if you prefer taking another go with a fresh pair of Aptitude Stones, that can be arranged."

"No, thank you," I returned with a polite smirk. At least, as polite as a smirk can be.

Lenoir flipped over the dossier's top sheet, her eyebrows raising almost imperceptibly. I suspected it was an act for my benefit, some trick to measure my nervousness. "We're investigating Mr. Algernon's poisoning. I understand you were the last person to see him before his dissembling?"

"So he *was* poisoned." I kept my sweaty backside planted in the metal and plastic chair, resting on the back half of its wobble. "Is he all right?"

"Simple 'yes' or 'no' answers will do, Mr. Yeager. Were you his last visitor?"

"Yes, but there might have been other people in—"

"A simple yes or no, Mr. Yeager," she repeated.

An uncomfortable pause lingered before I answered again. "Yes."

Lenoir nodded toward the granite cube. "If you would be so kind, place your hand in the *Bocca della Verità*?"

I returned the stone's frown. It occurred to me that I was the Brussels sprouts it would be forced to eat.

"Oh, you haven't had the pleasure of trying out Alpha's polygraph?" She patted the stone like a sleeping cat. "This is the real 'Mouth of Truth,' as opposed to its larger cousin in Rome. Though the one at the *Cosmedin* basilica is inspired by our little friend here, it is sadly just a tourist trap for the Mundanes."

She tilted her head, watching my expressions.

I matched her gaze with a tilt of my own. "It doesn't contain another *Turia Feir*, does it? The last one I encountered nearly took my head off."

"No elves. I promise. However..." Her half-grin acquired a cruel glint. "Perhaps a small demonstration. If you would indulge us, Mr. Pellagati?"

The unflappable gent reached across and placed his wrinkled left hand, its thumb and forefinger yellowed from tobacco, into the gaping mouth of the stone's face.

"For the record, Mr. Pellagati... Are you wearing sunglasses?"

"Yes." His vocal cords warbled, heavy with phlegm.

"Have you smoked cigarettes today?"

"No."

Stone teeth inside the rocky mouth clamped down on his hand with the speed of a bear trap. Pellagati remained still.

"Again, Mr. Pellagati. Did you smoke any cigarettes today?"

"Yes."

The *Bocca*'s teeth released him, and he returned his uninjured hand to his lap, unflappable to the last.

"You see, Mr. Yeager? Nothing to fear, as long as you're truthful. Now, please place your right hand in the *Bocca*."

I hesitated.

"I hate to be firm so early in our investigation, but you are not leaving this room unless you follow my instructions."

I inched my right hand into the *Bocca*. The stone was rough and cool. I focused on Lenoir's intent eyes.

"I am required to advise you the force with which the *Bocca* bites down on the liar's hand is proportional to the magnitude of the lie or its importance to our investigation."

"Now she tells me," I mumbled.

"Back in 1971, Alpha asked Mr. Pellagati if he knew anything about the mysterious disappearance of D. B. Cooper..."

Pellagati raised his unstained right hand and flattened his palm. His middle finger was missing its nail.

"I must be more observant the next time I shake hands." I jabbed my left thumb at the stenography machine pattering away. "Is all this necessary? Two scribes video recording and transcribing everything we say, a haunted polygraph, and you two escapees from *The Eurythmics* Fan Club?"

Lenoir's smile could crack Arctic ice. "Normally, this is where another investigator would assert, '*I'll* ask the questions, Mr. Yeager,' but I sense such a display would be of little use. Your rather jaunty interior monologue shows a level of disdain toward authority that borders on flippant." She gave a gentle shrug and a wink. "Nothing we can't handle."

She leaned in, folding her hands. "But we do need to address the situation at hand quickly, as an attempt on the life of an employee is a serious matter. I understand you had previous dealings with Mr. Algernon. Is this correct?"

"Yes. At orientation."

Lenoir leafed through a section in her folder. From where I was sitting, they looked like a course transcript. "I see... *Aliens 201*. Was that the only time?"

"No. He joined me at mess one day early on. He was interested in my encounter with the Euryale."

"How would you describe your relationship with Mr. Algernon during those times?"

"Yes."

"Excuse me?"

"I thought you wanted only yes or no answers." I cracked a grin and waggled my eyebrows.

Lenoir's deadpan rivaled Buster Keaton's. "Very droll, Mr. Yeager. Please answer as directly as possible, and we can end this unpleasantness."

"It was amicable enough. There really wasn't time to have much of a relationship."

"Is that so?" She advanced to the next page. "I understand you threw a chair after your first class with Mr. Algernon. That doesn't sound very amicable to me."

"I was frustrated that he couldn't tell me anything about the Euryale."

The teeth of the Bocca gently squeezed my right hand.

"I think you need to clarify that statement, Mr. Yeager."

"I was still upset that my friends were turned into monsters. I was forced to kill one of them." Even with Pellagati's silent urging, I couldn't bring myself to say Sindhu's name.

The teeth released my hand, retreating behind the stone's oval mouth. "Once Algernon explained all history of the Euryale on Earth was destroyed, things were fine between us. And that's it—just those two meetings before taking the Oath."

"About that—Why was your company orientation rushed?"

"I don't know." My hand flinched a tiny bit. I wasn't sure how the granite goblin would react to an honest lack of knowledge. "Let me know if you find out."

Lenoir wrote on a blank tablet in the other half of her folder. Pellagati continued his role as quiet observer. I scratched my scalp, but the itch wouldn't go away. As I watched him, I began to perceive small taps around my cranium, like flies landing on the skin before buzzing away a moment later. I hoped detecting his probes meant I had a chance to defend against them. Where's Ventnor and Hibara when I need them?

Lenoir finished her scribbling. "What did you and Algernon discuss before his unfortunate situation?"

"We discussed Sofia's latest vision—an impending death and the possibility of an assassin here at Eldridge Sacramento. Given the limits of her sketchy vision, we agreed that both of us were possible targets."

"Sketchy?" Lenoir's inquisitive stare was a challenge. "What leads you to that evaluation?"

"Scientific skepticism."

"And yet, there you were with Mr. Algernon, discussing Ms. Urdsen's prediction as though it were authentic."

I shrugged my shoulders. "Occupational hazard."

The teeth gnawed again gently on my knuckles. Lenoir leaned forward with her arms folded on the table. "I think there's more to it than that."

Pellagati's probes came at me. I couldn't see them, but I could sure feel them. The top of my scalp itched like head lice had found a new home and were having a square dance.

All right—if they wanted what's *really* on my mind, they'll get it. "I don't like fortune-tellers, okay?"

Pellagati twitched like a bug landed on his forehead.

"When they're right, they're a royal pain in the you-know-where, acting like God's gift to humanity," I said. "When they're wrong, there's always some excuse that can't be discounted. 'Ooh, the spirits are confused. Hidden forces are at work. My trick knee's acting up. Mercury's in retrograde.' They have no accountability when things don't pan out. Meanwhile, the rest of the ATP group gets the extra workload."

"Too bad. That's the way things are, Mr. Yeager." If Lenoir had a further opinion on the subject, she didn't show it. She did, however, glance at the *Bocca's* partially exposed teeth. They were still poised to gnaw on Yeager knuckles. She flashed me another wicked half-grin. "Are you sure that's all there is?"

Before I could craft a response, a Pellagati spectral fly bit behind my ear, and something spilled out. "The idea of seers goes against the grain of my science side. A future that's predetermined?" I scoffed heavily enough to flutter the pages on Pellagati's folder. What I really wanted to do was spit. "I think quantum mechanics would have a lot to say about that."

"Again, that is why we have ATP groups like yours. Not all predictions are reliable. Others may be of a *possible* future. ATPG's are necessary to sift the wheat from the chaff."

The *Bocca* still refused to release me. Lenoir's eyes seethed with concentration. My scar no longer itched—it burned. So did Pellagati's probe. I was between a rock and three hard places.

"We're waiting, Mr. Yeager."

"What do you guys want from me?" I shouted.

"The truth," said Lenoir with the patience of a glacier. "Maybe one that you don't realize yourself. What is it about seers you so dislike?"

"Sindhu," I shouted, jumping to my feet, my free hand pounding the table. Sweat rolled into my eyes. It mixed in with my tears. "Why the *fuck* couldn't they save Sindhu?"

Pellagati relented, and the *Bocca* released me. I collapsed back into my seat, with the rest of me sprawled across my half of the table. My lungs clutched at the increasingly humid air.

The concrete floor rumbled like it was the only thing separating us from the deep-throated growl out of some cavernous mouth below our feet. I sat up so fast, my back slammed against the chair.

The room shook, slightly at first. The legs of my wobbly chair did a tap dance. The room temperature inched up. I wasn't sure, but the orange-red molding and wastebasket base might have shifted a brighter shade of fiery.

Lenoir *tsk*-ed several times, wagging her finger in time. "Temper, Mr. Yeager."

She scribbled a few more lines on her paper tablet, then layered her hands on top of the open folder. Her quizzical expression searched my own. "Actually, you may have answered several questions for us."

"Like what?" I tired of her mind games.

"Like—Why you were assigned to ATPG 217, or to an ATP group in the first place."

"Care to clue me in?"

Lenoir leaned in, her eyes continuing to probe. "I think Director Ventnor anticipated your heavy resentment over the loss of your three friends."

I steeled myself for her to attempt to drill down into my company-disapproved relationship with Sindhu. Unless...

"It's not like we haven't seen this before in new employees," she continued. "I suspect the Director assigned you to an ATPG to demonstrate that psychic ability, magic, and super-science do not guarantee success. I would not be surprised if he relegated you to ATPG 217 because of its below-average record."

"Below average?" I repeated, slinging one arm over the back of my chair. "Now that Merrill's out and *I'm* in, maybe things will improve."

"Anything is possible." Lenoir chuckled. Who'd have thought the ice queen was capable of laughter? "Nevertheless, my condolences, Mr. Yeager." Her contemptible smile remained.

I wanted to explode at her amusement, seemingly at my misfortune. What reined me back was her assumption that Sindhu was dead. Which meant I didn't have to lie. With Pellagati taking a breather, I wasn't compelled to correct her either. Fine by me. If only the scar on the top of my head would stop itching.

Lenoir instructed me to place my hand in the Bocca again, and Pellagati's noodle prodded my cranium anew. "Let's get back to your sit-down with Algernon. After you agreed you both were possible targets, what specifics did you discuss?"

"While we waited for Jiā-lì's database search results, Algernon wanted more information on me, hoping to narrow down who else the target might be. Y'know—if we had anything in common beyond orientation camp and the ATPG. He showed me my employee record, which was the first time I was aware of my redacted data. After he showed me his own personnel sheet's redactions, we established a bridge and discussed our personal histories. We really didn't have much time to go all that deep."

"Then, you know the history of the Oovlid people."

"I know he's the last of his kind, but not much more."

"And it didn't occur to you *that* made him a prime candidate to match Ms. Urdsen's prognostication?"

"Of course it did."

Pellagati tried to shoulder his way deeper into my skull.

I bit my lip and took another breath, attempting to discipline my conscious thoughts. Mustering my best mental defenses garnered from Psychic Defense classes, I mixed it in with some pointers on tantric meditation Sindhu had shared with me long ago. Who knows, maybe that one section from her copy of the *Kama Sutra* would keep Pellagati out? Or gross him out.

A wrinkled smile creased Pellagati's jaw. Now, *I* was grossed out—he liked to watch! I had to scramble for a new defense.

"And what part of *your* blacked-out history makes you a prime candidate?"

His aura burrowed away, this time at my temples. A sudden urge to cry out "Elrameshe!" rose up, but the itch at the top of my head started to burn, stopping the impulse in its tracks.

"I wish I knew."

The *Bocca*'s teeth chittered with hesitation.

Lenoir pressed on. "Who redacted your data from your employee record?"

"I. Don't. Know." Each word of my reply required a Herculean effort, while I kept Pellagati's attack at bay.

He breathed with effort while sweat beaded on his forehead. The pressure increased. I expected to smell my own hair burning any second.

"Did you redact your *own* information?"

"Wow, are *you* barking up the wrong tree." I swallowed air in gulps, regaining my concentration. "I don't have that type of access."

"We are not accustomed to interviewing employees who have so much data unavailable to us. Not even my supervisor can gain access to your protected data. Why is that?"

"You're asking the wrong person."

"Is it because your information and Mr. Algernon's were erased for the same reason?"

"Do I *look* like an Oovlid?"

"No, but neither do we know what manner of creatures eradicated the Oovlid. How do we know you are not one of that species?"

"You're grasping at straws. If I were one of these bogeyman aliens, do you think I would resort to something as pedestrian as poisoning?"

"I'm trying to determine what you are, Mr. Yeager." She stood, her hands splaying out over her folder. "Let's get down to the basics. Are you *human*? I'm not convinced you are."

"If I'm not human, then what am I?"

"A shapeshifter? Maybe one of a race we've never met before, perhaps the one that erased the Oovlid? Maybe a mole who slipped through security?" Lenoir produced an employee sheet with its own photograph and slid it toward me. "Do you recognize this person?"

I squinted against the bright white of the paper. "I'm not sure. One of the janitorial staff, maybe? I haven't had many chances to network around Eldridge yet."

"Correct. We found him unconscious, locked in a closet. Yet, security footage shows him making rounds in your area, including entering

Algernon's office. Strangely enough, during a time when you were notably absent."

"But then, so was everyone else in my group." I measured my words carefully. "We were in a meeting. I noticed things in my own cubicle had been moved around."

She snatched back the photograph. "How long did you really know Algernon? Or did you know him by his Oovlid name? Did you finagle getting Mr. Algernon assigned to your group? Are you the assassin? Did you work alone, or is there another mole assisting you in Eldridge? Who's your handler?"

"Lady, now you're barking up the wrong *forest*," I said with a labored scoff. "I was born on Earth and raised by human stepparents."

"So you say. But how can we be sure you were born on Earth? You claim you have no memory before age six. Birth and adoption records can be falsified. With Mr. and Mrs. Pritchard conveniently passed away, we cannot confirm that they in fact *did* raise you, now can we?"

"You cold-hearted..." I growled. My relationship with my stepparents Erwin and Esther might have been a complex one—especially after she tried to kill me—but they still were family. Erwin and I had loved the memory of the person we had once known as Esther, before she succumbed to madness.

Sensing my anger distracted me from defense, Pellagati jabbed his aura again at me.

My itch began to burn again. "That's your best theory—I'm an alien sent to liquidate Algernon? If that's so, these aliens sure play the long game. You realize that means I had to have been planted sometime between twenty-two and twenty-eight years ago."

"Not necessarily. You might have replaced the real Michael Yeager at any number of opportunities after your adoption. For example, one of the many times your family pulled up stakes and moved to another state— an excessive number of times, as I see it. Was your stepfather a trouble-maker like you?"

I refused her bait this time. She had no idea how convoluted my family's relationships were.

"The opposite. Erwin was employed by the Forest Ranger Service. He got assigned to a new station every so often. Sometimes with a promotion."

Lenoir sat and flipped into a new section in my folder. "From the

Girdwood station near Anchorage to Lubbock in 1964, then San Fernando in '70, Rapid City in '71, Ft. Collins in '72, and lastly, the quiet little Mt. Adams station near Mt. St. Helens in '76."

"How'd you get that? I thought you said my info was redacted."

"Alpha has its ways... Goodness, five times in twelve years. That's an awful lot of relocating for a young family. Except Erwin Pritchard *wasn't* reassigned by the government service."

"*What*?" That little tidbit stopped me cold.

"It seems he always filed the transfer requests one day before he hustled his family to the next assignment. And every one was approved almost immediately." She extracted a sheet from the folder and slipped it toward me.

Pellagati's probes slithered into cracks of opportunity left unguarded while I dusted off my memories. Despite a sudden grumble from his gut, he kept up the attack.

The surprise—and sometimes shock—brought on by each of Erwin's announcements came rushing back. My recollection of our last move was the clearest. It had been burned into my memory because it hurt the worst.

The latch keeping my mouth shut popped off.

"That's impossible. The day before we moved to Washington, Erwin rushed into the dining room. I was finishing up my high-school Honors Chem homework when he announced he got another transfer. But we had to move quick. Man, I was so *pissed* at Erwin that night."

I would have clenched my hand into a fist if I weren't up to my knuckles in that blasted *Bocca*. "We had *finally* stayed in a place long enough to set down roots. I sure as heck didn't want to leave my buddies behind, not to mention a girl I had just started dating. Esther put up a brave face, but I could tell she was just as cheesed as I was."

Then it struck me—my stepmother's curious reaction at the time.

I spoke barely above a whisper. "Esther sat across the table from me, catching up on some notary work from the county clerk's office. Like me, she was dumbstruck by Erwin's news. Then she tore into him with a barn-burner of an argument. She loved Fort Collins and was involved in the community. For once, she had a circle of friends. She screamed at him she couldn't—*wouldn't*—leave. But when Erwin mentioned the person he would replace—some lady's name—Athena, Atlanta, *Atreyu*?—Esther's face went blank. She dropped everything to begin packing. It was almost like she turned into a robot."

I sniffed loudly, but my nose refused to clear up. "And Erwin, he looked a little off, too. At the time, I thought he was leery of the tirade Esther whipped up. But he was scared. *Really* scared. What could have done that?"

"Maybe he was scared of *you*," Lenoir said. Her eyebrows were those of a she-wolf on the hunt.

"Goddamn it, now you have me doubting my own memories."

The concrete floor trembled again with that hellacious growl underneath. It stopped, replaced by sounds of rasping claws scraping underneath my feet.

"Such language," said Lenoir, her hand raised to her mouth, covering a deceitfully coy pose. "Two strikes, Mr. Yeager. I wouldn't want to be in your shoes on strike three."

The stinging on the top of my head burned red-hot again. I shut my eyes hard, took a breath, and shoved Pellagati out of my head. He hiccuped, looking a shade paler, if such a thing was possible.

The crazy idea of visualizing a brick wall popped into my head, like the one George Sanders used as a mental block against the alien offspring in *Village of the Damned*. I tried not to linger on the fact his character died in the attempt.

"Is this how you sadists get your jollies?" One layer of brick. Not the best foundation, but I stuck with it.

Lenoir ignored my barb and charged straight ahead, her sickening half-grin leading the way. "Oh, we're just warming up, Mr. Yeager." Leaning closer on her elbows, she rested her chin on bridged hands. Pellagati followed suit, though he wasn't in lockstep with Lenoir. Easy to see why— his hands were trembling. I slathered on a layer of psychic mortar.

"Let's assume for the moment you were still the real Michael Yeager while your parents were alive. What about *after* their deaths?" She ran a fingernail down the next sheet, a series of transcripts. "You received your Bachelor's from the University of Washington one month after their passing. You then matriculated into the University of California graduate program the very next semester."

She leaned back in her seat, crossing her arms. "Curious, Mr. Yeager. Both events, done without missing a beat. Not would I would expect from a grieving son."

"You forget—At the time, I still believed I was their stepson." I wistfully peered into the hollow eyes of the *Bocca*. Cool and calm, it was the exact opposite of the turmoil inside me. "Our relationship was... complicated."

"Is that the reason you never refer to Esther and Elmer as 'Mom' or 'Dad?'"

"For some reason, it didn't feel..." I dared the stone teeth to move. "...proper."

Lenoir chewed on my response for a few seconds. "Tell me about your stepmother."

"What, are you my psychiatrist now?" Another sarcastic quip, another layer of brick.

"According to our records, much of your post-orientation evaluation, including the required final psychological assessment, was waived after your tussle with the *Habilitas*. From what I've observed so far, my report will strenuously recommend that you be examined immediately." Lenoir paged to the bottom of the paper pile in my folder. "Especially considering your family history. I see here that Mrs. Pritchard was institutionalized for a substantial amount of time."

"I think you'll also find she had recurring hemorrhoids." Another layer...

The albino was soaking in sweat. Lenoir was too intent on me to notice.

"It took some doing on short notice, but we were able to locate Mrs. Pritchard's psychiatric records. The supervising doctor listed her admission as due to a violent psychotic break." Her eyes focused on a line in the middle of the report. "There seems to be a police report referenced as well. We'll have to follow up on that. Unless you would care to explain what occurred, leading to her admission to the hospital's psych ward?"

I tamped down another layer to my brick wall before I answered. "She attacked me."

Lenoir's expression could have been that of a demon about to devour a soul.

"Heavens, Mr. Yeager. Whatever for?"

"For reasons that didn't make sense." That was true enough, but the *Bocca* detected my equivocation. Its teeth clenched on my hand. Not painfully so, but there was no way I could remove my knuckles from the thing's mouth. "The real reasons stayed locked in her head, and they died with her under tons of ash."

The *Bocca* still held my hand in its rocky maw.

I added another layer, this time with my bricks replaced with a row of *Boccas* face down, eating wet cement.

"You'll have to do better than that, Mr. Yeager."

Another layer, this time with bricks embossed with Lenoir's face.

"Tell you what, I'll take you up on that psychiatric examination, and you can read the doctor's report later. That'll be quicker for both of us. In the meantime, what does my dysfunctional family have to do with Algernon?"

Pellagati's gut burbled like a clogged toilet. Meanwhile, I was bolstered by the realization his probes failed to make me blurt out my desire to punch Lenoir in the face.

She finally caught on to her partner's condition, sitting back in her chair, her expression not as tenacious, but still dangerous.

I set another layer onto my wall, tall enough to shield my itching, burning head.

"Very well," she said with deliberation. "Let us instead focus on the time between your parents' deaths and your joining Eldridge."

The *Bocca* released my hand, leaving depressions in my skin.

The tension in my shoulders bunched my neck into a cramp. "You're still on this alien mole spy kick?"

"When you started college, did you know anyone there?"

"There was the admissions director, and—"

"That was not what I meant, Mr. Yeager. Was there already anyone at the University of California from Mt. Adams, Fort Collins, Rapid City, or any other places you lived? Anyone from your past that might have recognized you upon your arrival at university?"

"No."

"Surely you see the problem, then, Mr. Yeager. We are faced with a period of time during which you are an unverified single actor. A lone wolf. No family, nor friends—"

"I understood that to be the major qualification Eldridge looks for in a recruit. Nothing to gum up relationship rules one and two, right?"

"—nor acquaintances, nor academic contacts that you might see on a regular basis to maintain a continuity." Lenoir must have read the confusion in my eyebrows. "In short, no one can verify that the person who arrived at San Jose was the real Michael Yeager."

I leaned in. "You know, there's a couple of inventions in the Mundane world to handle this sort of thing. Perhaps you've heard of them. Drivers' licenses? Social security numbers?" Another layer of mortar to my towering defensive wall. "What does this have to do with anything?"

"You might have been replaced by a simulacrum."

"A *who*?"

"A double, a doppelgänger, a duplicate. Like your cohort who pretended to be a janitor?"

"So someone *was* mucking about my desk and Algernon's office." I almost jumped out of my seat. "I wonder if someone's trying to get back at Algernon for all the cold cases I closed. There was that one St. Petersburg assessor. Man, he was fit to be tied." I rapped the table with my free hand. "Maybe something in my cubicle was poisoned, too."

"Ridiculous."

"Your cleaning crew confiscated everything in my cube. How convenient." I flipped an accusing finger at her. "*You* check it out."

Lenoir's shoulders hitched with a sigh. "We did find the original janitor. Unconscious and rambling incoherently about his age."

"Looks like I'm not the one who should be wrist-deep in a *Bocca*. You know what else backs me up against this doppelgänger baloney? DNA. You guys made a big stink that my DNA proves I *am* Michael Yeager. Your theories are falling apart, Lenoir. How could I be target and perpetrator at the same time?"

"There is the distinct possibility you may have been reprogrammed, brainwashed, any number of scenarios."

I wiped my face, dragging my hand down slowly to exaggerate the impatience in my eyes. "How am I expected to respond to this endless parade of hare-brained conspiracy theories? How do you people sleep, thinking up goofy stuff like this?"

"We sleep much better when we eliminate security threats." Her grin revealed the return of her snarl.

"Here, let me help you." I clenched my free hand into a fist and conked the *Bocca* on its flat head. "Hey, *Bocca*—wake up. Did I poison Algernon? No, I did not." I mugged for Lenoir, hoping she understood what sarcasm looked like. "Am I an alien, mole, or simulacrum, bent on the assassination of Algernon and maybe the destruction of Eldridge? No, I most certainly am not." I shot her another dose of annoyed frustration. "Am I the real Michael Avery Yeager? Why, yes, I am, thank you for asking."

Though it probably wanted to chomp my fingers off, the *Bocca* remained still.

"Most amusing, Mr. Yeager." She closed my folder and opened the one underneath it. "If we may proceed? I have one last venue of questioning."

"If we must."

"Oh, yes, we must."

The underlying folder was thinner. Lenoir quickly ruffled through the scant few pages it contained. "About your fiancée, Ms. Sindhu Mehra."

My gut tensed, and my eyes became burning embers. "What about her?"

"Understandably, we had little time to prepare for your interview. Though security on the Mundane's governments' files is laughable, it is nonetheless time-consuming to work around. We would appreciate it if you could fill us in on some of her particulars that we lack."

"Assuming that's a lie, you want me to divulge something that will feed into your loony conspiracy theory."

"When did you first meet Ms. Mehra?"

Pellagati slipped past my anger. I winced at what felt like the bite of a horsefly on my temple. "The first week of graduate school." I regained my composure and bit the inside of my lips together to prevent myself from spilling out the details. The astral horsefly buzzed away. I tried to add another layer to my defense, but I was tiring quickly.

"I see Ms. Mehra emigrated with her mother from India."

I felt safe discussing what would be common knowledge. "Yes."

"What do you know about your fiancée's family?"

"Not much. Her father died before they left India. Once here, her mother began a successful snake-oil company, Yakshini Herbal Health." I failed at repressing a scoff.

"Excuse me?"

"Nothing," I said. "I meant homeopathic supplement company. I always thought Yakshini was a stupid choice for a name."

"I see," Lenoir said, trailing off. She placed a finger on her page, obscuring several lines from my view. "Curious."

Out of curiosity, I craned my neck, only to sit back rigidly when she slapped the papers down sharply.

"Do you know when they came to America?" she asked.

"Not exactly. I know it was shortly before my first year at Santa

Clara."

"And you don't find that an interesting coincidence?"

"That's all it is, a coincidence," I said more than a little defensively. "I would imagine lots of international students do that."

"*With* their parents?" she said.

"I wouldn't know."

"What did Ms. Mehra tell you about their family before they emigrated?"

"She was born in Varanasi and moved to New Delhi with her mother when her father passed away. She got her Bachelor's at Delhi University before moving to California."

"Curious," Lenoir said, scanning her papers.

"You keep saying that."

"Her degree seems in perfect order. What I find extremely *odd*," she said with a knife's edge, "is that there is no record of your Sindhu Mehra in New Delhi—nor in all of India for that matter..." She inhaled deeply, then spoke like she led a funeral dirge. "... before May 18, 1980."

My head snapped back with a violent twist, like I dodged a right cross.

The day Mt. St. Helens exploded. The day my parents died.

Lenoir leaned in, pressing her advantage. So did Pellagati's attacks, though he sat immobile. His gut was not. It gurgled loud as ever.

"You seem to be the focal point of too many coincidences, Mr. Yeager. And lies seem to swirl around you. Why did your parents lie about your adoption?"

"I don't know."

"Why did your fiancée lie about her previous life?"

"I don't..." My mind stumbled as it absorbed Lenoir's information. I leaned on my mental wall for support.

"Or is that a fabrication of your own making? Why did she bring you to Lick Observatory? Did she know about the Euryale? Did *you*? Were they the reason you tried to assassinate Mr. Algernon? Was he digging too deep into the Euryale's history for your liking?"

She flipped over almost the whole series of dossiers in her folder: me, Sindhu, my parents. Opening the last one, the upside-down picture of a blue four-armed giantess figured prominently. "And then there's Lt. Yadavi. She has logged a good number of times visiting Ms. Mehra in Long-Term Storage. Why is that, Mr. Yeager? Is she a part of this as well?"

She banged her fist on the table, and her voice increased to near shouting. "Was Ms. Mehra the mastermind? Was she even human? Are *you*? Did you sacrifice your supposed betrothed when she was no longer necessary?"

My mind spun at Lenoir's rapid-fire barrage of questions. I gagged on my own words.

Pellagati's tendrils struck from behind, boring into the spot on the top of my head. It burned like a torch.

I whipped my hand out of the Bocca and slammed both fists on the table. "You conniving bitch! My stepparents are one thing, but *Sindhu*? Your paranoid delusion has gone far enough." I stood, and she shot up to face me as well, challenging me once more with her deadly smile.

I shut my eyes so hard that tears and sweat tumbled out.

My first whisper to Sindhu rushed into my head. The sight of her perfectly formed ear, the touch and aroma of her scented hair. Our first kiss swam in front of my eyes. Its taste sent my nerves reeling. The sweet memory of our first night wrapped around each other, nothing but our mingling sweat between our bodies, minds, and souls. The laughter and tears on the day I proposed.

"She was human," I bellowed.

And then the horrible sight of my beautiful Sindhu, half-corrupted into a monster of stone, smashed my consciousness into wild fury. My rage and the top of my head burned hot as a furnace. My caution against opening my mind to Pellagati's incessant worming tore apart like tissue paper against the juggernaut of my fury. Using its immediacy, its undeniability, its power, I pictured myself shoving my brick wall over onto Pellagati, crushing him to powder.

"We— are— *human*!" I shrieked. The room rang like a giant bronze bell.

Shock swept across Lenoir's face, and the albino retched.

Pellagati threw off his sunglasses, and they clattered on the metal table. His eyes rolled up into his forehead, leaving only the bottoms of his creepy pink irises visible. Jumping up from his seat, he dashed toward the exit. He ducked his head into the wastebasket and puked.

Did I do that? Or did he overexert himself, having reached some physical limit?

The burning at the top of my skull shut off like a switch was thrown.

Lenoir's tortured rictus vanished, replaced with pure consternation. The door *whanged* open.

Petrakis strode through, holding a small attaché case. His ragged, stunted ponytail wagged behind him. "I couldn't agree more." He coughed, snatched a handkerchief from his pocket, and held it over his nose. "Good gravy, what is that smell?"

Pellagati spilled another load of his innards into the black and red wastebasket.

Petrakis minced over to our table while covering another cough. "Assessor Lenoir, you are hereby instructed to cease this interview with Mr. Yeager."

She snarled at the professor. "I wondered when you would show up and rescue your pet prodigy. You have no authority to—"

Petrakis opened his attaché and thrust a paper in front of her nose before slapping it on top of her copy of my dossier. "Quite correct. But Director Ventnor does."

I could almost smell Lenoir's mascara burning from the shade of crimson her otherwise pale and drawn face had turned.

Petrakis marched with purpose over to the recording machines. He popped the video camera and stenography machines open, confiscating their tapes. "There will be no media records kept of this interview." Walking to the door, with the recordings stashed in his case, he beckoned at me. "Come along, my boy. We have work to do."

I nodded at Lenoir, returning her death's head scowl as an appropriate courtesy, before accompanying Petrakis out. He closed the door behind us, leaving Lenoir to glower impotently at the signed order, and Pellagati wiping off his mouth.

"Thanks for rescuing me. I wasn't sure how much longer I could hold out." I wiped off my sweat with a handkerchief. "So, don't take this the wrong way. What are you doing here? Did we catch a break on who attacked Algernon?"

"No, the Alpha and Omega ATPGs have already divided that assignment among themselves. Something else has come up." He stuffed his handkerchief into his pocket and produced from his case a black-and-white fax of what looked like a frame from a security camera video. "Have you ever seen this person?"

I blinked in astonishment. The picture showed a woman using a walker, escorted by a nurse down a bare institutional hallway. Behind her was a fuzzy poster with a large letter Y in the center.

I recognized the woman, though she was older. Somehow, she had passed "Go" and collected two hundred years. But it was her.

"This is impossible," I said.

"That's what *I* thought."

"Where is this?" I swallowed to clear the hitch in my voice. "Where did you find Esther?"

CHAPTER 22

Driving north along the coast, we headed into the teeth of a Pineapple Express rainstorm. As he plowed through the never-ending downpour, he hummed and "*da-de-dah*"-ed to symphonic pieces that, to my ear, were recordings of an orchestra tumbling down an up escalator. I remained silent, my eyes closed, alone with my thoughts.

Though ATPG Alpha had spent hours of overtime chasing their collective tail, probing for my part in Algernon's assault, they did succeed in one aspect. They planted the seeds of doubt in me.

Why did my parents lie to me about my adoption? Why did Erwin need to fake his transfers? Who was Sindhu before she appeared out of nowhere? What other secrets had she kept from me? By God, I still loved her, but the knowledge that she had a past of which I had never suspected —and she had never revealed—left me empty.

By nightfall, I had no revelations, let alone the beginnings of an answer. Doubt still chewed at my insides, insisting I was missing something.

Something that tied it all together.

After a night of fitful sleep at a seedy hotel and another ten-plus hours of splattering rain on the windshield and symphonic carnage over the car's loudspeakers, we arrived at our destination along the southern side of the sprawling Tacoma-Seattle area.

We entered the metro limits late. The buildings loomed dark and forbidding, made even more so by streaks of black gutter wash. Petrakis turned off the cassette player in the middle of an atonal piece with *Nachklang* in the name by some sadist named Terzakis.

If there is a Hades, the symphonies of modern Greek composers must surely play on their speakers. The bozo who came up with the rule, "the driver picks the music, and shotgun shuts his cakehole," should have a permanent seat between two giant Marshall stacks down there.

We completed a circuit along the drives that serpentined around the Western Bay State Hospital campus. Streetlamps placed too far apart beamed down their baleful yellow sodium rays upon the asphalt and the greenery. Misty drizzle sparkled in their cones of light.

Along the outer loop, silhouetted armies of fir and spruce trees stood off against squadrons of elm and oak. They maintained their stalwart vigils behind a dotted line of dainty fruit trees. All the while, the hospital complex dominated the land, brooding over its fiefdom.

I couldn't shake the sense that the more prominent buildings watched us in the quiet night. Though they all shared an architectural style resembling oversized haciendas wrestling Gregorian monasteries, each regarded us with its own unique sentiment.

Stuccoed concrete walls eyed us with stern watchfulness. Squat buildings housing specific functions like laundry or maintenance lay frozen with fear, surrounded by their stories-high brothers. Long stretches of stone and masonry walls put up a happy front, like a tired aunt who still greets you with the best smile she can manage. One wing's corner was dominated by a circular structure with decorative stonework that tried to look open and welcoming. Instead, it gave off the vibe of a prison watch‑tower.

In the center of the easternmost facade rested a century-old edifice, the original sanitarium. It spilled over with prim and proper stuffiness, as it looked down its slate roof nose at us.

"Esther's in this place?" Despair tarnished my voice.

"Ah, you're awake." Petrakis turned onto the main boulevard along the campus's southern side, beginning his second pass at casing the joint.

"I've been awake since we left Eldridge. I can't sleep in a vehicle—plane, train, or car. And most of those pieces by Kalomiris, Markopoulos, and Whoozy-Whatzis aren't exactly lullabies."

"Apologies, my boy."

Somehow, I didn't get the warm-and-fuzzies that his *mea culpa* was all that earnest. I rubbed my eyes to full alertness. "I've just been trying to make sense of everything that happened yesterday."

"Yes, it has been a rather busy time for you, hasn't it? You're told your life may be in jeopardy, an attempt is made on the life of your supervisor, ATPG Alpha drags you in for interrogation, and now this."

"Any word on Algernon's condition?" I felt a slight pang of guilt for not having considered his situation earlier.

"I checked in last night. They have successfully flushed the poison out of his pieces, and he's on the mend. Sadly, there is no prognosis when he can fully reassemble himself and return to service."

"How was he poisoned?"

"A concentrated dose of the toxin produced by red algae."

"So, *that's* why his office stank. Couldn't he smell that?"

"I am afraid his nose is simply ornamental, my boy."

Our unassuming beige Taurus rolled along quietly, seesawing with minor grunts from its suspension as we crossed the loop's speed bumps. I wasn't sure what model of company car to expect, but I hoped for something better than my K-Car frump-mobile.

"Why couldn't we have taken one of the company helicopters?"

"Don't be silly," he said with a scoff. "They were necessary at Lick Observatory because covert containment teams were required. That, and Euryale intrusions occur like clockwork every forty-two years, allowing us to requisition everything needed well ahead of time. Routine assessments like this do not warrant a helicopter, magicked with a silence spell or not."

My head twitched in disbelief and grew a smile. "Wait... we're on an *assessment*?"

From day one at Eldridge Sacramento, everyone impressed on me that a member of an Advanced Threat Prediction Group getting attached to a field assignment was a once-in-a-decade event. Yet here I am, on my first assessment, after only a few months at Eldridge.

"Officially, yes—as far as APTG Alpha is concerned." He swiped his finger along the side of his nose. "We had to get you out of their grasp before their probing uncovered your... agreement with Vice President Hibara."

I snapped my head at Petrakis. I could feel the hairs on my eyebrows bristle. "So, this assessment is a red herring? My stepmother *isn't* here?"

Petrakis swatted my flash of anger away while we waited at a stoplight. "I'm not explaining this well, am I? You see, while you languished in Alpha interrogation, your scribe notified Namiki and Hadrian of your situation." His crooked smile dimpled one cheek. "Don't you find it rather interesting the lowest level of our Eldridge building habitable by humans is labeled 'Alpha?'"

"We have non-human levels?"

His shoulders sagged, pushing out an exasperated sigh. "Day six of your orientation."

"What non-human was underneath my interrogation room? It sounded upset and *hungry* every time I said... something non-regulation."

"Don't trouble yourself with details, my boy. Take it as another object lesson to constantly monitor your language while in any Eldridge building." The light turned green, and he raised a finger as though he were back at a USCA lecture hall. "After all, 'Death and life are in the power of the tongue.'"

"What grimoire is that from? The *Necronomicon*? The *Book of Shadows*? The *Clavicule of Solomon*?"

"Something infinitely more dangerous—*The Bible*. Proverbs 18, I believe. Anyway, our scribes alerted us that Ms. Lenoir was employing the *Bocca* polygraph and a revealer empath to scan you."

"Well, you arrived just in time. Lenoir gloated that Pellagati had a talent for making people talk, and I can attest to that. I had to scramble to keep the subject of Amelia, Hibara, and the Circle of Ageless Waters from spilling out."

"At least you remembered your training from Psychic Defenses 201. I was, however, rather surprised by Pellagati's violent reaction to your psychic block."

The sound of the albino puking his brains out still fresh in my mind, I chuckled with satisfaction at the agent's just-desserts. I debated if I should tell Petrakis how I had almost surrendered to Pellagati's probes before the top of my head burned like an acetylene torch.

"Getting back to the purpose of our little adventure—once your Pilot spread the word, Director Ventnor signed all the necessary paperwork to extricate you in a flash. As of this afternoon, in addition to my duties as an assessor, Ventnor has assigned me as your ATPG's interim supervisor. Therefore, as far as anyone else at Eldridge knows, you are accompanying me on an assessment requiring your biochemistry expertise."

"Which, of course, is a lie."

Petrakis took his eyes off the road to glower at me. "Shall I take you back to the Alpha interrogation room?"

"Gotcha, boss." I bit my lower lip as I stewed. I regarded Petrakis in a new light, one that revealed more than the jaundiced streetlights did.

More feints, half-truths, and obfuscation. Can I trust anyone in this company?

I looked at the dashboard clock. "Criminy, eight o'clock in the evening? We're not going in *now*, are we?"

"Heavens, no. I merely wanted to get the gist of the hospital layout. Namiki made reservations for us at a local hotel and an appointment with the hospital's Head of Psychiatry at ten o'clock tomorrow morning." He yawned expansively. "Excuse me—I'm not used to all this driving. Four hours last night, a rather lumpy bed, topped off with ten more hours of driving is terribly taxing."

"I offered to take the wheel each time we stretched our legs along the way."

"Thanks all the same, my boy, but no." He exited the grounds, turning onto the main boulevard heading back toward the interstate. "I requisitioned this car in my name alone. I was understandably in a bit of a rush and did not have the presence of mind to add your name on the forms. As a result, there would be... consequences if anyone other than myself tried to take the wheel."

A skittering of claws scratched behind the passenger-side airbag panel.

I pushed myself deeper into the passenger seat. "Point taken."

A hotel sign a quarter mile down the road beamed through the drizzle. We ran over a speed bump entering the hotel parking lot. My chin bobbled from the momentum. It must have dislodged something in my brain as well, and my jaw went slack with an epiphany. Maybe the thing I was missing?

"Doc, something has been bugging me about—"

"*Bugging*? Ha!" He swiped an index finger across his nostril at some pun I apparently had made.

"*Doctor* Petrakis," I said, gravity in my voice. "How did you get that photograph of Esther?"

He pulled the Taurus into the empty spot nearest the hotel's front entrance. He shifted the car into park and regarded me with a starkly sober look.

"An ATPG in the New York regional office filed a prediction about an intrusion somewhere in a Washington state hospital. Their seer didn't provide much solid evidence for their team to go on—"

"Do they ever?" I snapped.

"—other than a prophecy that 'Someone has returned, who should not be here,' adding a warning that 'They are a wolf in sheep's skin.'"

"Sheep's *clothing*," I corrected.

"They said 'skin,' and I suspect they *meant* skin. They also provided a sketch of a woman's face. The New York ATPG collected as much info as possible, then sent an official request for an assessment, which was forwarded to our Sacramento office."

The silence was filled with the engine idling. "Where did the photo come from?" I repeated, forcing my telltale eyebrows low, flat, and stern.

"Our Remote Viewing department. Using the seer's drawing, they searched for days. They finally located a match and documented it, adding it to the case file. One of these days, I must learn the process by which they transfer their mental images to photographic film. Getting magic and technology to talk to one another is not impossible, but it *is* exceptionally difficult. Believe me, I know."

I paused to unclench my teeth. "One thing I *do* remember from my rushed indoctrination: Assessment requests not marked 'Immediate Attention' are assigned in the weekly Assessor Bullpen." My thoughts fell into a flowchart order. "How long have you had the photograph?"

"Ah." His gaze veered away from me. "Two weeks into your orientation."

"You've been sitting on this for *two* months!?"

"I've hardly been sitting on anything, my boy."

"Stop calling me that." I punched the airbag panel in front of me. No sound of startled claws, thank goodness. "The only things I want out of you are an explanation and an apology."

Petrakis flashed a wounded expression. "I am attempting the former if you would stop interrupting. However, you shall wait a long time for the latter. A very long time, indeed."

"Let's have it, then. The explanation."

He stared through the windshield and rubbed his knuckles. "Your last day of orientation—the day you took the Oath—was filled with questions, puzzles, and contradictions. Why did the Aptitude Stones attack you? Why did your parents concoct the fiction about your supposed adoption? Why all the fuss and bother about admitting you into the Circle of Ageless Waters? I never quite accepted Vice President Hibara's reasons for admitting you to that prestigious group."

"Me, either." It dawned on me that Petrakis might not fully trust me, either. "All that's been preoccupying me, too."

Petrakis cut off a sarcastic snort. "You hide it well. My research began with your dossier and the DNA comparison between you and your parents."

"Like I told Dr. Fleischer, that's bullshit." I twitched in my seat, half expecting the thing inside the airbag to jump out in response to my slip of the tongue. No chittering of tiny teeth and claws, nor the rumble of a hungry Leviathan beneath the car. Apparently, company cars were safe, relatively speaking. "Esther and Erwin died years before DNA testing became available."

"Available to the Mundane world, you mean. Do you recall an event during your high school years involving the extended Yeager family?"

"Kinda," I said after a moment of thought. I caught my eyebrows dancing again. "There was some big family reunion in '75. Esther and Erwin each took a week off and traveled from Fort Collins to San Bernardino. It was to celebrate Brigadier General Yeager's retirement, I think."

"You didn't attend?"

"At the time, there was no question about me being adopted, remember? Besides, no one from the Yeager family ever visited us, regardless of where we lived. I didn't see any reason to spend days away from school and my friends to meet dozens of strangers who never gave a rip about us."

"That explains why we didn't have your DNA on file before you joined Eldridge. You see, the guest of honor used the event to collect specimens from all his direct blood relatives and a few spouses he suspected might have latent PQ—with the utmost discretion expected of an adjuster, of course. That's how we have Esther's and Erwin's genetic data on file."

"Why on earth would Brigadier Uncle Emeritus Whatever Chuck do something so gonzo?"

"Ever since the first witch was burned at the stake, there's always been the notion that paranormal abilities were passed along family lines. Eldridge put that hypothesis to the test with the advent of DNA testing. The brigadier general's extended family was one of the first ones the company sampled. Quite a few Eldridge scientists had egg on their faces when everyone in the Yeager clan registered as PQ-0, let me tell you." Petrakis shook his head with a snort. "Myself included. But I never gave up hope on the hypothesis—scientists must always be thorough, you know. After our little scuffle with the Aptitude Stones, I had your results double-checked. I called in a favor from our region's resident expert—you remember Dr. Fleischer's assistant?"

"P.A. Kovalenko?"

"She's a doctor now. Not only that, she's been promoted to Priestess of our local Druidic chapter. But that's neither here nor there. What's important is she confirmed your mita... meetokern..."

"Mitochondrial."

"Quite. Dr. Kovalenko confirmed that your *mitochondrial* DNA matched Esther's and your Y-chromosome markers matched Erwin's."

I slouched in my seat. The foundations of my reality took their final sledgehammer hit from Eldridge. "So, the DNA results were real," I whispered in defeat. "Esther and Erwin really were... my parents?"

My stomach shrank. I rubbed my eyes to chase away a headache. "That still leaves the question of why my parents pretended that I was adopted."

"The answer lies in something you said during your final day of orientation, when the Stones attacked you. You told me you remember nothing before age six. Nothing before the Good Friday Earthquake."

"Right."

"Therefore, to be precise, your parents told you that you were adopted—only as far as you remember."

I metered out my words, as I struggled to unravel the point he failed to make. "I don't see the difference."

"After Dr. Kovalenko confirmed your DNA, I went to Anchorage and did some digging in the public records. Specifically, newspapers and the office of the county clerk. The records from both sources before the quake were spotty, as half of the microfiche reels were destroyed. However, I did find something most unusual in the county records filed *after* the quake." Petrakis fell silent, staring wide-eyed through the windshield at the young poplar in front of our parking space.

"And?"

"You said Esther, that is, your mother, worked in the county clerk's office?"

"Yes, she found work in the local county office almost every time Erwin... *Father* moved us to a new state."

Petrakis pursed his lips and looked at me. His eyes were conflicted.

Which made my stomach crimp harder. "Out with it, doc."

"Your mother falsified two records. One was a death certificate for their six-year-old son. The other was an adoption record of a six-year-old child. Both were signed the day *after* the quake, and notarized by your mother."

"How do you know they were falsified?"

"On the surface, they appeared legal and correct. The death certificate was signed by the county medical examiner, likewise the adoption certificate by the head county clerk. I double-checked their signatures—all perfectly valid, no forgeries. Both notarized and placed in the county's records by your mother."

Petrakis must have noticed my skepticism. He reached behind his seat and pulled out a valise. From that, he ruffled through bunches of office material, pulled out a folder, and handed it to me. In it lay photocopies of the death and adoption certificates.

I scrutinized them by the parking lot light. My mother's notary stamp was nestled in between signatures that were professional scribbles. "I see what you mean. Who adopts a child the same day their own dies?"

"That's not the main thing." He handed me a second folder containing two more photocopies. "These other death certificates were filed *two* days after the earthquake."

I didn't recognize either of the scribbles. Someone other than Esther had notarized the papers. "Whose signatures are those?"

"The medical examiner and clerk from the neighboring county. They were called in because—"

I read the names of the deceased. My heart tripped over itself. "—because the Anchorage County ME and clerk perished in the Good Friday Earthquake. How..." I swallowed what tasted like cold sweat. "...how could they sign and date my adoption documents?"

The silence was taut as a hangman's rope.

"Something happened the day of the earthquake," said Petrakis.

"Yeah," I scoffed, no holds on the sarcasm. "My Mom's a two-bit forger."

"Don't be obtuse," Petrakis scolded. "Namiki and I compared the signatures against surviving volumes of microfiche. They are authentic."

"How can dead people sign documents?"

"Something *else* must have occurred that day. Something that made the impossible... possible. Something that made your parents attempt to hide your identity after the earthquake. Whatever that something was, I am left with only a few threads to pull on. One of them being your middle name."

"What do you mean?"

"The name on your death certificate was Michael Frederic Yeager."

"Michael and Frederic were Erwin's and Esther's fathers' names. Mine's Michael *Avery*."

"Yes, I know." He waggled his eyebrows and ran his finger along his nose.

"Well, what's changing my middle name supposed to mean? If they were really trying to hide my identity, why didn't they change my entire name, for crying out loud?"

"An excellent question, one for which I don't have an answer." He sat back with an expression of quizzical satisfaction and crossed his arms. "Though I am intrigued by its etymology. The Germanic root of the English name Avery is *Alberich*, after all—"

"It is?" Somewhere in my head, I heard Dr. Fleischer scream that name.

"—which means 'magical being.' The French origin is a bit more lavish, as it often is. 'Ruler of Elves' seems to be their definition, whereas Norse roots could mean anything from 'wealthy magical being' to 'elven kingdom.'"

"That makes me a bit of a disappointment, don't you think? Given that my paranormal quotient is a hop, skip, and a jump from Mundane."

"On the other hand, it may have something to do with Germanic and Norse mythology. Alberich was the dwarf who forged the Ring of the *Nibelungen*. You didn't happen to see a dwarf with a golden ring chased by three river nymphs before you left Anchorage, did you?"

I shot him an annoyed glance.

"Or it could refer to the Alberich Glacier field in the vicinity of McMurdo Station, Antarctica. Do any of these references ring a bell?"

I drew a blank. I was too tired and shocked to think.

Petrakis' pen clicked her cap open and closed in rapid succession. Amelia clicked in reply deep inside my jacket.

"My, look at the time! Thank you, Namiki. Come along, Michael. We'll pick up where we left off when we have time. For now, we'd best check in and get some sleep. We have a meeting at the hospital tomorrow morning, for which we have yet to prepare."

CHAPTER 23

A rapping on the door startled me awake. Wisps of a dream about Dwarves and Elves adrift on an Antarctic ice floe, engaged in a snowball fight, evaporated with the second round of knocks.

"Michael, aren't you up yet?" said Petrakis, muffled by the locked door connecting our rooms. I stumbled to the door, still in my boxers. Petrakis was dressed in a three-piece suit. It fit him well enough, but even with my bleary eyes, I could tell it was off the rack.

"Good gravy, man," he said with an edge of reproach. "Get shaved and showered, *tout de suite*. We meet with Dr. Azizi in an hour. I shall order room service to send your breakfast here—I've already had mine. Make yourself presentable and come over in twenty minutes." Still pointing at the floor behind him, he punctuated his instructions by shutting the door one decibel below that of a solid slam.

I made it in fifteen minutes, although I was only half dressed, my bathrobe making do until I finished eating.

Petrakis rattled off all the bullet points of a rushed briefing while I gobbled down a dish of Eggs Benedict, V8, and overcooked hotel coffee. Starting with a few stats about the state hospital, he slid me a single-page layout of the grounds and buildings. He switched gears, summarizing the lengthy *curriculum vitae* of his alias in stops and starts.

"...and I received my degrees in psychiatry from Johns Hopkins, and law from Stanford. We selected those schools, as Dr. Azizi's professional circle does not deal with those schools often." He roughly sorted one stack of papers and jammed them into a folder in his briefcase. "Now, we've made *your* part in this scenario as close to the truth as possible. We both shall keep our names during this assessment, as that is the single detail most often flubbed by Eldridge employees not accustomed to covert work. As your erstwhile legal representative, I am escorting you in the search for your mother. We have been spending the past month checking various facilities that accept 'Jane Doe's. After exhausting all other avenues, you are quite anxious to find your mother before the statute of limitations expires."

"My mother's a criminal now?" Bits of egg and Hollandaise landed on the table in a semicircle around me.

Petrakis snatched up the remainder of his papers, shooing off the offending morsels before they stained. "Of course not," he said with a frown. I washed down the better part of the mouthful with some coffee. "However, it being late October is fortuitous for our use. Your parents may be legally declared dead in a little over six months, seven years after Mt. St. Helens' eruption. We can use that as our cover, and the immediacy of finding your mother alive to keep Dr. Azizi and his staff from digging too deep into our story."

"Sounds like you've done your homework." The back of my neck itched, discomforted at the depth of Petrakis' snooping. "Except for one glaring hole—I already have my inheritance."

Pacing a small loop in the hotel room as he lectured, Petrakis stopped in his tracks. "How's that?"

"When I turned eighteen, the family trust became available to me. That's how I put myself through the remainder of my Bachelor's degree and the others. There was just enough dough to cover my tuition and expenses while I pursued my Master's and PhD."

"Your parents must have been quite progressive, entrusting such a financial responsibility to you at a relatively young age." His voice became softer and wandering. "Or perhaps they suspected they might not..."

I was grateful he didn't complete his thought, though I ended up where he was headed anyway. Were my parents in fear for their lives? Might that have been the real reason we kept moving from state to state?

Namiki and Amelia clicked their pen caps in unison.

"Leave your breakfast." Petrakis pouted at his wristwatch. "We must leave now if we are to be on time. Our intelligence indicates Dr. Azizi is a stickler for punctuality."

CHAPTER 24

The Taurus idled underneath the hotel's front canopy. I strolled out of the revolving door toward the car. More like I strutted.

Petrakis sat in the driver's seat, fiddling with the knobs of an aluminum box the size of a club sandwich. His jacket hung by the headrest over the back of the driver's seat.

Except for the box's smaller size, it reminded me of the electronics he shoved into the Lick Refractor that fateful night that changed the direction of my entire life. Out of one top corner protruded a small antenna. The top two-thirds of Namiki protruded out its opposite corner. Her enameled dragon looked somewhat unsettled as Petrakis talked, presumably to her.

After adjusting my shirt cuffs and silk tie, I took out my pocket square and swatted the passenger seat clean, refolded it and got in the car.

Peering wide-eyed over the bridge of his nose, Petrakis remarked, "What a transformation."

"Clothes maketh the man," I offered.

Petrakis remained silent, holding his metal box, his hand frozen on one knob in mid-twist. He gave me the full once over, his eyes demanding an explanation.

I indulged him. "It's a nice change from office casual, and I don't often get the chance to dress how I prefer."

"It's certainly a side of you I would have never guessed."

"Father always came home from work a mess—covered in dirt and his boots stinking of scat. His uniform was wrinkled like he slept in it, or frayed like he tore off a bushel of stickleburrs after fighting a mountain lion. Mother, on the other hand, kinda devolved into a grubby mess. I have some early memories of her being rather fashionable, often wearing fantastic dresses on happy occasions like anniversaries. But those instances soon grew few and far between. Later, she grew more..." I planted my head on the headrest, searching the car roof for the kindest word. "...disheveled. By the time we moved to Washington, she rarely shed her jeans and a sweatshirt. Between the two of them, my parents were Trout Lake's worst-dressed couple."

I stopped myself. For a moment, I reflected on how it suddenly felt acceptable to refer to Esther and Erwin as my parents. Not an easy thing to do, considering the black hole of despair that Mother had fallen into after we moved from Fort Collins, and how Father favored her well-being over mine.

I inspected my manicure and faced Petrakis. With his impish smile, he resumed twiddling the box's knobs. A row of green LEDs on top of the box zoomed to fully lit.

"While studying in California," I continued while he fiddled, "my general wardrobe wasn't much better. Being a starving Bohemian, I got used to wearing jeans, ratty T-shirts, and sweatshirts." A shiver went down my back from the memory of too-rough cloth against my skin.

"What about your inheritance?"

"Like I said, the family trust got me through my doctorate, but I was on the 'no-frills' plan. Now that I'm gainfully employed, I can indulge myself a little. Last month, I had a fitting at a superb tailor on Sacramento's K Street." I allowed myself a pensive grin. "I can't wait for Sindhu to see me decked out like this. She'd flip." My grin drooped into a wistful frown.

"In that case, I guess it's time for formal introductions." Petrakis extended his hand, which I shook tentatively. "Pleased to meet you, Mr. Yeager—I am Anton Petrakis, Esq." He reached behind him into his jacket and handed me a business card with Eldridge's legal branch's logo, annotations and all. He turned on the radio, dialing the tuner until the frequency of 86.5 came up on its digital display.

"Wait a minute, I thought the FM band only went down to 87."

Petrakis twisted a control knob on his contraption. "Correct. Now..." He cleared his throat, full of formality. "Mr. Yeager, may I introduce my assistant, Namiki. Like all Eldridge scribes, she has no memories of her previous life. However, I have determined through other means that she had been a musician under Joseph Haydn in some minor royalty's chamber orchestra."

Knowing this, he still chose not to give his scribe an appropriate name? I felt a maudlin shade of pity for her. Through an uncomfortable and embarrassed smile, I said, "Pleased to meet you... Ms. Namiki?"

Her pen cap clicked twice. Out of the radio speaker came a velvet voice with an accent laced with French overtones. "Pleased to make your acquaintance, Mr. Yeager."

My jump of surprise rammed my ribs into the door's armrest. "Whoa," I croaked. "I thought you said magic and technology were incompatible."

Petrakis set his radio box of tricks on the armrest between us. "No, I told you it is extraordinarily difficult to make them work together." He shifted the Taurus into drive and headed toward the parking lot exit. "Now, if you would be so kind, Namiki, please fill in Mr. Yeager with the rest of the assignment."

Her voice at first sounded demure, but undertones of firm resolve peeked through now and then. "Once the New York Remote Viewing department located the person of interest—"

"You mean my mother?"

"That has yet to be determined and is the purpose of this assessment."

"Yes, ma'am," I said, shooting a pout split between the radio speaker and Namiki.

"—I prepared the necessary application paperwork for visitation rights at Western Bay State Hospital." She continued for a few minutes, reviewing the Eldridge rules for assessments and the WSBH regulations for visitors. By the time we pulled into the facility's visitors' lot, I felt like the last of the hospital's rules going in one ear squeezed the Eldridge instructions out the other.

"One last related item—your scribe, Amelia..." Namiki almost sounded jealous. "...has informed me that an adjuster has updated your university records. They now reflect you received your PhD in Biochemistry, *magna cum laude*."

I sat up straight in my seat. "That's great! Thanks, Amelia," I said into my shirt pocket. She clicked her pen cap twice. I mulled over how my old advisor and the rest of the faculty had to be *adjusted* in addition to paper and computer records. I didn't care to ponder too deeply.

"I don't mean to sound ungrateful, but I thought Eldridge could graduate me with *summa cum laude*."

"We are not miracle workers, Dr. Yeager," said Namiki, with that hidden firmness rising again. "The adjuster assigned to the task reviewed your work and awarded what he felt was warranted."

"Congratulations are in order, my dear *Doctor* Yeager," said Petrakis, sitting a little taller and sporting a smile.

"Mister is fine," I said.

For some reason, I found the thought of my new honorific prickly and unsettling now. In my heart of hearts, I truly believed I had earned the degree. That confidence was not strong enough to sweep away a cold cinder of uncertainty—like the feeling hanging over your head when your tab at the bar was about to be called. In my case, someone at Eldridge held the IOU.

"Your personal preference may be moot for the purposes of this assessment, Dr. Yeager," said Namiki. "Dr. Aziki and her staff may already be aware of it, depending on when they completed their background checks."

"Background? Me?" I wasn't sure if I was proud or indignant about that.

"It is the standard procedure of institutions like these to perform criminal background checks for all visitors not directly related to a patient. There is a good chance they may have also pulled your academic records."

"I guess their precautions do make sense," I said, scratching my ear. "Wouldn't want impostors or con men manipulating their patients. Gosh, I hope they don't find out about that Honors Chem incident at Fort Collins High."

"Ammonium tri-iodide is a deceptively powerful explosive," commented Namiki.

I sunk into my seat.

The south complex spread out, forming a warm and welcoming embrace—a stark contrast against their cold, grasping reach last night. The east wing's façade shone brightly, appearing far less haughty in the morning sun, capped a stately Georgian portico that led into the main edifice. Apple blossom petals fluttered by, subtly accenting the coniferous breeze.

Once Petrakis parked in the closest visitor's space, he snatched Namiki from his device, switched it off, and slipped the box into the storage under the center armrest. I straightened my suit before entering the hospital. Past the portico, we were met by a male orderly in white behind the reception desk, accompanied by a security guard standing at stiff parade rest.

"We have an appointment with Dr. Azizi," stated Petrakis. We presented our driver's licenses for identification and signed in.

The orderly gave us directions, and the guard escorted us to the elevators. He leaned in and pressed the button for the fourth floor.

After the doors closed, I muttered, "Service with a sneer..."

"Now, now, my bo— *Dr.* Yeager. Your best behavior, if you please. This is an official assessment, and our scribes are required to record everything. They do so with the utmost efficiency."

I glanced at my pocket, seeing Amelia in a harsh new light. Would she sound equally pragmatic when plugged into Petrakis' thingamajig?

The doors opened, and we were met by another silent security worker-bee, who left us with Dr. Azizi's receptionist. I glanced at my watch —ten o'clock on the button.

The reception area was austere. Worn leather chairs rested on wall-to-wall Berber carpet, surrounded by drab beige walls. Nondescript and non-threatening abstract paintings hung on each wall. The place reeked of air freshener dumped over disinfectant.

"Good morning, my good sir," said Petrakis, showing his phony business card to the man behind the desk. "I believe Dr. Azizi is expecting me and my client."

The man phoned the inner office, saying, "Your ten o'clock is here. Yes, ma'am," before facing us again. His plastic smile annoyed me. "Dr. Azizi will be just a moment. May I offer you anything—coffee, tea?"

We both declined. Before I could decide where to sit, the inner door opened.

Dr. Azizi was somewhere between my age and Petrakis'. Her straight black hair, styled in a French bob, adorned a chestnut complexion. A muted raspberry jacket covered a deep violet blouse with a matching necklace scarf, and a black knee-length skirt matched her low heels.

My heart clenched between beats. My imagination didn't have far to go to envision Sindhu's face replacing Azizi's in that ensemble.

She extended her hand as she entered the room. "Mr. Petrakis, I presume. And Dr. Yeager."

Doctor. The title made my brain squirm. Glad Amelia saw fit to forewarn me, otherwise my eyebrows would have danced a confused jig. In turn, we each shook her hand.

"I believe my letter explained the reason for our visit?" said Petrakis with obsequious politeness.

"Yes, I understand you wish to interview our patients whose identities remain undetermined, with the hope that one of them might be Dr. Yeager's mother. We're happy to oblige if it leads to establishing one of our patients' personal histories. It would go a long way to adjust their treatment and hopefully improve their condition. I must confess, however, we were caught a little off-guard by the timing of your visit. We somehow overlooked your appointment until yesterday. My staff blames the new computer software." She glanced at her receptionist with a touch of reproach.

Smooth work, Namiki.

"We apologize for the inconvenience," Petrakis said with a nod. "We would be happy to reschedule, if it weren't for my client's pressing need."

Azizi surveyed my entirety before focusing on my face, as though it were a lens into my psyche. "Yes, the impending legal status of your mother." She motioned us into her office. "It's quite all right. However, I can spend only a limited time with you, as the rest of my day is occupied."

Dark oaken walls lined with even gloomier wainscoting laughed off the bleaching sun beaming through a pair of tall windows. An oversized Georgian desk sat near the far wall, with two large bookcases filled to capacity standing guard on either side. The one on the right was filled with textbooks and reference works on psychiatry; the left overflowed with general reference books. One shelf was devoted to photography books by National Geographic, Nature, and other photo-journalism notables.

In the far corner of her office stood an unassuming man in a white doctor's jacket, looking out a window at the visitor parking lot. A smattering of wavy black hair crowned a gregarious face adorned with circular black framed glasses and a thick black mustache. Add greasepaint eyebrows and a cigar, and you'd have a close match for Groucho Marx. "Dr. Levinson is the attending psychiatrist for our three 'Jane Doe's. He will be assisting you during managed interviews."

"Managed interviews?" The phrase felt odd in my mouth.

"Nothing inordinate," said Levinson. "I and an orderly must be present during your sessions. For the well-being of the patient, you understand."

Leaning forward, Azizi asked, "Mr. Petrakis, what other institutions have you searched?" She resumed scrutinizing my face while he answered.

"I have polled various nursing homes and hospices in Washington state that still accept charity cases, searching for those whose residents fitting Mrs. Pritchard's timeline. Yours is the first on our list to visit."

"About that," said Azizi. "Your letter was not overflowing with particulars besides her timeline. What circumstances are we talking about, other than seven years or less since admission? Why only patients found in Washington state? And what other details do you have concerning her disappearance?"

That was my cue. "My father died in the Mt. St. Helens eruption. His remains were discovered under a flow of ash. They had to resort to dental records to make a positive identification. Similarly charred partial remains of a female body were found near his, but there wasn't enough to confirm an identity."

Levinson eyed me over, as did Azizi. But I had repeated similar morbid statements often enough over the past six years, that it no longer fazed me. I was beginning to dislike headshrinkers almost as much as oracles.

"Dr. Yeager would prefer to find his mother alive, of course." Petrakis inched in, interposing himself between us before they could examine me further, including my eyebrows. "Consider this search as part of our due diligence on my client's behalf. Unless your 'Jane Doe's were transferred from out of state or have been here for more than seven years, my client would like to see them. Speaking of which, have you transferred any patients of interest to another facility?"

"None." Dr. Azizi stiffened, as if the thought offended her.

"Well, then," Petrakis stepped back toward the door. "I'm sure we will be satisfied, spending a short session with each of them—while adhering to your requirements, of course. If any of your patients recognize my client, or *vice versa*, it would be to both our benefit."

Azizi and Levinson exchanged glances. She seemed at least marginally open. The shadow of misgivings haunted Levinson's features.

"So it's been six-and-a-half years since you saw her last?" said Azizi, one eyebrow raised. "Then you should be able to identify her rather easily."

"I hope so. I didn't see Mother often during our last years together."

I regarded Petrakis with a thin-lipped pout. He was about to receive another unwelcome surprise, almost as bad as when I revealed my supposed adoption.

"After we moved from Colorado to Washington, my mother developed a..." While I could talk about most anything from my past without hitting a snag, this particular facet of my life always gave me pause. Skeletons in the family closet are never easy. "...an unfortunate mental condition. The doctors called it 'severe specific prosopagnosia.'" With a nod to Petrakis, I added, "To the layman, 'face-blindness.'"

"She did not recognize people?" Levinson asked.

"Just me. Like so many maladies, it started small. She would forget my name or ask me who I was, as if I were a perfect stranger. She would almost immediately correct herself when she registered Father's or my reaction of surprise. Her most common excuse was that it was 'a trick of the light' or some other circumstance. When it occurred with increasing frequency, we suspected early-onset Alzheimer's. Time progressed, and her condition worsened dramatically. Then, she presented with symptoms that didn't fit. In unguarded moments, she said outlandish things, like I 'took the place of her son.'"

Azizi rubbed the fingers of one hand against her other palm. "That must have been terrible. How did that make you feel?"

I ignored her ham-handed probe into my own psychological makeup. "For reasons he refused to explain, Father would not allow her to see a doctor... until the day she turned violent."

Petrakis strained to keep a straight face and preserve his cover. After all, an attorney should be acquainted with all the details of his client's case. The set of his jaw shouted his betrayal.

"I came home from undergrad school over spring break. It was my twentieth birthday, and Mother was preparing a trout Father had caught earlier that day. They were in the middle of an argument. From what little I overheard, it was about some unsavory people they met back in Anchorage. She took one look at me, and she changed into a madwoman. Her eyes burned at me with nothing but hatred. She screamed, 'What have you done with my son?' and lunged at me with her fish knife. Father tackled her. I dialed 911, and we kept her restrained until the EMTs arrived and sedated her. We had her institutionalized, where she remained for a long time. One year before Mt. St. Helens' eruption, the doctors declared her well enough to be released into Father's care. She remained on medication ever since. The meds controlled her psychotic episodes, but they rendered her a depressed blob of inactivity." Forever wrapped in rumpled jeans and sweatshirts.

"That's unsettling," said Azizi, regarding Petrakis sternly. "I wish you had notified us of such tendencies in your letter. At least for our other patients' safety."

"It's not my attorney's fault. I should have been more candid about my family's history."

She marched around her desk to the intercom and raised her assistant. "Please inform the orderlies escorting the Yeager interviewees that we've received an update on a possible diagnosis. Accordingly, they must be prepared for a severe physical reaction during the interviews." Returning to us, her glower of consternation disappeared as quickly as it came. She tilted her head at me, her eyes fixed on my features. I felt like a slide under a microscope. "Is there anything else we should know about your mother?"

"Not that I can think of."

Azizi opened the door to her receptionist's area. "Then I wish you the best success in your search. Please stop by my office before you leave. I would be most interested in your progress."

I wondered if her concern was more focused on her institutional patients or me as her newest case.

To her nodding assistant, she instructed, "When our visitors return, I will want to speak with them immediately, regardless of whatever meeting I'm in." With a forced grin, Azizi remarked to Petrakis, "Annual board reviews can be so tedious."

Levinson, carrying a clipboard laden with a thick stack of papers, led us to the nearest elevator, through a small maze of corridors, and a pair of automatic sliding metal and glass doors leading into a central courtyard.

Cedar waxwings fluttered between trees that shivered in slow motion to playful breeze. A handful of scattered patients sat on benches, staring in stupefaction at their surroundings. Others meandered, strolled, or were rolled in a wheelchair, each accompanied by a chaperone orderly dressed in white.

We stopped in front of a sad woman, sitting across a picnic table from her escort. She listened intently, or at least pretended to, as he described amusing anecdotes about the recent goings-on at the facility. Her vacant brown eyes never left the man entertaining her, ignoring the waves of her own medium-length blond hair with wisps of slate blown across her face.

Levinson cleared his throat at the orderly. "How's Ms. Beresford today?"

"Easily entertained today, doctor. Unresponsive, per usual," replied the husky young man, standing.

"Beresford?" I asked. "I thought we were to interview women without identities."

"Oh, sorry," Levinson said. "It's something of an institutional tradition. We've given our 'John and Jane Doe's temporary names. It's less dehumanizing than referring to them as a case number. Long before I came to Western Bay, the practice had been to name them after fictional characters in detective stories."

"Beresford's an Agatha Christie character, if memory serves," said Petrakis.

"Most of the names we use for the 'Jane Doe's are."

Levinson stood opposite Beresford, his air of dispassion replaced by one of contagious contentedness. "Ms. Beresford, look—you have a visitor. Would you like to speak to him?"

She tilted her head at Petrakis. Her jowls shifted, wrinkles smoothing out on one side of her face only to reappear on the other, leaving her despondent expression intact.

"His name is Michael Yeager. He's a doctor now, with a degree in..." He glanced at me, his eyes prompting me to speak.

I stepped into her field of view. "...biochemistry."

Her gaze returned to Levinson. I lay my pocket square on the bench and sat beside the orderly.

She looked nothing like Esther. However, I didn't care to brush the pitiful shell of a woman off. "Ms. Beresford? It's Michael. Do you remember me?"

She slowly rotated her head at me, said a non-committal "You're new." Her somber disposition remained unaltered.

Levinson and the orderly were another story. They shared an expression of bewilderment if not astonishment. "Those are the first words she's spoken in half a year," breathed Levinson.

"If not longer," whispered the orderly. They both looked at me with expressions that implored me to continue. I shook my head, afraid to say Beresford was not my mother in front of her. Levinson spurred me on with a sharp nod of his head.

"How are they treating you here, ma'am?" I pieced together my sentence, unsure if it was of any help. Overcome with dread that my words might break something in the poor woman, I cautiously added, "Do I remind you of anyone?"

The corners of her mouth drooped lower, turning her pout into a wrinkled parody of a Greek tragedy mask. She turned back to her chaperon, her face sad and her brown eyes vacant.

I shook my head again at Levinson and stood, collecting my handkerchief. He led me and Petrakis from the table. Once far enough away, I said, "That's not her. Wrong hair, wrong eyes, wrong voice."

"A shame," said Levinson. "If only you could spend more time with Ms. Beresford, get her talking..." With a shrug, he added, "That won't be a problem with our next patient."

I looked over his shoulder as he consulted a sheet in the middle of his clipboard's ream. He ran his finger up and down a schedule in spreadsheet form, annotated with handwritten notes filling every square inch. A quiet chuckle escaped me when a scribbled "When does this chatterbox breathe?" snagged my attention.

"Inform me if Ms. Beresford opens up again today," said Levinson to the orderly before leading Petrakis and me to another building across the central grounds. "We'll meet Ms. Oliver in the upstairs recreation room."

Petrakis leaned over as we crossed the lobby to an elevator. "One of Hercule Poirot's foils, who fancied herself a detective."

The cramped compartment smelled like baby powder. Its doors opened, and we walked down a short hallway, past a nurse's station with windows of wire-reinforced glass, into a large room containing a half-dozen round tables. Each held dilapidated boxes of simple board games and children's jigsaw puzzles. A handful of patients milled aimlessly under the watchful eye of an orderly in the room and a nurse in the enclosed watch room.

One patient sat at a table, fiddling with a palm-sized cardboard jigsaw piece shaped like a happy elephant. His shaved head exposed a C-shaped surgical scar surrounding a depression in his skull. His face peppered with a day's growth surrounding a lopsided mouth, he ignored the woman chatting at him.

Her whole being was a mish-mash of opposing forces. While she yammered away, she scrutinized the man's ear as though she were watching a television screen. Her face seemed pleasant, happy to take in the sun angling through the windows. One hand playfully twiddled with a lock of her brunette hair while the other rapped the table with a puzzle piece of a sleeping lion.

As we approached, my head spun with the torrent of nonsense she disgorged at her prisoner of circumstance.

"These are not the clothes I want to wear," she prattled. "They clash with my eyes of blue. I got them from my cat. Now what was his name? He wandered away when I was little. Cars went past our house all day long. Your hair is awfully thin, do you know that?" She twirled her hair even faster. "Not like mine. You need more moon dust in your diet. The nurses give me some every night. That's what made my hair the envy of my cat and your elephant, and all-l-l the jungle."

"Ms. Oliver," said Levinson, interposing himself between the two. He would have had more success trying to pry open a bank safe with a toothpick. He placed his hand lightly on her shoulder as he repeated her name more forcefully.

She turned toward him, stopped playing with her hair, and smiled with recognition. "Dr. Lohengrin! How marvelous to see you again. I'm afraid the bride never made it to the altar. The flowers were spilled all over the pews. It's all that darned horse's fault. How many times did I tell the silly beast that carnations are never to be eaten?"

"Ms. Oliver," said Levinson, "you have a visitor. He'd very much like to talk to you."

Not really. She wasn't Esther, either.

"Ms. Oliver?" I said. I pulled out an empty chair beside her but pushed it back in when I spotted the crusty remains of a dried spill on its seat. There was no way I'd trust a meager handkerchief to protect my one-month's-salary bespoke suit.

"You'll have to speak louder than that to pierce her shell."

"Ms. Oliver," I repeated stridently, my voice echoing over hers. "Do you recognize me?"

She ignored me, turning toward Petrakis. Fluttering her eyelashes, her blue eyes gave him the once-over with a flirtatious grin. "Shangri-La was never supposed to be there, of course. But we both know it is."

Ms. Oliver wagged her finger at Petrakis, then tapped it against her temple with a wink. "The weather there reminds me of Georgia, except the forests are the wrong type of trees. No magnolias or peach, just cypress. Not much snow, either. And some idiot put a pagoda made of stone right in the middle of the valley. What a picturesque valley, too. Such a shame."

Petrakis went a shade paler. He cleared his throat and skewered me with eyes twitching with consternation.

Ms. Oliver scrutinized his face, then followed his gaze to turn toward me. "What are *you* doing here? Your tall friends are looking for you. Now, *they* would love Shangri-La. They prefer trees and would love the temperate weather. Not me—I love the snow. I learned to ski when I was young." She sighed, holding her cardboard lion in front of her face. She moved it up and down, back and forth, romping in the snow globe of her imagination. "They called it a bunny slope. Do you know why? Because there were no lions there!" She tossed the puzzle piece over her shoulder, caring nothing about how it clattered on the table in front of her silent companion.

"Ms. Oliver, do I look familiar?" For a moment, I thought of mentioning one or more of my old hometowns. I decided against it. Why pollute her personal visions with details of the real world? "Do I remind you of anyone... from long ago?"

Her expression soured. "The *other* tall people are looking for you, too. You know, the white and the gray ones? You'd be in a peck of trouble if any of *them* found you. Fortunately, you've found a wonderful place to hide." She pointed a bony finger at me, almost touching my nose. "You know, one of *them* is here."

She placed her finger against a suddenly mischievous smile, and her head sunk between hunched shoulders. Her eyes swooped back and forth, looking for mischief. "Oo-ooh, if she knew you were here, she'd be quite cross. Fortunately, she's taking a nap right now." She slapped my knee and laughed. "It's just as well. I can't stand the sight of her. Her heart is black as tonight's new moon, through and through. Not to worry, she'll be right as rain tomorrow. Maybe *both* of them will. Every so often, she's visited by her twin, you know. Then they switch places. I've seen it happen."

She drew a long, sad breath. "Every new moon. Once in a while, though, someone here pays the price—saw something they shouldn't have. But not like me. I know when to be quiet!" Putting her finger to her lips, she hissed to shush us all, including the silent man. Just as quickly, her sullen mood evaporated. "Now where did my pet lion get to?" She searched the table, scooped up her puzzle piece, and resumed torturing her reluctant friend.

Petrakis glanced back and forth between Ms. Oliver and myself. I took a step back, as did Levinson. "That's not her, either, I'm afraid." I felt a twinge of dizziness. Not that I would faint, but her dynamic presence drained the charge out of my batteries.

"Do you need to take a break?" Petrakis steadied me, his hand on my elbow. He led me to the doors adjoining the nurses' station.

Levinson locked the door behind us. "If you need, we can take a moment or two and sit in the front lobby downstairs."

I waved both of them off, the enervation having left me. "No, I'm fine." With a self-effacing chuckle, I added, "She is quite the force of nature, isn't she?"

"Yes, Ms. Oliver does seem to suck all the oxygen out of the room." Levinson guided us back to the elevator. From his gait, he seemed a little worse for wear as well. "If you're amenable, we can visit the last patient. I guarantee she will be far less distressing than Ms. Oliver."

"Why's that?" asked Petrakis.

"In addition to her state of dementia, Ms. Marple has periodic bouts of narcolepsy. Sometimes that facet of her neuropathy lasts for days and is as deep as a coma. Unfortunately, she is suffering one of those episodes today."

"I'd still like to see her," I said. Petrakis stood silent in the elevator, clutching his valise as he contemplated patterns in the floor tiles.

"Very well," said Levinson. "I just didn't want to raise your hopes unnecessarily."

The doors opened to a circular counter, behind which two nurses and two orderlies tended to monitoring their screens, filling out paperwork, and updating a wall of three-ring binders. From the central area radiated three hallways at even angles. "A visitor for Ms. Marple," said Levinson to a pudgy nurse of color with a nameplate "Davis RN" over her voluminous bosom.

"Just a moment," said Davis, checking a monitor. "No change in Ms. Marple. I can accompany you if you like, doctor. It's time for my rounds, anyway."

The four of us walked down a long hallway of white marbled linoleum. Beige walls with rows of doors on either side opened to rooms, many brimming with sunlight. Halfway down the hall, we passed a safety poster displaying the emergency exits on the three corridors spreading out from the central area in the shape of a *Y*. There was a hitch in my step when I realized this corridor matched the one in Petrakis' remote viewing photograph.

More than once we walked past a darkened room with curtains closed that reverberated with snoring. In other rooms, I could spy patients sitting in barely-cushioned chairs, staring out their windows or at their walls. My nose crinkled from the whiff of feces emanating from one cur-tained room, its door propped open with a hamper stenciled with "Soiled Linens."

Davis guided us to one of the nondescript rooms near the end of the hallway. She peeked in and nodded. "She's still unresponsive," she said before entering. We followed, Levinson herding us in, as Davis checked various tubes leading into and out of Ms. Marple and the numeric readouts on the small stack of monitors next to her bed.

Despite the feeding tube taped into one nostril, and an oxygen can-nula strapped into the other, they couldn't hide her familiar features from me.

I stifled a gasp. My palms tickled with sweat.

It was Esther.

Mother.

CHAPTER 25

Her skin stretched over her skull like an old wineskin. As her image in the blurry photograph suggested, she seemed to have aged far more than I expected over nearly seven years. I tried to imagine what she must have gone through to survive Mt. St. Helens and how it might have exacted such a toll on her body.

She lay on a mechanized bed, its upper half inclined. Her faded floral print hospital gown was starched stiff as cardboard. Through its neck opening snaked a hydra-like bundle of EKG wires. A sheet and thin white blanket covered her body from the chest down.

"I think…" I hesitated. "…it could be her. Are her eyes hazel?"

"Last time we checked," said Davis, with a little chuckle. She gently lifted one of Ms. Marple's eyelids. "Yup. Still hazel."

"But she's so… old."

"How long ago did the hospital receive Ms. Marple?" asked Petrakis.

Levinson squinted one eye and scratched an ear. "Almost seven years ago. State police found her wandering along I-5 near Longview. About thirty miles from Mt. St. Helens."

I lifted one edge of the covers to satisfy my curiosity about the bulges over her wrists. What I discovered made me fume. I didn't care what my eyebrows were doing. "Are restraints really necessary?"

Davis shushed me, her close-cut Afro framing a suddenly stern expression.

"I'm afraid so." Levinson unhooked the clipboard from the foot of the bed and made notations. "She has a history of unusual behaviors when she arises from her comatose state."

"Such as?" asked Petrakis. He finished inspecting an empty institutional armoire, then began to inch around the room, scanning the walls and other sparse furniture.

"Nothing violent," began Levinson.

"Such as disappearing," said Davis. "She'd send the whole block into a tizzy."

Levinson replaced the clipboard with a loud clack. He shoved his hands into his jacket pockets. "It's not all that exciting," he interjected, with a stern glance at Davis. "Sleepwalking is a common behavior. On two instances, she wandered about when she emerged from her narcoleptic state without a sitter present. On many occasions, she also presented with dementia, apraxia—"

"Escaping from previous restraints," said Nurse Davis.

Levinson shot her an annoyed scowl. "What the good nurse means is that Ms. Marple was lightly restrained after her somnambulism manifested. We've had to resort to firmer restraints after she escaped them several times beginning... oh, when was it... two years ago? We couldn't have her harming herself or others."

Davis glanced at me with a smirk, then regarded Levinson with a long, forbearing look. Esther would shoot Erwin that same face to say, "you don't know what you're talking about."

"What kind of dementia?" asked Petrakis. He moved from the ajar bathroom door to the window, pausing to survey the central grounds far below. "Alzheimer's?"

"No, quite the opposite. She can remember things that happened recently, say yesterday or a week ago. She can even carry on a rational conversation. But she remembers nothing from before her last coma. It's as if her memory does a full reset, like a computer."

"Then she probably won't remember me," I said, tinted with regret. "What about this apraxia?"

"Hers is not a full-blown failure of speech, like aphasia. But Ms. Marple often affects an accent of sorts at first. It never lasts long after she emerges from her narcolepsy, though."

"It's no accent *I* ever heard," said Davis.

Petrakis turned away from the window and opened an empty end table drawer near her bed. "Is there nothing of Mrs. Pritchard's—" He caught himself with an apologetic chuckle. "Forgive my presumption—

Ms. Marple's personal belongings? I would have thought they would be kept in her room, to help restore her memory and identity."

"Her clothing and particulars found on her person were held for a time by the police to compare against their open missing persons cases. Once returned, we kept them with her until her narcolepsy began. When we moved her to this secure wing, they were put in storage."

Petrakis corralled Levinson by the shoulder, urging him toward the door. "If you can produce those items, we would appreciate it. It could have a bearing on my client's situation and possibly help him positively identify Ms. Marple."

"I..." Levinson stuttered, glancing at Petrakis' hand on his shoulder, "I'm sure we can locate her belongings. I'd be happy to set aside time later this week to—"

"Unfortunately, Dr. Yeager has another appointment at another prospective medical facility in two days." As Petrakis herded his mark down the hallway, the last thing I heard was, "How might we facilitate viewing these items later today?"

"Y'know," said Davis, "the doctor has a few details out of whack. He hasn't seen some of the things we've seen, either." She pointed toward where the central station lay.

"Like what?" I held up my hand abruptly. "No, perhaps you shouldn't tell me. You don't know me from Adam. For all you know, I could be a con man digging for a lost inheritance."

She squinted one eye at me and dismissed my caution with a flick of her hand. "No, I can see the family resemblance. And you knew about her eyes, something no grifter could know." Puffing up her chest, she declared, "Besides, I could tell you're honest. Now, your lawyer friend, he's another story." She summarized her assessment with a small soprano *humph*.

"So, what other things has..." I took a long look at Esther. "...Ms. Marple done?"

"She's a regular Houdini, she is." Davis lifted the cover on her side of the bed and inspected the other restraint. "She got out of these last month. If she escapes them again, we'll have to lock her room. Either that or use iron shackles." The nurse showed me a wry grin.

"Last month? Her episodes are that often?"

"Oh my, yes. About once a month, it seems. Ms. Marple sure keeps us on our toes. She'll be fine, all smiles for four weeks or so. Then, she turns into a mad dog. Screaming to high heaven the strangest things." Davis raised her hands, waving them in mock hysteria. "'I don't like it here. I have to go home. I'll *die* if I don't return—'"

"That kind of attitude's common for many patients with dementia, isn't it?"

"Yes, but then she'll work herself into a lather with outbursts like 'Where's my sister? She has to take my place!' Then *boom*—she collapses. Faints dead away. One time, her head flopped mid-sentence, right into her breakfast."

"Once a month? I'm no physician, but isn't she a bit old for..." My cheeks flushed with warmth. "...a visit from Aunt Flow?" Don't blame me, that's what Sindhu called it.

Davis craned her neck to peek over my shoulder and out the door.

"That's not all," she said, scarcely over a whisper. "We can even tell when her next coma is coming. The doctors don't wanna hear about it, more fool them. The day shift started a pool what time she's gonna black out...." She shot a disapproving glance in the direction of the central area. "The day before her coma hits, she spooks some of our patients like you never saw. It's gotten to the point, at the first sign of her stirring up the locals, we confine her to this wing."

"Does she yell or bully them? I hope she doesn't assault them." Or try to kill them.

"No, nothing like that. She doesn't *do* anything. The more delicate of our patients just look at her and lose it. They start yelling things even more craz— more *disturbing* than what Ms. Marple says."

"Like what?"

She looked over my shoulder again. "Like 'she turns gray,' 'she's crawling with white bugs,' and 'Her twin is here to send her back.'"

I caught my eyebrows dancing.

So did Davis, judging how she raised one of her own. "Say, you've *talked* to one of them."

"Yes, I think I met one earlier. Might one of them be Ms. Oliver?"

"Heavens, she's the worst one. If she's anywhere near Ms. Marple on those days, Ms. Oliver throws anything she can grab at her, real hard. All the while screaming the worst things you ever heard."

I remained silent. Most people can't help but talk if you just look at them expectantly. Count nurse Davis among them.

"Hand to God, Ms. Oliver would scream that Ms. Marple was 'searching for someone to take back to Hell.' Last month, we had to restrain Ms. Oliver as well, with her prattle about 'that she-devil's aiming to kill one of our patients.'" Davis suppressed a shiver. "Now, normally I don't pay no nevermind to such stuff. But the thing is, the day Ms. Marple woke out of her last episode, Mr. Wilson across the hall fell into a coma. Never came out of it, poor man. Looked like he aged ten years..." She pouted, gazing wistfully into the hallway.

Petrakis and Levinson came through the doorway. "It's all set, Dr. Yeager. Dr. Levinson will have Ms. Marple's personal effects brought up from storage before the end of business today." I bid Davis a rushed thanks and goodbye before Petrakis herded me back to the elevator. Levinson joined us after leaving instructions with the staff, only to have Petrakis bid him a hasty farewell and corral me out the nearest exit the moment the elevator doors opened.

"We can leave the details to the hospital. Meanwhile, it's past lunchtime. I'm starved, and I discovered a wonderful Nepalese restaurant just off 48th St. last time I was here."

"I thought Dr. Azizi wanted to see us before we left."

"Levinson arranged for her to join us for the unboxing at 4:00 PM."

I only hoped Petrakis' taste in food was better than his musical preferences. Once in the safety of the Taurus, Petrakis whooshed a sigh of relief and caught his breath from double-timing it to the parking lot.

"What's the rush? The restaurant's food can't be *that* good. Besides, I'm still full from a rushed breakfast."

He fumbled for his keys, peppered with a couple of grunts of frustration, before he managed to start the car.

"Was Ms. Marple your mother?"

"Yes, though I'm not sure why she's so decrepit. Then again, she survived everything Mt. St. Helens could throw at her. I've also heard these hospitals are not known for their four-star hotel treatment."

"Then it's good you left them with some uncertainty over her relationship to you. I wonder what would have happened if..." A fierce shiver overcame him.

"What's got into you, doc?"

"We had a close shave, there."

"The hospital?" I asked. "I've never been in a booby hatchery before —"

"Don't let them catch you saying that."

"—but everything seemed on the up and up. Drs. Azizi and Levinson were professional. I didn't get a vibe that anything was wrong."

"No, not the staff," he blurted. Beads of perspiration dotted the ridges of his forehead's worry lines. "The patients. Ms. Beresford reacted to you. Didn't that seem odd?"

"Not especially. She had never seen me before. I assumed strangers startled her."

"Then why didn't she react when she looked at me first?" Petrakis lifted the center armrest cover, inserted Namiki into his box of electronics, and snapped it on. "No, she responded to *you*. And then there was Ms. Oliver. Didn't you find her the least bit curious? Or dangerous?"

"As curious as an open fire hydrant. No doubt she has an active and fanciful imagination. I had a lot of trouble keeping up with her. But dangerous? Nah."

Petrakis bellowed a moan of frustration. "My boy, if I was thick as you during my formative years, my father would have boxed my ears."

"I said, stop calling me that." I blasted out.

"Then act like you've earned the privilege, Yeager. Eldridge employees that naïve on their first day in the field end up *dead*."

That was the first time Petrakis didn't use a title with my name. I set aside my temper before it matched his. "All right, doc. What did I miss?"

"First and foremost, Ms. Oliver's not a Mundane." He folded his arms over his chest. His jaw jutted forward. "That's no great surprise, by itself. There's almost always one patient in every institution who isn't. They fall into two categories we call Unawares or Untrained. They tend to be receptive to the paranormal. As a result, they experience events they can't explain. The lucky ones can ignore it, put it out of their minds, or find a way to explain the strangeness away and continue with their normal lives, unperturbed. The less fortunate ones are unable to cope with their abilities and the unearthly realities they uncover. Some become unsettled to the point where society thinks them mentally ill. The ones who simply cannot adapt end up in places such as these. Their Ms. Oliver is Untrained."

"So, she saw visions. What makes her dangerous?"

"Her first vision—"

"The one about Shangri-La?"

"She described it with unquestionable accuracy. Not only that, she identified the school of Eastern Magic established there, one that operates under the jurisdiction of Eldridge & S.Q.Amos."

"Eastern Magic... isn't magic all the same?"

"Good gravy." I'd never seen Petrakis that discouraged. "I truly am regretting Hibara's decision to rush your orientation."

Vice President Hibara decided? It made sense that he'd be the one pulling everyone's strings...

"Magical energies are essentially all the same," said Petrakis, "drawn from other planes, other realities. But there are many roads to reach the same destination. Western magic, African magic, Eastern magic... even *alien* magic. In Eastern magic, there are five schools: Air, Water, Fire, Stone and Metal. Ms. Oliver correctly identified the School of Stone residing in the mountains of Shangri-La. I was shaking in my boots that she might have picked up Dali Uulyn was the *sensei*—the Master—there, or worse, named him out loud. He is one of Eldridge's regional Vice Presidents."

With a nod, I said, "I guess he's the one I saw dressed in saffron robes in the Chamber of Ageless Waters. How could she get such information?"

"By reading it from *me*, hang it all." Petrakis pounded the center of the steering column. The Taurus beeped out a complaint. "I didn't realize the threat she posed, and my defenses were down. *Now* do you understand why assessments can be so dangerous?" He tried to calm himself with a deep breath. "It's water under the bridge, now. Let's think about what she might have read from you."

"From me?"

"I'm sure you didn't have your psychic blocks up either. She's more dangerous than Lenoir and Pellagati combined." Petrakis pulled his electronics out of the center compartment. "Namiki, please remind us what Ms. Oliver said about Mr. Yeager."

Her sultry voice sprang to life out of the radio speaker. She quoted Oliver's warnings about the tall gray and white people, how some patient here had a twin that traded places, and how someone would pay the price, all with the accuracy of a court transcript. Her alluring accent made it difficult for me to concentrate on the details. With her recitation complete, Petrakis plucked Namiki out of the device, slipping her in his shirt pocket.

"Thank you, Namiki. But which patient could she be talking about?" Petrakis asked the windshield.

"My mother," I replied, afraid of my deduction.

Petrakis turned to me, shocked. "How do you come to that conclusion?"

"Nurse Davis told me of strange goings-on while you were busy with Levinson."

"Don't leave me hanging, Yeager." His impatience stung.

"Maybe I should plug Amelia in and ask her to read them off?"

"No, my equipment is sensitive, and each scribe has a different freq —" Petrakis cut himself off with an unintelligible growl. "Just out with it, Yeager," he commanded.

"Nurse Davis talked about Marple's narcolepsy, that it was quite regular. About once a month. Not only that, the more sensitive patients— more Unawares, I suppose—can sense her coma coming on. But they're all *afraid* of my mother. What Davis described jived with Ms. Oliver's rants. And one more thing—when Mother arose from her last narcolepsy, a patient across the hall suffered a coma and died soon after."

Petrakis mulled to himself, "Our seer said, 'wolf in sheep's skin.'"

"Now you're saying she's *not* my mother?"

"All I'm saying is, keep your defenses up and be ready." He nudged the car into reverse and pulled out of the parking lot. "Enough. I can't think on an empty stomach."

Petrakis was silent, fuming during the entire drive to the restaurant, except for the occasional *humph* and stomach gurgle. Mine echoed every one of his.

Once we entered the unassuming mom'n'pop bistro, I scanned the room and relaxed a tad when I noted the clientele. It's always a good sign when a boutique eatery is patronized by their fellow expatriated country-men. We sat, ordered, and waited in silence. Petrakis' face was devoid of emotion, which meant he looked angry to the casual observer. Who knew what my face looked like, given I couldn't make heads or tails of our situation, nor could I talk out in the open about it. Our waiter regarded us with caution when he delivered our dishes. He probably expected to find us arguing like a married couple. He wouldn't have been too far off.

Life with Sindhu prepared me for tasty dishes like those I had ordered: samosa, potato dumplings laced with cumin, ginger, and chutney; and spicy-sweet Gorkhali lamb, the heat of which challenged even my jaded, but still essentially Western palette. Unfortunately, Petrakis' grumpy disposition detracted from my enjoyment of the meal.

On the road back to the hospital, my stomach decided it was not as pleased as my taste buds were. Or maybe it was the mood combined with the tension in the air. Regardless, every pothole renewed my stomach's objections to my culinary choices.

"Well, Assessor Petrakis," I said, hoping my mock officious tone penetrated his train of thought. "What's our plan of attack?"

"No attack," he said, his stern expression still firmly in place. "Mostly observation. We see what's in Ms. Marple's box and hope it has something to convince them she is your mother."

"She *is* my mother."

"Azizi and Levinson are the ones we must persuade. If we find nothing in her personal effects that proves your relationship with Ms. Marple to their satisfaction, we must improvise. I suggest you request to spend the remainder of the day with Ms. Marple."

"Doing what?"

"The things that relatives of coma patients do. Hold their hand, talk to them, reminisce about past events." He rapped the side of his thumb on the steering wheel, enumerating each item. "All the while keeping an eye out for anything that might explain why Eldridge New York suspected your mother is involved in an intrusion. Good gravy, my boy, must I think of everything?"

"*You're* the assessor, old man."

Petrakis veered into the first empty street parking space with an audible skid. He slammed the transmission into park hard enough to make the car rock.

"What is your problem, *Doctor* Yeager?" His voice trembled with anger.

I didn't care. "What's *yours*, Dr. Petrakis?"

"Too many to count. But my biggest one is sitting next to me."

My front teeth gnashed, ready to tear into meat. "Do tell."

Petrakis plucked Amelia out of my pocket and, with Namiki, tossed them both into the well of the center armrest. "Namiki has never heard me say anything uncouth, but I fear this is the only way to keep my record spotless."

"Your puns don't count?"

He slammed the armrest cover shut with a force that made the padding exhale a gust of new car smell.

Petrakis switched the radio to the AM band. The moment static came out of the speakers, the rage in his eyes vanished.

"Forgive my previous behavior," he said in hushed tones. "The situation required it. I can't keep our scribes in there long, so please don't interrupt. Having a scribe is a mixed blessing. You'll find they are handy when vanquishing mounds of paperwork, a time-saver for research, and absolutely indispensable when writing assessment reports, because they observe *everything*. At times like this, however, their all-seeing, all-hearing features are a distinct drawback."

His night-to-day transformation left me confused. "What are you saying? They're *spying* on us?"

"Not intentionally," Petrakis replied. "But your every word and action can be evaluated by a third party. Like our lovely Ms. Lenoir."

"Can scribes read our minds?"

"No." He squinted at the car roof. "At least, I'm ninety-nine percent sure they can't."

I suddenly understood why no one gave real names to their scribes. They were worse than a conscience. Maybe I should have named my scribe Jiminy.

My pulse stopped hammering in my ears. "Then you'd better say what you need to say."

"Vice President Hibara didn't give you a scribe as a favor. He wants to keep tabs on you."

"What is so damned special about me?"

"I wish I knew. Hibara invited you into the Circle for his own reasons. His pretext of rewarding your sacrifice, namely waiting for your poor fiancée, has no precedent. In fact, it is so maudlin and out of character for him, that it rings hollow."

"You know Hibara that well?"

"Not at all. I only know empathy is a painful luxury upper management in Eldridge can ill afford. Pray you never meet the company's president or board—I sometimes wonder what other traits of common humanity they sacrificed to attain their positions. In the meantime, the two of us are left to stumble about, following a trail of breadcrumbs we hope will reveal your true history. I have a feeling Hibara *already* knows everything about you."

"So, what do you want me to do?"

"Keep up the façade of us having a falling out. It is not a coincidence I've been assigned as your group's supervisor. Someone wants us together so they can watch us more easily."

"Hibara?"

"Most probably. Director Ventnor could be another possibility."

Petrakis surveyed the traffic and the sidewalk pedestrians. Worry was written all over the wrinkles on his forehead. "Whoever it is, let's see what they do when we throw a spanner in their works."

"I'm not sure how long I can keep up an act like that. I've been told my face is an open book." My eyebrows chose that moment to twitch.

"Then I'll have to make it easy for you." He flashed me a leering grin worthy of a silent screen villain, followed by a swipe of his nose. "Just keep in mind, no matter how difficult I may seem, I am doing this to protect you. If we're lucky, we can find the answers with both our hides intact."

"Why are you telling me all of this now?"

"I am *still* your sponsor, Dr. Yeager. You are my responsibility, which I take seriously."

"Bullshit. That's the shiny veneer reason. What's the real one?"

Petrakis peeped out a nervous titter. "Because... my curiosity will not be satisfied until I know your secret?" He followed the question with a half-hearted smile.

"And I thought *I* was transparent. Besides, you're assuming I only have one secret. Try again."

We both chuckled uneasily at my observation.

"There's something amiss about how Hibara favors you. I cannot tell if it is good or bad, but I cannot take that chance." He swallowed nervously. "The *world* cannot take that chance. I have to know if Hibara is true to Eldridge's mission."

"That serious?" I gestured down the road. "What are we waiting for? Let's find out."

"It's not that simple, my boy." He frowned so hard, his teeth gnashed. "What if I find out that Hibara is compromised?"

"Now you're sounding as paranoid as Lenoir."

"What if he poses a threat to Earth, and *you* are his instrument to make good that threat? You do understand what extremes I may be required to perform... if it comes to that."

My heart froze. My stomach acid went on overdrive. We stared wide-eyed at each other. I shifted in my seat with the uncomfortable memory of Petrakis poking Sapphire's knife in my back at the Chamber of Ageless Waters.

"I... understand."

He put his hand on the armrest latch. "Follow my lead. Ready?"

I set my jaw and nodded.

"And another thing," bellowed Petrakis as he tore open the armrest cover. I winced at the ragged anger in his voice. "When this assessment is complete, as your supervisor, I'm putting you on administrative leave without pay for a week."

"What?" I barked, except my indignation was one-hundred percent authentic.

"*Two* weeks," Petrakis snapped. He snatched Namiki from the compartment and stuffed it in his shirt pocket. "I am tired of your feeble excuse of a rushed orientation. As soon as Namiki and..." He flicked a mote of dust off the armrest. "...Pilot finish our post-assessment reports—"

"Her name is *Amelia*." I scooped her out of the compartment as well.

Petrakis slammed the cover down, barely missing my knuckles. "Whatever. Once they finish—which had best be in the timeliest of manners—I am restricting you to your apartment and Eldridge grounds until you know the entirety of the orientation material and Eldridge & S.Q.Amos' rule book backward and forward. And yes, there will be a test."

Petrakis started the car, revved the engine, and pulled out into traffic with tires squealing.

CHAPTER 26

A few white-knuckled minutes later, the Taurus rolled onto the hospital grounds. Petrakis' transition from horn-heavy leadfoot to calm, collected, milquetoast driver was astonishing. "Remember, we examine the box, convince Drs. Azizi and Levinson that Ms. Marple is your mother, then you spend the rest of the day observing her."

"What will you be doing?"

He snatched up his briefcase. "Observing everything else. Oh, and one last thing…" He flipped open the case, retrieving two thin pairs of spectacles. He put one pair in his coat pocket and handed the second to me.

"What are these for?"

"Those are your reading glasses."

"I don't wear—"

"Yes, you do, Dr. Yeager. You will also find they work excellently in all light conditions."

Peering through them, their arms still folded, they seemed perfectly normal. With a shrug, I slipped them inside my jacket opposite Amelia.

After we again collected our visitor's badges at the front, Levinson met us at the elevators. He exuded giddiness. "We've located Ms. Marple's belongings. They're in Dr. Azizi's office, but we haven't opened the container yet, out of respect for Dr. Yeager."

More like he and Azizi wanted to dissect my reactions.

"We appreciate your consideration," said Petrakis.

Azizi greeted us relatively formally, then guided us past her assistant to her own desk, on which a black plastic box the size of a large suit-case rested. She dialed the container's flimsy combination lock. Stepping back, gesturing toward the lid, the pressure of her stare resumed. "Would you care to do the honors, Dr. Yeager?"

I swung the lid open. A wallop of cedar floated up from a cheese-cloth sachet of wood chips dangling from the lid's interior. Layers of clear plastic bags sighed as they expanded and relaxed. The topmost ones con-tained Esther's usual Thorazine-inspired couture: loose jeans and a frumpy sweatshirt. They were cleaned, pressed, and folded, but their processing emphasized dozens of holes, tears, and burn marks.

I handed the bags to Petrakis. "I assume all the pockets have been emptied?"

"The police were quite thorough," said Azizi. "We cleaned and sani-tized the clothing once they were returned. The police photographed the clothing in the state in which Ms. Marple was found for their records." She opened a manila envelope on her desk and showed the pictures to Petrakis. Even from my angle, I could spot that the ragged clothes were soiled with human waste.

"At first glance, these clothes align with Dr. Yeager's information about his mother's last known location," said Petrakis.

"Mt. St. Helens? It seems plausible," said Levinson with a shrug. "What else does the box hold?"

I pulled out and set aside a sealed plastic bag containing women's sneakers. Underneath lay a baggie containing pocket-sized sundries. Unsealing the bag, I opened the ladies' wallet inside. It was cleaned out of anything that might help identify the owner.

"According to the inventory," said Azizi, "the wallet held some pho-tos. They should be in a separate envelope. Probably near the bottom?"

Ignoring a bag stuffed with sanitized undergarments, I dug out a sandwich-sized clear bag with two photos: one wallet-sized, the other folded into quarters. My impatient heart pressed against my ribs.

The wallet photo was a black-and-white baby portrait, stained sepia with age. Two small sections had been defaced with a pen.

"What's wrong?" asked Azizi.

My eyebrows must have given me away again. "Someone scribbled out the left eye and a patch near the top of the head." I handed the photo to Petrakis, then reached up and probed that part of my skull. Turns out, it was right at the part of my scalp that tingles when snow is in the forecast.

The part of my brain where Pellagati dug and dug. "A recent X-ray suggested I had an injury there when I was very young."

"Did your Mother cause the injury?" Azizi's scrutiny dialed up my paranoia.

"I have no recollection. It must have happened before we left Anchorage."

I unfolded the second photograph. My heart jumped. "That's my father, Erwin Pritchard."

Azizi and Levinson showed little reaction. Despite my certainty, my identification was no real proof as far as they were concerned. I scrutinized the photo for anything more.

My father stood in the center of the photograph, wearing a lumberjack plaid flannel shirt. His generous smile paraded his perfect teeth while the wind tousled his hair like a red-haired Albert Einstein. His arms gathered around the shoulders of two people. Surrounding the trio stretched a rocky field scarred by a faint trail, leading toward a backdrop of mountains painted with enormous swaths of gray and white granite.

To Father's left, Mother stood stiffly in his embrace. Her face was blurred, like she shook her head violently the moment the shutter snapped. On the right, a teenager in jeans and a purple sports jersey with gold piping waved at the camera. I could only assume it was me. Like the other photograph, there was a patch of harsh pen scribbles. Only in this instance, my entire head was blotted out with such force that the paper had a hole where my face would be.

Dejectedly, I handed the second photo to Petrakis as well. After a sigh, he passed them to Azizi.

"This could be anyone's baby picture," she said. "And as for the other one... most unfortunate. We're so sorry." She handed them back to me with a pout that I judged to be sincere.

Petrakis popped open his briefcase and handed a paper to the doctors. "Actually, I believe we can corroborate it is indeed Mr. Pritchard, Dr. Yeager's father, in the photo. Here's a photocopy of his last driver's license."

I tilted my head to examine the color snapshot more closely. "There's something else," I hedged. "My shirt—those are my high school colors. Fort Collins High, purple and gold."

"Did you play sports there?" asked Levinson.

"No. With a 'Lambkin' as our mascot, I couldn't take team sports seriously."

"You'll find Fort Collins is listed in Dr. Yeager's particulars attached to my letter," added Petrakis on the heels of my statement.

"And if I'm not mistaken," I said in hesitant syllables, "That's Long's Peak, about thirty miles from Fort Collins. We hiked there just before graduation."

Levinson snatched the photo from my hand and scrutinized it. Azizi hummed to herself as she strolled along the array of books behind her. She ambled to the end of her bookshelves, her finger running along the books' spines, before extracting a coffee-table book. Placing the sizable tome on her desk, she leafed through the pages of black-and-white photos on heavy paper. "I've always admired Ansel Adams' photography, especially his work in the Rocky Mountains. Here we are—Long's Peak."

We huddled around the book. Levinson held the snapshot over the stark mural of the mountain and its surrounding range. "It looks like this photo was taken from the opposite side of the mountain," he said, "but it does seem to match."

"It was." I pointed between one of the smaller edifices in the photographs. "Notice the white streaks of granite on the one mountain? Those strata cut all the way through. It's visible on both sides."

"Assuming these are your parents," said Petrakis, "why would your mother eradicate your face like that?"

"Like I said yesterday," I replied. "She was diagnosed with prosopagnosia. This picture was taken the summer before Father and I had her committed."

"I believe we have a confirmation of sorts," declared Azizi. Regarding me with new eyes, her stare of clinical assessment was gone. "Dr. Levinson and I have some final verifications to make, now that you have identified Mr. Pritchard. But for the time being, I believe we can afford Dr. Yeager visitation rights?" She blinked at Levinson, who nodded. "How would you like to proceed, Dr. Yeager, Mr. Petrakis?"

"Dr. Yeager's estate will be interested in moving Ms. Marple—excuse me—Mrs. Pritchard to more comfortable facilities. His insurance company will be responsible for any boarding and additional charges. Can someone give me a tour of the hospital's... less *spartan*... accommodations, while Dr. Yeager spends some quality time with his mother?"

CHAPTER 27

I sat beside Mother's bed. The monitor blipped out its monotone staccato rhythm. Once every half-hour, the head duty nurse or one of the orderlies poked their head into the room during their rounds.

Nurse Davis made her rounds at six o'clock. She burst into the room with her usual warm smile, a plastic water pitcher, and two paper cups.

"Two cups? That's rather optimistic, don't you think, nurse?"

"You never know..." she said with a playful shrug, interrupted by a stifled yawn. "Oh, excuse me. They have me on a double shift today. But don't let that bother you. You just let me know if you need anything, dear. I'll be at the central desk."

My stomach *blupped* after she left. I poured out a glass and sipped it, hoping to rinse the aftertaste of chutney and bile from my mouth. I wished I had thought to ask Davis for an antacid.

As Petrakis suggested, I spent the time talking to Mother, at first in a series of incomplete sentences and false starts. What the hell do you talk about when most of your new life has more secrets than the Knights Templar and the Illuminati combined? Not to mention when your audience is trapped between consciousness and oblivion, who may or may not be listening, who might or might not recall what you said?

I started off with the few snapshots of happy family life I could remember: the three of us riding at a dude ranch near our digs at Lubbock; our yearly day at Disneyland two hours away from our San Fernando home; hiking Rocky Mountain Park during the Fort Collins years. I eventually rambled into vignettes from college for a short time. After an hour of soliloquizing, I got around to the last events of my so-called Mundane life. I babbled about how my thesis advisor and the combined Astrophysics and Biology Departments of UCSC had screwed me over. My heart wasn't into it this time. The righteous indignation that usually laced my retelling was gone.

Why? Maybe because I had been awarded the doctorate—post the university screw-job—by an Eldridge adjuster? Or perhaps because I didn't care anymore?

By the time the sun dove behind Puget Sound's network of inner islands on the horizon, I got around to telling her about the greatest of my college exploits—meeting Sindhu.

"It was late '84, and I sat under the shade of an ash tree on the UC Quad, boning up on the NIH's latest recombinant DNA research papers. My half of the yard held a squad practice for the women's lacrosse team. Frankly, I didn't even know we had one. I was one-third into an article on a new gene that encoded the EGF receptor—believe or not, Esther, that's my meat and potatoes—when some blond girl body-checked an Indian beauty straight into my lap. Book, notebook, magazine, and I each tumbled in different directions. Me, I conked my noggin against the tree trunk. She showered a fountain of profuse apologies on me, which led to her buying me a drink at a local pub, followed by an evening of talk and laughter. Looks, brains, *and* a sense of humor? I hit the jackpot, and I wasn't even looking.

"I've long suspected that *accident* was planned by one or both of the girls, but Sindhu staunchly denies it every time I bring it up. I've never told her that I spotted her and the blond exchange winks at the end of their practice session."

I tried to chuckle, but I needed another swig of water to ease a dry throat. That, and try again to wash down the stubborn burn of undigested chutney.

"Her mahogany face framed by her black hair takes my breath away every time. She has turquoise eyes that shine like the sun on a Bermuda bay and are just as deep. She always smells of jasmine, but different—like the flower copied *her*. Her smile is bright and without guile, and can chase my darkest thoughts away. Every time I'm by her side, I'm happy. She's so beautiful in body, mind, and spirit... it hurts to be away from her." I shook my head and sighed. "But she's going to be away for a long time. A *very* long time, I fear."

The need for Sindhu's voice, her closeness, her touch overwhelmed me. Hollow inside, my voice hitched, and I swallowed a sob. "It hurts sometimes to even *think* about her, or worse, where she might be. I just wish I knew when I might see her again, Esther." An unexpected pang of guilt crimped my ribs. I shuffled my feet absentmindedly. I had been addressing my mother by her given name since I arrived.

All the years I called her by name must have annoyed her to no end. If I thought hard enough, I could recall how sometimes she would wince, lose her smile, or droop her shoulders when I said it. I wondered if it might have contributed to her eventual psychotic break as well? It struck me how terrible it might feel, even with all odds against it, that she might wake up to me still calling her by her given name.

The muscles behind my jaw ached, but not from talking for hours. "I think you'd like Sindhu... Mother."

Unbidden, Petrakis' voice echoed in my already crowded head, reminding me I should hold Mother's hand in addition to simply talking to her. I reached out and gently clasped her frail and wrinkled hand.

Scuffling my shoes must have built up a static charge, because a tiny spark jumped from my left hand to hers.

Esther's eyelids fluttered.

She whispered, "You're here. You finally found me."

Her eyes snapped open, and I recoiled back deep into my seat. Gone were the irises of hazel. Staring at me were two orbs of ebon, studded with glints of silver, like tiny stars swimming in a sea of gray ichor. Her lips pulled back to reveal a toothy snarl.

"Amelia! Alert Petrakis," I sputtered out at lightning speed.

The room plunged into darkness. The monitors went silent. The electromagnetic lock holding open the door behind me clicked, and the door swung closed.

Something cold and rubbery gripped my hand.

CHAPTER 28

"We have waited so long for you, *yon gorikuba elā*." With each word, the voice that began as Esther's slouched lower into something inhuman. The unseen thing around my hand squeezed hard enough to make my knuckles crack. "My brothers will rejoice, never having to return to this miserable place."

"The *hell* happened to the lights?" echoed Davis's screech down the hall, before the room's door latched with a *thump*.

I reached for the side table. My cup clattered on the floor, its water sloshing about in unseen directions. Searching in the barest gloaming that filtered through the window, the fingers of my free hand found the handle of the water pitcher.

"Month after month, we came here..." If a snake had a voice, it would have sounded only slightly less chilling than the thing in the dark. "...relieving our siblings with each new moon. I'm so glad you came on my watch, *yon gorikuba elā*. I dislike returning to *Phelek Lepan* empty-handed."

Something about his speech scratched at my ears. Was this the accent to which Levinson and Davis referred?

Emergency spotlights in the hall behind me snapped on. A cone of light beamed through the door's wired-glass window onto the room's far wall, framing the shadowy thing facing me.

It rose from the bed, graceful as a great cat in tall grass stalking its prey. Its eyes squinted away from the white light. One slender hand had already freed itself from its bed restraint, continuing to crush my fist. Swinging its legs off the bed, the thing's whole body shed the colors of human flesh, becoming gray and translucent. As I stared transfixed, the material that had mimicked human hair combined into thin tentacles, withdrawing into its smooth head. Its entire skin shivered from its misshapen head down to its legs into translucence, not unlike a cephalopod's camouflage. The creature's true form revealed itself, filled with the same gelatinous flesh that had first gazed at me, dotted with floating specks of silver. From the refracted light passing through it, I dimly discerned what might have been bones and organs within. It stood, and the creature's hospital gown slid off its frame, crumpling about its feet. The five adhesive EKG pads still hung from its chest, their wires bundled into a single cord that dangled about its waist.

I halted a gasp at the crawling realization this was the thing that Sofia had drawn.

I swung the pitcher at the thing's skull. Its pointy-eared head gave, deforming like I smacked a heavy sponge-covered rock. Its iron grip on my other hand never wavered. Water splashed everywhere. The pitcher bounced out of my grip as my adversary's head sprang back to its original shape.

"What an ugly shell the traitorous slave king chose," slithered out of its mouth.

"The *what*? Who'd I betray?"

A rippling ribbon of mauve coursed down its torso. "Who would have guessed it more grotesque than the human bitch that spawned it? It would be a mercy, killing such a hideous creation."

"Look in a mirror lately, fuck-face?" God, it felt good to curse again. I was only sorry that Amelia had to hear it. There was no time to puzzle out what this monster said, let alone what might be important, and I doubted it would pause to explain itself.

I reached into my jacket.

The emergency lights flickered twice, then blinked out. Shouts and curses filtered down the hall from the central desk again. From behind the door, the hallway echoed with inmates' whimpers and cries.

"Sorry, Amelia." I grabbed her in my fist and plunged her into where my persistence of vision told me where the creature's heart lay. I buried Amelia deep into something wet and spongy. My hand was expelled. Amelia was gone, sucked out of my hand.

My mind raced, trying to recall if there was anything else on my person or in the room I might use as a weapon. I reached into my other pocket, and my fingers wrapped around an unfamiliar object of metal and plastic.

Petrakis' stupid reading glasses.

I pulled them out anyway, grasping them like a knife. I did a double-take when their lenses glowed with a tenuous light. A flick of my wrist, their arms snapped open, and I slipped them on. I drew in a sharp breath of surprise to find I could see as though the room was dimly illuminated—though only with enough light as if from a single candle. After near-pitch blackness, it was enough. They probably lit a portion of my face as well, but I figured if the thing could see me in the dark regardless, it was no great tactical loss.

The barest end of Amelia protruded from the creature's shoulder. The thing seemed unfazed by the deep stab. Twisting my left hand, it drew me close.

I gritted my teeth from the pain. Its breath, rank with a stench like fungus growing on bat guano, made everything from my nose down to my bronchial tubes want to slam shut.

"I am directed to bring you back alive," the thing's voice writhed. "However, there is no order preventing me from inflicting pain."

The thing's free hand, each finger a writhing tentacle, reached for my neck. The monster hesitated with surprise when I ducked its grasp.

"Yeah? I wonder if you feel pain the same way we do." Reaching toward the monster's abdomen, I grabbed the EKG bundle. "You got anything like chest hair?"

I yanked for all I was worth. The pads tore off.

The thing shrieked in unholy agony.

A damp warmth enveloped my hand. Glancing down, I gawked at clumps of oozing flesh attached to the adhesive terminal squares. They dripped over my arm and pants leg. I uttered a cry of disgust like I stepped in cowflop. It smelled like it, too. I only hoped Eldridge had something that could remove creature stains from wool and silk.

A staggered flow of goop pulsed out of its wounds with the consistency of Jell-O being strained through a cheese grater. My stomach started making sounds similar to the muck splattering on the floor.

Through the locked door rolled Nurse Davis's voice, high and shrill. She called out each patient's name as she advanced down the hall, verifying they were safely in their rooms when the power outage caused their doors to close as well.

Holding my breath, I took out my trusty handkerchief and plucked Amelia out of the creature. The puncture wound she had made sealed up with no visible scar. I buried pen and handkerchief deep in my hip pocket.

The creature's shimmering translucent body continued to shrivel as its gelatinous fluid spread in an ever-widening puddle.

The door opened. Nurse Davis stood in the doorway, holding the door open as her flashlight probed the room wildly. "Ms. Marple, you okay? Not that you could hear—" The whites of her eyes stood out in the dark. "What the devil is going on here? Dr. Yeager, explain this mess." Her light came to rest on the monster, spurting out the last of its guts.

She inhaled, promising the mother of all screams, when a hand gripped her shoulder. The person behind Davis whirled her about and grabbed her by the throat. Davis's flashlight beam careened about until it exposed the face of—

Another Ms. Marple.

The old lady showered a benevolent smile at Nurse Davis. In a flash, her face transformed into an emotionless husk. She clamped her other hand around Davis's chin. Planting her feet, Marple rammed the nurse's head against the metal door frame. Davis's unconscious form crumpled in a heap against the door. Streaks of blood drew jagged lines down the length of the door jamb. Her flashlight rolled along the floor in a tight circle.

Ms. Oliver's words whispered in my ear. *"Every so often, she's visited by her twin."*

The new Ms. Marple drew close to Davis's face and inhaled. A tenuous mist emanated from the nurse's mouth, twining itself into delicate strands. The vaporous cord whined and groaned with what sounded like Davis's voice as it disappeared down Marple's gullet. The flashlight rolled past the nurse's head. The roots of Davis' mini-Afro had turned gray.

Marple's body shimmered, its entire surface vibrating into new shapes and colors. Her arm lengthened and darkened into another miasma of dark gray translucent flesh specked with silver. Her entire form writhed until, in the space of a few heartbeats, a second Nurse Davis stood before me, dressed in Marple's nightgown.

I reached into my pocket for Amelia but thought better of it. She didn't work too well as a weapon last time. I backed into the room's private bathroom. The thing that became Davis stalked toward me.

Desperate for a weapon—any weapon—I tore open the vanity's lower closet. My choices were somewhat sparse: toilet tissue, toilet brush, or toilet plunger.

My brain clicked with a hopeful connection. I grabbed the plunger.

Wielding the plumber's helper as a sword, I charged out of the bathroom and plowed its black rubber business end flat into Davis's face. The doppelgänger staggered back a step, and I tore the plunger cup away, quick as I could muster. The room reverberated with a sucking *pop* when it detached.

I jumped back a step, hoping to avoid the splatter of suctioned goo I expected would erupt from the monster's face. I instead stood opposite a Davis creature with a red circle centered on its angry face.

I shrugged. "It was worth a shot."

It clamped its meaty hand on my wrist and yanked me close. It twisted my hand hard, and the plunger fell out of my hand. Like it had done with Davis, the creature riveted its other hand on my chin and forced my head against the door jamb. Its eyes regarded my face with a burning hatred. "Such a feeble vessel. I could kill both of you with the barest flick."

Both? Davis and me? No, it meant something else...

"But the Circle of Elders commands otherwise. We are commanded to return you, the traitor's son, to the Great Cavern of the Five."

Its hand released my chin, followed by a lightning-fast recoil and a quick shot to my jaw. A Niagara Falls' worth of stars flooded my sight. I wasn't knocked out, but I was pretty sure I was horizontal on the wet floor. I hoped it was only water. My nose informed me it was monster goop.

Bit by bit, the waterfall of flashes dwindled, but I still lay stunned and half-blind as I perceived a large dark form lying near my head. After a few moments, along with several blinks and squints, I realized it was Davis. She wasn't breathing. I would have shivered if I could. More came into focus, and I realized she had been stripped of her uniform.

I had to get up. I laid my hands flat on the floor, but didn't yet have the coordination to push myself up. My strength wasn't up to snuff, either.

The sound of squeaking wheels approached. The doppelgänger wearing Davis's uniform and face pushed a gurney into the room. She stopped, with the gurney blocking the doorway. I couldn't see what she was doing on the rolling platform, but I heard the clink of glass. She lifted my arm and injected something into my forearm.

"Without sterilizing the area first?" I said through lips that were on a one-second delay. "My God, you *are* a monster."

Davis hefted me over her shoulder like a roll of carpet and flopped me on the gurney. Her nurse's smile belied a hint of savagery. "Quiet, now, Mr. Yeager. We don't want you to hurt yourself during our little trip."

My head rolled to the side and stayed there. My limbs felt like someone had turned gravity up to eleven. I barely managed to say, "Oh," when I read the label on the vial beside me. I tried to pronounce "succinylcholine" but couldn't. My lips worked as well as two overripe bananas.

"Enjoy the ride," I told myself, recognizing the drug was a paralytic. Depending on the dosage and whether she struck a vein or not, I could be mush for a long time.

Davis removed my glasses, and everything fell into darkness again. I heard them clatter on the floor tile, followed by a crunch. "You won't be needing those anymore."

She lay my arms straight along my sides. Covering me up to my neck with a blanket, she also slung a surgical mask over my face.

The gurney's wheels wobbled and squeaked their repetitive melody. The sound of a telephone ringing increased until we bumped into something.

"*That* human at least knew how to fight. Not that it helped him much." I heard a body being shoved out of the way.

Small wonder it was so quiet. Where the hell was Petrakis? Unless...

The elevator bell rang, and their doors opened. Fluorescent light spilled out into the hallway.

The gurney banged its way into the compartment. The doppelgänger stood next to me as the elevator descended. Gone was the gentle aroma of baby powder and disinfectant. The monster stunk up the place with old body odor, wet stone, and fungus.

Since my brain couldn't do much in the way of moving my body's parts, it entertained itself by reasoning out that Davis's soap, shampoo, underarm deodorant, and who-knows-what-else couldn't be duplicated by the monster, just like her uniform and shoes.

My stomach rebelled against the onslaught of odors. My brain switched over to worrying how the paralytic would interfere with the reaction of throwing up. I didn't relish the thought of aspirating my own vomit.

The elevator bonged, and the doors opened to the bright first-floor lobby. A night security guard blocked the way.

"Davis? Why's the power out on your level? What the hell's going on up there? We've been calling your level for a couple of minutes."

"Get a team up to the secure level," said Davis, a convincing urgency tightening her voice. "Ms. Marple has escaped her restraints again and has turned violent. She has disabled all but one of the staff and severely injured Mr. Yeager. The remaining orderly may not be able to hold her for long." She shoved the gurney ahead, and the guard hopped to one side. "He needs immediate attention."

"No, I don't!" At least, that's what I tried to say. All I successfully communicated was a pained groan.

"You okay, Davis?" The guard's eyes searched her face. "You sound weird. Sure you didn't get conked, too?"

"I am fine," the thing replied in Davis' voice, if not her manner. "Move."

The guard leaped into the elevator. The doors closed as he called into his shoulder mic, "Code Gray on secure level."

The Davis clone trundled my gurney through the doors leading to the central courtyard. A burly male nurse dashed past us, a roll of pennies clasped in his fist.

She buffeted my table along the paved curved walkway. The surroundings were dark this moonless night, and the trees blocked what little light leaked out of the circle of buildings' windows. Jerked to a halt, I nearly rolled off the table. Davis walked past me.

"You will soon rejoin your mother. You can die together, once we have the traitor's son."

First, this creature thinks I'm a traitor. So, who's the traitor's son? I wanted to scream, "Will you make fucking *sense*?" Out of my mouth came another nonsensical garble.

The ersatz Davis halted a step past my field of vision and began to utter more words of its strange language. "*Etra phen mbarda Phelek Lepan. Ni sam yon gorikuba elā.*"

His buddy said something similar in the hospital room. I got the feeling they were referring to me, somehow. I'd have to ask Algernon or Barandir when—*if*—I ever got back to Eldridge.

I lost count of the times it intoned those phrases. With each repetition, the wind stirred the tall firs towering on either side of the path until the surrounding copse of trees was whipped into a frenzy.

A flash of light—No, a pulse of darkness—appeared between the two firs, tearing a hole in the air. Streamers of gray condensation cascaded into the gaping circle of pitch black.

A cry from somewhere past my feet rang out. "What in God's name?"

Dr. Levinson ran up to the gurney. A second pair of footsteps clicked along the lane behind him, their nonchalant gait in sharp disparity against the doctor's. Leaning close, he pulled off my mask. "Dr. Yeager?" he cried over the whistling winds. His wavy hair clung for dear life to his scalp.

Levinson seized the drug vial. His face awash with stern anger, he stormed toward the doppelgänger.

"Kebwy," I said, being my best version of "Keep away."

"Nurse Davis, what is the meaning—" He stopped short, faced with the impossibility of the swirling dimensional gate churning in front of him.

The thing that was Davis grabbed Levinson by his shoulder. The sound of bone grinding against cartilage was quickly followed by the doctor's cry of pain. The monster kicked out Levinson's legs from under him. It clamped its other hand on his head and rammed Levinson's whole torso into the macadam. My stomach twisted at the sound of crunching bone. The creature rose, leaving Levinson's smashed head and shoulders half-buried into the walkway.

The second set of footsteps stopped. My lower eye muscles cramped as I tried to look past my feet. I spotted a briefcase being tossed to the ground.

"As an assessor representing the firm of Eldridge & S.Q.Amos, I would advise you to cease and desist," said Petrakis. "Whatever you are."

"Yutugyerdsfitymgyr," I said. The Mumble-to-English translation? "You took your damn sweet time getting here!"

Petrakis stepped forward, holding Namiki like a sword in his left hand, her silver nib pointed at Davis. In his right hand, two finger-sized rectangles of blue and red rubber.

Ink erasers?

The doppelgänger yowled, facing him. It advanced one step before hesitating. "The vessel, he is with you and your kind?" it growled with a vindictiveness that made my spine shiver.

If my spine could shiver, then maybe...? I focused my attention on moving my legs.

"Yes. He is under our protection," Petrakis replied.

The thing curled a wicked smile that could wilt flowers. "Oh, what joy it shall be tearing your cabal's secrets out of him, along with the traitor's son. The halls of *Phelek Lepan* shall echo with triumph."

By sheer force of will, I managed to dangle a calf over the gurney's side.

"That's assuming you can still get there." With a full-circled under-hand softball pitch, Petrakis rocketed one of the erasers into the mouth of the gate.

The streams of vapor coursing into the black circle scattered to the four winds. The gate spun, dancing about like a giant coin on a tabletop. It collapsed into itself with a pulse of black spray, followed by a clap of thunder, only played in reverse.

"Get it? I *erased* your spell." Petrakis chuckled, quite pleased with himself.

With a howl of rage, the doppelgänger charged Petrakis. My mentor dodged Davis' lumbering bulk like a bullfighter, planting the second eraser on the creature's forehead. It attached itself like glue.

The doppelgänger screamed and tumbled to the ground, its guise writhing and dissolving into the speckled gray humanoid shape that was its natural form.

I swung my other leg over the gurney's edge.

The gray monster breathed with difficulty.

Petrakis took a step forward. "Namiki, please begin containment protoco—"

Without warning, the slender creature launched itself at Petrakis. It wrapped its translucent arms about him, shimmering muscle bunching around gray bone. Petrakis fell back, stabbing the monster repeatedly with Namiki.

Its wounds closed up as if the strike never occurred.

"I cudda tode yuu dat wudnt wok." I pushed best as I could with arms of rubber. I almost sat up, but collapsed onto the gurney again.

With Petrakis flat on his back, the creature ripped the eraser from its forehead, yowling in agony as a patch of gray, speckled skin tore off its skull. Clawing at Petrakis' hand, it snatched Namiki out of his grasp.

"You may defend yourself, Namiki," said Petrakis.

Smoke began to emerge from the monster's grip. Screaming through the pain, it stabbed Namiki at Petrakis' head. Its hand deflected away, like one magnet repelled by another.

Petrakis barked out a sharp yelp. The creature jumped up, leaving

Namiki's point in his shoulder.

After a moment of the creature wrapping itself in concentration, we were faced again with Esther, though still in Davis's loose-fitting uniform. A rectangular wound on her forehead bled, lines of red coursing down her face. The palm of her hand showed a gruesome second-degree burn.

The monster pointed Esther's scrawny finger at me. "You shall never see your mother again. I shall suck the last drop of life out of her and savor her final misery." Showing that evil grin again, she turned and dashed into the front building.

I planted my legs on the ground and wobbled to a near-vertical position. As I did, I wished I could have left my stomach on the gurney.

With a grimace, Petrakis yanked Namiki out of his shoulder. A circle of red spread on his jacket as he clambered to his feet. "No apologies necessary, Namiki. You tried your best to miss. Thanks."

Corralling me in his good arm, Petrakis and I both limped after the creature in Esther's skin. My legs felt like I was dancing with three feet, all of them left.

"My mother," I mumbled.

No sooner had we entered the building, than the halls echoed with an alarm. Following the trail of prone guards and staff, my stomach stiffened when I approached their bodies. Pools of blood, shattered bone, and brains splashed from the necks of each of their bodies.

I spotted Dr. Azizi on the floor. She lay still, one arm bent at a gut-wrenching angle, and her head flattened into the concrete floor. Unbidden, the image of my mother's body, broken by the vengeance of the nameless shapeshifter, filled my sight. Instead of Azizi, the sight of Esther's face, violated and torn by bone and blood, burned into my soul.

I broke away from Petrakis and clutched my gut. A single wail of horror exhausted my lungs, and I crumpled to all fours. My stomach responded and emptied its contents by Azizi's broken arm.

"She was never here," I gurgled between heaves.

Without a word, a solemn Petrakis hauled me off the floor and dragged me along in pursuit. It was easy to follow the doppelgänger—the smashed exterior doors to the front parking lot were a dead giveaway. We maneuvered through the broken doorway, when Petrakis stopped.

He patted his pants pocket and frowned. "*Coconuts*! The confounded creature took my keys." His attitude struck me as rather complacent, considering a murderous monster had access to our vehicle.

The revving of our car's engine roared over the expanse of the empty visitor parking area. A quick but treacherous jaunt down the short quartet of concrete stairs, and I spotted our Taurus parked under a streetlamp.

Esther's doppelgänger engaged the shift. Surprise registered on its face when the shifter shoved itself back into park. The car's horn beeped twice, followed by an unfamiliar popping sound. The car's steering column airbag whooshed open, a white balloon filling the space between the wheel and the creature.

Except the balloon didn't stop inflating. It grew in size until it flattened against the driver's window. The inner lining of the airbag began filling with gray. A splatter here, a splash there. A sudden gush of gray liquid and silver flecks filled the translucent bag. The car beeped again, and the monstrous slime-filled airbag was sucked back into the steering column.

"Oh dear, I think Fido may have been a bit too rough. That's a shame. I had hoped we could interrogate the creature before putting it in cold storage."

I tottered over to the handrail and leaned over it. "Fido?" I wheezed.

"An inside joke, one the motor pool has never explained to me. Now you know why I wouldn't let you drive. Be glad your friend didn't have a chance to force you into the passenger seat. The glove compartment would have an even nastier surprise in store."

The rest of my dinner decided that was the moment to make a spectacular exit.

"Come along, Yeager." The "pissed-off Petrakis" came back full force. "Time to get yourself cleaned up, return home, and write our reports. After which, of course, you are immediately on two-week probation."

"Yes, sir," I said with muck still dribbling from my mouth.

"Namiki, please alert Eldridge. Intrusion confirmed. Send an adjuster to Western Bay State Hospital. Mark it 'Immediate Attention.' Only one intrusion. Intrusion has been removed. Several—"

"Two," I said.

"Two what?"

"Two intrusions. I killed the one that impersonated Esther."

"Correction. Two intrusions, one killed with remains still on the grounds, one with remains sealed. Several human fatalities."

I coughed, trying to spit out the taste of vomit. After wiping my mouth with my handkerchief, I sat on the cement steps. I didn't have to fake my despair or anger for the sake of the watchful Namiki and Amelia. "Where the hell were you, Petrakis? I told Amelia to contact you the second Esther changed into one of those doppelgängers."

"Watch your mouth, Yeager," Petrakis spat. "First of all, that was not a Doppelgänger. I have seen my share of that despicable species, and their natural form does *not* look like that. Our friends were something else."

"Then, what?"

"Write your report, and I shall try to figure that out. Secondly— Exactly *how* did you ask Pilot to contact me?"

"I don't know. I think I said, 'Amelia, contact Petrakis.'"

"There you are. You did not say 'please.'"

My head tilted so low, I had to stare at Petrakis through my eyebrows. "Excuse me?"

"There's a reason parents tell their children that 'please' is the magic word."

"Are you fu—" I took a breath to calm myself, squeezing my eyes shut to dry them. "Are you kidding me?"

"Not at all. Scribes are forbidden to take action of their own volition. As your scribe's keeper, you must predicate any request with 'please,' 'if you would be so kind,' or something similar granting permission. Otherwise, they are powerless to act. You could be dying, and your last words would be 'Help me,' if you didn't add 'please' immediately before or after."

His answer roiled me more than it should have. "How did Namiki damage the doppelgänger's, I mean, the shapeshifter's hand? Amelia didn't leave a scratch on the one I stabbed with her."

"Does your Pilot have a fire-breathing dragon on it?" His growing impatience rattled in his voice.

"This company is insane." I simmered for a moment, drumming the cement with my right hand. "The intrusions called me a traitor, a traitor's son, then a vessel. What did they mean?"

Petrakis stood over me, offering his hand. His face remained a stern mask as he helped me to my feet. "Too many questions. If I can, I shall let you know once I digest your report."

"Oof, don't say *digest*." I grabbed my stomach and gulped hard. "But I need to know what they meant. I need to help the people left inside. *Now*."

"You want to help? Fetch my briefcase. We're leaving."

"Leaving?" My mother could be dead. So many killed. I couldn't leave anyone else to die. "We should assist any wounded."

"Trust me, there's no one you can help."

"We have to—"

"That's for the adjuster to handle," he almost shouted. "Now hurry. The Mundane authorities are sure to arrive before the adjuster."

I wobbled back to the courtyard, averting my gaze from Azizi's crushed face, pile-drivered into the floor. Stumbling into the dark courtyard, I sucked in a lungful of air, holding my breath when I spotted a form in white between the trees ahead.

A gyrating nightgown supported by a pair of wrinkled legs, thick with varicose veins, crossed a stray beam of light.

"Ms. Oliver? What are you doing out here?"

"You got rid of her! I *knew* you would." she giggled as she grabbed my shoulders. Catching her breath, she leaned on me for balance. I stumbled under the sudden weight but steadied myself against a tree and righted ourselves.

A sudden surge of bitterness made me want to shake some sense into her muddled head. "She was my *mother*," I said, ending in a shout.

"No, dearie," she said with a schoolgirl's pout. "Not really, she wasn't."

"I... I know." I forced my hands to my sides. They balled into fists. "But that thing was the only clue I had left to find her. And now it's fucking dead."

Oliver slapped my face. "Watch your mouth," she said, pointing her knobby finger at me. Her stern face quickly sprouted a wry grin. "There's a lady present."

"You don't understand. For years, I believed my mother was dead. I thought I found her, getting the care she needed." My eyes welled up again. "Instead, I find she's gone, locked in a prison somewhere I'll never find." I pounded my fist against the side of my leg. "My fiancée's gone, too—I don't know if I'll ever get her back again, either. I'm all alone in this world."

I spun around, gauging the buildings surrounding me. Their darkened floors called to the blackest parts of my soul. "You're happy Ms. Marple's gone? Well, *good* for you! Look at who had to suffer." I grabbed her arm and marched her over to Levinson's corpse. "Look at who had to *die*," I almost screamed.

Oliver only shook her head with a sad "Tut-tut."

I stared at her, aghast. "Maybe this nuthouse is where I belong. The whole world is insane, and I'm the only one thinking straight? Maybe it's me who should be here." I pushed her away. "Maybe I should be dead."

"Oh, no... Don't say that, dearie," Oliver blurted. She bent to Petrakis' briefcase and plucked out the last ink eraser. She scrutinized it, as though it were the most unusual thing she had ever seen. Not taking her eyes off it, she softly spoke and patted my cheek. "Now, don't you worry. You'll see your mother again. And your girl, too. Oh my, she *is* a pretty one." A wistful smile crossed her face, and she caressed her cheek. "I was pretty once, too."

I gaped unabashedly at her prediction.

She handed me the ink eraser. "You'd better keep this. Keep it *close*. You're going to need it, and pretty soon. In a place that looks like a Chinese tearoom." With a gentle shove, she pushed herself away from me and began to pirouette, dancing into the darkness. "Now, I have to find my lion, so I can finish my puzzle."

Sounds of burly men moving into action percolated out from the secured patient wing. I collected the briefcase and hastened back to Petrakis.

CHAPTER 29

We drove south, the Pineapple Express at our backs. I had a sour taste in my mouth—not from food poisoning or puke, but from my aversion to putting up the front of being at odds with Petrakis. At least there was no music during the return trip.

I spent the entire distance weighing my options while I considered the monsters' statements that I could recall and Ms. Oliver's encouraging words.

Some questions I could answer even without Amelia's help. My mother was alive. They needed her to create duplicates as bait to capture me. She had aged faster than normal, subjected to the repeated effect I witnessed when the creature copied Davis. But she was *alive*.

The simulacrums were dead, so my mother was safe for the moment. I had bought myself some time, as the news that their 'vessel' had shown up had died with them. My hopes rose.

I will see Mother again.

I *will* see Sindhu again.

Restored and whole.

I *had* to.

Unfortunately, too many other questions were scattered in my path, blocking the way.

Who or what were those shapeshifters? Where were they keeping Mother? What am I to them? And who was this traitor and traitor's son they wanted so badly? And what did they mean by "vessel?"

I had the inkling of an answer, but I didn't like it. If I found that medico Alvarez, maybe a CAT scan, PET scan, MRI, or another pass with her Magic Mirror could give me a clue.

Then there's all the hoo-hah back at Eldridge I had to contend with. Where exactly was Sindhu? Why was Lt. Yadavi interested in my fiancée? Would the blue jarhead be a help or a hindrance?

Where was Dr. Fleischer squirreled away? And what did *Alberich* have to do with me?

What had Petrakis so spooked? Company politics proved to be more screwed up than university backroom wheeling-and-dealing, but now I had to deal with conspiracy theories?

I trusted Petrakis. Director Ventnor's contempt for me was there for everyone to see, and therefore could be trusted in its own twisted way. But was Vice President Hibara still one of the good guys?

Theories whirled about in my skull like a spinning Gordian knot. When I separated one thread from the rest, it made no sense.

I supposed that's when a scribe would come in handy. Writing all this down could be the best way to straighten it out in my head.

It was the first time in my life I actually looked forward to writing a report.

CHAPTER 30

The good news? Petrakis was right. Scribes made paperwork a breeze. Left to my own devices, it would have taken me hours to figure out how to fill out items like "Ambient PQ Level" or "Ectoplasm Half-Life." Amelia and I polished off the post-assessment report in less than an hour. And in my own handwriting, to boot. Not bad for a Monday morning.

I wondered if she could balance my checkbook.

The bad news? My two-week probation began the moment I sent the report to Petrakis, Ventnor, Central Records, and whomever else was on the copy-to list. A split-second after I hit the "Send" button on *Plan-10*'s newfangled e-mail software, Petrakis was in my cubicle.

"Here's my personal hardbound copy of the Eldridge & S.Q.Amos New Employee Handbook, Mr. Yeager. Keep your Pilot far away from it. I don't want to see any underlines or margin notes when you return it."

I was mulling over an appropriate smart-ass retort, when he steam-rolled over it.

"Report to my office at nine o'clock two weeks from today. I will have two exams prepped for you. The first will cover any material pre-sented during your orientation. The second shall focus on the handbook. Ten questions each. If you pass, you may continue your employment here at Eldridge & S.Q.Amos. If you fail—in the form of making more than one incorrect response per exam—your employment shall be terminated, and your memory shall be wiped. Any additional disciplinary actions will be at the discretion of Director Ventnor and myself, depending on how spectacularly you fail."

"Seriously?" My ears could fry eggs. "You're going to continue being a real hard-ass about this?"

"Diamond hard, Mr. Yeager. Last week, you displayed gaps in knowledge that endangered not only yourself, but myself and every innocent person at the intrusion—especially the Mundanes who perished at the hands of the shapeshifters. I shudder to think about what risks any future Eldridge employee who has the misfortune of accompanying you in the field might be exposed to."

He straightened his back, peering over the cubicle walls down the corridor. "I assume everyone has jobs to do," he pronounced sternly to the various employees pretending not to eavesdrop.

"Director Ventnor will be reviewing our reports along with those of the adjuster who cleaned up your mess at Western Bay State Hospital. He will then inform me whether the multiple Mundane deaths there could have been avoided."

His faux animosity was infectious, and I didn't have enough coffee this early in the morning to deal with it. "Did Ventnor review your report from the Lick Observatory Intrusion, too? What did he have to say about Gary's death, *hmm*? What about Cheryl and Sindhu? Could all that have been avoided, too?"

He slammed his leather-bound copy of the handbook on my desk, on top of my own soft-cover version of it. Small objects on my surrounding office furniture bounced. From over the cubicle wall came a chorus of rattles from Natalie's desk.

"I remind you, Mr. Yeager, that as of this moment, you are on probation. Don't make it worse." He paced my cramped cubicle, goose-stepping in slow motion a grand total of two paces before turning about-face. "You are hereby restricted to your apartment and this Eldridge facility until probation is lifted. Travel is permitted only between those two destinations. And, yes, you *shall* be monitored."

"What if I run out of food? Or, more importantly, *coffee*?"

"I suggest you adjust your schedule to fit our cafeteria's." He stopped to frown at a poster tacked to one of my cubicle's fabric walls—a close-up of the *Wolfman* paired with a headshot of *Lassie* and the caption, "Before Coffee - After Coffee."

"It was Director Ventnor's original intent to restrict you to this floor during this probation," he said to hairy Lon Chaney Jr. "However, I persuaded him to grant you access to whatever Eldridge resources you feel you need to pass your exams." Petrakis shot me one last crabby glance.

"I wish you luck." He turned on his heel and strolled out of my cube.

I had to repeat the mantra, "*It's only a movie, it's only a movie,*" to myself several times to keep my composure. Even so, I was filled with a familiar but dreadful anxiety—I thought I had kissed exams goodbye when I left the university.

My eyebrows arched before I forced them to lie still. Too late, I realized I still had questions to ask of him. I lunged out of my cube's entrance. "Did you ever find out what those doppelgängers were?"

The only thing listening was empty air. I craned my neck, looking up and down my line of cubicles. Petrakis had already turned the corner at the end of the row.

Not a single person peered over their walls. Those employees who I could spy through their cubicle openings had their collective attention fixed on their screens or paperwork. I waited for a few seconds. Not even my ATPG coworkers ventured to poke their whack-a-mole heads out of the sanctity of their cubicles.

I grabbed my coffee mug and headed to the break room. As I turned each corner, people dove out of the corridor into whatever nook or cranny they could wiggle their way into. News about the new company leper traveled fast.

After filling my mug, I poked around the fridge for any community snacks. My stomach growled its disappointment, though I was amused by one sandwich's Post-It note:

Sofia's Lunch
Warning: Contains Eye of Newt
Go ahead, steal this. Are you willing to gamble?

That's a hard pass on food prepared by our group's seer.

With a fresh mug of java, I stopped by Natalie's cubicle. Her attention was locked on her screen, displaying a star chart labeled "Predicted Gamma Ray Bursts Present-to-2010." Arrows from a dozen stars were drawn, all pointing towards the Sun. It looked like the galaxy had put out a hit contract on good old Sol.

I knocked politely and ambled in. Natalie spun in her chair like she was ready to draw at the OK Corral. I was surprised to see her wearing a pantsuit but was heartened by her refusal to ditch her Oklahoma belt buckle for the usual business fare.

"Stop right there, Alaska."

I arched my back, keeping my coffee from spritzing my off-the-rack, but nevertheless new, tie and white shirt.

"Alaska?" I said. "I suppose it's better than 'Unclean.'"

"You're *persona non grata* for the next two weeks. Now, git."

"So you heard?"

Natalie stuck her thumb, pointing toward my cubicle. "I think the whole office floor heard."

"Then you also heard Director Ventnor still allows me access to whatever Eldridge resources I need. Since Algernon assigned you as my mentor, and neither Petrakis nor Ventnor have countermanded his assignment, I think you still classify as a resource."

She emitted a sound somewhere between a growl and a whimper. Her voice dropped hoarse and dark, and her eyes were those of a cornered animal. "If you get me in hot water, Alaska, so help me..."

"Just some info. That's all."

She stood with her arms crossed, blocking me from entering her cubicle further. "Okay, shoot."

"Is anyone in our group good with languages?"

"European, Asian, Aboriginal...?"

"More like alien or cryptid."

"Algernon was our resident expert on aliens. Obviously, he's not available anymore. You could try asking around other ATPGs." She snorted back a snicker. "Good luck with that. I'd say your next best option is the company library. As far as cryptids and such, Barandir knows the most about earth-bound non-human jibber-jabber."

"Makes sense." I raised my mug to her and turned to leave. Thanks."

"Hold up there, Alaska. Tit for tat. I got a question for you. What's the story about our new boss?"

"Could you be a bit more specific?"

"Is Petrakis always that cranky?"

"No, he's usually pretty laid back." Then I shot her a faint half-smile. "Though he is a bit of a pun factory."

"Shoot. Then I got dressed up for nothin'. Why's he riding your tail so hard?"

"Things got a little hairy on our assessment last week. He feels my..." I searched for the right word and failed. "...inexperience and gaps in knowledge nearly got us killed."

"I *told* you, I ain't tellin' you again. You can't rely on that lame excuse about a rushed orientation forever."

"Maybe so, but I *do* remember how everyone in the company made it sound like riding along with an assessor was something to look forward to."

"Never said it would be a walk in the park." She unfolded her arms. Leaning in a little, she lowered her voice. "What were you up against?"

"Don't know. Shapeshifters of some type," I said. Natalie's eyes brightened with excitement. "That's why I need a linguistics expert. They said some things during our face-off. It was like they *knew* me. I think they might have even identified their home." I sipped my mug thoughtfully. "Okay, thanks. See ya."

"What'd they say? Did you see their natural form? What'd they look like?"

"Read my report, if Petrakis lets you. Otherwise, you gotta wait 'til I have more questions for you. Tit for tat..." I smiled and vamoosed. The spot between my shoulder blades itched. Even money it was Natalie's eyes stabbing my back.

Strolling past Barandir's cube, I didn't think anything was out of sorts when I spotted it was empty. On the way back to my desk, a hunch made me take an indirect path past Petrakis' office. Though his door was closed, the vertical blinds were not completely shut, affording me a zoetrope view inside as I passed.

Petrakis had beaten me to the punch. Their ties and white shirts were almost exact matches. A shame, as denim and leather suited Barandir far better than office formal. The only way to discern who was who, was by Barandir's long auburn ponytail versus Petrakis' stubby one of salt-and-pepper.

Leaning on his desk, Petrakis intently watched Barandir, who silently read a five-page memo. I had no doubt he was reading my report, which contained Amelia's word-for-word transcriptions of what the shapeshifters had said to me. With his back to me, I couldn't read his reactions.

His neck twitched, and he cocked his head in my direction. I hastened my pace, but it might have been too late to evade his elven hearing.

My eyes darted about, searching for other uninvited eavesdroppers. I whispered, "Amelia, is Namiki in that room?"

She double-clicked her cap.

"Can you get from her what they're discussing?"

No response.

"*Please* tell me what they're talking about?"

Still nothing from my scribe. I was pretty sure that was a "no." Please, or no please.

I slunk my way back to my cube and sat dejected in front of my terminal.

To one side of my Sun-3 computer stood my stacks of two-inch binders from orientation. On the other side, Petrakis' venerable copy rested on top of my paperback version, probably squishing its paper into coal by now.

Over the past month, I had tried to commit to memory some pages of the orientation material, diligently read others, and lightly scanned the rest—but for the life of me, I could not remember a single page of it. It took four weeks the first time to plow through the info, with a healthy dose of tutoring from Caltrop. Now I had a mere two weeks to tackle it all again, plus the added load of getting the Eldridge & S.Q.Amos New Employee Handbook under my belt.

After a minute of wallowing in my own pity party, a stray thought interrupted my vicious cycle of despondency. Namely, why did Petrakis loan me his personal copy? He had to have seen my virgin copy lying on the desk. I scoured my recollection of his instructions.

"*Keep your Pilot far away from it.*"

A spark of hope popped into my head. Is *that* what he meant?

Staring at his book, I said, solely for Amelia's benefit, "Well, I better get down to brass tacks. Only two weeks to go." I only hoped that would throw her—and any third-party voyeurs—off the scent.

I set down my mug and its potential coffee ring stain arm's length from the book and opened my top desk drawer. I swept a small cache of pens and pencils from the desktop into it. Removing Amelia from my shirt pocket, I placed my scribe in her gray plastic box and deposited it on top of the pick-up-sticks pile of writing implements. Before closing the drawer, I shrugged with an apology. "You heard the boss. No marks in his book. Can't make a mark if all my pens are out of reach."

I opened the book.

On the title page was a chartreuse Post-It note with Petrakis' handwriting in pencil.

Commit the following to memory <u>before</u> reading the other side:
Ref Lib - 355.31
Read pg. 47 <u>twice</u>
1st time aloud, 2nd time silently

I took the time needed to reread the instructions until I had them under my belt. Flipping it over, the paper said simply:

Open wide
Remember to chew 25 times!

Without thinking, I snorted a chuckle, a smirk wrapping around one cheek. If he thought I would—

The paper wriggled out of my grasp, folded itself twice in midair, and flew into my gawping mouth.

I coughed. I gagged. The paper bounced off one inner cheek, treated my uvula as a punching bag, then wedged itself between the opposite cheek and molar. Every inch of skin below my hairline jumped five degrees Fahrenheit. My entire face and neck beaded with sweat.

Reaching for my mug, I tossed a mouthful of its contents back lightning fast, trying to wedge the blasted thing loose with a coffee mouthwash. It wouldn't budge.

Forcing my panic down, I champed my molars together. The folded note obliged and slipped itself in between, offering itself up to be ground to bits. Downing the last of my coffee, I swallowed the gummy wad of *papier-mâché.*

When I could breathe again, I wiped myself down with my handkerchief.

Natalie called over the cubicle wall. "Hey, you okay over there, Alaska?"

"Yeah," I croaked out between gasps. "Just swallowed down the wrong pipe."

After my epiglottis finished seizing up, I made a beeline to the elevator. While checking the directory between the three sets of doors, another person stood next to me.

"Hi, Barandir." I wasn't sure if this was good or bad timing.

"Hello, Michael." He pressed the up button and stood statuesque, meditating as hard as he could at the doors, his hands folded flat against his abdomen.

Whatever Forest Elf genes he inherited, they were obviously the dominant pair. His stance might be regarded by a Mundane passerby as effeminate, but I could sense a strength hidden underneath his wiry exterior. In a way, it was not unlike the impression I got from Hibara's receptionist, Ms. Emerald—a placid exterior hiding dangerous mysteries.

The doors opened, and he gestured politely that I enter first.

"What floor?" I asked as I pushed the button for the floor housing the company library.

"Same as yours, apparently."

"You don't say. What are you researching in the library?" I ventured.

"Etymology."

"Sounds interesting." Pulling teeth out of Caltrop's mouth might be easier. "What language?"

"That's what I hope to discover."

"Good. You'll have to tell me all about it."

The doors finally closed. Barandir took it as the signal to ask his question. "And what of you? What sends you to the library?"

"Um, I'm reviewing my employee orientation. I need to clear up some confused notes I made at the time."

He bent slightly forward at the waist, his eyes scrutinizing my face, finally focusing on—what else—my eyebrows. "I see." He straightened up again.

Taking a chance, I said, "You read my report."

"Which report?"

I turned toward him, hang whatever my eyebrows were doing. "I may be on probation, Barandir, but I'm not dim. I know you read my assessment report and heard me outside Petrakis' office."

He faced me as well, his hands still neatly folded. "Neither am I on probation nor dim, Michael. Please do not treat me as such, either."

I heaved an exasperated sigh. "Okay, I read something in the new employee handbook that didn't make sense. So off to the library I go. I'm hoping it'll clear up some questions about my probation and last week's assessment."

Rationalizing something close to the truth disturbed me. I was more unsettled at how each lie came more easily than the one before it.

Barandir turned to face the doors. "Your shapeshifters used... I believe the human term is a 'dead language.'"

"They didn't sound like they spoke Latin or Greek. Not that I would recognize Aramaic or Sumerian. They're not used much in modern science. But I suspected it wasn't anything human. That's why I walked past Petrakis' office. I was looking for you."

He accepted my reason with a nod. "Their words sounded old, reminiscent of a primitive tongue from my world that was ancient when Qin Shi Huang became the first emperor of your China. Understandably, I am not well-versed in it."

"How would a book about a language from your world be in our library?"

"Eldridge has maintained relations with *Tawar Cevan* for some time. Some of our ancient texts have migrated here with us."

The elevator chimed, and the doors opened. Barandir and I headed down a short, wide corridor to the library entrance.

Standing floor to ceiling, the library doors were a ponderous affair of brass and wood. The scene carved in the doors depicted a collage of many ancient libraries. Amid the buildings of Greek, Babylonian, Chinese, and Aztec architectures, the only feature I recognized was the Great Lighthouse associated with the venerable Library of Alexandria.

"I suspect this is your first time in an Eldridge library?" Barandir paused in front of the doors. "Will you need assistance finding your way around?"

"Libraries are all the same," I said. "I should be—"

The doors glided open toward us, revealing a great stories-high room with racks and stacks bordering the central area. Commanding the center of the library was a two-story-tall replica of the Great Lighthouse. A beam of light slowly marched around the catwalk and cupola capping the structure. Several floors of balconies, each with its own phalanxes of towering bookshelves and rolling ladders, encircled the lighthouse and the cavernous open area.

"—I should learn to keep my mouth shut."

On either side of the entrance stood revolving case stands labeled "FAQ," holding dozens of small compartments. Each held copies of a different type of brochure or pamphlet. Barandir rotated the one closest to him. "The Eldridge libraries, due to their focus on specific areas of knowledge, are organized quite differently than libraries found in the Mundane world."

"Let me guess, that would have been covered on day five of my orientation."

"As yours was rushed, I cannot say. Even so, new employees often find it difficult to accustom themselves to the Eldridge library's unique methodologies." He plucked a green brochure from one of the pigeon-hole boxes and handed it to me. "This has two maps. The first is a general guide to the areas with overview to how reference material is organized. The second one is annotated with your cumbersome Dewey Decimal system. One of these should be sufficient to get you on your way."

"Is there a good old-fashioned card catalog?"

Barandir wore a slightly confused expression for a moment, then pointed off to his left. "If it hasn't already been computerized, it may be in that far corner. I wish you good hunting." With a curt nod, he turned and vanished into the nearest maze of bookcases.

I headed in the direction he had pointed. It took a few minutes and several wrong turns before I located the card catalog. Along the way, I passed one or two employees from the orientation classes I had crashed. They appeared equally lost.

If it weren't for the lighthouse as an anchor, my ATP group might have had to send out a search party for me. I gave the catalog cabinet, surprisingly small for a library of this size, the once over. But it wasn't the catalog itself I was looking for. Instead, I grabbed a few blank index cards and pygmy pencils on one end of the cabinet. At least *that* tradition hadn't vanished yet.

Referring to the brochure map, I headed toward the third level via one of the curved staircases spiraling around the central area between balconies. I strolled past corridors of bookcases that radiated outward from the library's center. Each hall was crammed with bookshelves and a triplet of personal reading rooms. Every closet-sized room contained a simple table, chair, and lamp. Entry was by an oaken door with a window laminated with a label declaring the rules and etiquette of the room.

Moments before I entered the first section, the row brightened for five seconds or so. My shadow whipped down one side of the corridor, then back up the other as the lighthouse beam soon paraded past me.

I peered down half a level, marveling at the mechanism of the lighthouse. In the center of the lantern room was a model of a great fire consuming a pyramid of stacked logs. I wondered if the 'flame' was an optical or magical display, as it threw off no heat. The lighthouse beam emanated from a four-foot-wide lens set in a gimbal mount. A moment's examination revealed the lens could be swiveled to point at almost any outward angle. Two stamped-metal clockwork men in ancient Egyptian garb pushed the entire assembly around the fire along a circular track.

I smiled to myself, comforted there still existed pockets of whimsy in the company.

Despite Barandir's disdain, the rows were still organized with some semblance to Dewey. I sang a small "Ta-da" to myself when I found a book with the number I wanted. My moment of victory passed quickly, as I soon realized dozens of books occupied the shelves above and below with the same Dewey designation 355.31 pasted over the bottom of their spines.

Running my finger over the titles, it became apparent all these books were penned by various assessors and adjusters, each claiming their book of recommendations, suggestions, and helpful hints was the authority on their profession. I scanned the rows for a book that might have been authored by Petrakis himself. No soap. Specters of doubt scratched at me as I pondered his directions, until I spotted what I hoped was the object of my search.

Bound in thick paper, its number was pasted upside down on a thin spine broken in several places. The title was eroded to the point of illegibility.

I pulled it out and snickered at the cover of *Uncle Billy-Bob Hatfield's Guide to Gaming the E&SQA System.* Other than the title and Billy-Bob's signature, the cover consisted of a black-and-white photograph of an extended family gathering. Many of the men were bare-chested, wearing only farmer's overalls. The women wore their best frocks and cooking aprons, which wasn't saying much. Most of the hayseeds were barefoot, standing in a proud array around a moonshine still, steaming away at full bore behind them. A slick-haired youth stood near the extreme corner, his chin thrust out high and proud. His head was bounded by a perfect red circle, and a red arrow swooped from the signature to the circle.

"Oh... *those* Hatfields," I said with a snicker.

I surveyed the rest of the bookshelves. It seemed this humble booklet had been referenced more often than all the other books combined.

The coast was clear—no rubberneckers to be found.

Opening the door to the nearest reading room, one rule on its placard was twice the size of the others—"No Casting of Magic in These

Rooms!"

I sat down and opened the book, setting aside the cards and pencils from the catalog downstairs. I took the utmost care leafing through, as the threadbare binding had been so abused that the pages might fly away with a stiff breeze. Not only that, but the book had been handwritten, each page completed with a different writing tool: pencil, pen, felt-tip, or Sharpie. I chuckled to myself at the down-home style of writing and the downright irreverent section headings. *How to Use Your Supervisor Just Like He Uses You, Some Aliens are Idjits*, and *Riddles to Tick Off Sphinxes and Brownies* were just a few.

The one on page forty-seven seemed no different at first: *Who Needs Those Fancy Spy Cameras?* Though the title was written in pen, the paragraph below was done in pencil.

What were Petrakis' instructions? *Read once aloud, read again silently.*

I didn't pause to wonder why the content was in Latin, or where a redneck from Appalachia had the chance to learn that language. I just read it aloud. I'm no slacker in Latin, but the paragraph made no sense whatsoever as I spoke it. Maybe this was why Petrakis needed me to read it twice?

I read it a second time, silently as instructed, and the text vanished.

I gasped, maybe adding something along the lines of "Yipe!"

A split second later, the room brightened like high noon in the desert. Looking over my shoulder, I grimaced at a column of light blasting past the door. It proceeded to flash red once every half-second.

My stomach flipped. Posted inside the door was a sign reminding the room's occupant, "No Spells!"

On cue, the water works on my forehead and under my armpits got to work. Staring at the blank page under the header, panic gripped my throat.

In a cold frenzy, I scooped up Uncle Billy-Bob's book. Angling through the window, then pulling the door ajar by a fraction of an inch, I eyed the corridor, exhaling a grateful sigh at the empty row. I slipped through the door and scampered down the row between the walls of books. My shadow, stark black surrounded by alternating white and red, danced ahead of me.

Crouching behind the stacks at the end of the hall, I snatched a peek back at the light. I stared straight into the blinding lighthouse fire. The mechanism had risen a floor above its previous height. Its clockwork apparatus had stopped, its lens focusing the fire's light down the length of my corridor. The cold flames pulsed their blood-red silent alarm.

From behind the stacks, a dark figure emerged, one hand fingering the railing of the central balcony. I pasted my sweaty back against the cool wood of the bookcase.

"We have detected the casting of magic in this row," a female voice announced. "Please show yourself and surrender all books immediately."

Oh, crud.

CHAPTER 31

Steeling myself to face the music, my brain scrambled for what to say. All I could think of was to jump out, saying, "Booga, booga!"

A door opened. I snatched a glance down the row. The door to *my* room stood open.

A thin figure exited, framed in grays and black against the burning lens. He calmly closed the door behind him. He raised one hand, holding a book. A ponytail rested on one lanky shoulder.

"Apologies, madam librarian," the silhouette said—with *Barandir*'s voice. "I am researching ancient languages. I sounded out the phonetics of a written sentence, which was particularly challenging. I did not realize it might have contained magical power."

The woman, bordered by magnified flames, advanced and held out her hand. "Mr. Robert Barandir Peradlon Boyce."

I almost blurted "*Boyce*?" out loud.

"You, of all people, should know better. I am afraid I must report this infraction to your supervisor. Depending on his response, your library privileges might be revoked."

"Understood."

The woman, dressed not too differently than the frumpy daughter from *American Gothic*, removed the book from Barandir's—or Boyce's—outstretched hand. "Assuming your privileges continue, you may have access to this book again after we have had a chance to examine it for spell-casting damage." She retreated to the balcony and disappeared behind the nearest stack.

The flames lessened in intensity, returning to their soft amber fluttering. Resuming their duties, the clockwork men continued slogging the lens about its track. The lighthouse lowered itself, returning the corridor's lighting to normal.

Barandir craned his head, cocking his ear toward me. I flattened my back against the bookcase end.

His footsteps approached. Given his ability for stealth, I surmised he wanted to be heard. He stepped from the corridor, facing me. "You forgot these."

He handed me the pencils and cards I had left behind.

I squinted at him. He watched my eyebrows. "Thanks. But why are you helping me? I thought I was the company pariah."

"Helping you?" he asked. "That remains to be seen." With an inscrutable expression, he turned and walked away. If he had worn a cape, he might have given it a flourish.

As loud as I dared, I inquired, "Robert Barandir Peradlon Boyce?"

He stopped. In a voice colder than ice, he grumped over his shoulder at me, "A name given to me by my parents. The first name was given to me by my father, and the last I inherited from him. The third was forced upon me by my mother's family. It is a name I do not care to hear again in its entirety." He turned the corner and was gone.

Frustration tainted my gratitude. So many questions remained unasked. First and foremost, did Barandir save my bacon on his own volition, or did Petrakis ask him to watch my back? While I puzzled, it struck me as curious that we shared the trait of middle names with shady pasts.

In the end, gratitude won. I whooshed out another sigh and fell back, knocking my head against the bookcase. I rubbed my eyes to count my lucky stars.

However, instead of being filled with the usual rainbow-hued sparkles of photopsia, the image of Uncle Billy-Bob's penciled paragraph occupied my dark field of vision. I opened my eyes then squeezed them shut again. In the darkness, I could see the Latin gibberish text plain as day. I opened the threadbare book back to the mystical page. It was blank except for the title and footer, the latter which read:

> *They say: "Be Kind, Rewind."*
> *I say: "Don't fight it, rewrite it."*

With a shrug, I whispered to myself, "Oh, what the heck. Why not?"

I inched my way back to the nearest reading room and cautiously took a seat. With one of the library pencils, I rewrote the first line of the spell. I halted, with my feet poised to vamoose out the door at the slightest twitch of light in the corridor. Encouraged by the absence of virulent red flashes, I copied the rest of the spell back into the booklet, word for exact word, right down to each curlicue onto the empty space. I suppose Amelia could have done a better job of it, but I couldn't let her know anything about this little caper. Besides, she was still back in her drawer.

I closed the book. My momentary relief was shoved aside by surprise. I could feel my eyebrows bouncing, because the cover photograph had subtly changed. Young Billy-Bob Hatfield now beamed a gap-toothed smile, thrusting two thumbs up at the camera. Attempting the furtiveness of a cat burglar—and no doubt failing—I returned the booklet to its rightful place in the bookshelves.

Straightening my shirt and tie and assuming a nonchalant poise, I strolled down the balcony stairs and out of the library.

When the ponderous double doors closed behind me, saw-toothed panic released my brain. But it was replaced by a new question. What did that magic spell do to me?

I closed my eyes again. Nothing. I held my breath and, this time, concentrated on the page containing the spell. In a flash, it appeared to me again, as legible as today's newspaper.

With a smile, I mumbled to myself, "That crazy Greek geek," and made a dash into the elevators and back to my cubicle.

Sitting at my desk, I placed the first orientation binder on my cleared desk and eagerly opened it to its first page. With an introspective voice, I said, "Time for a little experiment."

Once my breathing slowed to normal, I closed my eyes once more and willed Billy-Bob's page into view with ease. My heartbeat quickened in my ears. In my quietest voice, I recited the enchantment before me. Opening my eyes, I read the binder's first page. Once I reached its end, every word on the page vanished.

I wondered how long the spell would last. Would it only serve for one page, or could it handle more? Might it even handle a whole book?

I calmly read the next page and the next. Text and diagrams on every completed page disappeared. With each page, it became easier. By the time I reached the midpoint of the first module, I was skimming the pages before their contents evaporated.

How's *them* bananas, Evelyn Wood?

That's when the blinding headache hit. Twice as strong as the brain freeze from an ice-cold dessert, it wrapped my whole noggin in freezer burn. My field of vision became a wallpaper of white peppered with sparkles of silent fireworks. My eyes felt like someone was twisting ice picks in them.

I think I gasped or whimpered. Maybe even cried out? I was too busy pressing my hands against my temples until my brain warmed up again.

Just as quickly, it disappeared, leaving me breathing harder than Oliver Hardy running a 100-yard dash. I opened my eyes. My head rested on the open binder.

Over the cubicle came Natalie's voice. "Hey, Alaska. You okay?"

"Yeah," I rattled. "An ocular migraine. It's already gone."

"I didn't know you got those."

"Neither did I."

I was faced with a doozy of a quandary. What caused that major mental spasm? Did I reach a limit? Was it the spell's or my own?

Catching my breath, I clutched my hands into fists until the hammering heartbeat in my ears subsided. Even so, I remained oddly exhilarated. Despite my logical left hemisphere reasoning it was merely hypoxia, my emotional right hemisphere wanted to jump through the ceiling with the possibilities of my new ability.

I closed my eyes and concentrated on the material I had just read. One by one, the pages marched by. Giddiness overcame me as I found I could manipulate the pages—stop them, examine them at my leisure, scroll ahead or back to any page I desired, and zoom in to any paragraph or diagram. It was like Billy-Bob's spell had installed a personal photocopier in my brain.

My giddiness became elation. I whipped toward the last page I had scanned before the pain nailed me. I cringed, anticipating another crippling wave of pain.

Hooray, no brain icicles. I was good to go.

I spent a minute musing over the remaining image on the paper. The top started a little fuzzy, like an out-of-focus camera, but the bottom was crystal clear. It matched up with the picture I summoned up, but in reverse—I could envision only the top half of the image, and poorly at that.

Taking a break, I ate lunch alone in the crowded and bustling company cafeteria. It was just as well—I wouldn't have been good company. In addition to the usual ton of questions rolling around, my head was filled with an experience I dared not share with anyone.

By the time I finished my meal, I had formulated a tentative plan: I would spend the rest of the afternoon in an empty meeting room with my entire pile of orientation binders, testing the limits of the spell for the rest of the afternoon. However, I would need to be careful not to scream out in pain again when I hit the brick wall while on full display to any passersby.

After I found an unused room, I began with a simple check. Could I still bring up Billy-Bob's page after using it once?

I smiled inwardly. The simple answer was yes. Which meant I had a system at my fingertips: call up Uncle Billy-Bob's eidetic spell—though I doubt he'd call it that—quietly cast it, then memorize a block of information. Rinse with coffee and repeat.

Like Uncle Billy-Bob said, *Who needs those fancy spy cameras?*

The afternoon went by quickly as I cast the spell, memorized, tested, observed, measured. By the end of the day—and two more ice picks to my brain—I had learned the limits of the spell. I could *eideticize*—it didn't feel right calling it *Billy-Bobbing*—no more than fifty pages per casting of his spell. I also learned that I required ten minutes of downtime between sessions, and coffee was imperative during those breaks.

Along the way, I absorbed a few things in the handouts, of which I had no recollection from my four weeks of tribulation in employee orientation. *Cryptids 340: Cryptid etiquette*, for one—the lion's share of which was taken up by Forest Elf rituals. No great surprise there, but I'm sure my eyebrows wiggled at some of the others. Who knew ogres had their own version of Miss Manners? Apparently, there's a whole regimen devoted to the topic of when injuring your host is required. I scratched ogre shindigs off my bucket list.

I found one section interesting enough to read for pleasure before committing it to my spell-enhanced memory—the *Cryptids 220: Elves* seminar that had put me to sleep. According to the material, the Forest Elves granted asylum in our reality originated from a parallel earth they referred to as *Tawar Cevan*, or 'forest world' in English. That pleased my scientific upbringing—there was no way I could reconcile the existence of elvenkind and other fae with the Theory of Evolution.

Another section that caught my attention was the Eldridge system of sign language, the same which Petrakis and Yadavi used in the helicopter. At first, I questioned why the company didn't use an established system like ASL. The second page answered my question—"Because we don't want Mundanes to eavesdrop on what we're saying, Apprentice!" The third page wasn't too much friendlier. It concentrated on signals that distilled commands into a single motion—"Shut up, scum," "Because I said so," and the like.

I don't care for documentation that verbally abuses me.

Understandably, I committed to memory the rest of the signing vocabulary as quickly as possible, figuring plenty of opportunities for practice would come later.

By the end of the business day, I had committed the entirety of my twelve-volume orientation to memory. Returning to my cubicle the victorious hero, I plopped down the stack of a dozen empty binders next to my computer—I had dumped the blank paper in the recycle bin next to the floor's Xerox machine. As I retrieved Amelia from her desk drawer prison, I wondered what risks I would take by performing the *eideticize* spell in her hear-all, see-all presence. I relegated that thought to the pile of things I would consider later.

A quick check of my e-mail brought no new messages. Perhaps one of the perks of being the company outcast? Maybe I should get tossed on probation more often.

The hubbub of my fellow employees heading out for the day perked me up. Plowing through all four weeks of my orientation in one day was a definite cause to celebrate. I was about to grab my jacket until I realized no one from Eldridge would be caught dead in the presence of the company's red-headed stepchild. Besides, going to a Mundane eatery was *verboten*.

I snarfed a tasteless sandwich doled out by one of the machines in the commissary break room. After making a fresh pot of coffee for myself and whoever else might be burning the midnight oil, I resumed my place in my cubicle. The eerie quiet didn't bother me much, as I still enjoyed playing with my new, shiny, one-and-only spell. On top of that, it settled better with my work ethic that I got the job over and done with.

Setting Petrakis' rule book in front of me, I opened the beast up. Then immediately slammed it shut.

"Don't be an imbecile, Yeager," I grumbled. The last thing I wanted to do was blank out Petrakis' personal copy.

I set it aside and instead used my standard issue edition underneath it.

The first fifty pages went smoothly, and the coffee I had smuggled in from home was delicious. The opening material was the same as one might find in a company prospectus: mission statements, hierarchy of authority, head offices around the world and their jurisdictions, emergency situations, behavior while among Mundanes, and so on.

The second load was another story.

I ground to a halt in the HR section about *Relationships*. My low-acid coffee still managed to sour in my stomach. I quickly recalled the rules Natalie had recited a week or so ago. She nailed the first three rules almost perfectly. I could practically hear her voice as I read:

```
Rule 1 - Absolutely no relationships of an
intimate nature (including, but not limited
to: physical, spiritual, mystical, astral,
etc.) between Eldridge & S.Q.Amos employees
are permitted whatsoever;
Rule 2 - All relationships of an intimate
nature (as defined above) with person(s) out-
side E&SQA must be pre-approved by Director
level or higher;
Rule 3 - All relationships of a personal or
intimate nature (as listed above) between
human and non-human sentient being(s) must be
pre-approved by Vice President level or
higher;
Any violations of Rules 1-3, upon review
with participation of the offender and two
levels of their management, may result in ter-
mination of employment and mindwipe of both
parties.
```

Natalie never explained Rule 4, believing no one could be stupid enough to break it. She didn't know about Sindhu and me at the time. She still shouldn't, nor should any Eldridge employee outside myself, Petrakis, Director Ventnor, Vice President Hibara, and the other VPs.

As far as I knew.

But there it was, in black and white—the fourth and most damning rule, right in front of my gawking eyes. The words hit me like a sledgehammer.

<pre>
     Rule 4 - Relationships of a casual, per-
sonal, or intimate nature (as listed above)
with any Intrusion(s), individuals under the
influence of an Intrusion(s), or individuals
detained in any E&SQA facility, including
Intrusion Long-Term Storage (ILTS) units, are
forbidden;
     Any violation, upon review with participa-
tion of the offender and two levels of their
management, may result in immediate termina-
tion, not only of employment, but in all other
aspects as well.
</pre>

I crumpled in my seat, my entire psyche in shock.

The contradictions came roaring back at full volume. Petrakis *knew* about my betrothal to Sindhu when he recruited me, and her condition when he scooped both of us into the silent helicopter. Hibara had to have known all this as well. How could they allow me to sign the Oath, knowing I was signing my own death warrant?

How could Hibara initiate me into the Circle of Ageless Waters? That would only result in a monumental waste of time, as Petrakis warned me that I was not immortal.

Were *their* lives forfeit as well?

I slammed down my empty mug and jumped straight out of my seat. I wanted to scream. Before I knew it, I was stalking the halls of the mostly empty building, watching my feet eat up the industrial high-traffic carpet while trying to puzzle it all out.

Trying to find the missing piece that allowed all the impossibilities that I represented to coexist.

Trying to work out why I had been manipulated into Eldridge.

Yes, *manipulated*.

From the day I set foot on the helicopter that whisked me to Eldridge orientation, I was pushed, prodded, and goaded down a path with no other exits, and given choices that held only one viable option.

Janitorial staff gawped at me like I was crazy and moved their carts out of my path. With my approach, security guards on their rounds regarded me with wary eyes and hands poised over their walkie-talkies and tasers. The few day-shift people still working this late turned into the nearest aisle to avoid the company Untouchable.

I don't know how many laps I made around my floor, stomping down the hallways. I stopped in front of a large lobby window overlooking the city. Placing my hand on the jamb, I rested my forehead on the cool glass.

My eyes caught a glimmer of movement behind me in my reflection. In that fleeting moment, I glimpsed a thin silhouette of a man slightly taller than myself. A hint of pointed ears angling away from a dark head cried "shapeshifter" inside my skull. I whipped around, my upraised hands bunched into fists. My chest heaved like I just finished a sprint.

I was alone. On the wall opposite me hung a two-foot-wide Eldridge corporate symbol forged in bronze.

I needed answers, and the company logo told me where to go next. I walked, this time with purpose, to the upper-level elevator. Facing the sliding doors' onyx and mother-of-pearl version of the corporate logo, I placed my hand on the dark waist-level glass panel next to the door.

It flashed red.

Though I knew it to be an exercise in futility, I tried again. The panel flashed its denial once more.

I punched the glass. A fat lot of good that did my knuckles.

"Can I help you, sir?"

One of the security guards who had witnessed me stalking the corridors faced me. His expression was caught between a cautious inquisitiveness and the possible necessity for violence.

My shoulders slumped, a reflex of submissiveness to authority. Another thing I needed to work on after I got my eyebrows straightened out.

"No... *yes*," I stammered. "How do I get up to the Vice President level?"

"You'd have to get clearance."

"How do I do that?"

"If you have to ask, you won't get it tonight. Would you mind stepping away from the elevator, sir?"

"Never mind," I spat out in defeat as I walked past his watchful gaze. "I'll be in my cubicle if Vice President Hibara wants me." I didn't look back to see if the man was amused, angered, or relieved by my embittered sarcasm.

I continued pacing, this time confining myself to my cubicle's row while I worked out my next move. Each time I passed my cube, my sight was drawn to the remaining pages in the rule book waiting for me.

"Okay, time for that last brass tack," I said through gritted teeth. Despite the hour, reason told me that if I wrapped up eideticizing the blasted thing tonight, I could browse its contents at my leisure after a good night's sleep.

Maybe it could answer a few questions, like how much trouble am I in? How much is Petrakis? What's Hibara's game? Is there anything that gives me an out from the potential death sentence Rule 4 hung over my head?

The coffee in the break room was scalding in its pot. It seemed fitting to finish my task with the acrid stench and taste of burnt coffee that no amount of cream could mask. I cast the spell one last time and puttered through the final set of pages.

I tossed the emptied book onto my pile of empty binders.

It occurred to me that Petrakis' copy might have his own set of notes in the margins. Leafing through the hefty tome, I found none. Turning the last page, I was rewarded with another green Post-It stuck to the inside endpaper. In Petrakis' hand, it read:

Use your remaining time wisely.

"Sage advice for any occasion," I murmured. With my mouth firmly shut, I made sure there was no *kamikaze* text on its back. I stuck the note on the bottom corner of my computer monitor.

I rubbed my tired eyes. It felt better than getting a full-body massage. I could only imagine how bloodshot they must be. I glanced at my watch before giving my whole face a gentle rubdown.

"A quarter past nine already," I said through a yawn. After a quick cold-water wash-up, I'll head back to my apartment and—

CHAPTER 32

The scent of fir and spruce gave the cool air a gentle crispness. Trees surrounded me in every direction. Moss-covered trunks sprang out of old snow that had formed a thin crust of ice. With each step I took, the glaze crumbled, letting my feet sink into ankle-deep fluff.

I climbed a rill, basking in the morning sun, reveling in the songs of —nothing. The forest was silent. Snow-flocked tree branches devoured the crunch of the paper-thin ice beneath me, returning no echo.

Once over the crest, I came upon a clearing, a windswept outcropping of angular boulders. Snow had never touched this rock, and its surrounding earth lay freshly turned.

Down the mountain ran a wide, crooked gash of turmoil, as though some drunken god had dragged their finger down the face of the mountain slope. On either side of the crevasse, mammoth stone slabs lay strewn like dominoes. The youngest conifers, with their notoriously shallow roots, had toppled like bowling pins. Of those trees left standing, the snow had shaken off their boughs, and they tilted every which way.

A new odor made my nose wrinkle. Mixed with the earthy loam and oily spice of the trees lurked scents that hinted at even more destruction. It took a moment to recognize the sting of smoke was laced with the taint of raw sewage. Something else in the pungent mix explained the stinging itch in my mouth and nostrils—not the sweet aroma of wood burning in a campfire, but the noxious combustion of treated lumber, petrochemicals, plastics and metal.

To the west, a thin rain of cinders dimmed the setting sun. They billowed from the wreckage of a city on fire. I raised my hand to shield against the direct sunlight as I surveyed the distant ruination. A handful of business towers poked several stories above the black clouds churning in the city's center. The smoke remained motionless, neither rising from their heat nor shearing away from any wind. The burning buildings were laced with frozen fire.

Time stood still here.

On the nearest mountain to the east, ski lift towers strewn like broken toothpicks laced the open slopes near an expansive lodge. Halfway down my own mountainside stood the remains of a radio tower next to a large log building. The tower had snapped in two, blocking the service road leading to a highway at the bottom of the valley. A small avalanche had swept across the service road and highway as well, bringing down power and telephone poles alike. If anyone had been in the building, their access to escape, assistance, and rescue was blocked.

I viewed again the three areas where humans had left their mark across the majesty of the pristine mountains. I shook my head and gnawed on my lower lip. Everything looked so familiar, *smelled* so familiar. Yet I could not recall where it was that I found myself.

As I tramped down the hillside, the mortared log structure tugged at my memory. Following parallel to the crack in the earth, I was forced to double back when faced with another crevice filled with loose rock. Crossing over the first slab that forded over the fissure, I was soon surrounded by a thick copse of trees.

A dim trickle of orange sunlight far below beckoned me forward to what I hoped would be another clearing.

I took a step. A footfall echoed behind me.

I whirled about. The lessons of the wilderness Erwin—*Father*—had taught me flooded back. I scoured the snow for prints—deer, wolf, moose, bear. Hugging the nearest boulder, I peered into the forest as best as the army of drunken trees permitted.

Other than myself, nothing moved.

Finding a broken branch of sufficient heft, I stripped it best as I could with my bare hands. I reasoned a walking stick was needed for the uncertain terrain, though it sure would come in handy as a weapon in a pinch. I continued down the slope until I heard the crunch of glazed snow behind me again.

This time, my instincts told me to turn slowly. I gripped my impromptu staff with both hands. A startled wild animal, especially an

Alaskan moose or a grizzly bear, can spell the end for almost anyone.

Alaska. I'm in Alaska.

I hadn't been there since I was six years old. Even so, my earliest memories there were only of the day we had left Anchorage. I stared at the city with a terrible pang of recognition. The building nestled on the hillside below yanked out another murky memory—the national park office where Father had been stationed.

How did I get here?

Another crackle of ice shot me back to the here and now.

From behind a western columbine shrub and a toppled fir rose a slender humanoid figure made of shadow.

It stood with the strength and grace of a forest animal. Once fully erect, it surpassed me by an inch or two. Its silhouette in transparent gray froze my heart between beats—but only for a moment.

Unlike the gray shapeshifters, no bones or internal organs were discernible. In fact, its total lack of features tended to trick the eye into believing it was two-dimensional, like a living shadow puppet.

The gray figure tilted its head and sniffed the air like an inquisitive fox. Its shadowy outline suggested long, straight hair that gave way to expose pointed ears.

I gulped noisily when I put two and two together—it was this thing's reflection that I had glimpsed in the Eldridge lobby window high above the city.

The shadow took a step toward me.

I brandished my walking stick like a baseball bat.

"Greetings, Michael," it said, raising a flat, gray, open hand. Its voice was gentle and melodic, a snowfall of musical notes.

"You know me?"

"Oh, yes," it said in tones delicate as the touch of a lamb's fleece. "I have been with you, watching for a long time."

"Well, *that's* unsettling. And just plain rude." I choked up on my branch, ready to swing for a home run at its head. "Are you one of Eldridge's spies, a remote viewer? Or the cleanup crew for the shapeshifters?"

"You misunderstand. I have not watched you; I have watched *with* you."

It pointed at my green eye. "Through there." Then, its hand touched the top of its cranium and rubbed along a line. Exactly where my scar would be. "From here."

My shoulders twitched. "Oh God, it's a tumor. I'm having a halluci-nation. I can feel it metastasizing."

"I assure you, I am not a hallucination."

"Just what a brain cancer-induced hallucination would say."

"Would a hallucination help you vanquish unwelcome empaths?"

My heart pounded a handful of repetitions. "*You* protected me from Pellagati?" The branch grew suddenly heavy.

"That was I, though I still remained in my confinement."

"Elrameshe and the Aptitude Stones, too?"

"Though a friend, entry was still forbidden to Elrameshe. The Blue Watcher wished me harm. My silver prison repelled his attack."

"Elrameshe and *Turia Feir* were both elves. Why did one help and the other attack?"

"That is indeed a mystery."

My hostile stance faltered. "Who are you?"

It lowered its hand. Tilting its head to the other side, seemingly to look at the ground, it shook its head slightly, then faced me again. "I am not sure."

"*What* are you?"

After a pause, it replied, "I know what I am *not*. I am neither Euryale nor Elrameshe, nor the Blue Watcher, nor a gray shapeshifter, nor an Oovlid. Neither am I human."

"Why are you here?"

"Waiting for you, I think. We were both brought here." It advanced down the slope a few steps. Despite the androgynous quality of its voice, its profile and the way it carried itself suggested it was masculine. It paused several feet to my side, within reach of my branch.

"There is something here. Something we need to see." He continued down the slope, cautious and lithe as a cat. The ice crinkled lightly under his weight. His footprints were not as deep as mine, and their impressions were those of a bare foot.

"We?"

"Do you not feel its call, Michael?"

I lowered my makeshift weapon, resuming its use as a walking stick. I followed him, matching my steps next to his. We hiked along the edge of a snow-filled gully littered with a slurry of deep snow pocked by heavy stones.

As we descended, a hoary mist rose from those spots where sunlight struck the snow and ice, both in the trees and on the ground. The mist marked our passage only slightly. Everywhere else, curls of turbulent steam hovered without movement.

We clambered over fields of stone mixed in with rivers of snow from an avalanche. The lower we climbed, the spilth of snow gave way to a landslide, a river of mud and stone. Trees were sheared and smashed to shattered stumps. Trunks of once-tall trees, splintered as easily as twigs, had floated along the rapids of rock, piling along the sides of the stilled tumult like leaves trapped in the shallows of a rushing stream.

The morning sun bore down on the river of earth, driving up a roiling mist. I caught a last glimpse of the smoldering city before we trudged down into a damp layer denser than San Francisco's morning fogs.

My Shadow companion led us beyond the edge of the rock flow into another area of thickening trees, untouched by chaos. I followed him until we halted at the edge of a clearing, where we bore witness to a tragedy frozen in time.

CHAPTER 33

Seven figures had assembled, standing in a circle around a febrile glow. Their shadows sliced dark tunnels through the gray fog. In their midst lay two brightly lit bodies, arranged in repose on the ground.

Shadow and I advanced slowly, solemnly. As we approached, the mist parted, and the figures became clear, illuminated by a central ball of blue, green, and red swirls, burning bright as a star brought to Earth.

Beams from the sun streaked into the clearing, but did not fall in straight lines as Nature would dictate. They arced through the air as rays through a curved prism, diving into the multicolored sphere of energy.

From that orb of seething magic, two searing rays of the purest white beamed into the faces of the fallen figures. Their mud-caked, blood-stained bodies contradicted the reverential manner with which they had been lain.

The larger of the pair was a young Forest Elf, clad in silvered chain mail. From his chest protruded a tangle of flesh, metal, and nightmare.

Some *thing* had torn through the left plate of his armored chest like it was tin foil. Though blurred like smeared paint, I still could make out it had a chitinous shell and more digits than a human hand, tearing out several of his ribs. Sliced cleanly off at what could have been an elbow joint, the limb hinted at a monstrously large jet-black crab with hands instead of pincers. Its pitch-black blood stained a sizable patch of the youth's armor.

The other victim was a human boy, dressed in winter clothes torn by stone and wood, and streaked with blood. His scalp was a red chaos of gore.

"Good God, he's barely a child." In this place, my whisper seemed as blasphemous as the vilest curse flung at the heavens.

The crowns of the slain's heads touched at the feet of three figures. Though the central trio were undoubtedly elves, two of them were a type I had never seen before. The three stood over the broken bodies, each wearing a different color of garb, with unique circlets upon their heads and pendants around their necks.

I sucked a halting breath between gritted teeth. Over the child stood a female elf with a chilling resemblance to a shapeshifter. Unlike them, however, her dark ashen skin was supple and solid. Oversized eyes hinted that her species had evolved in a lightless environment, not unlike the denizens of the deepest oceans or darkest caves. Her countenance showed no malice. If anything, the elf's expression was that of pitiful remorse.

Upon her head rested a band of onyx. Captured in black stone, strange reptilian creatures with six legs ringed her long black hair, each devouring the tail of the next creature. Her hands, sleeved in a gown of radiant crimson that glowed as brightly as the carmine gem draped from her neck, guided one of the blinding curved tubes of white light onto the deceased boy's head.

In the center stood an elven sorceress of regal stature. Her auburn hair surrounded a sun-kissed angular face adorned with a delicate nose and eyes of stunning green.

"Elrameshe?" I cried out, stepping closer. Only then did I realize it wasn't the Forest Elf I expected. Whoever she was, she might have been beautiful without her timeless expression of frantic urgency.

Her head was crowned with a band of wrought silver consisting of two thin intertwined lines of salamanders. She wore an iridescent green gown that seemed like it had been carved from veined tourmaline. Circling her neck draped two silver chains, the links of which resembled the scales of a serpent. From one dangled a gem of emerald, precisely like the one Elrameshe had worn. The longer chain hung suspended between her neck and an amulet floating inches above her breasts. Drawn toward the ball of light like iron to a magnet, it contained three stones—sapphire, ruby, and emerald. All shaped like teardrops, the three gemstones were mounted in spirals of braided gold, silver, and steel.

The same shape as the knit bone sutures of my healed skull.

Between her outstretched hands hovered the ball of focused sunlight. In her face, lambent from the power she wielded before her, held wild eyes focused on the energy her hands commanded. I could only guess what words of power were being uttered from her open and tortured mouth.

The third sorceress, clad in blue, had skin so pale she seemed to have been carved from old ivory. Her face was surrounded by a waterfall of platinum blonde hair bound together by a headband of gold, depicting a chain of winged dragons with eyes of sapphire.

Fear and hope were harshly sketched across the white elf's face. Her hands and blue gemstone guided the second of the argent beams of light from the rainbow sphere into the fallen warrior's face.

At each of the slain's feet huddled a pair of mourners.

A man and a woman crouched near the child's supine body. Their features were curiously blurred, like they were painted from a broken memory.

The man's plaid shirt burned orange and black in the light, and his frazzled hair flickered with St. Elmo's fire. He held up one arm to shield his face from the searing light. His other arm dangled uselessly, the forearm wrapped in a makeshift splint of torn shirt and branches. Though obscured by mud-matted hair, the woman's smeared face still plainly painted a tormented pastiche of screaming grief. Kneeling by the shoulder of the child, she hovered over him, her hands near his glowing face. The arch of her fingers left no question that she desperately wanted to caress it but was held back by fear.

Near the other fallen body stood a pair of Forest Elves, male and female. Like the green sorceress, their heads were adorned with thin salamander bands. Hers sparkled in the light with highlights of gold, his with steel.

The female stood at the feet of her lost comrade. Her expression of grief was subdued, though it was pierced by her burning gaze, focused on the face of her fallen kinsman. At an earlier time, her tattered and torn clothes might have been fitting for a lady of some mythical royal court. In her hands, she held an ornate wooden box with platinum corners.

I gasped, retreating a step when I recognized the box the female held was similar in color, size, and shape—though carved with a different design—to the one Dr. Fleischer had possessed. The box that held the *Lapidibus Habilitas*, the Aptitude Stones that tried to crush my skull.

The male stood behind the female. His body faced obliquely away from the gathering, his right hand holding a curious longsword at a defensive angle. Though wooden, it still held an edge that looked like it could cut anything—and probably did. It dripped gobs of black blood. Every inch of his warrior's shimmering mail and armored joints was streaked with blood—both red and black—and strips of gore.

Bloodlust raged in his angular features, the only chink being the grief in his eyes as they focused askance toward his fallen comrade.

The Shadow tread quietly, circling the figures like a detective surveying a crime scene. He approached each of the five upright Elves closely, though never touching them. Finally, he knelt by the fallen elf. I approached the slain human child.

Their faces burned bright in the concentrated rays of redirected sunlight. Its radiance was so blinding that it obscured their features, though the youth's mortal wound was laid bare. Gray matter hung out of an open crater near the top of his head. Splinters of wood and shards of rock, caked in blood, clung to his hair.

I examined the faces of the humans again. Despite their smeared faces, their grief and terror, I felt I should have recognized them. My mind became as clouded as the dreamy frozen mists surrounding us.

"What on Earth happened here?" I said. "Who are these people?"

"Can you not see, Michael?" Shadow rose, standing over the fallen elf. "This is where we died."

CHAPTER 34

"Rise and shine, Alaska!"

For a split second, the sensation of falling overcame me, like my mind and soul were poured back into my body. My head jerked up, and my arms shot out, splaying over the desk. Empty binders crashed onto the floor, followed closely by a flurry of loose documents. The aroma of a coniferous forest marred by the stench of Anchorage in ruins evaporated, replaced with the hint of burnt coffee.

That *couldn't* have been a dream. For one thing, I've never dreamed in color. The memory of the sorceress's radiant gowns and the Forest Elf's blazing multicolored spell proved it. Besides, I didn't think it possible to smell odors in a dream. A vision, then?

"This is where we died."

I am often amazed at what the human mind is capable of. Failing to realize truths staring you in the face is one of them.

That child was me. The slain elven warrior was Shadow.

He died. I died.

That's why I don't remember anything before the age of six.

Intuitive leaps are another.

Those were my parents.

They were there. They knew I had died.

No wonder Mother slowly went insane, knowing I was not the same Michael she had lost.

That brain mass isn't cancer. It's the result of the spell cast by those three elves.

I was their vessel. I carried Shadow inside of me.

Nagging questions sprung up to replace the old ones.

How much of me is me*? How much is Shadow?*

Why did my parents go through the pretense of adoption?

Why was I shown this now—

"I said, wake up," said Natalie, her voice solid as a pipe wrench. "Sakes alive, you been here all night? That's a risky proposition."

I pivoted in my chair toward the voice while rubbing sleep gunk from my eyes. Natalie blocked the doorway of my cubicle. Her wardrobe had reverted to Oklahoma casual.

"I guess so," I managed to say through a yawn. "I just finished all..." A warning bell went off in my sluggish head—don't slip up about Uncle Billy-Bob's spell.

"I guess I conked out while studying," I said. "What's so dangerous about falling asleep here?"

"You have to ask? Loads of people on Eldridge's upper floors have a PQ of some level. Even when they call it quits for the day, they still leave dribs and drabs of ectoplasmic residue all over the place. I shouldn't have to tell you every inch of this place gets soaked with it. You open your sub-conscious up to all that leftover psychic energy when you sleep."

"I'll be more careful next time."

"No." She stamped her foot. "There will be no next time. Trust me, you don't want to be here on those random nights when the psychic cleaners come through. And you definitely *don't* want to be asleep."

Cocking my head at her, I switched gears. "Wait a minute, I thought you wanted nothing to do with me, being the company reprobate and all?"

"Petrakis backed you up," she said after an irritated sigh. "I'm stuck as your mentor." She leaned against my cubicle's entry. "So, you have any questions for me after your all-nighter?"

"As a matter of fact—"

"Too bad. Straighten up your cubicle first, then read the handbook, or get your butt to the library. See me after lunch if you still can't figger out your answers." She gave me a two-finger salute. "I may be your mentor, but I ain't your teacher or an instruction book."

Two cubicles down, she complained, "Criminy, it's cold in there. You better not have messed with the floor's thermostat, Alaska."

I stood to stretch but toppled back into my chair.

My legs had fallen asleep, and my feet were freezing cold. A quick look gave my spine another shiver. My shoes were damp. Shards of ice and melting snow clung to their laces. Faced with physical proof it was no mere dream nor some ephemeral ectoplasm, my questions gained extra urgency.

Who was Shadow? What kind of Elves were those two others? Did this vision come by random, or did Shadow show it to me? Or someone else?

Snapping myself out of my introspection, I decided to comply with Natalie's instructions. It was too early in the morning to put up a fight.

Once I kicked the slush off my shoes and stacked the binders out of the way, I collected all the papers and forms I had knocked off my desk. My inbox, to-do, and outbox piles had mixed themselves with my other office papers in a three-way Faro shuffle. Sorting the chaff from the wheat, I stalled when I came upon a multipage spreadsheet. After a minute of racking my poor, sleep-stunned brain, I recognized what I was holding—the snapshot of Eldridge employees meant for Algernon, courtesy of Jolly.

I wrestled with my conscience whether to toss the database in the circular file or fess up to Jolly, when an idea gave me goosebumps. At first, it didn't feel right to make a forever-remembered copy of employees' info, but where my skin is involved, rationalization is a powerful mind-changer. After all, I died once already, and any number of creatures were out for a second bite at the apple. I eideticized the papers and tossed the blanks away.

Once locked away in my noggin, it was a no-brainer what to do with that treasure trove of information—search for the people who held the keys to unlocking the answers I needed.

After a moment of concentration, I found the first one, plain as day.

Dr. Fleischer, accompanied by her data—including where I could find her. My heart stripped its gears, going from joyful anticipation to full reverse abject frustration.

"She's in Heidelberg?" I snarled under my breath. Recalling the pages from the handbook, I browsed through the list of E&SQA locations around the globe. Heidelberg wasn't one of them. The closest one was Prague.

So close, yet so far.

Or was I? I scratched my head over her phone number. In addition to the usual four-digit extension, it was preceded by a "#69#" prefix. I had nothing to lose, so I punched in the numbers on my desk phone.

A long string of electronic blips followed by an unfamiliar ringtone indicated my call had been forwarded to an international line. I wondered what time it was in Heidelberg. It was a quarter after nine here, so that made it—

"*Hallo?*"

"Hello, Dr. Fleischer?"

"*Ja.*" Her voice was a little hoarse, but that was to be expected. Ventnor explained she had to heal without the aid of magic.

"This is Michael Yeager. I hope you remember me from a few weeks ago. I'm so glad your voice has recovered. You were so badly wounded, I thought—"

"*Wer ist?*" she said, followed by broken English. "Who this is?"

"Michael Yeager," I replied slowly. "You did my post-orientation assessment."

"Your whats?"

"My PQ assessment after orientation."

"*Pey kew?* No such things at *Universität Heidelberg*." Annoyance grew in her tone.

"Don't you remember? We were interrupted when the Aptitude Stones attacked us."

"Attacks?" she screeched. "Young mans, I do not know who you be, but you picked the wrong womans to pranks and threatens. I'm reportings you to the *polizei*."

"Wait, do you know who Alberich—"

A harsh click, and the line trilled with a disconnection signal.

I smacked the receiver back to its cradle and glowered at the phone's keypad as I puzzled over what just happened. It was Fleischer's voice, but I was essentially talking to a stranger, like she had been...

I blinked at the keypad when it struck me that her phone number's prefix stood for the letters of the words on the tip of my tongue—Mind Wipe.

I rapped my desk in frustration. The one person who might enlighten me about Shadow's identity—and how it related to this mysterious Alberich—had been removed from the equation.

Did I say a quarter after nine? That meant Petrakis had already started the morning group meeting, and I was unforgivably late. I grabbed my journal and Amelia.

Slowing down as I neared our meeting room, I noticed the door was ajar an inch. I sidled up to get a preview of what I'd be walking into.

Petrakis and Barandir were discussing a point that pricked up my ears.

"Were you able to make a translation?" asked Petrakis.

"None that make sense. The most promising clue points toward a proto-Elven language. Ten words, two of them most probably proper nouns, are not a large enough sample to determine a language or their meaning."

"Proper nouns? You mean a person's name?"

"Their use of *Phelek Lepan* implies it is a location. But Eldridge has no previous record of that name."

"Do Elves have anything like fairy tales?" asked Sofia.

"Excuse me?" Barandir sounded like she tweaked his nose.

"Traditional fables elven parents tell their children before bedtime. Scary stories to coax them to behave."

"You know," said Hector. "Be a good little boy or the wicked witch will getcha."

"I resent that," said petulant Sofia.

"Take it up with *Abuela* Castellanos, God rest her soul."

"We know these creatures are evil," she continued, giving Hector the side eye. "Perhaps there is a Forest Elf fable of a place where bad little boys and girls go."

"The peoples of *Tawar Cevan* have no such stories," said Barandir. "But there is a cautionary tale among the *Kala-kwente*."

That made my ears prick up. Not the Forest Elves, the *Koire-kwente*?

Barandir leaned back in his seat, interlocking his slender fingers. "The story of *Laer-amrûn and Niquis* is a sad tale of two star-crossed lovers. The epic poem lasts up to three hours in its telling."

"A summary would be appreciated," said Petrakis. The room collectively breathed a sigh of relief.

"Laer-amrûn was the son of a mighty duke among the *Kala-kwente*, the High Elves, and Niquis the daughter of a lowly *Mori-kwente* Gray Elf peasant. They fell in love, despite the duke's wishes and the misgivings of the *Mori-kwente* elders. Moreover, they ignored the warnings of the Two Brothers, the most powerful mages of their peoples. Laer-amrûn and Niquis eloped, fleeing to a far-away land that had never seen the *Kala-kwente* nor the *Mori-kwente*. In the fullness of time, Niquis bore Laer-amrûn a healthy son, or so they thought. The child grew quickly, faster than they could believe. They resolved to return home, beg forgiveness, and seek the wisdom of their clans, but they never made it to either of their ancestral lands. One fateful night, the child transformed into a hideous monster that slew and ate both its parents. The story ends with the Laer-amrûn's and Niquis's abomination still prowling the lands."

"Cheery," quipped Natalie.

"No mention of this *Phelek* place?" asked Petrakis.

"None." Barandir took a long sip from his tea elixir. "Morality plays aside, I've reached the limit of what Eldridge has on file. If I am to pursue this further, I will need to travel and confer with my sources."

"Granted," said Petrakis. "Send me the paperwork, and I'll approve it immediately. You leave today."

That was my cue to join in. "What's all this about High and Gray elves? When was anybody going to tell *me* about them? I sure could have used that info before—"

Every head snapped toward me standing in the doorway. Their faces bore looks of alarm, except for Petrakis. He had a glower that could steam out the most stubborn wrinkle. "What are you doing here?" He stood up so quickly, his chair rolled back a few inches. "You are still on probation, Dr. Yeager. Return to your desk and continue your studies."

Petrakis shut the door in my face. I had to hop back a step to avoid getting my nose flattened.

My little "*it's just an act*" mantra didn't calm me down. I stormed back to my cubicle and stewed in my own juices.

I brought up the eideticized contents of that sleep-inducing class, *Cryptids 220: Elves*. Sure enough, there they were—High and Gray elves, the *Kala-kwente* and the *Mori-kwente*. Did I fall asleep a second time while I memorized this course? No, they were buried in the coursework foot-notes, easily missed while I digested four weeks of classes over one night.

Apparently, they came from a world other than that of the Forest Elves, a horrible wasteland named *Band Cevan*. These two species of elves, both described as wholly unsavory, periodically sent raiding parties to the Forest Elves' world, *Tawar Cevan*. But they didn't plunder or pillage. They kidnapped the forest folk and absconded with them back to the hellhole of *Band Cevan*, sometimes entire families and villages.

The saddest part? Once a Forest Elf was abducted, they were never heard from again. Understandably, little else was known of the *Kala-kwente* or *Mori-kwente*—other than these bastards were the primary rea-son the Forest Elves sought sanctuary on Earth with Eldridge.

I scratched my head, carefully avoiding my scar. The vision Shadow and I shared, and the elves in them, sure didn't match the villainous stereotypes that the footnote made them out to be. Regardless of race, every single one displayed not hatred, but regret, concern, empathy... and even love.

Love that I haven't seen since...

A well-deserved pang of guilt slapped me in the face. I had been so wrapped up in my own problems that I hadn't given a moment's thought about Sindhu. It was high time to redress my neglect. I had almost two weeks to remedy that and give her the consideration she deserved.

I closed my eyes, recalled Jolly's eideticized employee info dump, and poked around. The first hurdle was determining what the heck an ILTS-CA was, and where to find it.

The first clue lay hidden away in the damned Relationship Rules— it stood for Intrusion Long-Term Storage. From there it was easy to deduce the suffixes—CA, NY, UK, etc.—corresponded to Eldridge locations. I supposed there was a certain logic to it—not every Godzilla heads straight to Tokyo, after all.

A quick check of the company directory didn't shed any light on where Sacramento's intrusion stockyard might be.

Another curiosity made me sit up and take notice. I hoped no one was watching. They would have seen a guy with his eyes closed and eyebrows doing a Russian squat-kick dance.

All the recently-relocated staff associated with ILTS were Scandinavian. No expert in the etymology of surnames, I couldn't tell if they hailed from Sweden, Norway, Finland, or Denmark. Not only that, every one's new position was designated as security.

The "Position" column contained a menagerie of acronyms that was easy enough to decode. Us grunt employees were "EMPL," oracles were "SEER," and security staff were designated as "SECU."

But Sindhu's designation of "RPIN" in the "Acquisitions" table stopped me cold. I puzzled over it for several minutes, left with nothing better than a guess of "Registered Private Intrusion Nurse." A quick rummage of my eideticized material yielded nothing to clear it up.

So where to find out?

Two guesses.

CHAPTER 35

I shared the elevator with a group that included a woman wearing a toga and a mask of brass covering everything above her mouth. I shouldn't have been surprised Eldridge was crawling with oracles, as almost every ATPG has a seer. Typically, they're not this ostentatious. I tried not to stare, seeing that no one else did.

She turned her head toward me. A small scoff escaped her ruby lips, and her metallic mask flexed into an expression of disapproval as it met my eyes.

I've heard something called Botox is moving toward FDA approval. I swear I'll be first in line to have it injected into my eyebrows.

By the time we reached the library floor, everyone except me and Ms. Mask had left the elevator. When I exited, she remained inside. I regarded her with curiosity.

Her mask's metallic cheeks rose as if it were attempting to smile. Her flesh and blood mouth, however, remained flat. "The rejected man looks for you," she said. "Do not avoid him. He will help your search, and you shall learn hidden strengths." She pressed a button, and the doors slid shut.

"*Pfft*. And Jupiter is ascendant in the House of Pancakes to you too, lady."

Entering through the seemingly sentient ceiling-height library doors, I strolled around the information carousels on either side of the entrance. I soon found the booklet I hoped would be there: the layout of the Sacramento E&SQA building. Most floors were annotated with department locations. The inside front cover had what I needed—a listing of each level.

The first four floors above and below ground were strictly Mundane levels, housing most of the day-to-day functions of an everyday Nothing-to-see-here corporation. Security dominated every tenth floor.

The various other levels were organized haphazardly, at least to my non-MBA way of thinking. Logistics on one floor; accounting (including us lowly ATPG grunts), assessments, adjustments on another; earth-bound, magical, and alien research; oracle central; technology development —I couldn't make heads or tails of the method to the floor assignment madness.

The ATPG Alpha and Omega sections were the exception. Each occupied only one level: Alpha occupied sub-basement five, the lowest of the business floors, below two levels of executive parking and two more of shipping and receiving. Omega commanded the highest floor listed.

The twelve floors built below ATPG Alpha were listed as non-human residential levels. Given that something under the Alpha interroga-tion room growled at me, I couldn't help but imagine they were more zoo compartments than residences.

I bit my lower lip in frustration. Nothing to indicate where ILTS might be.

Not seeing any notation for a vice president level either, I reasoned Hibara and his workforce had to be on one of the upper unlisted floors. I didn't care to linger too long on what occupied the other eleven topmost levels, by my counting of the floors from the outside.

A statuesque woman approached me. Wearing a smart cactus-green pantsuit in the style that seemed the latest fashion craze, she regarded me with inquisitive eyes and a welcoming smile. A small patch of vitiligo resembling a small treble clef on one cheek marred her otherwise perfect complexion. After a second thought, I felt it rather enhanced her features, like an oversized beauty mark. About her neck hung a pendant of gold in the shape of an open book, its pages shaped from a deep lavender opal.

"Hello, Dr. Yeager," she said. "Your first time in an Eldridge library?"

My guts turned, trying to find the nearest rock they could crawl under. I recognized her voice. It was attached to the avenging silhouette who chastised Barandir when I cast Uncle Billy-Bob's eideticize spell in one of the reading rooms.

"No, I was here the other day." My voice warbled like a boy in the throes of puberty. "But I'm sure I barely scratched the surface of the library's content." I covered my mouth with the booklet and cleared my throat. "You know me, Ms...?"

"Ms. Mertens, Head Librarian, Sacramento Branch," she said, shaking my hand. "Not directly. I'm an old acquaintance of a relative of yours."

"I suppose you mean Uncle Chuck? I'm sorry to disappoint, but I never met him."

Her smile continued unabated. "You certainly have the Yeager nose."

"I thought the entire company had a directive to avoid me at all costs."

"Yes, I've heard of your recent misadventures." A cunning smile leaked out. "That doesn't affect my responsibilities in the slightest. Is there anything in particular you're looking for today?"

I waved the booklet. "Just this, but it's not complete. You wouldn't happen to know on what level I might find Intrusion Long-Term Storage?"

Her face registered disappointment, almost to an abject extreme.

That did it. I had no defense against a pout that earnest. "On second thought, Ms. Mertens, I *am* curious about one of my uncle's exploits. My mentor told me about an incident involving a djinn guarding the sound barrier? Is his intrusion assessment report available?"

"Actually, he was the adjuster assigned to that case." She beamed a bright smile. "But yes, all his records are on file. If you would follow me, please?"

Past the central lighthouse, up a stairway or two we went. The pair of us turned the heads of librarians and readers alike. Uncomfortable memories rushed back. The last time this many people barraged me with gawps of surprise and sneers of disdain was when Ventnor dragged Petrakis and me up to my audience with Hibara.

I followed Mertens from the top floor's central open area to an unassuming desk next to a door and a card reader. The door was labeled "Controlled Access – Central Records," under which hung a plastic placard listing a small army of rules and regulations.

On either side of the door, windows afforded a panoramic view overlooking the outskirts of Sacramento. I sidled up to one window pane, trying to eye where the secured door led. The corridor I presumed to be there, *wasn't*—only open air.

The young gentleman seated behind the desk shot us an inquisitive glance. "Yes, Ms. Mertens?"

"Myself and Dr. Yeager," she replied. The gatekeeper opened and spun around a leather-bound visitors' book, which we both signed. He stood, taking out an access card with a slick lighthouse design.

"No need," said Mertens with a lilt. She produced her own card and slid it through the reader.

She opened the door, not to open air but to the cavernous interior of a gigantic warehouse. A few paces away, another desk faced us, staffed by a bookish woman of an olive complexion. Three pencils stuck out of her hair. One rested above each ear, the third skewered her hair bun like Excalibur in the stone. A wooden nameplate announced "Central Records Librarian" in gleaming brass letters.

"Good evening, Ms. Mertens," said the woman, with a heavy Middle Eastern accent.

"Good morning, Ms. Mostafa. How are things in Alexandria today?"

"Stifling hot. Thank goodness for air conditioning."

As we walked past the desk, Mertens said, "No need to bother yourself. I know exactly where I'm going."

"I should hope so," said Mostafa with a cheery chuckle.

I looked over my shoulder when I heard another door open behind us. The wall through which we had entered stood lined with not one but several doors. On either side of ours stood a row of identical doorways, with labels such as "New York," "Tokyo," and every primary E&SQA location from around the globe.

"Oh, I get it. *Central* records."

We walked past at least a city block's worth of towering bookshelves, each with a rolling ladder attached. One Cyclopean bookshelf held arrays of dusty scrolls in diamond-shaped cubbyholes, guarded by a placard requiring the use of cotton gloves.

"How far back does the library go? I mean, how long has Eldridge been maintaining records?"

"Since the first cave painting," Mertens replied, "since the first cuneiform. Since the first oral tradition evolved into a written language. Since the very first Old Magic."

"I'd hate to pay the overdue fee for the Babylonian who failed to return the first stone tablet."

Mertens obliged me with a polite giggle. She made a right turn, heading down a hall of bookshelf ends. Every bookshelf was stuffed with an array of identical black clothbound binders. Each oaken panel was adorned with a lamp fixture and a range of numbers.

"His records are here?" I asked, baffled by the placards and their indecipherable organization method.

"Just a few more rows," she said. The clack of her heels echoed down the intersecting corridors. "And here we are," she said, turning left into the next aisle. From a waist-high shelf, she tilted out a binder. Running her finger down the row, she pulled out another.

Watching her, I noted the two binders and every one in between bore the same series of digits on the spine. "Is that his employee number?"

"Correct." Mertens pulled the third from last from his volumes. Opening it, she thumbed through its pages. She handed the binder to me.

The section divider was well-worn. I skimmed through the report, avoiding the more technical sections, including the dreaded "Ambient PQ Level." The actual event description read like an old pulp fiction novel, ending with Uncle-twice-removed Chuck driving the X-15 experimental rocket jet straight through the heart of Irhuriji, Archduke of Aircraft Gremlins.

"Thank you, Ms. Mertens. Quite riveting," I said before handing it back.

"Yes, it is." After returning all the binders to their original positions, she advanced to the next row and pulled out another of the ubiquitous binders. At the end of a shelf only half filled, it was one of a pair that bore my employee number. It held quite a few pages, many more than my recent Assessment Report. "It seems the family penchant for adventure has rubbed off on you."

"Believe me, I've been trying to keep my adventure to a minimum."

"Really? I guess only time will tell." She scanned the last of the pages, nodding her head in approval. "Impressive. Your report is well written and complete—quite unusual for a new employee."

I clasped my hands behind me. My feet shifted uncomfortably, and my collar had a touch of dampness. "Dr. Petrakis is a good teacher."

Mertens replaced the binder, sashayed past me, and invited me to follow. "Is there anything else you'd like to see before we leave Central Records?"

"I'm not sure," I said while catching up to walk beside her. "An hour ago, I was unaware of this area's existence or what it might contain. But as long as you're asking, is there any documentation on Eldridge's ILTS facilities? I couldn't find it on our building's map. Does it occupy a common space like this?"

A look of concern troubled her face. "Why are you so interested in the ILTS areas?"

Thinking fast, I managed not to stumble over my own tongue. "My ATP group seems to have run into a dead end trying to determine the nature of the creatures that attacked me and my supervisor. I was wondering if we had anything similar in storage."

"Oh, yes." she tapped her chin. "That explains a recent incident with one of your group members, Mr. Robert B. P. Boyce."

"Yes, Barandir was trying to determine the language they used. I hope he isn't in trouble on my behalf."

"Not terribly, but now that we know that little tidbit, I'm sure his record will be expunged."

"Thank you. That'll be a load off both our minds." Retracing our steps to the Sacramento exit, the silence begged to be filled. "Not to be a broken record, but about the ILTS? Is there a way I can visit or at least view a list of the creatures housed there? If I can examine the ILTS, I might spot an intrusion like the ones I faced, or a similar creature that can clue us in as to what we're facing." The thought of Sindhu stashed away in ILTS made my mouth taste of copper. A dozen different horrors flipped through the movie theater of my mind, imagining what her facilities might look like.

Mertens gave her head her shiver. "Yes, the ILTS. I apologize—my mind was elsewhere. Each Eldridge location has their own intrusion storage area, with its two-letter designation."

"I kinda guessed that on my own, though I wasn't sure why each location required one."

"A surprising amount of intrusions are tied to a place. Move them far enough away, and undesired effects can result. Like every ILTS, ours is located at the lowest levels of our building. But access is severely restricted. You can't just pull out an intrusion like a reference volume."

My shoulders sagged. "I understand."

"However, I can arrange for you to visit their Green Room—their nickname for their first security zone." She waved again at Mostafa as we passed her desk.

"You should receive clearance in two weeks or so."

"That long?" It was my turn to pout.

"Not until you've been released from probation," she said with a polite smile. "I read Dr. Petrakis' report along with yours. I'm sorry, but those are the rules."

As she signed us out at the outer desk, I nodded my defeat. "I understand. Thank you for the tour."

I maintained a polite smile until I left the library. Teeth clenched, I brooded at my brushed steel reflection in the elevator door. Frustrated beyond words, I hammered the elevator door frame. After stomping my way back to my cubicle, I was about to plop down in my chair for a good sulk, when I noticed the message light on my phone blinking.

"Mr. Yeager, this is Mr. Pellagati from ATPG Alpha. I hope you remember me from last week?"

Like I would soon forget getting my mind raped.

"I'm sorry for the last-minute notice, but could you stop by my office at your earliest convenience? By the end of business today in any event."

I wrote down his office and phone numbers. He said them extra slow, which I appreciated. One of my pet peeves is cretins who rattle off their numbers at light speed, not realizing the listener isn't familiar with the speaker's info.

While spending a leisurely lunch alone in the cafeteria, I wondered if any of the people—and a few *non*-people—walking past worked in Sacramento's ILTS. Dawdling with the café's terrible coffee until the lunch hour crowd had left, I worked off the calories by strolling around the levels between the cafeteria and my lucky number 13th floor.

I had an ulterior motive as well—I hoped to chance upon a stray clue pinned to a cubicle indicating its occupant worked in the storage facility. None of the SECU security staff from Jolly's eideticized tables had cubicle numbers I could locate. I lost track of time until I gave up.

Actually, "giving up" wasn't the real reason. I tend to do my best thinking during long walks. However, no matter how hard I tried to concentrate on finding Sindhu or how to wrangle my way into ILTS, I got distracted, gnawing on the old bone of getting my mind drilled by Pellagati.

"Enough," I told myself. "Time to get this over with."

CHAPTER 36

I rode the elevator down to the ATP Alpha level.

A female receptionist behind a desk looked inquiringly at me as I exited the elevator. Behind her was a disc of the darkest wood I'd ever seen. Embossed in brass, the corporate logo lay encircled with Latin text —*In V, in M, et S, Mea Fidelitas in A Præcedit.*

I had no idea what the initials might have stood for, but the "loyalty to Alpha first" came as no surprise. Categorizing ATP Alpha as a bunch of gung-ho psychic Marines fit Lenoir and Pellagati perfectly.

The floor's receptionist had dressed in subdued gray and black. Her glasses didn't reflect an image from the computer screen before her. "With whom do you have an appointment?" Her voice had as much inflection as a robot.

"Mr. Pellagati." I added the room number, but she rattled it off, finishing before I did. She pointed down the long hallway, illuminated only where cross halls intersected. "He's expecting you, Mr. Yeager. Third hallway down, turn left, third door on your right."

Following her directions, I noted the main difference of this level. Not a cubicle to be found, only full-fledged offices with doors at regular intervals. No floor-length windows, either—a series of two-foot tall glass transoms along the tops of walls allowed light in or out of each office. The walls soaked up the sound of my footfalls.

I was just about to knock on Pellagati's door, when I tilted my head, my ear close to the doorjamb. Someone was humming a strange tune.

Humming? In this dank, foreboding dungeon?

I knocked. The humming stopped, and Pellagati opened the door. The room reeked of cigarette smoke.

"Come in, Dr. Yeager." He gestured toward a chair inside. Pellagati appeared almost exactly as he did during my interrogation—the same black suit and tie, same pointless comb-over—except he wasn't wearing mirrored aviator frames. I could plainly see his pinkish irises. And he sported an amiable smile.

The room was mostly stark and bare. His desk had been cleared of anything indicating a flesh and blood person ever worked there, save for the ubiquitous computer terminal and a cardboard box filled with office paraphernalia and personal items—photographs, awards and so on. Two items remained on the otherwise emptied shelves lining the wall under the transom windows. A Polaroid X1000, presumably the one he and Lenoir used to measure my PQ, sat on one shelf. A curious box of black pebbled metal lay on the next lower shelf, surrounded by dust bunnies that could no longer hide behind the knick-knacks that had once stood there. Other than its wires, the box had a single feature, a single slot four inches wide on its front panel.

"What's going on?" I hesitated between each word. There were a handful of possibilities: he quit, was fired, or... "Have you been promoted?"

Whatever his reassignment, it happened after Jolly printed out her list.

"Transferred, actually." He signaled again that we both sit. After a pause, he rested his arms on the desk. "And I have *you* to thank for that."

My liver and stomach wrestled to see which could hide behind the other. Though I had eideticized *Psychic Defenses 101*, I still haven't had the chance to study it, let alone practice.

"Me?" I squeaked.

A second of silence felt like an eternity.

"If you're worried I might dive into your psyche and make you spout out embarrassing secrets again, you can put those fears to rest. I've lost my ability as a revealer empath."

"How did that happen?" I knew the answer, of course. Shadow knocked his psychic block off. I was curious where playing dumb would lead.

"I'm not sure. Our medical staff says I suffered a 'psychic whiplash' of sorts."

"And I was the cause of it?"

"It would seem so. I'm sure you recall my physical reaction when I slammed into your psychic defenses."

I did. A measly but climbing PQ-3 at the time, I expected my mental brick wall to hold up as well as a mobile home in a tornado. Seeing Pellagati toss his cookies into the wastepaper basket, though satisfying, was a total surprise.

"It was easy enough for me to slip past your initial defenses and push whatever buttons Ms. Lenoir needed to get you to open up. When you resisted, I did what was required of me. I pressed harder, further in. What I found was quite unique. Even now, I'm not sure how to best describe it."

Pellagati rose out of his seat and leaned against an empty wall while his eyes scoured the floor. "It was like I found a room inside the center of your mind. A room constructed of one-way mirrors. I could sense something was contained within, looking out, watching, listening. At first, I was confused. I felt no avarice, no kindliness, no fear, no emotion of any kind surrounding the area. It was a *tabula rasa*, a blank slate. I tried again and again to pierce the shell, open the door, break through the walls. Until the enclosure moved. It shoved me away—*hard*. It felt like I had a front-end collision without a seat belt or airbag. The doctor who later examined me confirmed I had a mild concussion, an actual physical manifestation from a psychic event."

Like snow on my shoes.

He faced me with his arms crossed across his chest, but his eyes still swept the floor. "I didn't discover I had lost my empathy until my next assignment. Lenoir and I assisted an assessor in questioning witnesses of a routine UFO sighting. I found that I couldn't exert any influence on the Mundanes. My ability was gone—somehow, I knew it was gone for good. As a result, I'm no use to Alpha anymore."

I hoped he didn't expect me to say I was sorry. I folded my arms across my chest as well.

He collected the camera off the shelf and handed it to me. "I know you have little reason to believe me, given Alpha's reputation for duplicity and our personal past history. But you can verify my claims for yourself. In order to be a revealer empath, one has to have at least a PQ-8."

Standing clear of his desk, he planted his feet at shoulder width and spread his arms. "Go ahead, Dr. Yeager, take my measurement."

I raised the camera and shot. The film rolled out, and I took a gander. Who knows what my eyebrows were doing, but the photographic evidence was plain. "PQ-4?"

"Just so," he sighed. His arms flopped down against his side, and he resumed his seat, his back rounded slightly more than before. He kept a brave face and sounded pleased enough, but it didn't jibe with his body language. "Alpha wrote up my transfer papers within one day."

"How is Lenoir taking it? Badly, I hope."

"She's not the type to develop strong attachments. I'm yesterday's news. She's already found another partner, a Mr. Odutola. He's not quite the revealer empath I was, but he still gets the job done."

I set the camera on his desk. Sitting erect, I fixed guarded eyes upon him. "Why are you telling me this? I know you were doing your job, but don't expect any sympathy. Not after what you and Lenoir put me through that day."

"Nor would I expect any." Pellagati stood again, staring at the camera. He stuffed his hands into his pants pockets. "Consider this as my making amends of sorts. Whether you accept it or not, whether you believe me or not, I feel that I must..." He looked me in the eye and cracked a wan grin. "You know, I had a whole speech prepared. The truth is, we here at Alpha never make apologies. So, you'll have to forgive my inexperience. However, now that I'm no longer in Alpha, I feel there are some crooked paths I should make straight."

I slumped back into my chair.

He tilted his head back slightly, looking down his nose at me. His expression didn't strike me as snooty. There was a dire warning in his albino eyes. "Be on your guard. Sable Lenoir is gunning for you."

"I kinda figured that. Last I saw her, I could almost smell the smoke coming out of her ears." I grinned with smarmy satisfaction.

"I don't think you fully appreciate the situation. You don't know her like I do."

I swung one leg over the other. "Enlighten me."

"During the interrogation, Ms. Lenoir wasn't merely barraging you with questions to trip you up, like any good interrogator. She firmly believed you were the perp for Mr. Algernon's poisoning and still does. When Dr. Petrakis whisked you out of her clutches, she took umbrage and harbors it against you and Director Ventnor." He poked a tar-stained finger at me. "She can't do much about a director, so that leaves you."

I shifted uncomfortably in my seat.

"As you might guess," Pellagati continued, "Lenoir demanded every detail of my experience while in your psyche be laid out in my interrogation report. What I described only strengthened Ms. Lenoir's suspicion that you were a mole. I disagreed, as I felt your mirrored bunker was a construct of your mind related to your memory loss at age six. Probably a defense due to some trauma from the Good Friday Earthqua—"

"How the h—" My feet stamped the floor. "How did you find out about that?"

"Alpha has its ways, Dr. Yeager." He shot me a glance of disapproval. "In this case, Lenoir generated a transcript of your conversations with Dr. Azizi at Western Bay State Hospital, courtesy of Petrakis' scribe, Namiki."

I glowered at the floor in consternation. Petrakis was right—scribes are a two-edged sword. At least, there was a silver lining.

Alpha didn't know about Amelia.

"That is but one example of the lengths to which Ms. Lenoir is prepared to go. The details about your 'room of mirrors' in my interrogation report have only focused her. She's handling it... poorly."

It was my turn for a tiny sarcastic gloat. "Gee, that's too bad."

Pellagati placed both hands on his desk and leaned in. "That's not what I mean. You have become her obsession, Dr. Yeager."

"Aw, shucks. I'm flattered," I said, rolling my eyes and flashing a melodramatic smirk. "But I'm already engaged."

"Oh, yes... Your Ms. Mehra. Dr. Yeager, I implore you to take this seriously. If not for your own self-interest, then at least for Sindhu's sake."

That got my attention—and how. My back bolted straight in my seat. "Don't you *dare* threaten her."

"I am not. Neither can Lenoir, even if she wanted to. What I mean is, Sindhu's future looks rather bleak. I don't think it shall improve, if Eldridge is left to their standard procedures."

My blood burned in my cheeks. "What do you mean? I was promised the company would work on a cure for her Euryale infection. Are you saying she might be harmed?"

"She is in no foreseeable danger. But let me ask you a question. Has anyone in E&SQA indicated what priority her cure has been assigned?"

I responded with an irritated, drawn-out "No."

"Despite its unique mission, Eldridge in many ways is similar to most large Mundane corporations. We are constantly pressured to 'do more with less.' As a result, there is always some high-priority project, some threat to Earth, some disaster *de jour* that will take precedence over Ms. Mehra's cure. I'm afraid unless someone stumbles upon a remedy for the infection during an assessment or adjustment, your fiancée will languish in ILTS for a long time. Like forty-two years long, after the next Euryale attack. It's not deliberate, malicious, or managerial laziness. It's just a fact of life."

It became somewhat clearer why that bastard Hibara admitted me into the circle.

Pellagati waited, observing, while I chewed on my thoughts. I went over the events at the Fountain of Agelessness. I couldn't shake the feeling there was something else behind Hibara's seeming beneficence. Sindhu was —to borrow a phrase from science—a necessary but insufficient condition for Eldridge to stop my biological clock. Hibara had another motive, but what was it?

"You might be leaving Alpha, Pellagati, but you still have a knack for ruining my day."

"I am sorry, Dr. Yeager, but if I'm to help you, it's best you know."

"You're *sure* Lenoir can't get to Sindhu?"

"Positive. ILTS has strict rules about interfering with the recovery of a surviving victim. However, *you* are fair game. Lenoir has spent almost every waking moment examining your history, your reports, and everyone you have come in contact with. You are her pet project, and she'll be watching you like a hawk. She's waiting for any slip-up or infraction, any excuse to get you into interrogation again. If you give her the opportunity, you won't just cross swords with her—she will dissect your psyche." Pella-gati grimaced. "Maybe more."

"Is she watching us now?"

Pellagati glanced around the room with a shrug. "I'm pretty sure the answer is 'no.' My position in Alpha isn't high enough to warrant a scribe, and my workstation's microphone is disconnected. Besides, it's considered poor form to surveil one's coworkers without cause, even in Alpha. 'Honor among thieves,' and all that. However, the moment we leave this room, it's best to assume she'll be keeping her eye on both of us."

"Understood." Another chasm of silence as we stared at each other. I didn't feel any probes. "And... thanks."

"Good. Now, let's see what we can do for Ms. Mehra." He retook his seat and rolled up to his computer keyboard. He called up a program, and a request form filled the screen. While he typed a mishmash of information into the blank tabs, he said, "I can grant you access to our ILTS level and maybe even locate where Ms. Mehra is kept—"

"ILTS-CA 2E-718."

Pellagati halted, his hands hovering over the keyboard, as he turned an inquiring eye toward me. "Gold star, Dr. Yeager. Maybe your talents are wasted in ATPG 217. Ever think about a position in Alpha?"

"No, thanks. I'd be spreading my legs and bending over too often." We shared a chuckle, and Pellagati resumed typing—then suddenly stopped.

"That's unexpected. She's been moved recently."

I jumped out of my seat. My eyeballs were ready to do the same out of their sockets. "Don't tell me she's not in Sacramento anymore."

"No, she's still here. Just relocated to a different row. She's now in 2D-141."

"Why move her?" I rubbed my forehead, managing to coax out a memory. "Wait a minute. Algernon told me that ILTS units are undergoing upgrades using his newly-adapted alien tech. Now, what did he call it...?"

"You mean the Void capsules?"

I snapped my fingers immediately after he spoke. "Yeah, that's it. Pretty gruesome name, though."

"That couldn't be the reason for her move. Both rows use Void technology. In any event, the farthest I can get you into ILTS is the security check area."

"The Green Room," I said with a nod.

"I wish you the best of luck finagling your way past there." He tapped the return key with a flourish, and the black box on the shelf growled to life. It spat out a plain gray card, a magnetic stripe on one side and the Alpha seal on the opposite, which he handed me.

Eyeing the newly minted card, I asked, "What do the letters V, M, and S stand for?"

"*In Vita, in Morte, et Sequitor*? In life, in death, and whatever follows."

"I should've guessed. That phrase is buried deep in the Oath. Like they hoped it would get lost in the fine print." I scrunched my shoulder blades to quash the shiver that ran up my spine. "Aren't you afraid of what

Lenoir might do in retaliation for helping me?"

"What *can* she do? Kick me out of Alpha?" He punctuated his statement with a carefree *humph*.

Pellagati turned off his computer. With a restive sigh, he rose to inspect the contents of his moving box. He extracted a box of business cards and dropped them in the trash. "I won't be needing those anymore." Satisfied, he folded the top leaves of the box closed.

"You're not taking the camera or the card printer?" I got to my feet as well.

"No, that's Alpha's inventoried property. Someone will collect them by the end of the day."

"You never told me where you've been transferred to."

"My transfer request to Accounting has been approved. I'm actually looking forward to my new supervisory position."

My heart quailed. It would just be my luck if he became my—

"I'll be in charge of five assessors. I'd prefer to stay out of management and be an assessor. My new PQ-4 is just high enough to squeak by." He rolled his albino irises at me. "But my appearance hampers my ability to blend into a crowd."

I paused my breath. A sigh of relief would be rude. "If they're anything like Assessor Petrakis, you'll need the patience of a saint."

"I think I can handle it. I wish you good luck, Dr. Yeager." Hefting his box in both hands, Pellagati walked out the door. "Turn off the lights, will you?"

I swung the door out of the way, only to find the light switch was not where I expected it. A quick survey of the other walls yielded nothing. I stuck my head out the doorway to ask, "Where did they hide—"

Pellagati had disappeared. My voice was swallowed up by the hungry walls as well. Scratching the back of my neck, I gave up on finding the little bugger. The light switch, that is—not Pellagati.

I was about to leave with the lights on when mischief crossed my mind. I plucked one of Pellagati's business cards from the wastebasket and shoved it in my wallet with the magstripe card. Picking up the camera, I held it at arm's length. I flipped the bird at the lens and pressed the shutter button.

"Chee-eese! A little gift for you, Lenoir, you bitch."

I intended to leave the picture between two rows of keys on the keyboard when I blurted out, "What the—?"

The orange aura near the top of the brown blob that was my head indicated I now registered as PQ-4.

I shoved the photo in my pants pocket and skedaddled off the Alpha floor as quickly as I could, before any sudden onrush of sweaty panic gave me away to any Alpha grunt I ran into along the way.

CHAPTER 37

I crumpled and ditched the photo in our break room trashcan under a fresh pile of coffee grounds. By the time I got back to the relative safety of my cubicle, I must have connived and summarily rejected a half dozen ILTS break-in scenarios. Hovering over my desk, I spent several minutes vacillating over whether I should keep Amelia with me, let her witness all my high jinks, or let her wallow in my top desk drawer for a little longer. The list of pros included her ability to call for help in a fix; the cons began with her as the primary witness against me for a mindwipe.

"Sorry, Amelia. You're sitting this one out, too."

Leaving the drawer closed, I did a double-take. Petrakis' Post-It note had been moved from where I put it on my computer monitor. A splotch of red diffused through the paper. I peeled it off and examined the other side. Stamped in red ink at the center of the paper lay a circle circumscribing a design that looked like Mozilla's Firefox logo.

Was someone trying to convince me to change to a new web browser? If they thought anything would replace Netscape anytime soon, they had another thing coming. A quick scan of my cube indicated nothing else had been moved this time.

I placed the Post-It back where I found it, then stuck my head over the cube wall. "Hey, Natalie."

Her eyes skewered me with annoyance. "What is it, Alaska? Couldn't find the library?"

"No, I was just wondering if someone was looking for me while I was out."

"Nope."

"Did a cleaning crew come by?"—which was my code for "Were we visited by a rogue shapeshifter in janitor's clothing again?"

"It's been quiet. Let's keep it that way."

A shake of the head, and I headed for the elevators. When the doors opened, I hesitated.

The sole occupant was the brass-masked oracle. I began to wonder if she was stalking me. The exposed lower half of her face was as expressionless as her mask. Decked out in a white and gold paisley dress, matching clutch bag, and high heels that seemed carved from polished brass, she stepped to the side, allowing me in.

Taking Pellagati's ATPG Alpha card out, I inserted it in the open slot underneath the elevator panel's matrix of buttons. A new series of buttons lit up below the slot. I held my breath as I pressed the one labeled "ILTS."

The oracle exited the elevator on one of the garage levels. The smell of exhaust wafted in, and she turned to face the doors as they closed. With a wrinkle of a one-sided grin, she said, "Told you so."

The one time I was beginning to take a shine to an oracle, and she had to screw it up by acting like a know-it-all. "Yeah, go drive in rush hour with your mask on," I grunted at the doors.

With each floor I descended, I shuffled Pellagati's business and Alpha magstripe cards while constructing my spiel.

The doors opened to a white concrete walkway seemingly floating in a sea of fern green. Stepping into the spacious square room, I had to blink a couple of times to be sure where the floor ended and the walls began. The concrete path led straight to a control console behind which two men sat.

Their faces were partially illuminated by the board over which they fretted. They looked like they were ready to tell ghost stories at a campfire. "'Let's transfer to *Eldritch & Squamous* ILTS,' you said. 'It's nice and quiet,' you said," groused the taller guy.

The shorter one shot back hoarsely, "You wanna go back to the psychic cleaner department? Those machines give me the creeps. And don't call the company 'Eldritch.' If the boss hears you, he'll—"

They both raised their heads when I stepped out of the elevator. Suspicion was written across one of their faces. The taller guy bore a harried look as if he expected to be handed a mop and pail.

I surveyed the rest of the room as I approached. On either side, the green floor dropped away in a series of steps as wide as the length of the walkway. I wondered at the need for "riot stairs," with the dimensions of their shallow rise and long tread spaced to prevent people from rushing the console or elevator. The treads were covered in green outdoor carpeting, the type one could conveniently hose down to remove pesky blood stains. The large drain grates at the stairs' bottoms seemed to confirm my conjecture.

At the base of each of the stairs also stood two wide metal cabinets next to a metal door and a large window, their sashes and rails lined with frost. Through the windows, I spied long rows of cylinders, each large enough to house Goliath.

"Hello," I said, concentrating on keeping my eyebrows frozen. I snapped down the magnetic card on the top counter of the console, making sure the Alpha logo faced up.

The plastic daisy performed a small hula dance at the sound of my voice. Not far from it lay a placard riveted to the console, declaring, "No Liquids on the Control Board!" Old coffee mug ring stains bookended either side of the placard.

"Alpha sent me down to check on the status of the intrusion in 2D-141."

"Confirmation number?" said the short guy with a suspicious face.

I tilted my head and shot him a confused look. That was the easy part. I picked up the magstripe card and asked, "Isn't that what *this* is? This is all Mr. Pellagati gave me."

He exhaled a heavy sigh. "Name and employee ID number, please." I rattled them off slowly as his thick fingers struggled to keep up. "There's no record of you being assigned a confirmation number," he said with a voice like a dirge.

"Look," I said, setting Pellagati's business card on the counter facing him. "Mr. Pellagati needs my visual confirmation and report on 2D-141 before the end of business today, and it's already 4:30. Call his extension, and he'll give you my confirmation."

His partner picked up one of three phone receivers from the console's built-in cradles. I hid my relief that he didn't select the red phone. He examined my face while the phone rang. "No answer."

"Could you leave a message for him to call back? He really *does* need this information. I can wait." I pinched my leg to stop it from twitching.

He hung up in the middle of Pellagati's outgoing message and stood. His expression was the embodiment of "Here we go again."

The suspicious man leaned forward in his seat, his index finger above a black button. "I'm sorry, sir. Without confirmation, I must ask you to leave."

"All right." I shook my head in defeat. I snatched my cards back, taking a step away. "I'll tell Pellagati and his partner that they have to come down in person. Man-oh-man, Ms. Lenoir is already on the rampage. This is really gonna set her off."

"*Sable* Lenoir?" His finger twitched away from the button.

"Yeah, she's the one." I leaned in a smidgen, lowering my voice. "I heard Pellagati is leaving Alpha for accounting, and Lenoir is the one pushing him out. I just left the both of them, and—*hoo-boy!*—there's no love lost there."

The two leaned in as well. The button man laid both hands on the console's wrist rest. "Lenoir was in here the other day, looking for the remains of some critter that got chewed up by a Fido. When I told her she couldn't because VP Hibara put his seal on its cylinder, she went ballistic. That broad is one nasty piece of work."

Pellagati was right. The harpy was digging for dirt on me.

"Hibara?" I said. I swallowed against a dry throat. Why was he involved? "He put his what on it?"

"His personal seal. No one can look at it or its status panel without himself present."

"Wow-w-w..." I tucked both cards into my shirt pocket. "Anyway, I'm not sure why Pellagati needs a visual check-up 2D-141, but I think he's gonna use it to pin something on Lenoir as a parting gift."

"In that case," said the button man, "I think I just found your confirmation number." He sprouted an eager grin tinged with a soupçon of malice.

His assistant started down the left set of riot stairs. "Follow me. By the way, the name's Beaumont. That's Kenny," he added, pointing his thumb behind us.

"Michael."

"Yeah, you already said. We still require that you have an escort in the storage area."

"Fine by me. I'd probably get lost trying to find the right cylinder."

He led me to the metal cabinets and opened one. Freed of their shackles, my eyebrows scaled my forehead. Inside were a pair of gloves, face mask and goggles, a fleece cap with ear flaps, and two suits. The first was a jumpsuit made from the latest cold-resistant, water-wicking synthetics. The larger consisted of a roughly sewn-together mélange of black and blood-red strips of fur.

"I can guess the reason for the Arctic suit, but what in blazes is *that*?"

"Snow-warg pelts. Large Arctic wolves from Middlin' Earth. Slip the Arctic suit on first, then the warg stuff. Use the other cabinet to change."

Beaumont leaned against the cabinets while I donned the gear. With the last snap in place, I gave him the once over. "What are you going to wear?"

He pulled back the cuffs of his sleeves, exposing his wrists. A band of burnished metal encircled each wrist. Crossing his forearms, he rapped the circlets against each other twice.

"Clap on," he said, mimicking the commercial.

"You're kidding."

"Inside joke," he said with a shrug. "These keep me plenty warm. We would've had a pair attuned for you if your visit had a confirmation number." He walked around me and keyed a handful of digits into the door's numeric pad. The door slid open, revealing an antechamber. A fog spilled out along the floor around our legs. Beaumont strolled in while I, swaddled in my Arctic suit, warg overcoat, and leggings, tottered along like Karloff's *Frankenstein*.

The door behind us closed, and the next one opened. A blast colder than anything I ever experienced bit through the Arctic mask. Despite the goggles, my eyelids were one degree away from freezing open.

"Follow me," said Beaumont. "And try to keep up. You can only last fifteen minutes tops in the suits."

We proceeded down the primary hall, lined with the giant fire-engine red cylinders on either side. Some looked more like capsules with their smoothed tops and bottoms, and weren't covered with as much hoar-frost.

"Are those the new cylinders using the new Void tech?"

"Right-o," said Beaumont.

Each had a transparent faceplate at eye level, an identification number in military-style stencil above it, and an electronic touchscreen below. As I passed more capsules, I made the correlation that the ones with active screens were occupied. The faces—and things that *weren't* faces—peering out of the cylinders matched nothing that I could recall from fairy-tale books and Disney animations. Or horror movies.

We made two turns at consecutive intersections. At each one, Beaumont urged me again to hustle my butt. My teeth ached from the cold, and I could hear my sinuses crystallizing. Whenever either of us exhaled, our breath instantly turned to snow.

We passed a capsule, indistinguishable from the rest, except for its faceplate riveted shut with a metal plate. I paused to examine the touch-screen, quietly blaring out "Access Restricted," underscored by two symbols, each in their own red circle. I had seen both earlier: the three ginkgo leaves gracing Hibara's doors, and the spiraling fox tail on Petrakis' Post-It note. Petrakis was down here? That didn't make any sense.

"Let me guess, that's the one Lenoir was itching to examine."

"Yup." Beaumont huffed, a miniature snowstorm billowing around his shoulders. "And you can't touch it either."

"Did Hibara himself come down here?"

"No, one of his assistants did it. Man, what a knockout."

"What color stripe did she have in her hair? Green, blue?"

"White," he said, his irritation building.

"Are you sure?" Did Emerald and Sapphire have another sister? I was about to ask another question, but Beaumont's single-mindedness got in the way.

"Can it, Yeager. You have no business with this capsule anyway, so *move* it."

One more intersection and we arrived.

"2D-141," he announced, standing before an occupied capsule with a blinking touchscreen.

I shuffled as fast as I could manage up to the faceplate. Beaumont keyed in his passcode on the touchscreen. A wan, baleful light in the cylinder's interior shone down on the occupant.

Inside stood my Sindhu. My beloved, beautiful, *horrific* Sindhu.

Her face seemed to hover inches from the faceplate. My poor Sindhu's countenance bore witness to a losing battle. She had stared into the power of a Gorgon and was now caught between the grim boundaries of life and death, flesh and sentient stone, beautiful innocence and scowling malevolence.

The hideous half of her stone face was encased in a latticework mask of wood, engraved with glowing sigils that quivered with mystical energies. The undefiled portion of her face was as I preferred to remember her: dazzling turquoise eyes piercing out from a complexion like polished mahogany, a slender nose over a mouth I longed to kiss again, her visage of grace framed by straight black hair pouring down like spun ebony.

It killed me to see my love's face torn by an expression of terror.

"No change," I muttered. "Three months, and no change."

I wanted to scream. I wanted to hit something. I wanted to tear off the capsule's door and hold her next to me again.

The top of my head itched. The scar that predicted snowy weather felt like it caught poison ivy. I was surprised it took this long to complain in this deep freeze.

I tapped a rectangle labeled "Status" on the touchscreen. My fingertip stung with the first stage of frostbite. Columns of data and paragraphs of info scrolled by. I tried in vain to slow it down, catching only bits and pieces.

The avalanche of info terminated with a list of dates when the cylinder was accessed: the initial date of "Void subject attunement"—whatever that meant—initial storage, monthly inspections, a series of visits all with the same employee number, her capsule's mysterious transfer to this row two weeks ago, a single visitor last week whose number didn't match any others, and today's date with Beaumont's and my IDs. I surmised the first group of visitations were probably logged by gruff, four-armed Yadavi. The date of Sindhu's last visitor left me baffled. Until the date clicked—the day after Alpha grilled me in their dungeon.

"Lenoir," I snarled. I faced Beaumont, not bothering to hide my dismay. "Do you know what she was doing here?"

Beaumont held up his palms facing me. "Whoa... Kenny and I monitor and maintain the storage floor. We don't stick our noses into visitors' business—especially Alpha's."

"No one accompanied her?"

"No, she had a valid confirmation number." Beaumont's wristwatch beeped rapidly. "Five minutes left. We head back—now."

I took one last look at Sindhu, after which my guide got no more arguments from me. My toes felt like they were ready to snap off.

Within a minute, we hustled and made the second of the three turns back to the control room. Halfway down the long, straight concourse back to the Green Room—the nice, *warm* Green Room—stood three towering blue humanoids. Two impossibly big bruisers had cornered the smaller against a row of cylinders. I could recognize a shakedown when I heard it, even in Scandinavian.

"Frost Giants. Exactly what we *don't* need," said Beaumont through clenched teeth. "Just keep walking along the other side. Give them a wide berth."

"What are intrusions doing here?" I whispered.

"They're not intrusions. They're refugees under Eldridge's protection."

"How many refugees does Eldridge take in?"

"We employ them to supply security for ILTS. They can handle most anything in the unlikely event an intrusion manages to escape or leak out of confinement."

At least, this explained why all the new security staff had Nordic names.

He nudged me from behind. "Now scoot. Leave them alone, and they'll leave us in one piece. If we're lucky, it'll only be a union dispute." He pushed again, urging me to move as fast as I could waddle.

"They have a *union*?"

"Same as ours." A shove from Beaumont ended his reply.

This was no union dispute. With their fists clenched, the two bullies were shaking down the shrimp hard—with "shrimp" being a relative term. Even Tiny looked like he could bench-press one of the Void capsules with ease.

A few paces safely past them, the top of my head stung. I wondered if it was even possible for my skull to get frostbite. Before I realized it, I froze in my tracks and turned.

Beaumont hissed, "What do you think you're doing?"

I tottered over to the hulking giants. The big brutes looked down their noses at me. The honkin' big angular blue wedges in the middle of their faces dropped teardrops of frozen snot.

"Leave the little one alone," I said. My stomach shrank two sizes in an instant—its version of screaming, "What the *hell* are you doing?" My eyebrows didn't move. They couldn't have. They were frozen in place.

The two blue hulks laughed cruelly. Their guffaws sounded like glaciers clashing. Leaning down, the middle-sized one let his fists hang down, dangling on either side of me. If he clapped, I'd be an icy red patch on the floor. "Run away, little human," he growled.

I stood my ground. Meeting his stare, I said, "I am Yeager."

I'm not even sure that sounded like my voice. Or Shadow's.

The two monsters stood erect, and their bodies shook with riotous howls and whoops of derision. "Oh ho, a *Jeger*, he says?" The blue runt giant did nothing but gawp at me, his glossy black eyes large as saucers. In his case, quite literally.

The middle-sized bully leaned down again, his massive face snarling at me. "The only thing you hunt for is your own death." He raised his giant's fist inches above my head.

I lowered my Arctic mask, and the not-me voice spoke again. "*Etra phen mbarda Phelek Lepan. Ni sam yon gorikuba elā.*"

The giant halted. His hand spasmed open. The largest giant behind him snapped erect like he'd been zapped by a high-tension wire. Then his back curled, his enormous shoulders crunching together into a slump. His blue knees nearly knocked together.

With a shake of my head, I gaped in astonishment at the backs of the two behemoths running as fast as their telephone-pole legs could carry them. The floor trembled with their receding footfalls as they screamed, "*Jegerne er her*! *Jegerne er her*!"

In front of me crouched the littlest giant, his torso large as an SUV, as he huddled himself face down at my feet. "Spare me, hunter! Please me spare," he groveled piteously. "Do not me take to your infernal home. Spare unworthy one me."

I patted his head as I turned to Beaumont with a shrug of my shoulders. The expression on my escort's face was indescribable.

The giant, however, continued his moaning pleas for mercy. Patting harder didn't stop his bawling either. I pounded the back of his head with my fist as hard as I could. I thought my fingers would break off. Nursing my crumpled hand under my armpit, I said—in my own voice—"Get up. I'm not going to harm you. You are free to go."

"Thank you, *Jeger*," be blubbered. "Hagebjørn forever your debt is in!"

Beaumont's watch beeped again. "One minute left. Move yer ass, Yeager, or you're one giant icicle," he said. If Beaumont hadn't yanked me back as well, I think Hagebjørn would have kissed my feet.

Beaumont hauled me into the anteroom.

My legs were numb. My hands were frozen stiff. My face was burning. With the outer door closed, he opened the inner door. Room-temperature air rushed in. It felt like the most wonderful sauna in the world. I collapsed onto the green carpet.

Beaumont slipped off his wrist bracers and fitted them on me. He forced my wrists together, clicking the circlets twice. My whole body flooded with warmth, like I dove into a warm bath.

"You flippin' idiot," he shouted, his face blazing red and his jugular and carotid standing out in near apoplexy. "You almost got yourself killed out there. And me too! Pickin' a fight with *Frost Giants*? You're friggin' nuts, you know that?"

"He did *what*?" called Kenny. He jumped up from the console and loped down the riot stairs.

I wiggled my toes and fingers back to existence. They suddenly hurt like someone smashed them with a hammer. "What's the problem? We're still alive."

After my eyebrows, I'm gonna need to work on my false bravado.

Beaumont's circulatory system returned to normal pressure. "What the heck did you say to them? I never saw Frost Giants run like that." His glower of anger was replaced with begrudging respect. "From *anything*."

"No idea. Something I heard on my last assessment. A little birdie told me it might be useful." I placed my hands over my face. "Oh, good. My lips and nose are still here."

Kenny and Beaumont grabbed my forearms and lifted me to my feet. I took a couple of deep breaths. I felt like a million bucks. I shed the warg coat, dove into the changing cabinet, and peeled off the suit, handing them to Beaumont. I frowned at my fingertips, covered with a dusting of white, flaky skin and the beginnings of a blister or two.

"You okay?" asked Kenny.

"Yeah, looks like I made it back in time. Mostly frostnip and only a touch of frostbite." I looked at my watch as I slipped on my work clothes. "Shoot. Speaking of time, I gotta get back to Pellagati pronto. Thanks, guys —I owe ya."

I tossed Beaumont's bracelets back to him and made a dash for the elevator. Once safely inside, I collapsed against the back wall and exhaled the largest breath of relief I ever took. I only hoped my charade didn't get them in deep doo-doo.

As the elevator climbed, so did my spirits. I reviewed my day, trying to sort out what I learned.

The shapeshifter is in storage. Only Hibara has access.

Sindhu hadn't changed since that night three months ago.

Pellagati could be right—despite Algernon's samples, no one is actively looking for a cure.

The only people who bothered to visit her so far were Yadavi and Lenoir. Lenoir, I understood, but Yadavi? She didn't strike me as the sentimental kind. As for Lenoir, that's gonna stop if I have any say about it.

Frost Giants understood the shapeshifters' lingo, including Phelek Lepan.

What made me repeat the shapeshifter's crud anyway?

It couldn't have been Shadow, could it?

Last but not least—somehow, I'm a PQ-4.

How long can I keep secret a PQ that continually gets stronger?

And what's causing that?

I slapped my palm against my head. With all the excitement, I never got a chance to talk to Barandir. After this latest escapade, I needed to speak with him before he departed for Middle Earth, *Tawar Cevan*, or whatever it's called.

CHAPTER 38

While I headed down Barandir's row, a discussion floated over the eye-level cubicle walls.

I poked my head around the corner of his cube's opening and knocked on the wooden and metal jamb. Jolly, barely contained by a spandex tube top, filled out a loose-fitting crop top dotted with neon-bright shapes and a matching pair of jogger's sweatpants beautifully. Her wrists sported pink wristbands, and her short, straight black hair was circled by a matching sweatband.

Immune to her provocative display, Barandir busied himself by stuffing an assortment of papers into a small backpack.

"Three sentences and ten words isn't a big enough sample to find an answer quickly," said Jolly. "I've written a program to search all records for the language's vocabulary and sentence structure." Sitting on the edge of a neighboring table, she drew a circle on his desk with her index finger. "But it keeps dumping core, reaching a hardware limit. I decided I needed a break. I'm heading down the block to the gym. Do you want to join me and work up a good... sweat?" She gripped the edge of the table, shoving everything above her abdomen forward.

"Excuse me, Barandir?" I rapped the jamb again. Jolly shot a sour glare at the person who dared intrude on her little soap opera of unrequited lust. It quickly changed into a worried look when she realized it was the company outcast.

"No, please excuse *me*," said Jolly. She scrunched her arms against her sides and skittered past me like she feared my probation was contagious.

"Don't believe everything you see on *Dallas*," I called after her, hoping it came across as whimsical.

Barandir paused with an Elvish/English dictionary in his hand. "Shouldn't you be studying, Dr. Yeager?"

"I have something I need to ask you before you go. And maybe offer information that will help your own field research."

He shoved the book into his backpack and set the bulging bag down. It was his turn to lean against his desk, facing me with his arms folded. He flipped his ponytail behind him. His cynicism weighed down the surrounding air. "Be quick. I must depart before the sun sets."

"I don't know what *Phelek Lepan* is, but Frost Giants do."

Barandir stood ramrod straight. His eyes skewered me with their intensity. "You were in Intrusion Long-Term Storage."

"Yes. I repeated the phrase one of the shapeshifters said to me at Western Bay. The one that went, '*Etra phen—*'"

"*No!*" Barandir barked, lunging a step forward. His hand was inches away from clamping over my mouth. After a gulp and a deep breath, he regained his austere composure. "Do *not* utter those words again, nor anything else those creatures may have said."

"Is it a spell?"

"I believe so, at least part of one. Regardless, I fear it is a cursed and baleful language. No good can come of speaking it aloud here."

"That's in line with the reaction I got from the Frost Giants."

"What did they do?"

"Two of them ran for the hills, screaming all the way. I don't speak Swedish or Norse or whatever, but it sounded like 'the hunters are here.' The third giant's reaction caught me by surprise. He practically worshiped at my feet, before the ILTS technician dragged me away." I showed my frostbitten fingertips to Barandir.

"Hunters…" Barandir mumbled. He rubbed a knuckle against his lips briefly while his eyes scrutinized the air. "That implies the giants are hunted by these shapeshifters as well," he reasoned. Then he shook his head. "I can think of no creature that Frost Giants fear. No *smaller* creature, that is."

"The guys at ILTS said something similar. Maybe this will help. You were correct in thinking *Phelek Lepan* is a place. One of the giants referred to it as the shapeshifters' 'infernal home.'"

"That is most helpful. And troubling as well. But at least now I know where I must go."

"Where?"

"The lands that border the Frost Giants' homeland."

"Which is where? Peoria, Oshkosh, Punxsutawney? Frost Giants don't appear in the news all that often."

"*Tawan Cevan* first. From there..." He lost his severe expression. "Who knows?" Barandir zipped his pack shut and slung it over one shoulder. "It is getting late," he said. "The portal lasts only a short time around sundown. And I have miles yet to travel." He rattled keys inside his pants pocket.

"You... drive?"

Barandir shot me a look of reproach.

"Guess I never thought about half-elves on the freeway." I shrugged my shoulders and extended my hand. "Well, as you say, good hunting."

Barandir didn't shake my hand. Instead, he eked out a wan smile. For him, that was almost a belly laugh.

I followed him to the elevators and silently watched the doors close. I stretched and tried to stifle a yawn. It only made a larger one overtake me. Patting my shirt pocket, I realized Amelia was still stashed away in my desk. I rescued her from her prison in my desk drawer. She weighed heavy in my hand, giving off the vibe she was distressed from being alone for most of the day. I was about to leave when I recalled Petrakis' gift and our little pretense. I took his copy of the handbook home—if only for appearance's sake.

CHAPTER 39

My apartment is truly a dilemma.

Each time I first enter, I'm comforted by the familiar surroundings. The furniture Sindhu and I rescued from a consignment store fits me like a fine Italian leather glove. The Indian rugs she brought from her hometown of Varanasi made the living room appear as grand as a palace. The faint aroma of incense and saffron still clung to its fibers.

Eldridge had quite literally spirited all our belongings from our San Jose apartment. Everything, down to the plastic treasure chest bubbling happily away in its aquarium, had been transported. No muss, no fuss, nothing broken, nothing chipped. Easiest move I ever made.

Two steps in, and I remember *she's* not there.

The first night alone was rough. Damn rough.

I didn't sleep at all, rattling around an empty apartment, sighing and simpering with every memory that hundreds of household items brought to mind, only to bawl my eyes out over the nightmare vision of Sindhu violated by the Euryale. After two months at work, the pain of separation remained, but it was no longer crippling.

Tonight, however, wore on me more heavily than that first night. Sindhu's half-tortured, half-serene face in the confines of the Void capsule brought my loneliness rampaging back again. Worse, my thoughts were consumed with what Sindhu might be enduring in her frozen confines.

I woke up on the sofa with a half-consumed bottle of tequila on the end table and a whacking great hangover. First stop was the medicine cabinet and the ruddy tan bottle of brownish-yellow powder inside. Sindhu never divulged the ingredients of her concoctions, saying she was sworn to keep the "old family recipes" secret until we married. But I can attest one-quarter teaspoon of that horrible-tasting miracle mixed in a tall glass of water cleared up any alcohol-induced pain in less than half an hour. No wonder Yakshini Herbal Health was so successful, despite its ludicrous name.

After a solid breakfast, I put on a pot of my best Moroccan coffee, some study music on the stereo, lazed in my recliner, and closed my eyes.

The pages of the eideticized employee orientation binders appeared at my whim. I read them leisurely, at a cursory level. When any section caught my interest, I dove into the details—like the ink erasers Petrakis had used against the shapeshifter. According to *Equipment 310: Field Camouflage*, their differently colored halves effectively neutralize two different magics.

If I had my druthers, I'd call up whatever information I wanted by topic or situation. For example, if I faced a creature in the field I had never seen before, having the necessary info pop up instantly would be most helpful. Sadly, that's not how it worked.

Instead, I had to memorize the old-fashioned way that the critter info could be under either *Cryptids 101*, *Cryptids 202: Monsters by State and Provenance*, *Cryptids 205: Mythological Beasts*, or *Cryptids 210: Non-Zoological Familiars*. Only afterward could I summon it the Uncle Billy-Bob way.

I spent the better part of that morning doing exactly that, first with the orientation material and then the handbook. Throughout the process, the feeling that something important was missing grew stronger. Only after I completed my giant mental task did I realize what the material failed to cover.

I grabbed Amelia and the last of my coffee and went into the second bedroom. During our first week living together, Sindhu had repurposed it into her craft room and our study. The bookcase was stuffed with text-books from every class we ever had at UC Santa Clara. The top row was reserved for my biochemistry books, the second highest for her astronomy and cosmology texts, the hierarchy determined by our respective heights. The room's far corner was reserved for Sindhu's latest craft project—a sand mandala. Rings of dust had gathered around her work, solemnly standing vigil over her incomplete twelve-sided lotus masterpiece.

After clearing off my desk and drawing the curtains, I took out a fresh legal pad. My hand, poised with my scribe, hovered over the blank top sheet.

"Amelia, I'm not sure how this is supposed to work. There's nothing in the New Employee Handbook or any orientation material about scribes. I suppose that's because newbies aren't supposed to have them. I think it's time we get to know one another."

I cleared my throat ceremoniously. "I know you observe everything, at least when I take you out of the box."

She double-clicked her cap.

"Other than clicking your thumb cap or shifting around in my pockets, the only other times I witnessed you move of your own volition was when we copied Sofia's vision of the shapeshifters, and when we filled out the Intrusion Assessment Report. By the way, you draw much better than I ever could."

She double-clicked.

So, she's either a wise-ass or honest to a fault. Was that a trait all scribes shared?

"What else are you allowed to do?"

Amelia remained silent. She didn't move. Perhaps I asked her too broad a question? I clicked my tongue when I realized I had forgotten Petrakis' most important instruction.

"Amelia, *please* tell me what else you can do on your own, without me saying the magic word."

She shifted in my grip and began to write, pulling my hand along with her. Her letters weren't cursive but were still perfectly shaped, almost as if they were printed by a computer.

```
   1) I may answer simple "yes or no" questions
directed at me, except when in the presence of Mun-
danes.
   2) I may assist you in filling out any regula-
tion corporate forms. You must be within an E&SQA
facility during this function.
```

"I know this already. What else?"

```
   3) I may produce a copy of any visible infor-
mation. I am permitted to perform the entire task
without guidance or complete what you have started
by triple-clicking my cap.
```

"I'm pretty sure I never did a triple-click. How were you able to draw Sofia's vision of the shapeshifter?"

Amelia remained still.

I sighed my growing annoyance. "Amelia, please tell me how you were able to draw the shapeshifter."

You said, "Oh, please," after attempting to draw it yourself.

"I did…? Son of a gun, so I did."

I paused, thinking how to best phrase my next request.

"For this session, please answer my questions in writing. The magic word and my holding you are not required for each response. Can you do that? Can we have a simple conversation without all the formality?"

Amelia wrested herself from my fingers and jumped onto the paper. Yes.

She stood upright on the period, just like Ventnor's pen, Hadrian, had done. She turned her pocket clip toward me and leaned slightly to the right. I got the feeling she was looking straight at me. My spine jumped with a shiver. I chewed my lip, mulling over what I should ask next.

"Petrakis says Namiki might have been a musician before the French Revolution. Scribes don't remember their previous lives?"

They do not.

"Well, that's just plain-old sad. Do you remember your name, at least?"

Pilot Hi-Tecpoint D6.

I rolled my eyes with a sigh of mild exasperation. "'Pilot' is what everyone else calls you. But that just feels wrong. Do you mind me calling you Amelia?"

No.

"Why does everyone else call their scribes by their make or model?"

Strongly advised by management. Underlying reason unknown.

"You anticipated my next question. That's a tad scary." I folded my arms, tapping my chin with my fist. "I need to ask some difficult questions. I'm apprehensive about asking them, but I must. I need to know if I can trust you, Amelia. Can scribes lie?"

In general, scribes may not report information known to be false. That does not prevent them from presenting inaccurate or untrue information if the original source is false, unknown to the scribe. Scribes are responsible for prefacing information known to be questionable with any appropriate cautions. Scribes may commit a lie of omission if directed by management, Director or above.

"If I were to give you personal information, or you witness anything of a sensitive nature, even if it related to Eldridge, who else has access to it? Are you able to keep secrets? *My* secrets?"

Information written by scribes into official reports is accessible to any E&SQA employee. Except for situations previously discussed, scribes cannot perform any function of their own volition. Therefore, scribes may not divulge anything of their assignment's activities, including information transmitted in confidence, with two general exceptions: observations that are work-related, if requested by supervisor or higher, or required by Central Records; observations of a personal nature if requested by vice president level or higher.

"Has anyone made such a request, yet?"

No.

"I can't tell you how much that relieves me. Okay, here's a secret." I leaned close and whispered with a smile, "I'm madly in love with Sindhu Mehra."

That is no secret. I am already aware of that, as is every member of ATPG 217, acting supervisor Petrakis, Vice President Hibara, supervisor Pellagati, and Assessor Lenoir.

My gut response was to order Amelia never to say that shrew's name again, but giving in to such a whim could have unexpected repercussions down the road. "Here's a real secret. Somehow, I got bumped up to a PQ-4. How is that possible?"

Increasing one's PQ level is achievable through training with another person with a sufficiently higher PQ. The methods and processes vary, but training is difficult and time-consuming. For example, advancing from PQ-1 to PQ-2 takes two months on average. Advancing to higher steps takes proportionately longer.

"My jump from PQ-1 to -4 occurred over less than three months. Without training. You're sure there's no other way?"

It took a while before Amelia replied.

Certain magic items and alien technologies are known to facilitate this. Some are contained within certain E&SQA storage facilities, but are restricted due to their deleterious side effects. E&SQA Sacramento possesses no such items. Company procedure is to contain, neutralize, destroy, or disassemble them once discovered.

No other processes have been documented by
E&SQA.

"*You* might be rock-solid sure, Amelia, but I can't help but wonder." She stood at attention while I drummed my fingers aimlessly. "I was almost killed by the Euryale, visited by Elrameshe twice, attacked by a Watcher named *Turia Feir*, discovered I have a peculiar growth in my brain, which then got drilled by a manic revealer empath, two shapeshifters tried to abduct me to *Phelek Lepan*, I cast a spell on myself, had a doozy of an ectoplasmic dream, capped off by spooking Frost Giants with shapeshifter gibberish."

I winced, kicking myself for being *too* honest.

I am unaware of any spells you may have cast.
Which spell?

"Wow, you can ask a question," I said, trying to recover from my gaff. "That makes this a real conversation."

Amelia wasn't fooled by my feeble distraction. She underlined her question.

"Sorry, Amelia. I wasn't entirely honest there, and you deserve honesty since you're forced to be straightforward with me. I cast a simple spell I found in the library to help my studying ability. As for the dream, it was more of a psychic experience. Physical evidence was left behind. Could any of those events have been responsible? Maybe a combination?"

Neither am I aware of any psychic vision.
When did these two events occur?

I had to answer carefully. There was still the cover story that Petrakis and I were at odds while he dug for reasons why upper management was so interested in me—and while I dug for what might be inside me. "I unwittingly cast a memorization spell while you were in my desk drawer two nights ago. As for the vision, it occurred when I fell asleep after studying the employee handbook."

Can you describe this vision?

I stared at Amelia for a full minute. "I'd like to tell you. I really would... Perhaps someday soon. For now, let's just say it was something from my childhood." I wondered what she made of my hyperactive eyebrows all that time.

Very well.

Even written out, that packed a punch. Whenever Sindhu said that, I'd rush out for an apology bouquet.

I have updated your employee record with your

```
current status of PQ-4.
```

"*What*? No! Why did you do that? *Undo*!" I pounded the desk. "Amelia, *please* undo."

```
     I  cannot  comply.  Central  Records  requires
scribes  keep  their  assignment's  personnel  records
current.  Director  level  or  higher  is  required  to
undo or redact.
```

"*Shit*. That's only gonna raise questions. You *know* Lenoir will get wind of that. Which will get me in hot water with Hibara." I rose from the desk and rammed its chair back into its well. "That's enough show and tell for now, Amelia." I paced around the room, working myself into a lather over Amelia's duty-bound tactlessness.

Should I tell Petrakis? Who's going to be the first to find out? Who am I kidding? It'll be Lenoir, no doubt.

The phone in the kitchen rang, and Amelia fell over.

"That was fast." My heart cramped when I picked up the receiver.

"Yeager, Petrakis here. I realize your probation is not even half over, but a situation has arisen." He spoke like an angry robot. "Come in tomorrow, please. You are still required to take the reinstatement exam first. Are you prepared?"

"Yes, I'm ready. What happened?"

"My office. Tomorrow morning. Nine o'clock." He hung up.

This "pissed at Yeager" act was getting old.

CHAPTER 40

I knocked on Petrakis' door at 9:00 AM on the button. I wore my unexciting, company-issued, Navy blue suit for the occasion. Except for the shirt—its cuffs irritated my wrists, so I subbed my favorite Yves Saint Laurent instead.

He called me into his office, which he had rearranged from Algernon's old layout. The room looked like it was vacuumed to within a millimeter of its life, and smelled like it had been immersed in disinfectant. His desk and two tables had been placed in a horseshoe, with him sitting in the center. The table nearest me had been cleared off, except for a short stack of blank paper and a Bic pen.

I placed his treasured leather-bound copy of the employee handbook on the table. "Thanks for the loan. I found it... memorable."

I expected Petrakis to brush-swipe his nose, acknowledging the jest. His poker face was granite.

He stood, snatched up the book, and placed it on the highest bookshelf above his computer monitor. He slapped two printed sheets of paper face down next to the stack of blanks. "For the next hour, you may not leave this room. You may not use any reference material. Your Pilot, if you please." He thrust out his hand.

I surrendered Amelia without a word.

He placed his scribe on the corner of his desk, its enameled dragon's eyes looking straight at me. "Namiki shall proctor this exam. Use the Mundane pen provided. I shall return in one hour *exactly*. Best of luck, Dr. Yeager." He shut the door. A split second later, it opened a smidgen, with Petrakis' head near the opening. He nodded at the room corner behind me. "One last thing. Hands off the machine." With that, he closed the door behind him.

I was pleasantly surprised by the beat-up Cuban espresso contraption rescued from Lick Observatory.

With a deep breath, I turned over the exam and hunkered down.

The questions pertaining to my employee orientation were not particularly difficult. Thanks to Uncle Billy-Bob's eideticize spell, I blasted through the twenty questions within a minute each. I budgeted my remaining forty minutes to answer five essay questions covering the employee handbook. Most of them were situational questions, consisting of "this particular event happens, which gives rise to this dilemma, what do you do?" They were relatively transparent because each could be resolved by one specific rule from the handbook. My essay responses were short paragraphs, ending with phrases that quoted the rule.

The last question, however, stopped me in my tracks with ten minutes to go.

```
You are on assignment in the field, search-
ing for an alien device of immense power. Your
partner discovers said item, which seems to be
in a countdown mode. Your partner begins act-
ing strangely after commandeering the object.
They claim they are not under duress or influ-
ence, yet insist the Earth is in immediate
danger, and they must employ the device to
save the planet. However, your mission brief-
ing indicated any use of the alien technology
would almost certainly kill the user and those
nearby, with the worst-case scenario resulting
in the destruction of everything in a ten-
kilometer radius. Describe and explain your
next action(s).
```

I stared at Namiki. I could almost hear the dragon snicker. I sneered back and wrote:

It depends. How much do I trust my partner? How much do I trust Eldridge? How much do I trust myself? How much time do I have? Depending on the answers at that exact moment, there are any number of actions I would next take: I might agree with my partner and let them activate the item; I might subdue my partner, killing him/her if necessary; afterward, I might attempt to disassemble or destroy the artifact; I might transport the artifact to E&SQA; I might activate the artifact myself and accept the risk of sacrificing myself.

If the company did not sufficiently prepare me for such an impossible situation, I shall remain as faithful as possible to the Oath. But in the end, I shall answer only to my own conscience. If that's not in line with company policy, then screw E&SQA.

No sooner did I put down my pen than Petrakis walked in. "Everything in order, Namiki?"

She double-clicked.

"Good, now let us have a look."

I made to leave.

"Please stay, Yeager. This won't take but a minute." He scanned the papers, theatrically harrumphing at each answer. I grinned coyly when my last wiseacre response raised his eyebrow.

"Almost perfect, Yeager. Only one error. Congratulations, you passed." A whisper of a smile crossed his face. I gathered he would have popped a few vest buttons with pride if he didn't have to keep up the act that we were still on unfriendly terms. He handed Amelia back to me and shook my hand. "Welcome back into the fold, Dr. Yeager."

"How badly did I flub the last question?"

"That was not the error. Your answer concerning employing a silver table knife when assessing if an intrusion were a vampire was incorrect."

"You don't stab them or make a cross with it?"

"No, you would first use it to check their reflection *before* stabbing them. Silver is the only metal unable to cast their reflection. In earlier days, Mundanes rationalized it because it was a "holy" metal. The actual reason has something to do with *tau neutrinos* interacting with silver's $5s^1$ electron, or so I'm told. In olden days, mirrors were silvered on one side. Modern mirrors are useless, as they are anodized with aluminum.

"Your final essay answer was adequate." He frowned, with a corner of one nostril scrunched up. "Though highly inappropriate."

I celebrated with a triumphant waggle of my eyebrows. "All right, then. What was so important that I had to be called in a week early?"

"Dr. Fleischer is dead."

Yeah, I'm sure my eyebrows jumped. "*When*? I just spoke with her."

"You did?"

"Yes. Two days ago. I called her company extension, which was forwarded to Heidelberg."

"How did you determine that?"

"I was connected to an international line. Fleischer answered the phone in German and mentioned the city's university." I shuffled my feet under my seat, discomforted by my small deception about eideticizing her number's extension. "Did you know she had been mindwiped?"

"No." Petrakis' face turned dour. "I had hoped hers was a simple retirement."

"How did she die?"

"Another professor at Heidelberg and a fellow Druid—"

"They're everywhere, aren't they?"

"—went to pay Dr. Fleischer a visit when she failed to show for her classes. Her study was torn apart, and her along with it. Eldridge got wind of it and sent an assessor and an adjuster. From the extent of the damage, signs of conflict, and blood spatter, they confirmed she had been killed by an intrusion. But she didn't go down without a fight. A goodly amount of blood was from her attacker." Petrakis lowered and shook his head.

"Wow. Never mess with a Druid on their home turf. What kind of intrusion?"

"One we haven't dealt with before. From the height and size of the claw marks on walls and scrapes on the floor, it's big. Seven feet tall or more. Along with its blood, Fleischer's Druidic scythe managed to break off several chips of a chitinous shell."

"How the heck does a seven-foot-tall crab move around Heidelberg without being seen?"

"I doubt it's anything like that. The claw marks indicate one of its hands has eight digits."

I stood silent while I digested Petrakis' info. My stomach swilled with guilt. "What color was the creature's blood?"

"Strange you should ask," he hemmed, his eyes narrowing. "Black, though it may have simply turned that color by the time they arrived."

No, I was sure it was black to begin with. "Was she targeted because I called her?"

"Possibly. Why did you call her?"

"I was convinced she had information about the shapeshifters. They said things that reminded me of her outburst during the Aptitude Stones' attack."

"We'll just have to sit tight on both fronts until either Barandir returns from his portal, or Prague calls with an update." He tapped the Bic on the table while he chewed on his thoughts. "In the meantime, there are a few other items I would like to clear up while we're alone."

He shot a clownish glance at Namiki, whose dragon's eyes were still trained on me. "I've been informed something remarkable has happened." He paused, observing my face, especially my eyebrows, dagnabbit. "How in the world did you increase your paranormal quotient?"

I slumped in my chair and sighed at the ceiling. "I wish I knew. If I were to guess, maybe it grows every time someone like Pellagati or Aptitude Stones messes with my brain?"

"I also understand you met with Barandir before he left."

"Yes." My jumbled thoughts danced a jig. I wasn't ready to update Petrakis about my visit to ILTS while Namiki listened in. I grabbed the first explanation that would suffice for the moment. "I gave him my insights about the shapeshifters."

I lowered my chin, aiming my forehead at Petrakis. I had an outlandish hope that my newly minted PQ-4 could shoot Petrakis a telepathic command to shut up and not press further. Saner expectations took ever, so I glowered at him instead, slowly shifting my head from left to right.

"Then you had best append those insights to the Western Bay Intrusion report." He said slowly, running his finger along one nostril. "Pilot will show you how." Petrakis rolled his chair away from the table. "Well then, that's about it. I'm preparing your next assignments. You can begin working on them this afternoon. Unless you have any requests, we can—"

"As a matter of fact, I do. I asked Head Librarian Mertens to request a pass allowing me to visit my fiancée in Internal Long-Term Storage, Capsule 2D-141. Is there any way you can speed the process up? If I could visit Sindhu aga—" I coughed overly loud to cover my flub. "—*before* I dive back into my ATPG duties, I would really appreciate it."

Petrakis sat up like someone goosed him. "How on earth did you find her—" He held up his hand, palm facing me. "Never mind, I do not wish to know." He swiveled to his computer terminal and started pattering away on its keyboard. "Meanwhile, I'll submit your request. I cannot promise you'll receive permission today—or at all. These things take time and require high-level management approval. I'll let— Hold the phone..."

I craned my neck to view his screen. "What's wrong?"

"Nothing. You already have a standing confirmation number, issued this very morning." He questioned me with his eyes. Bewilderment ran roughshod over his face.

"What does 'standing' mean?"

Petrakis scratched the roots of his short ponytail furiously. "You're allowed to visit Ms. Mehra at any time, up to once per week, providing it doesn't interfere with your duties."

"Who approved it?"

Petrakis tapped the print button on his computer. A familiar whir cranked away from its other side. He pulled a gray plastic magstripe card from a familiar black box hidden under a disheveled pile of paper and handed it to me. The three-leafed pattern printed on one side was all too familiar.

"Vice President Hibara."

CHAPTER 41

What a difference one day makes.

Taking advantage of my last half-day before the nine-to-five grind kicked in again, I first took a leisurely stroll around the living, breathing city, followed by a relaxing early lunch around nice, safe Mundanes. The corporate café was all right, but I needed to indulge myself.

I found two inviting deli joints about five blocks from the Eldridge tower. Not too far, but far enough to put myself out of the reach of most of my fellow employees who also chose to chow down *al fresco*. I was in no mood to be cornered by any gawkers who heard through the company grapevine that I was no longer the corporate outcast. I had my growing list of puzzles to occupy myself.

Scoping out a sunny table-for-two, I savored the best pastrami Reuben on the West Coast in peace. Finishing my sandwich, I stared at my plate overflowing with coleslaw and unanswered needs: a cure for Sindhu's Euryale infection; locate Mothers' prison of *Phelek Lepan*; the riddle why the gray shapeshifters considered Shadow the son of a traitor; why he was murdered in the mountains near Anchorage, and by what; the identities of his elven friends; why three sorceresses put Shadow in my head; where was Elrameshe; and what in blazes Vice President Hibara's machinations had to do with all of it.

After complimenting Mrs. Goldman on her excellent New York-style delicatessen and her *geshmake* eats, I headed out. Unfortunately, whatever goodwill I earned with her was immediately blown, when she gave me the hairy eyeball as I entered Brönderburg's deli across the street.

After a lengthy discussion with Mr. B. about Norway's favorite foods, I left with a package wrapped in butcher's paper and twine in an overpriced lunchpail. The insulated canister was a necessity, otherwise every stray cat in Sacramento would be following me by the time I walked back to Eldridge.

Back at home base, I slipped Hibara's access card into the elevator reader, and the doors soon opened to the Green Room. Beaumont poked Kenny, who had his nose glued to the console monitor.

"Hail the conquering hero," said Beaumont, a silly grin on his kisser as he raised his arms and bowed at the waist.

"Behold! Michael Yeager, giant slayer," quipped Kenny.

I leaned on the padded console ledge. "What the heck are you guys talking about?"

"The Frost Giants have been real quiet the past day," replied Kenny. "A welcome break."

"So what gives with the 'giant slayer' guff? You know I didn't lay a hand on them." My eyebrows jumped from an unpleasant thought. "Is Hagebjørn okay? Those other two bums didn't return to pick on him again, did they?"

"Hagebjørn's fine," said Beaumont with an *OK* sign. "As for the galoots that were hassling him, Uttrag and Knock— Kanuck—?"

"Uttrag and Knokehode. The Fist-Thumper brothers. Two of the nastiest characters in Frost Giant security. They thought they ran sub-level NH5. Good riddance. They were nothing but a pain in our *assets* here on the containment floors."

"What happened to them?" I leaned in, eager for their current events.

"Not quite sure," said Beaumont. "I think it was honor killings by their kinfolk. Word got around New Jotunbyen that they ran from a mere human, and *sch-ch-chk*." He drew his thumb across his throat.

"New Jotun-*what*?"

"New Jotunbyen. That's their community, way down in the non-human sublevels."

"The Frost Giants don't live in the ILTS?"

"No, they punch in for work, using the Red Room entrance down-stairs for non-humans."

"Never mind that," said Kenny. "Why didn't you tell us yesterday you had a confirmation number? It would have saved us a lot of paper-work."

"Sorry, I just found out this morning. I'm told it's a standing confirmation."

"Yup," said Beaumont. "You can go on the containment floors anytime you want."

"Hold up." Kenny raised his hand like a cop at an intersection, his eyes riveted on the screen in front of him. "Yours comes with one restriction. Admittance is limited to only once a week."

My head sunk between my shoulders as I slumped on the console ledge. "Oh..."

"I-i-i think we can let yesterday slide," said Beaumont with a wink to his compadre. "That one was on Pellagati's dime. Besides, anyone who helped nix Ugly and Okeydoke—"

"Uttrag and Knokehode," said Kenny.

"Whatever—can get special accommodation once."

Kenny punched a button under the console ledge, popping open a drawer. He pulled out a pair of the red copper bracelets. "Put these on, so's we can attune them to you." I did as Kenny asked, after which he passed a copper bar flashing with a black light over them. "You remember how they work, right?"

Beaumont silently mouthed "clap on" while pretending to click his own bracelets together.

"Okay, just keep in mind they only work for fifty minutes at a time," said Kenny. As I slipped them on, I looked for a charging plug. He shook his head. "It's a built-in limitation on the magic."

"It enforces our union's demand for ten-minute breaks from the containment areas," said Beaumont through a smirk of satisfaction. "Going to visit 2D-141 again?"

"For the most part. I'd also like to talk with Hagebjørn. Is he around?"

"Yeah, he still works this shift. Just like us poor schmoes." Beaumont handed me a sheet of paper. "Here's the layout, so you don't get lost."

I snapped my fingers when an idea hit. "Say, can you guys look up another location for me?"

"Let me check my busy schedule." Kenny spun a full circle in his chair. "Yeah, sure. What are you looking for?"

"There should be another intrusion that came in with 2D-141. Do you have a record of it? Her name used to be Cheryl Greenbough, if that helps."

Kenny's fingers did a little dance on his keyboard. He squinted at his screen. "Yeah, it's here, but one level down. 3F-142."

"Why was one moved to another row, and the other a level down? Same day, same intrusion, same infection."

Beaumont chimed in, looking a little confused. "Yeah, that *would* be normal procedure. In this place, who knows? Some paperwork screw-up, probably."

"You can't visit *that* one, though," said Kenny. "You're only cleared for here—Level 2."

"How many levels are there?"

"Just the three." Beaumont shrugged. "High-priority cases are on Level 1, one floor up. Maintenance cases sit on this level. The hard luck cases get ditched into Level 3. Hardly nothin' ever comes back from The Cellars."

I gave the boys a quick thanks and headed down the ungainly steps. I halted in front of the anteroom when a troubling idea wormed its way to the surface. Though sad for Cheryl, I was also confused as to why Sindhu wasn't on the priority level. Hibara's highfalutin promises would make anyone think Sindhu rated the penthouse suite. On the other hand, did Hibara register Sindhu as RPIN—whatever that meant—so she could avoid the level of no return?

"Everything okay, Yeager?" called Kenny.

"You're not coming with?" I said over one shoulder.

Kenny shrugged his. "You got confirmation and a map. No escort needed. Don't worry. We got cameras all over the place if you need help. Have a blast. Make sure you're back before your fifty minutes are up."

Beaumont wagged his finger at me. "If I have to pull you out a sec-ond time, it'll be with ice tongs, dead *or* alive." His smirk indicated he wasn't kidding. I shared a nervous chuckle with them.

I clacked my bracelets twice and held my breath as I exited the ante-room. The air felt bracing, a refreshing breeze on my exposed skin. I exhaled, and a miniature sleet storm materialized in front of me. Poised to dive back into the Green Room the moment my sinuses froze, I inhaled. The air felt springtime cool. However, the room stank to high heaven with the odors of old refrigerant, dirty compressors, and cleaning fluids.

I made a beeline to Sindhu's cylinder. Turning the last corner, I froze in my tracks—my immunity to the Arctic environment notwithstanding.

Facing Sindhu's capsule stood Yadavi.

Her azure skin stood out against her dark green uniform and the bright red containers. Oversized red copper protection bracelets pinched her upper wrists. With her eyes closed, her four palms were pressed together in two pairs of prayerful silence. The three-carat ruby in the middle of her forehead smoldered the color of fresh blood.

I approached quietly until I stood beside her.

After a moment, she bowed respectfully toward the capsule. She folded her upper arms across her chest and faced me. Her lower hands hung by her sides with elbows bent and poised to strangle something. "I did not expect to see you here."

I shot her an incredulous glance. "Why shouldn't I? She's my fiancée, or didn't you know? I would've thought Petrakis told you that at Lick Observatory."

One blue hand shot out and grabbed me by the Windsor knot. Lifting me, she rammed me against a nearby cylinder. One of her lower hands pulled out a knife that would make Jim Bowie piss himself.

"Betrothed to an *intrusion*?" she bellowed. "I should gut you where you stand."

Dangling from her grip, I clasped onto her arm, hoping my strength was sufficient to prevent my cervical vertebrae from separating. Dropping the lunchpail, I scrambled to produce my card with Hibara's crest. I could hardly hear my own oxygen-starved rasp. "I have clearance."

Yadavi snatched the card from my grasp with her fourth hand, squinted harshly at it, then released me.

My knees crumpled under the fall. Through a spasm of coughs, I said, "Is *everyone* with blue skin trying to kill me?" Once I could draw a clear breath, I stood, shuffling forward half a step to face her down properly.

"Why have you waited so long to come here?" said Yadavi, still glowering down at me.

"I was lied to. I was promised Eldridge would work to rid Sindhu of the Euryale. I only recently found out she was relegated to storage and forgotten."

Yadavi regarded me with a jaundiced eye, then relented, facing Sindhu's prison again. "Then it is good that you found her. She is relieved you are here."

"I heard you were hanging around ILTS. Even so, I'm kinda surprised to find you here today." I interposed myself between her and Sindhu's capsule. "So, why are you here?"

"She is afraid and despairs. Her dismay calls to me."

"Then you're in violation of Rule 4 just as much as I am," I blurted with a scoff. "The way I read it, 'relationships' as specified in the Rules could include your casual interest."

"You are free to try to report me," she said, skewering me with angry eyebrows hooded over her eyes. Who knows what mine were doing. "I am told you have a respectable PQ ability, Yeager. Do you not hear her calling?"

I squinted harshly at Yadavi. "What are you talking about? She's frozen solid. Besides, this is one of the new Void canisters. How could she say anything?" I snapped my fingers at a revelation. "Are you saying Sindhu has a PQ, too?"

"I thought that obvious by now. Even to you."

"Then why would she speak to *you* rather than to me?"

Yadavi clicked her tongue. "Typical human male. Listening with their pelvis, rather than with their heart."

"And *you* gotta work on your insults, sister."

I examined the capsule exterior. It remained untouched from yesterday. Like before, Sindhu stood silent, the same statue frozen in time, her face a triptych of hatred, pain, and terror. The glowing mask of enchanted wood still hid the worst of the Euryale infection that had consumed half her flesh.

I explored the touchscreen display, reading at leisure the information that had scrolled past at blinding speed yesterday. Some of the data made sense to the biochemist in me. The rest was as indecipherable as nuclear physics or occultism. For all I knew, it could be a combo of both.

I gritted my teeth at the end of the list because it reminded me that other than Uttrag, her only visitors since containment were Yadavi, me, and Lenoir. Not one med-tech in the bunch. I did, however, spot that strange acronym RPIN again, next to my employee number.

Was that a good thing or a bad thing?

I burrowed into the details of the transfer to her current location. There were two employee numbers—one probably belonged to a Frost Giant, the other one struck me as vaguely familiar.

I closed my eyes and tried to reach Sindhu with whatever PQ-4 gave me. Nothing.

I placed my fingertips on my lips. Not long after, the faceplate. "I *will* find a way, Sindhu." I only wish I was as certain as my voice sounded.

If I knew how to pray, I might have done so at that moment. It was probably best I didn't try. I wouldn't be able to keep any sense of decorum for long. In any case, whatever passes for a Creator in this hostile new world of aliens, magic, and spirits wouldn't appreciate getting sassed by the likes of me.

"See you in a week, *mera pyaar*, my love," I whispered, stepping away from the device.

"Why did your Oovlid supervisor move her to this Void canister?"

"*Algernon*?" The halls echoed with my outburst. "It couldn't have been him. They've been trying to put him back together in the hospital for the past week. I thought this was more like your idea. You've been visiting her more than I have."

"Not I." Yadavi folded both pairs of arms, daring me to contradict her. "A Frost Giant managed your betrothed's transfer. I came upon the ugly creature while he finished his task. His name was Uttrag. He said it was at Algernon's request."

I closed my eyes again and brought up Jolly's eideticized transfer info. Sure enough, Algernon's employee number matched the unfamiliar entry for Sindhu's move. My mind filled with dark apprehension. "Did you *see* Algernon here?"

"No."

"Uttrag and his brother are dead. Someone or some *thing* murdered them last night. Made it look like an honor killing, or so I'm told." My head spun with conspiracies and theories of conspiracies. I leaned against the capsule next to Sindhu's for support against a whirlwind of sudden vertigo. "Uttrag was fooled into moving Sindhu. Then again, he wasn't the sharpest icicle on the glacier. He thought I was something called a *Jeger*."

"You *are* a Yeager."

"Don't *you* start... Follow me."

I checked my watch along the way—plenty of time left. We stopped in front of the cylinder marked off-limits with Hibara's seal.

"In this container are the remains of one of the two creatures that attacked me and Petrakis last week." I gave Yadavi a quick summary of our exploits at Western Bay State Hospital and a physical description of the shapeshifter. "When I fought one, I discovered their Achilles' heel.

Although they're impervious to sharp and blunt weapons, they bleed out quickly if enough skin is torn away. They also have a 'tell.' They prematurely age the people they copy."

"Why are you showing me this container?"

I stared at Hibara's seal, lost in wide-eyed thought. "I believe one of these shapeshifter bastards is here in Eldridge."

"Why have you not raised an alarm?"

"No real evidence."

"Who, then, is this creature's prey? Frost Giants? You?" Yadavi's voice acquired an edge that promised violence. "Your betrothed?"

"Me." Rather, Shadow inside me, but I couldn't tell Yadavi that. She already took one shot at me today. She'd finish the job, thinking I harbored another intrusion. "Our seer warned us of the danger, though it was fifty-fifty that either Algernon or I was the target. She was right—soon after her vision, we were attacked. I believe a shapeshifter took the form of a custodial staff. It took its shot, but guessed wrong with Algernon. My gut tells me I was the one they wanted.

"Then, by accident, Petrakis and I walked into their Plan B—a trap they set two years ago, which is where this guy came from." I stopped for a moment. "Or *was* it an accident? Some oracle from New York…"

I shook my head to get rid of the conspiracy mania. "With their failure there, the bad guys went with Plan C. After they landed Algernon in the hospital, he would be the perfect person to copy—unconscious and totally alien. I don't think anyone could detect rapid aging on an unconscious Oovlid. Ditching its cover as a janitor, it posed as Algernon and tricked Uttrag to move Sindhu's capsule. I wouldn't be surprised if the shapeshifter killed Uttrag and Knokehode after I scared the big dope into blabbing to every giant in New Jotunbyen about *Jegers* and their intrusion into Eldridge. It's possible the shapeshifter felt threatened and killed them to hide his tracks."

"You believe these *Jegers* and shapeshifters are one and the same?"

"I think so, but I need proof." Before I realized it, I found myself pacing. "The shapeshifters want me out of action, but they never seem to come after their target directly. Not at Western Bay State Hospital, and not with Algernon. I wonder what their next flank attack will be."

"What does that have to do with anyone moving your betrothed's capsule?"

It was my turn to glower an accusation at Yadavi. I rubbed my sore neck to make sure she got it. "Maybe they hoped *you* would do the job for them. You almost did." I resumed my pacing. "But I think you're onto something. Sindhu was moved here, from an older container to this Void capsule, for a reason. But why?"

Yadavi's extra-large wristwatch rang, and she tapped it off. "I must leave or suffer the cold."

"Before you go, tell me something. You mentioned Sindhu called to you."

"I ask again, Yeager. You do not hear her call?"

I scratched the scar under my scalp. "Nothing. What do you hear?"

"She is *not* alone. She is afraid. And I am powerless to help her." She faced me. For the first time, something brittle lay exposed in Yadavi's countenance. "Can you help your betrothed?"

"Her name is *Sindhu*," I said, challenging her. "Sindhu Mehra. Not once have I heard you call her by her name. Why is that?"

"That is a human name. It is not her true name."

I shook my head, like Yadavi herself had slapped me. "*What?*"

"Does that surprise you?"

"What *is* her true name?"

"If your betrothed has not told you herself, it is not for me to say." Yadavi cocked an ear toward me. "There is a voice inside of you as well. I did not hear it before, but it is there now."

Everything froze in place. Every color jumped out at me—the capsules of Golden Gate red, crusted with wisps of angel-white hoarfrost, Yadavi's cobalt skin highlighting her baby blue knuckles, the knurled umber hilt of her knife, the glowing red crystal in her forehead.

Yadavi tilted her head forward.

The gem in the middle of her forehead opened. A third eye gazed down at me.

My legs itched to run. I didn't dare move. The mouse stared at the huge three-eyed cat.

"Your voice has a name as well. Many names."

The thunder of adrenaline in my ears drowned out the racket of compressors hissing and fans rattling. If Shadow answered, it was lost in the cacophony.

The Durga warrior scrunched her forehead. Her eye burrowed past my defenses, but I didn't suffer any brutish strike from a psychic pile driver. She glided through my skull with the painless precision of a surgical drill. "You choose to call him Shadow. His names are *Anor Cuithas, Tawar Caun, Árātō Taurē—*"

"Who or what is an Anor?"

"It means nothing to Shadow. None of his names do. Not unlike your own *Alberich.*"

"Elrameshe called me by those names back at Lick. Dr. Fleischer, too—though jumbled around—just before the *Annulus* of the Attribute Stones attacked me. She never had the chance to explain what it all meant before an intrusion silenced her." I swallowed, afraid to ask the next question. "Does that make *me* an intrusion?"

"No. Your Shadow is of the *Koire-kwente* who sought sanctuary in this world and were welcomed by Eldridge long ago."

Yadavi's third eye closed, its eyelid transmuting back into an oversized ruby. Her remaining two continued scolding me.

"One more question—"

Her watch beeped again, this time more frantically. "Ask me on the way. I must leave. Now."

"On second thought, I'll catch up with you later." I held up my lunchpail. "There's someone else I need to talk to."

CHAPTER 42

I strolled around the ILTS floor, taking random turns at intersections that looked promising in my search for Hagebjørn. Who was I kidding? Except for the section and row designations, they all looked alike. The ILTS map was helpful, but I kept returning to Sindhu's cylinder to make sure I didn't get lost.

Wandering through the rogues' gallery of aliens, fairie, monsters, and straight-up nightmares, it wasn't until my third return touching base that I noticed something peculiar staring me straight in the face. Most of the capsules around Sindhu were empty, their faceplates unlabeled and touchscreen monitors off. All except one.

I tapped the screen of the capsule to the right of Sindhu's, bringing up the listing of its inhabitant. With my nose close to the faceplate, I wondered if I might see Cheryl's face, albeit twisted by the Euryale infection. After all, like every company, things get misfiled all the time.

I tapped on the light and jumped back with a start.

An Asian man, most probably Chinese or Mongolian, stared through at me with a hateful snarl that would give a Euryale a run for the money. Plumpish and bedecked in finery from some forgotten dynasty, his frozen hands clutched empty air, choking some neck that was no longer there. I wondered why he had not been fitted with an enchanted rowan wood mask.

I glanced at his name—*Bin Sun*. It didn't ring any bells. Ancient history ain't my strong suit.

"*Jeger*," croaked a massive voice from behind and two feet above my head.

To say I nearly jumped out of my socks would be putting it lightly. Before my wits reassembled themselves, my back had pressed itself against the Asian gent's cylinder. I puffed out snow, hard as a chain smoker with emphysema. The lunchpail rolled in a tight circle around my feet.

"Hagebjørn?"

"*Ja, Stor Jeger*, Great Hunter." The giant hunched over and spoke softly. He fretted a frown under lost puppy eyes and wrung his hands with such force, I thought they would tear themselves apart. "So relieved I am to see you in health. I hope you are good feeling after you *frostskader* get?"

I held up one hand, fingers spread. "Almost back to normal."

The Frost Giant knelt down on one knee. "Hagebjørn cannot believe you spared him. My life nothing is. But it is yours to use." It looked like he was going to prostrate himself at my feet again.

Picking up the lunchpail, I slapped his hand hard. No doubt to him, it was barely a love tap. "Stop that," I said in my most commanding voice. "Get up. Stand straight."

He snapped up so fast it took my breath away. I think all of his joints cracked at once. His expression was that of a recruit getting dressed down by his drill sergeant.

"Relax, Hagebjørn. But let's get a few things straight. I am not one of these hunters you are so afraid of."

"You... not *Stor Jeger*?"

"No. My name is *Yeager*—Michael Avery Yeager." Hagebjørn blinked so hard, he crossed his eyes.

Why did I feel like I just started *Who's On First*?

The overhead lights down the row flickered. Every touchscreen up and down our row went dark, flickering back to life one by one.

"Not again," worried Hagebjørn. He held his breath and cringed. Sticking his bony fingers into his bright blue ears, he glanced at the PA horns at either end of the row.

"What's wrong?"

The giant waited a few seconds before unblocking his ears. "Nothing now. Something *Bow-Man* calls a 'power glitch.' Sometimes alarm sound if it bad."

I shrugged. "Okay, then. Can I ask you a favor, Hagebjørn?"

His face brightened, beaming a smile showing craggy teeth with a bluish tint. "Anything, *Stor Jeger*!"

"Yeager, not *Je*— Oh, never mind. I heard Uttrag and Knokehode are dead. Something about their families and honor killing?"

He peeked around the corner at the end of the row. "Not what I hear. Not what I see."

"You *saw* them killed?"

"I see it happen. It start with little man like you, but made of gritty stone. He talks like he gargling."

It was strange, feeling my face flush with heat in this Arctic corridor. My guess that a shapeshifter had taken Algernon's form turned out correct. "Is that who killed them?"

"No, he meet with Uttrag and Knokehode at their home. He gives Uttrag orders, something about moving a Void Can again. Uttrag gets real mad, tell little stone man he was almost caught last time. They argue, and Uttrag tries to beat him up. That little man tough. Uttrag hit him. He hit Uttrag, Knokehode hit him, he hit Knokehode..."

Hagebjørn punched the air, followed by wild swings in every direction. Ducking a stray jab that got too close, I shouted, "Yeah, I get it—they fought."

The giant calmed down, overcome with an embarrassed grimace. "They hit him, and he not hurt."

"Yeah, that sounds about right. So that's when the stone man killed them?"

"No, he die with the rest."

"All *three* of them?"

"*Ja*! Something I never see before appear. It walk right *through* wall. Hagebjørn so scared, and I not even in room! It ripped Uttrag across face, then Knokehode across chest. *Rip, rip...*"

Hagebjørn slashed the air above my head twice, stretching his claws to frightening lengths. "It have hand with eight nasty fingers. Each one sharp as a knife."

"Eight?" My head spun. Things didn't add up the way I expected.

"That is what is one more than seven, no?" His eyes crossed as he counted his own fingers. "*Ja*, eight!"

"What did it look like?"

"Big. Almost as big as Uttrag. Big black bug, but no feelers on top of head, and it stand like man."

"No feelers—you mean no antennae."

"*Ja*. Two legs, four arms—but one arm cut off at elbow. Didn't matter. One hand enough to kill Uttrag and Knokehode."

Oh, crud.

"What about the stone man?"

"He get sliced, too. But he heal up real quick. Like that," he said, snapping his enormous dark blue fingers. "I thought he get away, until big bug pick him up and bite him in two." Hagebjørn smacked his fists against the sides of his mouth, bit down hard, then yanked them away as his mouth made a tearing sound. Somehow, I successfully managed not to flinch.

"Wait a minute. How did you see this? How did you escape the big bad monster?"

Hagebjørn pursed his lips and drew a line in the frost-covered floor with a toe. "It not see me. I look through window."

I couldn't hold back a chuckle. "You were spying on them?"

"No," he said. He stood erect, with an injured pout, as if I accused him of something. "I... wanted to make sure Fist-Thumper brothers not following *me*."

"Okay, relax, Hagebjørn. You did good. Did you see anything else?"

"Once stone man was broken, he turn into gray, slimy *dritt*. Then I run away, before big thing see me."

"Hold on, Hagebjørn. What do these *Jegers* look like?" I got the feeling Shadow was chuckling at how long it took me to figure out something obvious to him.

"A little taller than you, friend *Jeger*. But they all gray, pointy ears, no hair, and can their skeleton see."

Every inch of my skin crawled one inch clockwise. "Do they have transparent skin and sparkly innards?"

Hagebjørn's face contorted into confusion. "Ja, but you already know this, no? You *Jeger*, too."

I stamped my foot. "I am not a *Jeger*, *consarn* it! My *name* is Yeager, and that is all." My outbreak echoed back from each intersection. "Look here, Hagebjørn—I can prove to you I am not one of these *Jegers*, these hunters."

The poor lummox looked like he was getting one of my headaches.

"Do *Jeger* hunt other *Jeger*? Do they ever kill one of their own kind?"

"No, they hunt us. They kill only what they are told to kill."

"Like their Circle of Elders," I mumbled to myself. I pointed down the row of containers. "You know that capsule that's marked off-limits?

The one with the big red circles on the screen?"

"Yes," he said with an exaggerated nod.

"One of those *Jegers* is in there."

Hagebjørn cringed again, glancing with dread where I had pointed. "Alive?"

"Relax. He's dead."

"How you know he dead?"

"I killed him." I winced at the realization of what I had unleashed. I tried correcting myself—that a Fido killed him—but it was too late.

The giant jumped with a whoop. The floor trembled when he landed. His blue-toothed grin punched through his awe-struck expression. "*Jeger av Jegere*! You are not one who hunts us. You are hunter of hunters."

"I give up," I said with a shrug. "Now that you know about me, what about your story? Tell me about Hagebjørn."

"I last of three brothers. Me runt of brood."

"Are your brothers here, too?"

"No. Only Hagebjørn exiled from Jotunlands." He hung his head, looking at his toenails, filed into dagger points.

"Whatever for? You seem to be a fine Frost Giant to me."

"Because I like..." He glanced over his shoulder, ostensibly looking for other Frost Giants. "...to garden. Chief of clan banish me before my ceremony of gianthood."

"That's too bad. I think it's great you like gardening. My fiancée tried her hand at that for a while. Turns out she has a brown thumb, worse than mine."

"Fee-yan-say?"

"My betrothed. See here?" I tapped on her faceplate light.

"You... want to marry *monster*?"

"No, she's human, just like me. She was *attacked* by a monster. Eldridge has promised me they will look for a cure. Make her human again."

He examined her through the faceplate. "Even behind wood mask, Hagebjørn see she very pretty."

I wanted to dope-slap the poor goofball. Punching his hip would have to do. "That's the *monster* half, Hagebjørn."

"Sad... So sad. Jeger all alone. Not like Hagebjørn." He puffed his chest out. "I have new neighbor. She shunned, exiled from Jotunlands for reading. Even worse, a book from Midgard. A long book." Hagebjørn's grimace could crack a mirror. "Something called *Pride and Pitcher of Ice*."

"*Pride and Predjud—*"

"She is pretty, too. And smart. I will take her as mine."

"Doesn't *she* have a say in that?"

"She is different. She is cousin. We will make many strong sons."

A shiver ran down my spine, but not from the cold. Time to switch topics before I yakked. "Listen, Hagebjørn, about that favor."

"Of course, Jeger." I half expected him to hop in excitement again.

"My fiancée's name is Sindhu. I will be visiting her once a week. I would appreciate it if you make sure nothing happens to her. Y'know, just keep an eye out for her? Most of all, let me know the minute any doctors visit her."

"Yes, friend Jeger." Raising his hands, he tapped his index fingertips together rapidly. "But how I let you know? We not allowed to use human things like *telly-fone*."

"Tell Kenny and *Bow-Man*. They'll let me know."

I opened the insulated lunchpail and held it high above my head. Its contents were "room temperature," still wrapped in butcher's paper and tied with coarse twine. Rising wisps of water vapor froze in the frigid air, immersing the bribe in its own snowstorm. "Here. This is for you."

He leaned down, plucked the package from the insulated bucket, and gave it the once over. Rubbing his chin's stubble, he gave it a sniff. His eyes popped—kinda like mine when the first whiff of its odor used my nose as a punching bag.

"*Lutefisk*?!"

"Yup."

"Is it fresh?"

"*Is* there such a thing?" My nose wrinkled again as he sliced open the package with his little fingernail. "Nothing but the best for my fiancée's caretaker."

Hagebjørn bit into the crunchy ice shell that formed during our conversation. He purred like a saber-toothed tiger who found catnip. "Still warm. Thank you, Jeger. It be so many years since I taste." He tore another potion off with his teeth, paper and all.

Leaving him to savor his delicacy, I checked the capsule's status. After a moment, I located the section detailing the device's power usage. Everything seemed in order, except for several momentary power outages. "You said there's been a few of those power glitches?"

"Yes. First happened..." Hagebjørn sucked another hunk of lutefisk from the wrapper. His mouth full, he spluttered, "...one day after Jeger's *fee-yan-say* was moved here."

He was right—graphs don't lie. A power glitch sometime in the middle of the night after she was placed in this row.

An alarm screeched from every point of the compass. I flinched at the klaxon—the Seventh Trumpet of Doom would be more soothing. The floor trembled. The alarm stopped abruptly, and from its vanishing echoes grew a howl. A series of howls, in fact, from throats larger and more savage than any wolf.

"*Snø ulver*," hissed Hagebjørn. "Snow wargs."

Two massive heads, each larger than a Frost Giant's, snorted the floor at the intersection. A cross between the worst parts of a pit bull and a timber wolf, only three times larger, they spotted me. They emitted snarls that made my nightmares run for cover. The stomping thunder of several pairs of massive feet approached behind them.

Hagebjørn gagged on the last of his mouthful and spat out what I hoped wasn't a curse in Giantish. Grabbing me under my armpits, he lifted me off my feet with ease. He opened the empty capsule left of Sindhu's and flung me into it. I barely had a chance to regain my footing when he clanged the hatch shut.

The warg's toothsome maw rammed the faceplate. In a rabid frenzy, it clawed, pawed, and gnawed the outside glass.

A coarse, ragged whine switched on inside my capsule. My skin crawled at its grinding dentist drill's screech.

As I watched in confusion, the rage of the slavering monster intensified—but slowed. The creature's fury froze in mid-snarl. Its baleful hazel-blue eye stared hungrily at me. Behind it, Hagebjørn stood moored to the spot, caught immobile as he struggled to pull the warg away from my capsule.

The keening stopped like a knife's edge—not even the slightest hint of an echo filled the sudden emptiness.

Gravity and the floor ceased to exist. The rectangular faceplate zoomed away to a pinprick and vanished.

"Hey!" My call was an exercise in futility. My voice was swallowed up by empty space.

Blackness. I raised my watch. I couldn't see it or my hand. I flailed my limbs, hoping to find anything which to grab or cling to. Emptiness forever in every direction.

I shouted pointless words into the void. And again. Did a minute pass? Or was it an hour?

Some poor souls incarcerated in isolation are known to go mad after a month, a week, or even less.

Panic squeezed my heart. Dread stabbed at my soul from every direction in the emptiness darker than lampblack. Hour after hour, day after day, week after...

How did I count off a year and still retain my sanity?

How did I scream for that second year and still retain my voice?

My mind, soul, and spirit were ground down into a pitiable state of surrender. The floodgates of endless nothingness yawned wider, and I had no more power to resist.

The terror of utter isolation settled on my mind like a crown of razor wire. It ripped down my face, tore my chest, clawed at my limbs, lacerated every muscle, slashed my genitals. The darkness ate my tortured screams.

Peeling away the outer rind of my consciousness, all sense of time drained out of my being. My thoughts slowed, eroded, and sloughed off— each one dragged off whimpering into its private oubliette of torture.

I was everywhere and nowhere.

One final scream... ripped from my lungs... became my entire universe.

My eternity.

My everlasting torment of solitude.

My Void.

Forever and ever and ever and...

CHAPTER 43

A light.

Despite being the smallest of pinpoints, it brought me immediate solace, drawing my focus away from the yawning gulf of eternal nonexistence.

The dot grew in intensity and in size. As it neared, I could make out a shape of white and blue, the boundaries of which ebbed and flowed.

Across the expanse of black nothingness, between my enfeebled thoughts, wended a deathless song. It surrounded me, washed over my never-ending scream, soothed it, diminished it, silenced it.

The form drew even closer until I perceived a woman wrapped in a diaphanous flowing gown and a halo of blue. The horror of the infinite evaporated.

Her body so sensual, she danced for me. Her face so familiar, her eyes so radiant, her hair a deep ultramarine, her smile so tender, she sang to me. From her forehead glowed her inner light, lighting my emptiness with a mandala of lotus blossoms. It pulsed with life and her song.

She reached for me. Like a passing leaf in a brook, her hand wafted through me. Her connection sewed the scattered shreds of my mind together again. Her sweeping song filled my soul, drowned out my dread.

Terror dissolved into warm serenity.

Despair became contentment.

Fear transformed into love.

I beheld her smile—the one I had not seen for more than a forever ago.

Sindhu, my beloved Sindhu.

Whole and free of the Euryale.

I reached out to touch her, to draw her close, to receive her absolution. Her other hand rose to caress my forehead.

The chorale of her placid thoughts faded, washed over by a plainsong of regret, sorrow, and her own terror.

A vision struck me like a freight train.

I beheld a petite elderly Chinese woman, her face stretched taut in a death rattle. She lay sprawled on the floor against a desk of dark cherry, its side carved with Confucius meditating under the leafy curtain of a willow. Her lifeless eyes stared at a four-fingered claw with ridged skin like mummified okra. Its long, bloodied talons withdrew from a gaping hole in her chest. The rest of the creature's limb was diffuse, like living glass. But the woman's glistening heart and the insectoid appendage that clutched it were as solid as the desk. The claw closed, forcing her heart into a toothy maw in the center of its palm, and down the stalk of the limb's green exoskeleton.

My addled brain struggled with the vision. The woman was awfully familiar, as was the nightmare-spawned appendage. Where had I seen them before?

A voice composed of whirs, hisses, and clicks made every chamber in my soul shiver. Yet I understood its gloating taunt. "Do you not remember my lessons, Seng Ling? 'Take advantage of your enemy's unwariness, make your way by unexpected routes, and attack unguarded spots.' Have you forgotten my ways still work?"

Sindhu's wan cry floated above it all. "I tried to stop him. I tried to warn her."

My vision winked out. Having passed through the width of my soul, her hand left me—more like her tender touch had been torn away.

She drew away, floating on the irresistible current of some invisible river. Her light diminished. I cried her name. My screams for her return were swallowed by the inky void. I steeled myself against the onslaught of naked nothingness, though in my core, I knew my feeble mind could never withstand the infinite nothingness.

The light that was Sindhu continued to shrink, not into a pinprick swallowed by the hungry emptiness, but the rectangular faceplate of my prison.

All the particles of thoughts and memories that made up Michael Avery Yeager, sealed away in their separate hellholes and unique tortures, ran screaming back to me, slamming back to reassemble my mind.

Time, space, and gravity returned, and I collapsed on the capsule's metal floor.

"Sindhu," I called out, followed by a dry retch.

Why was her hair blue? And a mandala—*her* lotus mandala—in her forehead? Yadavi's words punched me in the gut. "*That is a human name. It is not her true name.*"

The door inched open. Hagebjørn peeked around the edge of the cylinder door, panic painted in stark lines across his face. Somewhere behind him, the snow wargs whimpered and whined for permission to destroy their prey.

"Let..." I rasped. My vocal cords seized up, from eons of screaming. "Get me out."

The giant tossed something in. The lunchpail clattered at my feet. He clanged the door shut.

"No, don't! Hagebjørn—"

The Void engine inside the capsule ramped up its grating whine once more.

"Not again..." I mewled.

The incomprehensible emptiness of the Void returned with a vengeance, ripping a scream from my soul, stretching it into another endless howl.

Another unending span of solitude.

Another hellish dose of eternity.

My meager consciousness, alone and fragmented, surrounded by endless void.

I learned once more the enormity of eternal punishment.

Until...

Until my ageless suffering was broken by another light.

But this godsend remained silent. It shone a different hue and not as pure. It moved unsure, as if searching. Then, having found me, it approached. My agony of shrieking throughout eons, meaningless as the single tick of a clock, ended.

"Michael."

"Shadow," I gasped.

Swirls of red fog stirred by a gentle breeze wrapped around us. As the haze coalesced into the Alaskan forest vision-world where Shadow and I had last parted company, I surveyed the terrible diorama of death and rebirth in new and unexpected clarity.

Where there once were blurred features, I clearly saw my mother's face as she grieved over my dead six-year-old's body. Father held her away from the magic coursing into my split and bloodied skull. The slain elven warrior clutched his hand over his red chest. The elven lady in her courtly finery, shredded and muddied by struggle, still hoarded close her carved wooden and platinum box. The soldier gripped his wooden sword, bloodied with black gore, guarding against some unseen enemy.

"Thank God you rescued me, Shadow—but why are we here again?" I asked as I surveyed the sorceresses, joining the dead with rays of fiercely burning magic fed by the setting sun.

"I am not sure." His gray transparent form approached the three as well. He circled each one calmly, inspecting their expressions of grief, desperation, and wary concentration. "These people seem so familiar. But I still cannot recall who they are or why they are here."

I stood over my dead body. "Things are clearer now. I can actually recognize my parents' faces. Maybe the two tending you are your parents?"

Shadow faced the elven woman holding the ornate black box clad in platinum. "My heart tells me this is my mother. Her eyes tell me that my father had already been slain. I believe..." Tentatively placing his hand on the container, then grasping the lid, he tried to open it, but it remained stubbornly shut. "There is something of mine in that box."

I drew close to the black chitinous limb buried in the young elf's chest. No longer smeared like spilled paint, every ridge, every bump, every one of its eight talons was plain to see. My shoulders squeezed together in a futile attempt to stop the chill of recognition that ran up my spine. "Is this what killed Fleischer?"

"Along with the shapeshifter pretending to be Algernon. The *Turiathurin*."

"Come again?"

"The 'Guardian of Secrets.'"

"This guardian doesn't also happen to have a limb with four talons around a mouth, does it?"

"The thing that killed the woman called Seng Ling is unknown to me."

"Great. Now I have three monsters to worry about."

"But there is one thing I now know." Shadow faced me. His gray figure attained depth, becoming somewhat translucent and no longer featureless. His face faintly bore the features of the slain young elf. "I know *why* we are here."

"Why?"

"There was a spell. One that you had cast."

"The eideticize spell, in the library?"

"Yes. I have watched your life with you, beginning after the day we died so long ago. When Elrameshe discovered me in you, I was made aware that I was not you—that *I* existed, that I was separate from you. I was locked in a silver palace, with all but one of its windows shuttered. I stood by that solitary window during your entire life, Michael. Watching, hearing, feeling.

"By learning that spell, you had unlocked all of my silver prison's windows. I wanted—needed—to know who I was. Since then, I have visited the portals, one by one, opening them, reliving events that have occurred throughout your life, revealing events that occurred in *my* life. Some are others' memories as well... Sometimes the glass is clear, other times my view is distorted or darkened. This window is clearest."

The top of my head began to itch. "Is this your memory?"

"It should be obvious it cannot. Nor can it be yours." He made an expansive gesture, sweeping around the clearing, until he pointed at the multicolored globe of light guided by the Forest Elf enchantress's power. "This window opens unto a memory belonging to someone else depicted here. I suspect it belongs to the green sorceress of my people, the *Koirekwente*."

A horrid epiphany slipped into my train of thought. "Or maybe this memory belongs to someone else. Someone inside your prison with you?"

Shadow remained silent.

"Who was it Yadavi spoke to?" I demanded. "Who spoke through me to scare off the Frost Giants? Who did Elrameshe speak to? Whoever it was, it knew your names."

Shadow did not answer for a long time. "I do not know," he finally said, regret in his voice. "He is with me. He has always been with me. Whether he is my keeper or imprisoned with me, he will not say."

"Why didn't you *tell* me?" I stomped in a small circle. "Don't you realize this puts me back in danger? Your keeper is an *intrusion*, Shadow. If anyone finds out, I'll end up as a Void Popsicle, this time for good."

I halted, and my entire body trembled. "Oh, God," I whimpered. "I can't go back in there again. I'd sooner die."

"But you *are* there."

I tousled my hair, and my voice vented my frustration at the sky.

He approached close. "Have I harmed you, Michael?"

I stared at Shadow, dumbstruck. If he wasn't an illusion, I might have taken a swing at him.

At first, I thought he had asked rhetorically, pleading a case to convince me he wasn't a malicious intrusion. But his tone and his bearing overflowed with concern—for me.

"So, how did you find me?" I pulled at my hair near the burning at the top of my head. "Or is the capsule doing this? Did the Void finally drive me insane?"

"No. You are here. Here, because of Sindhu. When she called to you, I heard her exquisite song as well. She saved you from the Void's solitude, but I was also drawn to her call."

"You were subjected to the Void, too?"

"Yes, but I was not alone."

I nodded with grim understanding. "You and your keeper saved each other from the Hell I went through."

Shadow stood and faced me. "I heard her song, and I followed. She led me to you. I saw your mind and soul trapped and torn apart in the endless Void. I wanted to help, but her presence stayed my hand." His gray form shifted his feet in the snow like an embarrassed schoolboy. "She needed you, and you needed her."

"Then she was taken from me, and I was trapped in the Void a second time."

"But Sindhu could not rescue you a second time. She was gone, taken by something else in the Void. But I could help. I entered this window—this memory—and brought you with me to save you from madness."

Guilt poked me in the eyes. "I'm sorry I snapped at you, Shadow. I apologize. Thank you for saving me."

"Merely self-preservation, Michael."

I chuckled fatalistically. "Yeah, you're a Forest Elf for sure. You sound just like Barandir."

He placed his hand over where his heart might be and scanned the sky. "There is still much of myself that remains trapped. But her song released me from my silver castle... at least, another part of me."

He opened his eyes. In his translucent face floated two eyes of piercing green. If the eyes were indeed a window to the soul, Shadow's allowed me to glimpse into one graced with the beneficent qualities to which any spirit should aspire.

"I see the memories in my castle's windows more clearly now. Through me, you can as well."

"I noticed. I can see everyone's faces." I pointed to the severed claw. "And this. Is this *turiathurin* related to the shapeshifters?"

"No." The taint of disgust stained Shadow's voice. He peered into the fog surrounding the clearing. "The shapeshifters are *urkāphan*, spies and agents who serve the king of the *Mori-kwente*, those who are sentenced to live in darkness." He pointed to the monstrous claw that still pried apart his ribcage. "The *turiathurin* is a servant of the *Kala-kwente*, those who live in light."

Shadow faced me, his eyes boring into me. "They both search for me. The *Mori-kwente* want to imprison me. The *Kala-kwente* wish me dead."

"You remember who you are," I whispered.

"I... I..." Shadow struggled as though he were stirring from a dream. He sighed in disappointment and defeat. "I do not."

"Your keeper knows. He told Yadavi your names."

"He revealed the words. They hold no meaning for me." His verdant eyes held me fast. "But this I *do* know. The *urkāphan* who had infiltrated Eldridge may be dead, but they and the *turiathurin* still search for me, and you will suffer my fate if either finds us."

A distant roar whistled atop the mountains.

The silhouette of Shadow's gray hair fluttered in a strange updraft. "Heed my words, Michael. The *urkāphan* are not finished. It is anyone's guess where the *turiathurin* is now. And the creature that killed Seng Ling holds Sindhu."

A torrential wind rushed down the foothills, scattering the forest and everything in it before its hurricane force.

Before he was swept away as well, Shadow called out, "Remember Sindhu's vision. Her witness. Her warning." The last of his being to wink out of existence were his fervent green eyes.

CHAPTER 44

The Void capsule opened again. I rolled out of the hatch, curled tight in a quaking fetal position. I threw up near Hagebjørn's feet. He sidestepped the mess before it froze. Yanked to my feet, my knees refused to support me. My blue giant friend steadied me against the metal exterior of my timeless prison.

My mind was still picking up the pieces, reassembling itself. One idea was at the forefront. "Stop him," I gibbered. "Warn her."

"Wake up, friend Jeger." He tapped my cheek with his open palm. My head recoiled as if I was on the receiving end of a right cross. "Are you all right, good friend?"

I shielded my face with both hands to fend off another one of his tender ministrations. "How long," I rattled, ending in a cough. "How many years?" I examined my fingers, expecting shriveled skin on ancient gnarled bone. They were as supple as the day I joined Eldridge.

"Leave him be," said a man with a smoky sienna complexion and high cheekbones wearing a white lab coat. His breath fell about me as fine snow in the bitter cold. Red copper bracelets hugging his wrists hummed with a febrile glow. "Can you hear me, Mr. Yeager? I'm Dr. Hatahali. Can you see me? How many fingers?"

"Eight? No... four?"

He glowered and shook his head at a second man in a white jumpsuit. "Compensation unit, stat. Prep a *soma* mask." Together, they lifted my bent form onto a UFO gurney.

I blinked away stinging tears that couldn't decide if they should freeze or not. Through my murky vision, I could still make out the rows of red Void capsules lining either side of the corridor, including mine with the open door. Flat on my back, I stabbed an accusing stare at Hagebjørn. "What happened? Why did you throw me in that blasted cylinder?"

"I sorry. The alarm. Something *bad* escape from Void can. Very bad." He twiddled his thumbs like a guilty child. "Other giants with snow wargs came looking for it. I afraid wargs would kill you. Or bad thing get you. So I hid you."

I grabbed the medico's wrist. "How long was I in there?" I could feel my eyes quivering, unable to focus on the man's face. Instead, they were drawn to the open door of my darkened capsule. I shook with the fear that the yawning chasm of endless night would reach out and claim me again. Despite my double vision, I perceived the vacant space where Sindhu's capsule had once stood.

"Gone," I whimpered. "Where?" The fearful possibilities crowded together in a maddening collage.

"You were in the Void unprotected for ten minutes," said the doctor.

I repeated the number in disbelief.

"We have to get you to the ER as soon as possible," he said.

"What happened to the chamber next to mine? Where's the woman who was in there?" My eyes pleaded with Hagebjørn. "Where is Sindhu?"

"Please, Mr. Yeager. You were in an uncalibrated capsule. We must get you—"

"No," I demanded, my voice cracking with anger. "Where is Sindhu?"

"Later," Hatahali said with finality. He grabbed the back of the gurney and pushed. "You need to be in a compensation module and soma mask as soon as possible."

A twitch of black in the distance caught my eye. Something crawled out of my opened capsule.

I struggled to my elbows but collapsed as we glided around a corner.

"Mr. Yeager, you've been pulled out of a Void capsule that wasn't prepped to house a human psyche. We must get you hooked up to a soma mask, or you will be rendered with permanent mental or physical brain damage. No one withstands the Void without it."

I tossed back and forth again, calling Sindhu's name and the warning in her song.

"Mr. Yeager," he scolded. "Please calm yourself. Or I will have your giant friend sit on your chest, and then we *will* sedate you."

I froze. Not because Hatahali's tone convinced me to settle down, but because of what pursued us.

A vertical black pool flooded the end of the corridor. It rippled as it barreled toward us, swallowing everything it touched, floor to ceiling. Like falling dominoes, stasis capsules submerged into the advancing wall of Void. Inky tendrils sprang from its roiling black edges, striking out toward Hatahali as it closed the distance between us.

"Look out! Don't you see it?" I cried.

Doggedly pushing the gurney, he ignored the oily tentacles lashing about his face. He put up no resistance as the malevolent blackness devoured him.

I screamed my uttermost terror before the Void engulfed me again.

CHAPTER 45

The doctor, a white jacket over his ER jumpsuit, stood at the side of my bed. I was still in my street clothes, though my copper bracelets lay on a table in one corner. Windowless white walls surrounded me. An open door beckoned me toward an empty hallway.

My sleeve was rolled up, revealing a transdermal patch. I smiled stupidly, relieved they didn't cut my YSL shirt.

A monitor displaying an image of my brain beeped on a nearby stand. Phosphors of red, yellow, and green chased each other over its convolutions.

When I tried to turn my head, an unexpected lopsided weight pressed it into my pillow. I raised my hand to search my face, but the good doctor pinched my wrist and took my pulse.

"Welcome back, Dr. Yeager."

"Thanks, Doctor...?"

"Hatahali. I'm in charge of the entities contained in our storage facility. Even the ones that *shouldn't* be there." With a smirk, he handed me a small mirror from my bedside table. My face was half encapsulated by a wooden mask similar to Sindhu's, except this one had fewer glowing runes. He shone a penlight into my unmasked eye, then tapped the mask with his instrument, adding another mystical symbol. "You were hallucinating on the way to the ILTS ER. That wasn't the best of signs, but we got you into the compensation module in time. You were asleep during your session there and were still unconscious when we attached your soma mask. How are you feeling now? Calmer, I should hope."

The blinding light washed away the stain of the Void and the clawing madness of everlasting nothingness. Or maybe it was the mask. "Better. What happened to me in stasis? Please tell me Sindhu doesn't have to endure that hell in her chamber."

A twitch troubled his brow. "Sindhu? Oh, the half-human you were examining. Despite her current intrusion, she should be experiencing dreamlike tranquility, if anything. Her capsule was properly prepared."

"Somehow, I find that difficult to believe." I returned the mirror. "You never answered my question back in the deep-freeze. Where is Sindhu? Her capsule is gone."

"She's safe."

"You better tell me she was moved to the high-priority floor." I tried to keep the growl out of my voice.

"Her stasis chamber was transferred to a high security area."

I hammered the doctor with an incredulous stare. "What place is more secure than the ILTS facility?"

A shadow crossing the door made my butt scoot to the far side of my bed. I could breathe again when I realized it belonged to Petrakis. He cobbled a smile together, but it was no match for the darkening storm across his forehead.

"So, this is how you spend your half-day off?" said Petrakis. "Tracking down a rogue intrusion?"

"What intrusion?"

His fake smile vanished, frightened away by the intensity in his eyes. "And you just happened to be in the vicinity of the stasis chamber from which it escaped? How did it get out?"

This was not part of the "pissed at Yeager" act. He was way too distraught.

"Honestly, I don't know what—"

"You're telling me you were standing in front of the rogue entity's stasis tube, and you saw *nothing*?" He twisted the bed's gooseneck reading lamp and shone it straight into my eyes. "What buttons on what capsule did you push?"

"Seriously, the third degree, Doc? And I thought *I* watched too many old movies."

"Answer me," he said, close to shouting.

"You're saying *Sindhu* was the rogue intrusion? You, of all people, know that's not possible. And I can prove she isn't."

Hatahali interposed himself between us and swiveled the light away. "Dr. Petrakis, is this necessary? My patient is still recovering from the Void's psychic trauma. It might be days until he recalls events from the long-term storage facility."

"It's all right, doctor." I sat up in bed and swung my legs over the side of the bed to face Petrakis. "I recall it. Every blighted second." Except for the singular Hell of the Void, thank God. I could sense the mask unraveling that nightmare like a cheap sweater. In a way, it was good Petrakis was raking me over the coals. It focused me to stand guard around the cherished memory of meeting Sindhu in the Void, protecting those precious moments from obliteration. That, and the visions—the warning that Sindhu gave me, and the unfolding mystery of Shadow.

"Very well then, Dr. Yeager. Your report, please." Petrakis set his legs apart like he stood guard.

"Sindhu—or her astral self?—was in my Void chamber."

"That's impossible," said Hatahali. "No human mind can escape or enter a sealed Void capsule."

"Not without help." Petrakis regarded me with all the warmth of a rectal thermometer. "Did she say anything to you?"

"Not at first." The mask itched my forehead. I squeezed my eyes shut, shoving its magic aside to recall. "Sindhu showed me a murder. A Chinese woman. I think her name was Seng Ling? I couldn't see the murderer's face—I don't think it had one. It had a mouth surrounded by four talons on an arm colored a sickening green. It remained incorporeal until it plunged its claws in and tore out her beating heart. Then it ate it."

Something in the back of my mind insisted I knew what that monster was. I shook my head—it couldn't have been a *turiathurin*, not with a green circular buzz-saw of a mouth instead of a misshapen black crustacean claw.

When I opened my eyes, Hatahali scowled at Petrakis, who occupied himself by chewing his lower lip. "I think Sindhu showed me what she witnessed." I continued. "When the vision ended, she said she tried to warn Seng Ling and stop '*him*.'"

"More likely, *she's* the murderer." Lenoir entered the room. I swear the lights dimmed in her presence.

"What is *she* doing here?" I spat.

"An Eldridge employee has been murdered at the same time when ILTS registered an escape of an intrusion. Then I receive a report that my favorite person of interest was visiting ILTS—right next to said intrusion."

Her eyes burned with the desire for retribution.

I slid off the bed to face her, my indignation versus her vengefulness. My fist trembled with the urge to deck her, woman or not. "Use your head, Lenoir. Sindhu is frozen in mid-transformation. She might be half-Gorgon, but her hand would have five fingers the color of living stone. Not a grotesque mouth from some alien insect."

"Are you sure of that?" Her sneer mocked me. "She could have shown you whatever she wanted in those cylinders. You would accept it without question after your mind had been ripped apart by the Void."

I didn't flinch or have the slightest doubt. I recognized Sindhu's face, her voice, her spirit. I knew her when she touched me. Blue hair or not. Mandala or not. No pretense, no masquerade, *nothing* could be hidden from the Void. "I'm positive."

Petrakis' anxiety waned. Lenoir's peevishness didn't. "Then why was Ms. Mehra witnessed at the crime scene?"

"I don't know. Who was it I saw murdered?"

"Dowager Sengling, Vice President of the Eldridge Beijing branch."

"Oh, crud," I muttered. No wonder Petrakis' nose was out of joint. "You mean Seng Ling?"

"*Sengling* wasn't the first," said Lenoir. Petrakis and Hatahali recoiled like they both had been dosed with smelling salts. "Last week, Vice President Hagane in E&SQA Tokyo was slaughtered. The week before him, the Korean branch's VP was taken out. Like Sengling, they were killed just as you described in your vision. A spectral shape, Ms. Mehra's presumably, was seen at all three locations. This time she registered on video and is clearly identifiable."

The itch near my cowlick told me Shadow was trying to get my attention.

"What was the name of the Korean vice president?"

"Daeyang. What does that matter?" Her eyebrows rose above narrowed eyes.

"Are you onto something?" said Petrakis.

"I'm not sure yet." I wanted to yank Amelia out and dive into research. Too bad I left her in my desk drawer. Even if she were here, Lenoir would go bonkers.

Something about the names bugged me. Not just theirs, but another name. One I saw earlier today. I rapped my head in a playful gesture to bring it to the forefront.

"I wouldn't do that, Mr. Yeager," said Hatahali. "Soma masks are delicate."

"Does anybody have a scribe handy?"

A chime rang in the hallway. The bell was followed by a deceptively calm female voice. "Code silver. Alert, code silver."

"Intrusion in the medical unit," said Hatahali through gritted teeth.

The dread of the Void lurking in the hallway rushed at me like a charging rhino. So much for the soma mask's effectiveness.

Lenoir glowered at me, pointing her arm straight at my nose. "You stay put."

From the shoulder holster underneath her jacket, she pulled out an oversized water pistol. Transparent green plastic revealed two reservoirs filled with white liquids and a barrel with two nozzles set close together. She hugged flat against the doorway, assessing the situation with her gun pointed at the floor, then ran toward the cries of distress.

"Doc, if your pen is a scribe, can I borrow it?"

Hatahali returned an expression like Miss Manners caught me using a shrimp fork to pick my nose. Shadow's itch on my scalp crawled down the back of my neck, making every hair stand up along the way.

"Use mine," said Petrakis, offering me Namiki.

"No, I think I better use his."

From behind me came a dulcet voice, the one that saved my mind from the ravages of the Void two eternities ago. "He's coming, Michael."

Hatahali and I wheeled around. Petrakis whispered, "*There's* something you don't see every day."

Floating a foot above the ground, Sindhu stood translucent, a vision of pastels painted on the air. Free of the stony embrace of the Gorgon, her face radiated the color of warm chestnut. Yet this was not an image of the flesh and blood Sindhu that last drew breath high atop Hamilton Mount. Her blue hair and lotus mandala burned bright.

Regardless, my heart shouted with joy. I reached to touch her, but she flitted away, inches from my hand.

"He has killed the metal, water, and wood. He hungers for the hearts of the air and stone." Her spirit drew closer again, but something pulled her back like a rubber band. "He knows you saw him. Inside and outside. Now he comes for you, *mere pyaar*."

"My love," I echoed, scarcely above a whisper.

The echoes of heated battle rumbled through the doorway. It was getting closer. "*Who* is coming?" I said.

"Sun Bin." Her delicate voice acquired a harsher edge.

Why did that name sound familiar?

"The thing that *infested* Sun Bin. He and his fathers before him, beginning with the general who taught the world how to war."

At his name, the scar under my cowlick burned.

Knock it off, Shadow.

Her translucent eyes of turquoise scrunched together like she suffered the mother of all headaches. She covered her face with her glowing hands and whimpered, "He's pulling me, stealing my power. I—" Her spirit vanished, leaving a wail trailing off to nothingness.

Calling out her name, I grasped for her ephemeral hand.

I lost her—*again.*

I wanted to punch the wall, but there was no time for the luxury of fury.

"What's a sunbin?" said Hatahali.

"Why's that so familiar? Think, Michael, *think*," I spat out between clenched teeth. "Sun Bin. Passed down through generations. A general." The maddening taunt of Sengling's killer tumbled back to me. I repeated it out loud.

"That's Sun Tzŭ," Petrakis ventured in a whisper.

"Who's that?" said Hatahali.

"A merciless general," Petrakis breathed uneasily. "He wrote *The Art of War* over two millennia ago."

"You're taking the word of an intrusion suspected of three murders?"

"In a heartbeat, Doc," I said. "Your scribe, please. *Now.*"

Hatahali pulled a filigreed pen out of his pocket—a Levenger Classic. "You'd better let me," he said, pointing his scribe at the monitor. "Levenger, please access the storage manifest. Display location of stasis chamber holding Sun Tzŭ."

"No, not him," I said. "Sindhu told us it's Sun Tzŭ's descendant. Levenger, please check for *Sun Bin.*"

The screen, displaying the mask readout from my brain, was replaced with a line of text.

```
Who's this bozo, Dr. Hatahali?
```

"Michael Avery Yeager," I said with a touch of imperiousness. I'm not used to a scribe giving me guff.

```
Why don't you use your own scribe, slacker?
```

My entire face burned. Petrakis jerked like someone stepped on his toes, and our eyes locked. There we were, two criminals trying not to look guilty.

A crash and electric gunfire popped in the hallway. "Please do as he asks, Levenger," said Hatahali.

A frowning emoji sticking its tongue out filled the screen, followed by the status of the capsule containing Sun Bin. I slapped my forehead with a growl. "The capsule label had the stupid name in the wrong order—Bin Sun. I was looking right at him and didn't even know it. He's in the tube next to Sindhu's."

Scanning the monitor, Hatahali declared, "Everything's running. He's still safe in stasis."

And there it was. I tapped the screen. The next breadcrumb. "Maybe his body is secure, but not his astral body. See this, Doc? A power glitch. I noted a few of these on Sindhu's capsule as well." I scrolled the timeline on the graph and tapped my index finger on the screen. "And these, too. Interruptions a week apart on his capsule. I'll bet each time roughly coincides with the three murders. Not only that, they'll match the time-codes when Sindhu's stasis chamber glitched."

"What are you saying?" From his expression, I could tell Hatahali reached the same conclusion, but refused to believe it.

"Sun Bin, or the spirit of Sun Tzŭ to be accurate, in life, could somehow move from one body to another. That's what Sindhu told us a minute ago. Now he's found a way to escape stasis."

"But why is he using Sindhu?" said Petrakis.

"Someone moved her capsule to 2D-141, right next to his. She said he was drawing her energy. Or maybe he's tapping into her Euryale half. Who knows what other powers they have?"

"How do you know *she* isn't Sun Bin—I mean, Sun Tzŭ?" Hatahali's attention snapped toward a crash down the hall and the shouts that followed. A blazing blue searchlight swept past our door. Its electric hum set my teeth on edge.

I turned to face the doctor's pen. "Levenger, please, who captured Sun Bin?"

The dossier appeared on the screen, scrolling past many documents, jumping down chains of linked pages, before coming to rest on a digitized image of a centuries-old scroll. Half the image was covered with black bars, as was its translated text next to it.

"*Crud*!" I spat. "Five names redacted?" My eyes sped down the report until a "Five Schools" entry caught my attention. The fuzziness left by the mask's footprints in my brain muddied my thoughts. I yanked at the wooden artifact. It may as well have been superglued to my skin. But the spark of intuition still came to me.

I kept snapping my fingers, trying to keep the spark alive and form my thoughts into words. "Five schools of Eastern magic... Right, Petrakis? That's what you told me back at Washington Bay with Ms. Oliver.

"Levenger, please tell us the etymology of the murdered's names. Sengling, Hagane, and Daeyang."

The screen hummed and blipped out a whole paragraph.

```
Closest translations: Sengling, Mandarin for
'forest;' Hagane, Japanese meaning 'steel;' Dae-
yang, Korean for 'ocean.'
```

I pounded my end table. It was as loud as the close-quarters combat down the hall. "That's it! Three of the five schools of Eastern magic. Wood, metal, water—just like Sindhu said. Okay, Levi, this is the big one."

```
LEVI?!
```

"Which Eldridge personnel of Asian descent have names closest to the meanings 'stone' or 'air?' The higher ranking they are, the better."

The monitor blanked, then Levenger spelled out,

```
Pound sand, sport.
Their names were redacted for a reason.
```

"Then don't tell *us*," I barked at the screen, then at Hatahali's pen. "Warn whoever *they* are that Sun Bin is on the loose, and they're dead if we can't stop him."

"Please do it, Levenger," ordered the doctor.

A second passed.

```
I have notified their scribes.
```

A weapon blast I couldn't identify made the walls shake. Lenoir slammed her back against the door in retreat, her gun still raised. Another blue flash silhouetted her body. A man screamed. She returned fire. Her gun made a squirting sound, and two columns of plastic string streamed out. Something hideous in the hall roared in response.

"Get out of here!" she roared.

Hatahali corralled Petrakis and me toward the exit. "We gotta go!"

"I'm not finished." I made a grab for Levenger, but Hatahali was too fast.

"Yes, we are." He dragged me along by the wrist, and we exited with

Lenoir covering our retreat.

Down the hall behind us, a security crew arranged themselves into a diagonal row. One of the men held a projector beaming out a cone of cyan brilliance so intense, the air about it crackled and hummed. Wherever the light fell on the creature, it solidified into a giant crawling horror, towering above them all.

Half indigo praying mantis, half cockroach tank, its two forelimbs attacked whatever living thing was nearest. Its insectile head bore three enormous compound eyes and a mouth filled with chitinous mandibles. They munched, stabbing and crushing, on the remains of a uniformed leg. Thick cords of cobwebs dangled from its long articulated neck.

Algernon's diagrams from *Aliens 201* clicked into place. I blurted out, "A Valdaan?"

Lenoir fired her souped-up water pistol. Out of its nozzles sprayed streams that combined into a single strand like Silly String. It splattered against the thing's head and a nearby wall. The web solidified. The creature strained its neck, pulling back with its four massive legs. Concrete crumbled down as it freed itself.

"*That's* what infested Sun Bin?" exclaimed Hatahali.

"Valdaan... I know this," I remarked to Petrakis. I called up the eideticized pages. "Valdaan: Warlike and extremely territorial aliens. No known intentions toward Earth. Argh—where's their biological info?"

"Big, nasty, and just the type to hold a grudge for thousands of years," said Petrakis.

One of its forelimbs struck at a guard. Covered with crooked parallel ridges, it terminated in four razor-sharp claw nails surrounding a toothy maw. "That's what Sindhu saw. That's what killed Sengling."

The Valdaan peered over the diminishing crowd of fighters, its head and its three compound eyes pointing directly at me. It bellowed a hateful cry and charged. The remaining security men tumbled against the walls. The blue light flickered off, and the Valdaan began to fade. It advanced *through* the fallen bodies and wreckage.

"Follow me," yelled Hatahali. We dashed down the nearest corner. "Levenger, please open the pharmacy door, stat." His voice was firm and free of panic. The door at the end of the hall swung open.

We sprinted down the remainder of the hall. Diving through the open door, it slammed shut behind us.

"Levenger, please lock down the pharmacy."

A heavy *clank* and the room was bathed in yellow. I pressed my nose against the door's square of reinforced glass. My heart skipped a beat when the Valdaan, nearly invisible except for its milky spectral aura, bounded straight for us.

"I don't think this door's gonna be much help, Doc."

"What do you suggest?" His eyes belied his calm voice.

"It materializes at will," I shouted. "Maybe it's vulnerable then."

"Where do you keep the scalpels?" said Lenoir.

"This is the pharmacy, not surgical supplies." Hatahali rummaged through shelves of plastic bottles and boxes with the zeal of a bargain hunter on Black Friday. As for myself, I could only gawp at the whopping great room filled with containers of medicines, basic chemicals, and spell components. To one side of the door stood a small sink accompanied by an eyewash station. Its decontamination safety instructions included a graphic indicating to not use the wash if tentacles sprouted out of your eyes.

"Doc, you got anything to kill a Valdaan? I hope you passed your exobiology courses with all A's."

The blue beacon burned through the door window. The Valdaan became solid a split-second before ramming the door.

Stunned by the impact, it shook its head and scuttled around to attack the ray's source. I could only watch impotently as the Valdaan eviscerated the first of the remaining security team.

Bottle by bottle, Hatahali disgorged the contents of a cabinet onto the floor. "DDT is the best I've found. But I don't think it will take a Valdaan down fast enough."

"What on Earth is DDT doing in a pharmacy?" said Petrakis, his face contorted with confusion.

"Epsalians use it as their anesthetic," replied Hatahali. Another box of plastic bottles hit the floor.

The memory of Sengling's beating heart flashed in front of me. "Do we have anything else that could act like a poison or nerve agent against them?"

Hatahali's fingers raked his forehead. "Potassium chloride! It jumbles their synapses. But they would have to ingest it. Dusting the Valdaan with it won't do anything."

I had an idea, but my body wasn't going to like it. "That's perfect, Doc. Where is it?"

"Chemical salts, cabinet three, right behind you. What are you planning?"

I ripped open its doors and plowed through the contents inside. Thank goodness they alphabetized this mess. I found it moments before the blue light flickered out, accompanied by a piteous scream and the crash of glass.

I popped off its lid and spritzed the contents with water from the eyewash station.

"Dagnabbit, my favorite YSL." Tearing open my shirt, I smooshed a hefty handful of the salty paste on my exposed chest, with an extra helping slathered over my heart. Tossing another quart-sized container to Lenoir, I said, "Do the same if it comes after anyone else. Hope it's *you*!"

The door strained with a squeal like hot iron quenched in water. The Valdaan's pearly spectral forearms oozed through the door, their clawed mouths hungry to find my heart. Its head flowed through the glass. I backed into a corner between two shelving units. More of the monstrosity passed through the door. As the creature neared, it coalesced into translucent solidity, filling its form with dark purple putrescence.

Hatahali flung his plastic container against the beast's thorax. Liquid DDT splattered along its side. It bubbled and sprayed onto the floor as the Valdaan exhaled through spiracles lining its ribbed abdomen. Ignoring the distraction, it advanced unfazed.

Petrakis dove for cover, away from the splash zone.

Lenoir shot at one of its limbs, rising high and poised to strike me. The epoxy string webbed the limb against the ceiling. Her gun whined like a camera flash recharging.

I grasped the vertical rails of the storage shelves. Gripping them tight kept my hands occupied, rather than idiotically punching at the creature with my bare fists. I thrust out my chest. "C'mon, Sun Tzŭ, you lousy sonova—"

Its other forelimb shot out, straight at my heart. Salt paste drenched its arm as I recoiled from the strike. Searing pain stronger than a sledgehammer struck me as four barbs of steel pierced my flesh. The mouth chewed through my skin. It burrowed deeper into my chest, its talons spreading my ribs as the fang-rimmed maw bored its way to my heart.

I fell back, yowling in pain as I collapsed in the corner. Another spasm of red agony, and my world spun. Just like Petrakis warned—eternal agelessness is not the same as eternal life or invulnerability.

The misery relented. That is to say, it wasn't a fifteen out of ten on the hospital pain scale anymore.

When my vision righted itself, I could make out the outline of the Valdaan twitching. Its forelimb, covered in salt and blood, thrashed about. My heart was still safe in my bleeding chest. It would have hurt loads less otherwise.

Shelves and cabinets toppled as the creature lost its balance and collapsed on its side. Its legs flailed as if it were running at top speed.

Lenoir opened her canister and rammed it into the end of the webbed forelimb, its mouth dangling from the ceiling. The screaming horror halted, as sudden and severe as if time had stopped.

Gravity seemed to go sideways on me again, and I almost passed out. That is, until Hatahali slapped his hospital jacket, folded up into a makeshift compression bandage, hard on my chest. I howled in pain again, then fell into the comfort of painless oblivion.

CHAPTER 46

I came to, flat on my back in my hospital bed again. Except this time, I was stripped down to a pair of paper-thin drawstring trousers. My soma mask was gone, a large gauze bandage was taped across my chest wound, EKG patches were plastered over my torso, and an IV bag dripped saline solution into my arm. Hatahali stood over me, wearing a fresh clinical jacket, keeping one eye on my heart monitor and the other on me. Behind him, Petrakis wore a sly grin and tapped his nose with his index finger at me. Lenoir stood in the corner, brooding with her own thoughts.

"Dr. Hatahali." I expected my chest to scream bloody murder at me when I spoke, but it was silent. "Glad to see you guys made it." I tilted my head. "You too, Lenoir."

Her jaw shifted from side to side. I hoped that was crow she was chewing on.

The hall echoed and trembled from something enormous moving, followed by a cavernous *"Jeger!* I am so glad you live." Hagebjørn's enormous blue head filled a quarter of the doorway as he peered into my room. Dripping gallons of sweat, he nonetheless beamed a huge grin. He must have crawled down the hall on all fours.

I shot him a smile and a finger pistol. If Sindhu were here, even if only in astral form, she would have completed the reunion. My heart hurt, but this time, it was a good hurt.

"All right, visiting time is over. I have to talk to my patient," declared Hatahali before herding Hagebjørn's head, Lenoir, and Petrakis out and closing the door.

Before Hatahali could address me, I asked, "How is Sindhu?"

Hatahali professional concern was replaced with a wise grin. "She's fine. Body and spirit are unharmed in her stasis chamber, which is back in its original place. Far away from Sun Bin."

"I know Sun Bin used the power outages and Sindhu to escape. Heck, he probably *caused* the power glitches. Even so, how did he manage to escape the Void?" My heart skipped a beat. The hope that Sindhu might duplicate the Valdaan's Houdini act on her own lightened my spirits.

He scratched the back of his neck. "The techs are still working that out. Their best guess is the Valdaan somehow drained energy from its chamber and Ms. Mehra's."

Maybe from Sindhu herself—in her newly revealed blue-haired mandala-bearing form. I shook my head, wondering when or if I could talk to her again, and in what form I would find her. I could sense a headache creeping up on me.

"*What* is she?" I mumbled to myself.

"It's an interesting riddle," he continued, oblivious to my own woolgathering. "How the mind of a Valdaan existed in a human host and could jump from body to body, one generation to the next."

"Don't forget the ability to physically manifest itself in its true form."

"That too. Thank goodness your hunch was right—that when corporeal, the creature was vulnerable to its physical weaknesses." He folded his arms and gazed at the door. "Now we're left wondering what to do with Sun Bin himself."

"He's not dead?"

"We won't know until we attempt to revive him from containment. In theory, what remains should be human." Hatahali tapped his chin in thought before turning his attention to the monitor. "Levenger, please bring up Sun Bin's RPIN contacts. Let's make sure we don't have another surprise waiting for us."

I sat up like I leaned on an electric fence. "What's an RPIN?"

"It stands for 'Rehabilitate Pending Intrusion Neutralization.' It usually comes with a list of next of kin, but in Sun's case, it will probably list employees assigned to assist with rehabilitation. I wouldn't be surprised if the two surviving targets are included in his RPINs. In any case, I want to verify we don't find another Valdaan in hiding."

My heart was ready to leap out of my chest with hope again. Like getting two cones from the Good Humor man for the price of one. "Doc, I could *kiss* you!"

Eyebrows take a holiday—I didn't care how silly a shit-eating grin was plastered across my face. Spring had sprung again, God was in His heaven, and all was right with the world.

Sindhu was designated as having an RPIN. And my employee number was it. I was free from the death sentence hanging over my head!

Hatahali seemed amused by my expression, but his humor faded when he returned his attention to the monitor.

"As if simply reviving him wasn't a challenge enough, we must also consider his psyche. We don't know how old he was when the Valdaan possessed him. We could be dealing with the mind of an infant in an adult's body. That's in addition to any adjustments he'd have to make to successfully adapt to a world twenty-three hundred years in his future."

I was feeling magnanimous. After a moment, I thought aloud, "Maybe you could ship Sun Bin to the Eldridge office in Shangri-La?"

"That's not a bad idea. One less aspect of future shock for him to deal with."

I sat up in bed, testing how tender my ribs and chest wound might be. "Wow. No pain. Thanks, doc."

"I didn't do anything yet. Perhaps you can explain that to me..." Hatahali reached over and, with a single quick yank, ripped the bandage's adhesive strips off. I sucked air through clenched teeth. "...along with your medical record. It's redacted more than those reports on Sun Bin."

My chest was smooth. No wound, no jagged teeth marks, only a hint of a scar—though my ribs still ached. A benefit of the Circle of Ageless Waters, I suppose? Peeling off the remaining dissolved sutures, I regarded Hatahali with a friendly smirk. "Good genes?"

His arms folded tight against his chest. Accompanied by a severe half frown, it was plain he wasn't buying it.

"Lemme put it this way, Dr. Hatahali. Is it all that strange in a company like Eldridge?" I swung my legs off the bed. "I'll make a deal with you. After I have all the pieces of the puzzle, I'll let you know." I eyed the entire room. "Hopefully not under circumstances like today's."

He regarded me with concern, then relented. Unfolding his arms, he removed my IV and EKG pads. "Try to stay out of trouble, Dr. Yeager," he said, stilted and unsure. "I'll sign your release forms and escort you out when you're ready."

Closing the door behind him, I opened my closet. Everything was

still there, torn YSL shirt and all. Even the copper bracelets. They beckoned me to visit my Sindhu again.

I dressed, pocketed my bracelets and tie, and headed home. I preferred to savor the fresh memories of my beautiful fiancée—blue hair,
mandala, and all—over ugly Euryale reality.

CHAPTER 47

I slept like the proverbial baby—waking every couple of hours to fuss, cry, or scream.

It actually wasn't all *that* bad. Most times, I would wake up grateful I had made so much progress. Knowing that Sindhu's mind and spirit still lived on gave my hope the shot in the arm it desperately needed.

If only I could stay in that frame of mind for long. Instead, I'd end up contemplating her terrible struggle against the Valdaan, whether she was safe from the Void's terror of eternal loneliness, or why her essence chose to take the form it did. I dreaded the times when despair stalked my waking night hours as I considered the long road ahead to be reunited with my beloved. Worst of all was waking to the night terrors of an *urkāphan* shapeshifter crushing my throat.

When my alarm went off, I woke up in a good mood. I celebrated by showing up to work in an off-the-rack ensemble by Brooks Brothers. Even though it was far from their best, I still looked darned spiffy walking through the office maze of cubicles.

My high spirits, however, spilled over the cubicle divider too strongly for Natalie's druthers. More than once, my humming was answered by, "Knock it off, Alaska."

No sooner had I finished my supplemental report about the Sun/Valdaan Intrusion and faxed it to Central Records than I paid a visit to my grumpy mentor. "Has Barandir returned from wherever he went?"

"Nope, and when he gets back is on my 'Don't Care' pile."

"Wow, what burr got under your saddle?" When in Rome's cubicle, speak their lingo.

New graphics and star charts blipped onto her screen faster than popcorn while she typed furiously. "I swear the seers in London have it out for me. They dumped another stack of potential astronomical disasters on my to-do pile last night, and Petrakis expects an update on all of them before lunch."

"Could have been worse. Petrakis could have continued Algernon's tradition of having daily progress reports at nine o'clock."

"Git!"

I backed out of her cubicle, the only sound I dared make an empathetic chuckle.

Since Barandir wouldn't be available for the foreseeable future and had taken his translation dictionary along to *Tawar Cevan*, I went to the only logical place.

Quick-stepping my way once more to the library, the trusty card catalog sent me to the reference area, where I found precisely one English-to-Elvish dictionary. The ponderous tome was about as helpful as I feared it might be. If you weren't already familiar with Elvish, it was as easy as pi —to the hundredth decimal place.

It contained a phonetic glossary, but searching the volume by taking potshots at sounding out *Anor, Árātō, Caun, Cuithas,* or *Taurē* could take forever. On top of that, the red stripe at the base of the book's spine indicated the book was not allowed outside the library. So much for borrowing it for a few nights.

Strike one.

Several minutes remained before the group's pre-lunch round-up. I strolled to the upper levels, slinking my way to the shelf where I had found *Gaming the E&SQA System*. I wondered what other gem Uncle Billy-Bob could offer me.

I checked every book with the same Dewey number. Scanning the shelves above and below as well yielded squat. I was faced with two possibilities: either it was Petrakis' personal property, like his special-edition handbook; or the library figured out someone cast a spell from it and confiscated it. Which could spell big trouble with a capital *M* for *Mertens*.

Strike two.

I headed to the library exit, wondering what strike three might be after whiffing at Elvish and Billy-Bob. I got my answer at the top of the staircase leading to the main lobby.

"Good morning, Mr. Yeager."

Sable Lenoir leaned against the end of the bookshelf, staring laconically at the central lighthouse. Dressed in a mansion-white Armani business pants suit paired with a black satin shirt, she topped it off with a blazing red tie that matched her shade of lip gloss. With one hand in her jacket's pocket, she sported a sickening grin at me.

"*Guys and Dolls* called," I taunted. "Sky Masterson wants his suit back." If only I was as unconcerned as I sounded.

A spindly black gentleman wearing a suit and tie that would have been a perfect photographic negative of Lenoir's getup stepped out from the neighboring row. Not knowing what to expect from her new psychic muscle, my defense wall shot up. I could tell it was stronger from my recent PQ boosts, but I had not been keeping up with my practice drills. Any Alpha worth their reputation could still get past.

"Relax, Mr. Yeager," said Lenoir. "Mr. Odutola won't be assisting me on any interrogations today."

"What happened to Pellagati?"

A flash of annoyance soured her grin. "Please, Mr. Yeager. No games today."

"That's *Doctor* Yeager to you." I still disliked using the moniker, but I made a willing exception in her case.

"We *both* know he's quite happy in his new position," she bulldozed on. "However, given recent developments, I would like to have a chat. I've reserved a room on the library's main floor. If you care to accompany me?"

"Said the spider to the fly."

She gestured down the staircase. "There will be no Alpha tricks, I promise. As a matter of fact, I want to *give* you information you might find to your benefit."

If we were climbing the stairs instead of heading downward, it would have been the perfect allegory for ascending to the gallows. Especially if she knew Shadow lived inside my head. The three of us spiraled around the lighthouse, almost keeping pace with its slowly rotating search beam.

Lenoir led me and Odutola to a side room next to the librarians' offices. "Thank you, Mr. Odutola. I'll be fine. Wait for me back on Alpha Level."

In silence, he nodded to both of us with a smile I associate with those who come to my front door armed with religious tracts.

Lenoir bade me take one of two seats near a hefty machine occupying the room. Large as a desk, a central back-projection screen loomed over an apparatus with large glass platens bookended by two spools. It reminded me of an oversized View-Master on steroids. On its left side, a work area held a small pile of film canisters and a stack of photographer's binders.

"Is that a microfiche reader?" I squinted at the contraption. "I don't think I've seen one quite like it."

"Nothing but the top of the line for Eldridge. It reads every format of microform."

While I sat, Lenoir kicked a stopper under the door to keep it from closing. "Knowing we've met previously on less than friendly terms, I thought you'd be more comfortable with an easily accessible exit. As an added bonus, no one, including Mr. Odutola, can approach without being seen."

Taking the operator seat next to me, she pulled a halt-lex out of her jacket and placed it in front of the screen. Tapping the top of the tiny tetrahedron, all four corners lit up red. After it flipped over, Lenoir gave it a spin. It rotated faster until the three corners blurred into a ring of crimson. "Now we can talk in complete privacy."

"Thanks for the extra precautions, but you're assuming I'm as paranoid as you are."

She shot me an incredulous glance, focused on my forehead. "You aren't?"

Next time I see Shadow, I'll ask if he can give me a hand getting my eyebrows under control. I sat back and folded my arms. "What is it you wanted to show me?"

"Some old newspaper headlines from around the country."

I watched her face intently, waiting for a hint of her Machiavellian side to emerge.

"As Pellagati no doubt told you, I had believed you to be a shapeshifter mole during and after our interrogation session. Since yesterday's experience with the Valdaan, I am now convinced you are not. Not even a Doppelgänger could sustain such injuries and maintain an alternate physical form."

As she loaded the first microfilm reel into the machine, she asked, "Refresh my memory, Dr. Yeager. Your memories begin at age six, beginning with the Good Friday Earthquake near Anchorage. Then your parents moved to...?"

"Lubbock, Texas. The southwest outskirts."

"That's right," she said with a patronizing tone appropriate for a first-grade teacher leading her class. She spun the reels, stopping here and there along the feed. "Where did your father work?"

"Carlsbad Caverns National Park in New Mexico most times. Sometimes, he had to cover Hot Springs National Park in Arkansas."

"That's quite the commute." Her eyebrows bounced in exaggerated surprise, mocking my own fuzzy semaphore flags, no doubt. "If my math is correct, that's a three-hour drive to Carlsbad and at least eight hours to Hot Springs."

"Nine. Father stayed in park lodgings during the week and came home for the weekends—except on holiday weekends, which especially sucked for Mother and me."

"I see." She paused spooling the reader, stopping at the local section of the *Lubbock Avalanche Journal*. Nothing jumped out as newsworthy unless you considered "Local man bites local dog" consequential.

"Do you remember when you moved from Lubbock to sunny California?"

I scrunched my cheeks in thought. "1970, sometime in mid-May. I remember it was the weekend. Father came home Friday night with the news of a promotion—"

"Now, now, Dr. Yeager." She wagged her finger at me playfully. "I thought we cleared that up. Your father *requested* his transfers."

"Regardless, I was not happy. What twelve-year-old would be? We spent the weekend packing up and jack-rabbited it out of Texas that Sunday night."

"All right, then." She turned to the viewer and began spooling again. "Let's take a look at Sunday the Tenth. Anything in the *Avalanche Journal* social register about the Yeagers leaving town?"

Some people have a gift for comedy. Lenoir didn't. That day's headline described trouble at a capital rally protest.

"Let's try Monday. Nothing there either. How about Tues—Oh, dear..." I was pretty sure Lenoir wasn't asked to perform in any high school plays, either.

I read the screen.

Twister Smashes Lubbock
20 Dead, Hundreds Injured

"My, you certainly were lucky. Missing such a terrible catastrophe." She scrolled to one of the day's side stories. "Look at that. The twister demolished your own neighborhood, to boot. Goodness, 'lucky' doesn't begin to describe it."

My hands gripped my chair's armrest.

"Where was it in California that you moved next?"

"Sunland, a suburb in the armpit of Los Angeles. The only place we could afford was in a dump of a mobile home park, while father worked in Angeles National Park."

Lenoir loaded in several sheets from the top binder. "I think you told us the next place you resided was in South Dakota. What date did you leave Sunland?"

"First weekend of February, 1971. We were there only eight months, thank God. Then it was '*déjà vu* all over again.' Father got the news Friday night, and we piled everything into the wagon for Rapid City that Sunday."

The viewer flashed. Lenoir maneuvered a small joystick, and the screen jogged around an array of pages from the *San Fernando Valley Sun*. Zigging up and down, zagging left and right, she paused on the headlines of each day of February's news. She stopped on Wednesday the 10th. Lady Machiavelli turned to face me, grinning maliciously.

```
              24 Quake Dead
        50 Missing; Bridges Collapse
     Dam Badly Cracked; 2 Hospitals Wrecked
```

My jaw ached from gritting my teeth so hard. "You said 'no games,' Lenoir. What are you getting at?"

"Wait, Dr. Yeager. There's more."

She zoomed through the next spool. The *Rapid City Journal* from June 12, 1972, splashed on the screen. A lurid photo of a woman face down in water, drowned in a tangle of roots, took front and center. The headline blasted:

```
        Torrents, Then Major Disasters
     At Least 105 dead, $100 Million Damage
```

"*Whoof,*" Lenoir exhaled enthusiastically. "And on the very Sunday you left for Fort Collins, Colorado, too. Looks like you got out of Dodge by the skin of your teeth." Her sinister chuckle would get a thumbs-up from Mephistopheles himself.

The *Fort Collins Coloradoan* scrolled past next. The headline of August 1, 1976, shouted its accusation at me.

Floods Roar Down the Poudre Canyon River

My eyes skittered across the photos, quotes, and statistics. Over a hundred souls perished, again on the day after we had vamoosed for the relative safety of Mt. St. Helens.

I gnashed my teeth at the screen. "Where are you heading with this, you sick, twisted bitch?"

"I'm well aware of your opinion about me." She clicked off the screen and rewound the spool of microfilm. "I assume I don't need to show you the headlines from the Portland newspapers the day after May 18th, 1980."

"Heartless, soulless, God-forsaken wretch." My hands spasmed into fists. "Are you trying to tell me my parents caused these disasters?" I laughed a pitiful laugh. "That mold-infested Roach Motel you call a brain is crazier than I thought."

"Flattery will get you nowhere, Dr. Yeager." She seemed to revel in that despicable grin.

I stood up and flexed my jaw forward before their muscles seized up. The veins in my neck pounded. "Oh, I'm just getting started, you vile little ambulatory defecation. I hope you feast on botulism soup and anthrax pie in the hereafter. And as soon as possible."

The halt-lex certainly worked its magic. I shouted loud enough to topple Jericho, and the library outside continued on its merry way.

Her devilish grin disappeared. "Finally gotten that out of your system, Dr. Yeager? We still have business to discuss."

"Have a wonderful soliloquy, *Maleficent de Vil*. I'm outta here."

In stabbing, sharp syllables, Lenoir called after me. "Don't you wish to know *why* your parents died?"

I wheeled a step away from the door. I gave her my best glower while I panted like a spent horse. "My mother is still alive, bitch."

"Possibly. We do not have verifiable proof of that."

"I think we do. The gray shapeshifters need a live body to create their doubles. I saw them extract some form of life energy from Nurse Davis. Doing so ages their subject. They've copied my mother so often, she's been artificially aged at least into her eighties. She'd still have to be alive to make their latest copy at Washington Bay."

"How do we know their last copy didn't age her into an early death?"

"One shapeshifter told me he would torture both of us back at *Phelek Lepan*."

"You're so sure they haven't disposed of her, now that their gambit has failed?"

"Both the shapeshifters are dead. How could their leader find out?"

"If one of my agents failed to return from the field on schedule, I would immediately assume something had gone wrong. Surely, the shapeshifters are at least that intelligent." She patted my seat. "Come, let us reason together and put your doctor's brain to the test. The future of E&SQA Sacramento may depend on it."

Our eyes fenced one against the other, after which she relented. "I must apologize for how I treated you just now, but I had to assess your reaction and ensure it was an honest one. However, I'm afraid I still have several difficult questions to ask."

"You said you had information that would benefit me. Tell me, how did dragging me through that memory lane of pain help?"

Lenoir slid her chair a few inches away from me. "Please?" I brusquely accepted her invitation. "Now, Dr. Yeager, difficult question number one: You left the sites of all those natural disasters immediately before they occurred. How do you explain this?"

"I can't. I never made the connection before today."

She cut a *harrumph* in half, then peered at me as though I were a germ under a microscope. "You expect me to believe you had no idea about these miraculous coincidences? That you were blissfully unaware of the news that must have been blasting on every radio and TV in the nation?"

Her voice was on the edge of maniacal.

"We were on the road." I stared at the floor as I searched my memory. "Mother was in control of the radio and the 8-track during trips. Nothing but music. Father never got the local paper at our new digs until a week after we settled in. The movers didn't bring our stuff until a week later, either—including the TV. Besides, I was just a kid. I watched movies, went to games, and listened to music. Girls and school were my priorities, not the news."

She chewed on that for a few seconds, then moved on. "When did you last spend time with your parents in Washington?"

"I spent a long weekend between classes at our home near Trout Lake. I left May 17th, the day before the volcano blew."

"So that time, it was *your* decision to leave, not your father's." She leaned forward, her eyes more intent than ever. "Another lucky coincidence?"

Rubbing the back of my neck, I said, "I planned to leave Monday morning. Father said he got a phone call Saturday and had to work Sunday. Mother, of course, was zoned out on Thorazine and whatever other anti-psychotic cocktails the doctors prescribed. I offered to look after her while he worked, but he insisted I leave the middle of Saturday."

Her sardonic grimace burned straight at me. "Dodging a bullet from Mother Nature once is luck. Twice is a heck of a coincidence. If you count Anchorage, surviving six doomsdays is an undeniable pattern."

"What are you driving at? You still can't think my parents—"

"Someone wanted the Yeager family dead. *Really* wanted them dead. It's also quite obvious someone else was warning your father."

My head jerked like some long-buried memory punched me in the snoot. "I never heard the phone ring at Trout Lake," I mused hoarsely. "Thinking back, every time we moved, we only had Father's word he received orders to relocate. And that name he said to Mother at Fort Collins. It practically turned her into a zombie."

Like Donald Pleasance uttering the Russian mole agents' activation key-phrase in *Telefon*.

"Yes," said Lenoir, spurring me on. "I believe you said it was a woman's name beginning with 'At,' like Athena."

"You're suggesting someone—or something—was throwing natural disasters at us? If we weren't both employed by Eldridge, I'd say you're certifiably nuts, lady. Who would have that type of power?"

"I don't know yet." Lenoir rubbed her palms together. "Let's refine our search. Who was the intended target? Your father, your mother, or you? Did anyone make threats on your life?"

"Ridiculous. My parents were wonderful people. And Mother, once sedated, didn't bother anyone. Besides, what Mundane could lob tornadoes, earthquakes, and floods at us?"

"Even with your short experience here at Eldridge, you know any number of beings could have appeared to your family as a Mundane."

"No," I repeated. "No one ever made threats."

"Then once again, we are left with the conclusion the target of all these catastrophes... is you." She interlocked her fingers into a ball of white knuckles. "What about you made Mother Nature draw a bullseye on your back? What are you hiding, Dr. Yeager?"

The scar at the top of my head burned. I gasped at the intensity. Two bombshell ideas collided in my head.

Shadow!

All these years, all this damned time, *that* was how they've been trying to kill Shadow? That elven warrior who became Shadow—his murderers have been looking for him since I was six. My parents, my six-year-old self, hundreds and hundreds of innocents, from Mt. St. Helens all the way back to Anchorage, were merely collateral damage to these fuckers.

My eyes brimmed with wetness.

"Ah." Lenoir leaned forward in her chair. "We've hit upon something."

"Something the shapeshifters said—they kept calling me a traitor's son."

...and Shadow is the son of their traitor.

"Father had nothing to do with shapeshifters."

"How could you know at that young age?"

"What could Father have done that marked him as a traitor? Chop down a sacred tree? Shoot Smokey the Bear?" I could sense a monster tension headache building. Saying "Father" every time I meant "Shadow's dad," or saying "me" when I thought "Shadow" exacted a toll.

Part of that toll was the specter of distrust toward Shadow. Who or what was the thing imprisoned with him?

After clearing my wet throat, I said, "Let's try another angle. Whoever is after me, why would they use 'natural' disasters? It seems there are easier ways to take out a single human."

"Unless the disasters *were* the point," said Lenoir. "A display of force is a classic strategy. Send in the big guns to soften the enemy up. Instead of Howitzers, they used earthquakes, floods, and twisters."

And afterward, the enemy would send in the foot soldiers with big eight-fingered crab hands, like the one that killed Shadow after he survived the quake. At the other 'natural' disasters, we left before the events, so we wouldn't have had the chance to spot those crustacean nightmares. Or maybe Father *did* see them, and that's why he left. No matter what, I need to find some proof and figure out who was the general issuing the orders.

But where to start?

"Then again, maybe not." Lenoir scratched one cheek in thought. "What's the point of continuing the display of force if you keep missing?"

"Maybe I wasn't the target. What about the 'someone' who kept warning Father? A more powerful target, one who actually required the force of a natural disaster."

Like a Forest Elf sorceress dressed in emerald who resurrected me, who saved her fellow *Koire-kwente* Shadow in the vessel of a human child brought back to life. It wasn't a far stretch to imagine she was the one who forewarned my Father of each disaster. But I wasn't going to tell Lenoir that.

I had to get to Mt. St. Helens. The answers were there.

"Interesting, Dr. Yeager. Any ideas?"

I stared at Lenoir in silence while I dreamed up red herrings.

She shoved herself back into her seat and scoffed out the side of her mouth. "I hope you're not pointing the finger at someone in Eldridge."

"This organization has boatloads of seers and oracles. I can't spit without hitting one in this building. Are you telling me not a single one of them saw these disasters coming? Either that means Eldridge's precious prognosticators couldn't *oracle* their way out of a paper bag, or someone saw it coming, and it died a quiet death in the Assessor's Bullpen. Frankly, I think a third option is the most plausible."

"Oh, I simply *must* hear this." Lenoir's sarcasm dripped acid.

"Let's assume Eldridge seers *did* foretell some group, and they decided to take matters into their own hands. Some group with a lot of resources, and is large enough for an intrusion to marshal a large-scale offensive in the form of a natural disaster. Some group that could pull such an operation off, yet be totally off the books." I tapped my chin playfully. "Let me see, what group do I know that would be that full of themselves?"

"You are accusing *Alpha*?"

No, I was throwing spaghetti at the wall as fast as possible to see what would stick.

Her smirk could cut glass. "I can't tell you how many rules that would break. Not to mention, they'd have to be flying under Eldridge's collective radar for the past twenty-odd years during the span of these disasters. No star chamber is *that* good."

For a moment, I considered telling Lenoir about Shadow. The situation was getting too big and complicated for me. And the longer I drew this out, the worse my chances to slip up.

"I'm afraid I've had my own little epiphany, Dr. Yeager." She stood, leaning over me. I spied the strap of her gun holster under her suit. "I believe the shapeshifters are tied to the disasters following your family."

"Let's assume you made that point."

"Trouble is, it's been seven years since the last attempt on your life. They must have believed, or at least hoped, you died with your father. To cover their bets, they used your mother as bait to draw you out."

"Go on."

"The shapeshifters now know you are alive, your identity, and probably your location. These intrusions from *Phelek Lepan* could be conjuring an earthquake with Sacramento's name on it as we speak. Perhaps we should pack you away into ILTS and ship you to a random Eldridge location."

"You are aware," I said as flat as possible, "that ATPG 217 is already investigating the problem? Barandir is searching the other side of a portal in *Tawar Cevan* to determine what these shapeshifters are and where *Phelek Lepan* is."

Lenoir snapped her fingers, and Madame Machiavelli reappeared. "What a wonderful idea, Dr. Yeager. So noble of you to *volunteer* to assist Barandir. By going to *Tawar Cevan*, you'd be protecting Sacramento. I could even push the paperwork for new orders through by the end of business today."

"No, I'm staying right here on Earth." I stood, staring Lenoir down. "I'm heading to Mt. St. Helens."

"Why? What do you hope to find there?"

"None of your business."

"I think the bones of a female Forest Elf, lying next to those of your father's under yards of volcanic ash, are *definitely* my business."

I wobbled, almost collapsing back in my seat before I managed to lock my knees.

"So you see, Dr. Yeager, I agree with your previous hypothesis. There *was* a Forest Elf warning your father, perhaps even running some sort of 'Elven Witness Protection' program to keep you and your parents hidden. You might even be correct in that the disasters were aimed at this mystery Elf. That still leaves the question—What is the connection between her and your family?"

"Do the world a favor, Ms. Lenoir. Take a nap on the Capitol Corridor rails during the morning rush."

"Why, I don't understand, Dr. Yeager." Her expression of faux concern made my blood boil. "I would think you'd welcome the chance to find out, once and for all, why so many elves, shapeshifters, and other intrusions are so interested in you. Most of all, I would think you'd jump at the opportunity to join Mr. Robert Barandir Peradlon Boyce, find *Phelek Lepan*, and help rescue your mother."

"No, I have to get the hel—*far* away from you and think things out on my own. We're finished here." I marched to the open door.

"Stop where you are, Dr. Yeager," she barked.

The *swish* of cloth followed by an unfamiliar sound jerked me to a stop inches from the door.

CHAPTER 48

I glared sourly out the doorway into a library sparsely occupied with knots of employees, absorbed in their own research. If any of them bothered to look in my direction, they'd see a nondescript—though impeccably dressed—employee standing in the doorway of the microfilm reader room, mumbling silently at no one and everyone, before closing his eyes for a few seconds.

Turning around slowly, I said one last word.

"Please."

Rising from her chair, Lenoir held an alien black and silver pistol trained at my chest. Definitely not the type that shot instant concrete Silly String. "We are decidedly *not* finished here. Close the door."

I complied.

"I can't let you be a free agent, Dr. Yeager. You are too dangerous."

"*I'm* dangerous?" I scoffed. "I think you have that backwards, lady. I'm the one who's been hip-deep in danger ever since I joined this Looney-Toons company—which I did under duress, I might add. I've been attacked by no less than two alien species, an Elven spirit in a magic item, two shapeshifters, two giant escapees from Nordic fairy tales, threatened by a Durga, and now a paranoid Alpha operative with delusions of humanity."

"That's precisely my point."

"Your lack of decency?"

"I find your insouciance tiring, Dr. Yeager." Lenoir gestured with her pistol, waving me away from the door.

Raising my hands, I sidled toward the far wall. "Oh, dear God.

She's going to monologue at me."

"In the entire history of Eldridge & S.Q.Amos, no one has ever been in so many skirmishes within their first year of employment. You attract danger, Dr. Yeager. And I have to wonder why."

"If you find out, clue me in, too."

"I scarcely know where to begin. From the beginning, I sensed something was wrong with you. At first, I believed you only to be a mole, a plant, a spy. However, once Alpha discounted that possibility, your many other allegiances to entities outside Eldridge quickly became apparent. You desire to rescue your mother, held by the shapeshifters from *Phelek Lepan*. You pine for your fiancée, forever lost to you, doomed to spend eternity in the Void of her ILTS cylinder. There is a reason why Eldridge recruits only from those with no family ties and existing relationships. Yet here you are, your allegiances pulled in a multitude of directions. That in itself is a threat to the company.

"Threat number two? Now that the shapeshifters have proof that you are alive, of your connection to E&SQA, and quite possibly your location, I believe the risk of an *un*-natural catastrophe destroying Sacramento increases with every passing day. Even your ATP group's seer, Ms. Urdsen, prophesied, 'The earth shall rise, the waters shall flood, the sky shall fall.' Did she not?

"Threat number three. For no apparent reason, and without training, your paranormal quotient has risen three notches to PQ-4. How is this possible?"

Ever scowl so hard you can see your own eyebrows? "I don't know."

"Threat number four. If your growth continues unabated and without an explanation, the danger to Eldridge increases with every PQ point."

I pretended to yawn. "How high do your threat numbers go?"

"Number five. Your incessant willingness to skirt the rules of the company. The latest of which was making friends with a Frost Giant and turning New Jotunbyen upside down with the deaths of two others."

"Now, wait a minute..." Taking a step forward, I dropped one hand and wagged a finger at her.

Lenoir raised her arm, aiming at my head. "You shouldn't even have *been* in the ILTS. And yet that was your second visit."

"Threat number five sounds pretty lame to me. Besides, I don't know what floor New *Jarlsberg* is on."

"The real threat is that you seem to have someone looking out for you. Protecting you, pulling your fat out of the fire every time your flippant disregard of Eldridge rules gets you in hot water. Petrakis, who was preoccupied with recruiting you in the first place and rescued you from the Euryale; Director Ventnor, who pulled you out of my interrogation; Ms. Mertens, who practically afforded you *carte blanche* in Central Records; and Pellagati, who gave you access to ILTS."

"It's called being friendly. You should try it sometime."

"No, Dr. Yeager. It's called by another name. Nations call it treason. Eldridge has harsher words for it.

"Let's suppose for a moment you actually have a paranormal quotient far higher than a paltry PQ-4. Some PQ-15s have the ability to hide their true quotient. Pellagati, while he still registered as PQ-8, had the power of suggestion. At PQ-15, that talent becomes far more powerful. Such people can wield the power of Command. In untrained minds, even those unaware of it, the threat is labeled by Eldridge as an Interloper.

"In a trained mind, they become an Intrusion.

"If someone else is behind it, pulling the strings of Pellagati, Mertens, Ventnor, Petrakis, then it's a Conspiracy Level Threat."

I applauded slowly. "Oh, you've outdone yourself, Lenoir. An astonishing bit of circular reasoning there. Well, then—if I'm a PQ-15, then I *command* you to kiss my ass."

"You pose a threat to this organization I am sworn to protect, Dr. Yeager. Before we are finished, I *will* know what that threat is."

The last time Lenoir had me under her microscope, she had me doubting myself down to my core. She almost had me doing it again, but things were different this go-round.

"Lady, if you're trying to scare me, it won't work. After surviving three months of magic and monsters, I'm not impressed. And what about Sindhu? You forgot her in your paranoid list of helpers. Is she part of this vast conspiracy surrounding me as well?"

"Yes, let's discuss your fiancée, shall we? Languishing in ILTS, yet a part of her escapes to come to your rescue. How do I know that was really her and not another shapeshifter?"

"It was her. I could tell."

"Then she's an *intrusion*. No human, not even their astral self, can leave the Void of an ILTS capsule."

"Dr. Hatahali believes Sun Bin dragged her out of containment for her energy."

"Even so, you are in violation of Rule 4." She flexed her arm to the point her elbow almost bent double-jointed. I stared straight down the barrel. "You *are* familiar with it?"

"I'm acquainted with it. So what?"

"You've flouted it ever since you've joined Eldridge. But this time, it is not just a minor skirting of regulations—you are in blatant violation. Your fiancée, Ms. Mehra, is an intrusion. Personal relationships with an intrusion result in termination. *Full* termination. I am therefore authorized—"

"Stop right there, Lenoir. Believe me, I am intimately familiar with Eldridge's precious Rule 4. And you're way off base. The rule states that termination occurs only after a formal review that requires my participation along with my management's. There has been no such review. That means you have no authority to terminate me. Or are you judge, jury, and executioner, all in one?

"You know what I think, Lenoir? Perhaps *you* are the mole with the sole mission of killing me."

Lenoir's eyes twitched.

"And what about the mess down in New Jotunbyen? Something big and nasty killed those Frost Giants, and it wasn't for their family's honor. There's a mole somewhere in the heart of Eldridge, Sacramento—but it ain't me. I was under probation, so I'm sure you had my every move under surveillance. I should be the one asking where *you* were when they were slaughtered."

My neck relaxed. Shadow's scratching at my skull and the headache vanished. Maybe I should play mind games more often.

"Second, are you familiar with the designation RPIN?" There was her twitch again. "It stands for 'Rehabilitation Pending Intrusion Neutralization,' in case you forgot. I am officially designated on Sindhu's RPIN list and therefore excluded from Rule 4. Put your popgun away, Lenoir. You are without cause."

This was fun, but I began to wonder where the blazes was the cavalry? I lowered my hands. "Let me clue you in on another regulation I'm familiar with—Section 8, Paragraph 2. It states, and I quote, 'Drawing a deadly weapon on an employee of E&SQA *without cause* is a violation of company policy.' And another thing—"

The door opened, and Ms. Mertens popped her head into the room. "There you are, Dr. Yeager. I heard you were having problems with the

Multi-Micro—" Mertens' engaging smile vanished. "*What the Sam Hill is going on here?!*"

The vitiligo on her cheek almost glowed bright red. She flung the door open, banging it against the wall.

"I was about to explain to Ms. Lenoir that the New Employee Handbook, Section 14, Paragraph 3 unequivocally states 'No weapons are permitted within E&SQA library areas.'"

"And what's a halt-lex doing in here?" asked Mertens in that shouting whisper only librarians can execute flawlessly. "They're not allowed to operate in the library, either."

I snapped to sunny alertness, like someone offered me a mug of Blue Mountain. "Oh, really? I missed that one."

Lenoir lowered her head, though her eyes and gun kept a bead on me. She said through gritted teeth, "I am placing Dr. Michael Avery Yeager under arrest. By the authority of ATP Alpha, I—"

"Young miss, I don't care if you're Alpha *or* Omega. Frankly, I don't care if you're *The* Alpha and Omega. I am the Head Librarian, and you will holster your weapon and shut that halt-lex off immediately. Who is your supervisor?"

"I think there's been a misunderstanding." I stepped to the side, out of Lenoir's line of fire. "Ms. Lenoir was doing her duty, presenting her case as to what she believed a danger to Eldridge."

"Do you normally discuss work holding an Epsalian Carbon Bond Disrupter, Ms. Lenoir?"

"I believe Dr. Yeager is an operative under the influence of one or more intrusions," hissed Lenoir.

"What intrusions?"

"Shapeshifters. Frost Giants. The Sun/Valdaan Intrusion in ILTS. Take your pick."

"I addressed each of her arguments," I continued. "I had hoped to her satisfaction." I lowered my head to match Lenoir's demonic scowl. The atmosphere bearing down on me reminded me of my disastrous dissertation back at UC. This time, *I* wasn't going to be the one to get screwed. "But apparently not. If Lenoir insists, we can bring her official concerns to Director Ventnor."

"I agree." Mertens inhaled deeply. "Your weapon, Ms. Lenoir. I'm waiting."

I was so focused on the barrel of silver and black alien zappiness, that I missed that Mertens had raised her book-shaped pendant, its chain taut and its lavender-turned-black pages facing Lenoir.

Lenoir glanced at Mertens and her pendant. She lowered her gun at a snail's pace and holstered it.

"Stalemate, Dr. Yeager," she muttered. "For now." Tapping the halt-lex, it stopped spinning, and she swept the device into her jacket pocket.

Lenoir's mouth turned downward. She approached until we were nose to nose. Her bared teeth behind crimson lipstick made her face look like she carved her frown with a knife.

She kissed me. Hard as a lover escaped from prison. I remained frozen, torn between a transparent attempt at a brave laugh or wiping her taste off my lips and burning the handkerchief. Stepping to my side, she breathed into my ear, "Next time I kiss you, I'll kill you."

Lenoir then showed her malicious grimace toward Mertens.

"I take it, Dr. Yeager, that you do not intend to file a complaint against Ms. Lenoir?" Mertens lowered her pendant. Its pages returned to its lavender opalescence as she straightened her collar.

"No. No complaint from me." I strode to the doorway. Pausing next to Mertens, I looked over my shoulder at Lenoir. "However, Ms. Mertens, feel free to lodge your own grievance. Section 14, Paragraph 3 concerning weapons in the library... and don't forget the regulation that disallows a halt-lex in the library."

I smiled a devilish grin at Lenoir, who could have fired bullets at me from her eyes. Leaving the room, I beat a hasty retreat from the library into the sanctuary of an empty elevator.

"Thanks for saving my bacon, Amelia. Ms. Mertens answered your scribe-to-scribe alert in the nick of time."

She replied with a pair of clicks.

I punched the button for my floor extra hard. "I don't know about you, but I'm tired of constantly being under the gun. I'm sick of corporate secrets, conspiracies behind every pair of eyes, and being manipulated. I tried playing their games back there—and it left a bad taste in my mouth." I took my scribe out of her pocket.

"Amelia, how do you feel about doing something stupid and go after the big fish?"

Again, she clicked her cap twice.

CHAPTER 49

Back at my cubicle, I snagged my suit jacket and the Post-It note hanging on for dear life to my terminal screen, slipping it into my shirt pocket next to Amelia.

"Why is what I need always at the bottom?" I grumbled as I dug around my desk drawer. After a few more moments of rummaging, I found my prize and stuffed Petrakis' ink eraser into my pants pocket.

"Thank you, Ms. Oliver, *whoever* you are. You are a rare commodity—a seer that I *like*."

I thought of calling in my coworkers to tag along on this hare-brained crusade but couldn't bring myself to do it. I'd be exposing them to dangers I could only guess at. Outside my group, there's Hagebjørn. He'd be nice to have along, but he wouldn't fit in the elevator.

In any case, there was simply no time to explain everything to whoever would choose to join me on this fool's errand. There was no telling how quickly Lenoir would be back on her crusade.

So it's just li'l-ol'-me and Amelia facing one or more adversaries, whose powers were a colossal unknown, while running full tilt from a host of intrusions and one insanely dangerous Alpha chasing me from behind.

St. Michael was ready to face the dragon—except his horse was stuck in ILTS, his lance a pen, his suit of armor made of wool blend and silk, and his shields a Post-It note and an ink eraser.

I stamped my way to the elevators. I issued a non-committal *humph* at the group waiting at the regular ones on the left, across from the singular mystical elevator on my right. My first thought was to skulk in a regular elevator to its highest floor, then engage the upper management's car. I tossed that idea in the trash. If I gotta go, let it be with as many witnesses as possible.

I placed my hand on the frosted translucent panel next to the door. It glowed an unfriendly red. A few snickers behind me tugged at my ears. I took out the Post-It, slapped it on my palm, and flattened it on the panel, red insignia side down. Though a little surprised, I was relieved when the reader turned green and kept my hand in place.

The hallway denizens behind me must have been surprised as well. The assorted chortles were terminated by several soft *gulps*.

The reader blinked off. Not sure what to expect, I stepped back. The red spiral fox-tails stamp had disappeared from the back of the Post-It. The other employees in the hallway made themselves equally scarce.

The steel doors opened, dividing the onyx and mother-of-pearl corporate logo in two. In the center of the compartment stood Ms. Emerald. Her distinctive stripe of fine spun green gemstone hair raced down in front of her left ear. Wearing the same outfit and hairstyle from when I first met her, she greeted me with a formal bow and beckoned me to enter.

The doors closed, and we stared at each other's smiles for a second or two. Hers was a serene summer night, while I had to bite my lips to keep mine from trembling. I waited for the elevator to speak, but silence reigned.

"Don't we have to tell the elevator a destination?"

Emerald pressed her palm over her heart, and with her ever-present knowing grin, she politely shook her head. The doors opened.

Stepping out onto the office floor, she turned sideways and beckoned me to follow. I trod the familiar path to Vice President Hibara's office. To the left was the room-length mural depicting catastrophe upon catastrophe. The giant canvas left me wondering if more lava flowed from Mt. Fuji than before, if the *kaiju* had closed the distance between itself and the dormant volcano, or if the fearsome red eyes peering out of the ashen plumes had intensified. Then I spotted the hands, removing all doubt. Gigantic fingertips with nails forged from innumerable blackened skeletons had emerged from the smoke.

The array of plush chairs faced me on the right, and nearly every seat facing us was occupied. Like my previous visit, only half the gallery was human. Among the non-human types I counted were two trolls, three ogres of different skin colors, and a Dwarf. All were dressed in the closest things they could assemble into business attire. The Dwarf pulled it off with his beard braided into a makeshift tie with a perfect Windsor knot, but the trolls' disheveled three-piece suits of burlap, moss, and hides would have been laughable if they weren't so disturbing. As before, almost every warm body seated there held either a red envelope or a scroll tied in a red ribbon. Some had both. I wondered if they were bribes to sweeten their petitions.

Emerald's twin, Sapphire, smiled benevolently behind the receptionist's desk. The two exchanged nods in perfect synchronicity, their docile expressions raising the hairs on the back of my neck. When little kids trade smiles like that, they're up to something.

A roar erupted from the waiting area.

"Not again," cried a single-horned red ogre bedecked in painted lacquered strips tied around his torso and upper limbs by leather and silk. He pounded his fist on his chair's arm, making the floor *thrum*. "This is the *second* time that weasel has jumped ahead of me. I will not stand for it," he bellowed as he stood.

Irony is lost on ogres.

At least seven feet tall, its armor, painted to resemble a business suit, rattled with each tromp toward us. Sapphire rose from her desk as well. Emerald stepped forward to guard my left. Two giant paces away from us, the ogre tossed his envelope and scroll to either side. He raised his formidable arms, his hands clenched into boulders.

A sudden puff of a breeze ruffled my hair. The ogre froze in midstep and emitted a guttural squawk. From behind him curled Sapphire's petite arm, holding the glittering edge of her short, straight-edged ninja sword against the creature's neck. Emerald stepped from my side and retrieved the monster's discarded papers.

I quietly backpedaled one step. Then another.

Emerald raised the ogre's scroll to him, then his envelope. With each item, she quietly displayed to the beast that they had already been neatly sliced in two.

The ogre lowered his massive fists. His shoulders dropped almost as much as the corners of his mouth. I'd never before seen a more piteous frown. Sapphire, her sword's point firmly against his back, quietly escorted the tamed beast to the elevator. Emerald, with her head angled forward, continued to glare at him.

Two more steps, and my back was against the massive carved

wooden double doors to Hibara's office. I held my breath and tugged at the half depicting the samurai general's shouting face, spear point, and head of his *kirin* mount. It glided open, and I slipped in between the slimmest of openings. My last sight of the waiting room was Emerald smiling her enigmatic best. She tilted her head at a scolding angle and wagged her finger at me.

I closed the door and surveyed the inner meeting area.

The room had changed since I saw it last. The far wall of painted wooden panels had been replaced with a wide landscape of gray and red hills on silk panels. A pink sun reflected off snow-covered ground, and icicles hung from a single leafless cherry tree.

Hibara's chair remained in its previous place. But instead of two large couches on either side, a matching sumptuous black leather chair faced it. Each chair was paired with a large black ceramic pot, from which grew climbing wisteria. A black coffee table rested on a white rug between the chairs. Incense burned in a ceramic holder in the shape of a dragon's head.

Did I mention *another* of the Gem Twins waited for me in the conversation pit? An identical triplet of the other two, she stood sideways with her hair's ruby red stripe facing me, her hands folded in front of her hips.

A moment passed while I vacillated over staying put or attempting my gambit.

"Now or never," I muttered to myself.

I strolled to the center of the room and nodded to Ms. Ruby. She returned a slight bow, graced with the Gem Sisters' trademark smile. Turning to face the right wall, I mumbled the eideticize spell and concentrated on the two-foot-tall *kanji* on the rice paper hangings.

One of these spells had to create Hibara's teleport doors. Once I got that enchantment under my belt, I could go to Mt. St. Helens, Heidelberg, or, with luck, maybe even *Tawar Cevan* at the drop of a hat. Or so I thought...

The Chinese ideograms remained stubbornly in place. Seeing that a ninja sword had not been placed against my throat, I repeated the eideticize spell with the same results. Except I could feel a headache building. It disappeared in a flash when I got zapped by a light electrical discharge. It resembled the sensation of putting your tongue across a nine-volt battery, except it covered my entire body.

One of the back wall's silk panels slid aside, revealing the Gem triplets had grown to quadruplets. How many of these women were there?

Unlike her three sisters, she wore a kimono of white and black, depicting flocks of black herons hiding among whirlwinds of white cherry blossoms. I recognized the same garment, the hem of which I had spotted behind the screens the last time I was here. The familiar aroma of cherry blossoms—and musk?—floated across the delicate scent of wisteria and incense.

Closing the panel, she revealed a plush rectangular pillow of folded cloth tied to her back. It bore a similar pattern, except the herons were blue and green, surrounded by red camellia blossoms. She showered me with her sisters' familiar smile when I spotted the stripe adorning her hair, white as brightly lit diamonds.

"Good afternoon, Dr. Yeager," she said. Her sultry voice almost purred with the subtlest of accents. "Hibara-*sama* will join us presently." She glanced at my forehead and raised her hand to her mouth to hide a quiet giggle. "Yes, I can talk."

The heck with waiting for Botox—I might resort to curare to get my eyebrows under control.

"I'm sure you have noticed the magical contrivance you attempted a moment ago has failed." Under the veil of her kimono, her delicate steps gave the illusion she floated across the floor toward me. "Each of these wall hangings wards this place against various threats. One of them prevents spells cast by visitors. Another exacts a delayed retribution after such attempts."

"I didn't experience any—" A massive migraine smashed into my temples, blinding me. The pain was shouted down by another electrical discharge, this time with a kick of a car battery. Steadying myself against the nearest chair, I said, "Right, *delayed*. Let me guess, it also increases with each infraction."

"Quite so. I would advise not trying a third time."

The door behind me opened. Whispered buzzing from the gallery of Hibara's petitioners tiptoed into the room, followed by Emerald. I stood stock still, in case she and her sword were going to escort me out for my infraction. Instead, she and Ruby bade me sit in the guest chair. Diamond stood behind Hibara's empty seat.

"Would you care for anything to drink, Dr. Yeager?"

"If it's not out of line, I could use a mezcal Paloma, Ms. ...?"

"You may call me Kit," said Diamond. She seemed unabashedly fascinated that I inquired after her name. "And no, it is not uncalled-for. You are our guest."

"Guest?" I asked. The invitation in question didn't have Hibara's trademark ginkgo pattern. "I take it that red stamp was yours?"

"So," she confirmed with a nod.

The more I observed Kit, the more I questioned her appearance as Hibara's assistant. It wouldn't be the first time in history that the real power was wielded by someone in the shadow of the figurehead formally holding the office.

She reached behind the seat facing me, producing the drink in a tall glass, complete with a slice of lime. Kit remained there as Emerald placed my drink on the table—coaster, napkin, and all. As expected, it was exceptional.

"I wonder if I might ask a question, Ms. Kit."

"Certainly."

"I get the feeling matters for Vice President Hibara are..." I paused, not for dramatic effect, but because it took a while to find a diplomatic word that wouldn't get my throat slit. "...becoming complicated. The mural outside reminds me of the Union of Concerned Scientist's Doomsday Clock. It seems to have inched closer to midnight. And the silk tapestry depicts scenery more forlorn since last I was here."

"Most observant, Dr. Yeager."

"What do they mean? What's going to happen?" A sufficiently long period of silence passed, that I felt I had to fill it. "Do you need more time to consider the question?"

"Not at all, Dr. Yeager. You may ask. However, I am not obliged to answer."

If my third-grade teacher were still alive, she would have declared Kit her sister from a different mother. They were both the sort who replied to "Can I go to the bathroom?" with "I don't know. *Can* you?"

Ruby slid open the center panel and stepped into the darkened room beyond. I stood when she reemerged with Vice President Hibara. From that vantage, I could see most of the serving table behind his chair. The area from which my Paloma came was empty—not even a water ring.

He entered slowly, with the assistance of a black cane with a silver handle. I was puzzled at his appearance—did the Valdaan manage to get to him before it came after me? He favored one leg, and Ruby hovered close by. Wearing a dashing black suit, he had his jacket draped over his shoulders, covering an arm in a black mesh sling. Dressed even so, the cut of his apparel made me want to shake his tailor's hand.

Behind them, Petrakis and Ventnor emerged from the darkness. However, they stopped millimeters before crossing the main room's threshold. Petrakis swiped his nose and folded his arms. Ventnor kept his at his side. His face fairly glowed with the color of a man about to have a brain aneurysm. His pince-nez glasses hung onto the end of his sweaty nose for dear life.

I shot Kit a glance filled with exasperation. "I should have known," I hissed softly at her. "You've all been waiting for me. I hope I haven't kept you waiting too long." Ventnor's apoplexy told me I had.

Barely above a whisper, Hibara leaned his head toward Kit and said, "Green tea, please."

Despite his injuries, he glided into his seat without a groan, showing only the slightest wince. "I am gratified you accepted my assistant's invitation, Dr. Yeager. Forgive me for receiving you in such a state."

Kit produced a rude pottery mug from the empty table behind Hibara and placed it, steaming with tea, in front of him.

A subtle contradiction suddenly clicked for me. Though no spells could be cast, apparently magical items—like the serving table?—still operated in this room. I could use that to my advantage. "No forgiveness necessary, sir. I wanted to thank you personally for granting me access to ILTS."

I sat, desperately wanting to chug the rest of my Paloma. "I feel I should ask *your* forgiveness, Vice President. I thought we had killed the Valdaan before it got to you."

"But you *did*, Dr. Yeager. Had you not, I would have had a far more difficult time with today's visit from..." He shifted his arm's sling. "...a competitor."

Hibara raised a finger, which Kit acknowledged with a subtle nod. Ruby flitted past Petrakis, disappearing into the darkened room beyond. "Because of that, Eldridge & S.Q.Amos would like to show you their appreciation for your service."

"Thank you, sir."

Hibara sipped his tea. I resisted the urge to toss my drink back in one gulp.

"Do not thank me yet, Dr. Yeager. I have read the reports from you and Dr. Petrakis with interest. I am pleased you have established a fine working relationship with your scribe.

"After considering the various reports and memoranda from ATPG Alpha concerning you, I was on the verge of pulling back on Ms. Lenoir's reins. I am informed you resolved the situation rather handily earlier today."

I doubted either Lenoir or Mertens had time to file anything official about our little scuffle—further proof that anyone up the management chain could get an immediate info dump on what Amelia observed.

"However, I must confess I share some of Ms. Lenoir's concerns. Therefore, before we proceed, several questions must be answered, a few avenues explored, and certain things verified."

Ruby entered the room, holding a camera—not Polaroid's X1000, but their high-end folding model SX70. Standing at the edge of the white rug, she snapped a photo of me and handed it to Hibara. Examining the image, his expression remained poker-faced. He returned it to Ruby, who in turn passed it to me.

"As you can see, Mr. Yeager. Your ability has increased to PQ-6. Considering your initial rating was PQ-1, that is an astounding increase in the space of less than a quarter of a year. How do you account for this?"

"Six?" I gawked at the developed photo as Emerald peered over my shoulder. There I stood in PQ outlines, an amber glow at the top of my skull where the green sorceress had enmeshed Shadow's and my life forces together. No doubt about it—I somehow climbed to a PQ-6.

Umber outlines of the wall hanging's *kanji* barely registered against the photo's black background. Emerald was nowhere to be seen. How could her presence not be recorded on the film? I glanced over my shoulder, almost knocking heads with her. Where she had stood, she *must* have been in the shot.

"I'm not sure I can." Shadow scratched under my scar. I got the inclination that he was afraid. I understood his anxiety, surrounded by powerful magics and three women who could easily slice'n'dice me into a pile of julienned Yeager.

Don't worry, Shadow. I think I got us—and Elrameshe—covered.

"Although..." I rubbed my chin dramatically. "I think I've detected a pattern. There've been several contacts and outright attacks directed at my psyche since I joined Eldridge. Dr. Kovalenko first measured my PQ-1 and prescribed psychic calisthenics. Caltrop made sure I did them—*all* of them. They must have worked, as Dr. Fleischer later confirmed my ability as PQ-2."

As long as I leave out Elrameshe of the story, that is…

"Plausible," said Kit.

Hibara lowered stern eyebrows at Kit then peered over his glasses at me. Did they see through my cover story for Elrameshe?

"The first attack came from the Aptitude Stones, after which Lenoir and Pellagati determined I had advanced to PQ-3. I have to conclude my PQ jumped a point in response to that attack.

"During their interrogation, Pellagati invaded my psyche, and I defended myself. I later used his camera to discover our tussle had pumped me up to a PQ-4.

"Then I was subjected to the ILTS Void… twice. Maybe one or more of those events boosted my PQ to its current level."

"What about the ill-advised spell you tried to cast in my sanctuary?" asked Hibara.

"A spell I picked up after orientation. It enhanced my memory, but hurt like heck before I mastered it. I suppose it could be a candidate for a PQ boost."

Kit hid another single-syllable giggle with a hand draped behind her kimono sleeve. I shot her a glance, one of surprise and confusion. I whispered to Emerald, "Don't tell me Uncle Billy-Bob was yours, too?" All four Gem sisters nodded.

"Perhaps this room's protections qualified as an attack, thereby raising your PQ another step?"

"It's possible." My gut told me otherwise, but adding an unknown to Hibara's calculations helped buy time to keep Shadow secret. "All in all, there were plenty of attacks that could have pushed me up to PQ-6."

I straightened my jacket. "To be perfectly frank, however, I don't feel any different. Certainly not more prescient or mystical."

I wasn't sure I could stand myself if I were.

"How is it you survived the Void, your mind intact?"

"I almost didn't. The spirit of my fiancée rescued me." I held back that she saved me only the first time. I felt Shadow tremble under the scar. "I'm surprised the Void didn't wipe out my PQ entirely."

"Which brings me to another concern. How did Ms. Mehra escape her containment?"

Why was he asking *me*? Surely, middle management or the scribe spy network would have clued him in by now.

"Last I heard, ILTS technicians were still puzzling that out. I assumed it involved with Sun Bin stealing her energy or her capsule's." I leaned forward in my seat. "Let me assure you, if you're concerned about Sindhu, you have nothing to fear from her. Her spirit, separated from the Euryale, tried to warn Dowager Sengling. She helped me against the Valdaan. You should also credit her as the one who warned you and the other surviving member of your fivesome of Eastern magic.

"By the way, which one of you two is 'fire' and 'air'?" I sat back, embarrassed at how surly my voice had gotten. I was relieved Hibara seemed to ignore it.

"Your personal attachments to Ms. Mehra aside, the method of her escape is something we need to determine. To your knowledge, did she possess a paranormal quotient?"

"I couldn't tell you. I didn't even know *I* had one three months ago."

"Have you seen her astral form since the Valdaan was disposed of?"

"No." A jab of panic shot me forward in my seat again. "Wait—I assumed she returned to her cylinder once the Valdaan died. Where is she? Has she returned?"

"As you said, the ILTS technicians are still working that out."

His equivocation made me sick to my stomach.

Was her mind, spirit, soul—what ever you wish to call it—lost? Did she die with the Valdaan? Is she...?

"I need to know one thing, Hibara. And you *owe* me." Kit and her sisters twitched in unison. They all wore the same nonplussed expression. Didn't I show the proper respect, ladies? Tough leechee nuts.

"I need to know Sindhu is safe. I need to know she is not suffering anything close to what I was subjected to in that hellish Void."

"I assure you, Ms. Mehra is safe." Hibara squinted, eyeing my suit. "If that is settled, let us turn to the subject of your mother. I can imagine this may involve many complex emotions on your part—the surprise and happiness of the discovery she is alive, the despair over her being a prisoner of the shapeshifters, the anguish of not knowing if she still lives.

"However, as an officer of E&SQA, I cannot be swayed by these facts or such sentiments. And neither must you. I am sure you are aware of Eldridge's rules concerning personal relationships. They have been wisely instituted over millennia and have served this company well, protecting the company and its fellowship."

"Believe me, I'm painfully aware of them. Lenoir was willing to kill me over Rule 4. Frankly, I don't see the wisdom behind them. Until I found out about Sindhu's RPIN—which I had to discover on my own, I might add—I spent every day at Eldridge afraid of... my own shadow. The Rules, as they stand, seem insanely restrictive and borderline regressive. What should I expect from Eldridge next? Arranged marriages?"

"Returning to the topic at hand, consider your recent exploits, Dr. Yeager. Shapeshifters killed several Mundanes trying to abduct you, using your mother as bait. They used up countless years of her life as they played their patient game. All this they did while unaware of your status. Imagine what they might have done, had they known you were employed by E&SQA. Imagine what they may do now."

"All the more reason for me to find my mother."

"Is it, Dr. Yeager?"

Hibara moved to stand, and Kit glided to his side. I rose out of my seat as well. Trying to maintain a casual demeanor, I slipped my right hand into my hip pocket. Hibara proceeded to amble around the room, surveying the wall hangings, and contemplating their calligraphy, all while speaking between taps of his cane on the wooden floor. I continued to face him as he shuffled past each hanging.

Tap. "This is precisely why we search for candidates with no family or ties outside the Eldridge community."

"That rings hollow, sir," I sniped. "You brought me into Eldridge, knowing full well Sindhu was my fiancée."

Tap. "Your impetuous reactions are precisely why Rule 4 exists."

Tap. "Ask yourself, Dr. Yeager—Who would you sacrifice to wrest your mother from the clutches of the shapeshifters?"

Tap. "Who in Eldridge would end up wounded or dead, if it meant returning Ms. Mehra from the scourge of the Euryale?"

I tried to scream at him at the top of my lungs. Something held me back.

Tap. "Could you let your mother die in *Phelek Lepan* to save others?"

Tap. "Could you let Ms. Mehra languish forever in the dreamless sleep of a Void capsule?"

Tap. "Could you willingly make those sacrifices to save the world?"

My mind felt clouded, my will sapped away. I tried to grasp the ink eraser in my pocket. My hand refused to budge.

Too late, I asked myself if it was magic or simple hypnosis.

CHAPTER 50

Tap. "Many of the forces against which we defend Earth think nothing of human lives as long as they achieve their aims. We at Eldridge & S.Q.Amos, as it has been called these past few centuries, accept the dangers of dealing with forces that rarely trouble themselves with thoughts of the billions of people inhabiting Earth."

Tap. "How dare we, in good conscience, expose any family, friends, or other loved ones to those dangers? This is why Eldridge seeks out, Mundane and gifted alike, those who are loners, those who are orphaned, those who are rejected by the world."

Tap. "This is the horrible truth of Eldridge that you now face."

Tap. "It will tempt and haunt you forever, so long as your mother and Sindhu are alive."

I was vaguely aware Kit stood next to me. In both hands, she held a silver tray, on which lay a curious object. Its hilt, wrapped in leather and facing Hibara, hinted at it being a weapon. Instead of holding a blade, a foot-long central tine protruded straight outward, terminating in a sharpened point. Like a misshapen trident, two pieces of metal sprouted on either side of its base.

A bead of sweat crawled down into my eye. It stung, but I couldn't blink.

Tap. "Where do your loyalties lie, Dr. Yeager? Eldridge and the fate of the world or your loved ones?"

Tap. Hibara stood facing me. "Eldridge, or the being that resides within your consciousness?"

"*He knows, Michael,*" I heard Shadow say, sharp and stinging as a paper cut.

The scar along the top of my head burned like a cattle prod shoved into my brain. Shadow's trepidation transformed into anger, burning a hole in the power that held me. I punched through that hole, and the blanket of somnambulant compliance vanished.

I clutched the eraser in my pocket. Whipping my arm fast as I could, I slapped it on Kit's throat.

With a whimper, she staggered back and collapsed onto her side. Her tray clanged on the floor. Ruby and Emerald shimmered into nothingness. A glittering cloud sprung up around Kit, vanishing in the blink of an eye.

Her head transformed, half-human but covered in fur, with the contours of red, black and white markings of a fox. Her hands and feet reformed into a cross between human appendages and paws. The pillow on her back had been replaced by four bushy fox tails, each tipped with a different color—sapphire, emerald, ruby, and diamond white.

I scrambled to grab the strange weapon. Swing and a miss—it had already disappeared from the tray. The clatter of Hibara's cane hitting the floor preceded the prick of the fork's center tine at my neck. "I still await your answer, Dr. Yeager."

I forced myself to not look at Hibara. Petrakis stood petrified with fear. Ventnor swaggered in rapt attention like he had the front row at a sporting event. "You expect me to give answer honestly at the point of your oversized salad fork?"

"I had planned to use this only if needed. A necessary precaution, seeing that your first action here was to remove this room's protective wards. It seems you have forced my hand."

"Why should I be honest, when almost everything about Eldridge is a lie?"

"I assure you. No one has lied to you."

"Then let me be perfectly frank as well. My answer is the same as what I wrote on the final question on Petrakis' silly exam. Despite being ill-prepared for what this company sent me into, I will try my best to remain faithful to the Oath of Service, but I ultimately answer to my own conscience. And blazes take this company if that isn't good enough.

"No one has lied to me? *Ha!*" I shouted loud enough for the outer waiting room to hear. "Pure sophistry, which is a lie framed in a pretty picture. A lie of omission is also a lie. I'm tired of secrets. I'm tired of being watched like a lab rat. Nothing is as it seems in this blasted organization. Just like you, I've told all the truth I dare tell. If you don't like it, then get it over with and kill me.

"And here's one more little bit of truth, Hibara. I'm willing to bet this company has a method to return from the dead. You better hope I don't find it."

The entire room waited for Hibara's next move.

Without turning his gaze to Petrakis, he said, "What say you, Supervisor?"

"He has betrayed none of my confidences."

I halted myself mid-inhale. I wanted to shout and lay bare Petrakis and his conspiracy-laden warnings in the car when our scribes were sealed in the armrest, and his scribe-radio doohickey was disabled.

He must have read my thoughts, or at least my eyebrows. "My concerns about a hidden conspiracy were real, my boy—I mean, Dr. Yeager. At the time, things did not add up where you and your fiancée were concerned. However, once assigned as your supervisor *pro tem*," he said, glancing an accusation at Hibara, "I was made aware of the situation."

"Which was?" I hoped my voice portrayed my fraying patience.

Petrakis lowered his head, leaving only a hangdog look at Hibara.

Hibara remained a statue. "And you, Director?"

"You know my objections, Vice President. They still stand. My evaluation notwithstanding, he has not been indiscreet, despite ample opportunities to break confidence with Messrs. Pellagati and Barandir, or Mss. Lenoir and Mertens." As a parting shot, we exchanged sneers dripping with sour persimmons.

"Congratulations, Dr. Yeager." Hibara withdrew his weapon from my carotid.

"That's it? All is forgiven? I don't buy it, Hibara."

"There is nothing for you to *buy*, Dr. Yeager."

He limped to Kit's side. Handing me the weapon, he said, "This is not, as you called it, a salad fork. It is a *sai*." His voice sank into reflection. "A peasant's weapon, it has been at my side since I planted rice fields as a youth in Japan four hundred years ago. Among my many struggles and crusades, it helped me free Netsumi from her captor."

"Netsumi... You mean Kit? Most interesting," I said after a mawkish yawn. I set the *sai* on the large coffee table.

"I'm glad you find it so," he said in a deadpan that cut like a knife.

"You met Netsumi's jailer quite recently. She was imprisoned by none other than Sun Bin." Bending at the waist, Hibara plucked the ink eraser from the creature's neck.

Netsumi stirred. With a slow fluttering of her eyes, she awoke.

Hibara straightened, assisting the vixen to her pawed feet. "Netsumi is a *kitsune-kame*, a fox spirit."

"Another shapeshifter," I said, acid on my lips. "A living lie."

She bowed her head, her eyes focused on the floor. Her tails curled behind her feet. I'm no great reader of fox expressions, but she exuded shame.

With a kind smile, Hibara gently raised her chin. "And yet, she is my trusted friend. When born, these gentle creatures have nine tails."

"Gentle?" I blurted. "I've seen how gentle they can be in your waiting room."

"Is that so, Dr. Yeager? Tell me, when was it that you saw Netsumi or her images draw blood? Their only true weapons are their wiles and their power of illusion. With each tail, they may generate a duplicate of themselves or grant a wish."

"So if I see a fox spirit with one tail, they have only one wish left?"

"Which they guard jealously. Granting their last wish ends their existence." He regarded me with rebuke, like I had stated the obvious. "When I freed Netsumi from Sun Bin, the Valdaan within him had already used up four of her tails to achieve its aims. Once freed, she vowed to serve me until my passing, or I used one of her tails to grant a wish. Neither I nor poor Netsumi had any inkling that I would partake of the Fountain of Agelessness afterward."

Nine tails? I re-counted. Netsumi only had four tails. Where was the fifth?

Hibara cast a forlorn look at his servant. Did he pity her? "Countless years later, I finally used one of her wishes to defeat a samurai possessed by a powerful demon, causing her to lose a tail and one of her images. Her vow was satisfied, her service complete. Yet, she still chose to stay by my side as friend and aide."

"That's all well and good, but I'm looking for answers, not fond memories."

"Very well, Dr. Yeager. Let us trade answers. I still await your declaration of your loyalties."

"Signing the Oath wasn't sufficient?"

"The Oath is only as powerful as its perceived punishments. I have witnessed it is all too common for a man to sacrifice his very soul for fleeting power." With Netsumi's help, he retrieved his cane and shuffled to his chair. After a long, slow draught of tea, he looked me straight in the eye. "Tell me what else you believe to be a lie, and I shall attempt to make things clear."

Sitting across from him, I finished my Paloma. "Let's begin with you, Hibara."

"Hibara-*sama*," hissed Netsumi.

Hibara raised a finger, and she fell silent, though her fox's eyes still burned, locked on me as though I were a rabbit. "Go on."

"How do I know *you're* not another shapeshifter? I've run into so many since I joined Eldridge, I've almost lost count. The gray shapeshifters from *Phelek Lepan*, and now, a fox spirit. On top of that, I was almost killed by a Valdaan that could hide itself in others and turn invisible. Then there's the other thing, a giant cockroach that can walk through walls—I'm told it's called a *turiathurin*—that eviscerated two Frost Giants and a shapeshifter that had somehow breached security."

A flash of consternation flitted behind Hibara's glasses. He *didn't* know about that.

"When I look around my immediate vicinity, I see a grand total of two humans and a fox spirit. How do I know it's not myself, a fox spirit, a blob of walking Play-Doh from *Phelek Lepan* pretending to be Hibara, and a roomful of invisible Valdaan or *turiathurin* at his beck and call? In short, Hibara-*sama*," I said with disdain, "how do I trust *you*?"

"Because I would know," said Netsumi, her voice high but firm. "By your own actions, you now see me in my true form. I have nothing to hide from you. What Hibara-sama said is true. I have been by his side for centuries." She raised her arms away from her sides. "Illusion is my stock-in-trade. I would also sense another's illusion. He is an ageless human, just as you are."

"Okay, let's say I can trust what you both seem to be," I said to Netsumi before fixing my gaze on Hibara again. "But the core of my question still stands. How do I trust your intentions?"

He sighed through a frown of granite. "Sadly, nothing I say would thoroughly convince you. No matter how detailed, no explanation of my actions would be impervious to the little worms of doubt that constantly nibble away at the truth. At this juncture, all I can say is, how strongly do you affirm your own Oath to E&SQA? The same Oath *I* swore in blood hundreds of years ago. Whose actions are a better example of their fealty to that Oath?

"I have done what I must to preserve and execute my Oath, Dr. Yeager. My loyalty is first and foremost to this organization, created long before my humble birth, and to the world it protects. My decisions and actions toward you, whether you deem them helpful or harmful, are a secondary consideration. So it comes to this, Dr. Yeager. Only *you* can convince yourself if you trust me."

The silence was broken only by the thrum of my heart.

"I shall reserve my decision for now." I pouted at my empty drink. "Your turn. What's your question?"

"Let's begin with a question you have yet to answer. Who is the being hidden inside your mind?"

"How did you find out about that?" I figured he gleaned that little gem from Pellagati's report of my blocked psyche. I waited for Hibara's reply, but his patient smile could probably outlast me by another hundred years.

"I call him Shadow. He doesn't know his name. Or rather, none of his names mean anything to him. He appears to me in visions, in the place where both he and I died."

Both Hibara and Petrakis raised an eyebrow at that little tidbit. I described the Anchorage scene—my six-year-old self, my parents, Shadow and his people, our mortal wounds, the three sorceresses who wove our souls and bodies together, and the monstrous severed limb buried deep in Shadow's mortal wound.

"Each time I talk with him, we learn a little more about each other... and ourselves."

That struck me as a good place to stop. "Now, it's my turn for a question."

I rose and, much to Netsumi's chagrin, walked to the serving table behind Hibara's leather seat. He raised a finger to keep her place.

"Mezcal margarita, kosher salt, please." I returned to my own black-as-midnight seat and took a sip.

Perfection.

"But I'm feeling generous, Hibara-sama." I began, raising my glass to him. "Besides, you might need this info to answer my question fully. During my visions, Shadow enlightened me about the dangers surrounding both me and him." I indulged myself with a glower at my supervisor and director, waiting in the wings. "Which is far more than most members of this company have done."

I could almost feel Shadow using my voice as I paraphrased his words. "Shadow calls the shapeshifters the *urkāphan*, servants of people he named the *Mori-kwente*, 'the ones who live in darkness.' Together, they search for 'the traitor's son,' who I deduce can only be Shadow. He fears they wish to imprison him, and that has the ring of truth to it. The *urkāphan* who captured me could have killed me without breaking a sweat, but he said I was to be brought before their Circle of Elders."

Paraphrased was not the best word to describe the task I was performing. If anyone else had spoken to me using the Elvish language, I'd be totally in the dark. But with Shadow speaking his native tongue, I knew the exact import of every word, every idiom, every nuance.

I took another sip, watching my audience for a reaction. "Now, I've been so busy dodging monsters and ATPG Alpha, I haven't had a chance to look them up in an Elvish dictionary. If you know what an *urkāphan* is, now would be a good time to share."

Nothing.

"Then there's the critter that killed Shadow near Anchorage and caused the carnage down in New Jotunbyen. The *turiathurin*."

"From your description, it sounds like your Shadow is correct," said Hibara. "We have heard of such a creature from the world of *Band Cevan*. However, its seeming ability to pass through walls is new. I am concerned neither the *urkāphan* nor this *turiathurin* were detected within our walls."

"Shadow also says the *turiathurin* are assassins for the *Kala-kwente*, 'the ones who live in light.' That's the High Elves, right?"

That got a rise out of Hibara—a tremble in his right hand. On him, that twitch looked as severe as a heart attack. "This Shadow accuses the High Elves?" he said before regaining his composure.

"Yes, he does. As do I. What I find curious is all these *-kwente* are supposed to be Elves, right? Why does Eldridge only give refuge to Forest Elves but not the other types? I've double-checked all my orientation material—they hardly mention the High and Gray Elves. Why is that?"

"Eldridge has few records of the *Kala-kwente* or *Mori-kwente*. Mostly legends."

"Yes, I heard one of those stories from Barandir—*Laer-amrûn and Niquis*. I think I'll call them High and Gray Elves, if it's all the same to you.

My jaw's gonna get whiplash with all this Elvish talk." I took a lip-full of salt and a sip of my drink.

"What little else we have is anecdotal evidence from those Forest Elves whom we granted sanctuary."

"Then the High and Gray are a giant question mark. Barandir could be in a lot more danger than anyone thought. *We* might be in a heap of danger, too."

"How is that so?"

The smart-ass in me wanted to let Mr. Vice Prez twist in the wind. He was in the hole by a truckload of questions. I let the moment pass, as I was sure he was keeping count as well.

"The *turiathurin* did us a big favor, killing the *urkāphan*. However, it means we still have a monster lurking somewhere inside Eldridge Sacramento."

"Not necessarily," said Hibara, "if your report of its ability is reliable. It may have already left if it has completed its task."

"I'm not sure New Jotunbyen was its mission."

"Regardless, the necessary security alerts have already been issued."

Already? He wasn't telling me something. Again.

I regarded him suspiciously. "So here's my question, Hibara-sama. Between High Elves and their *turiathurin*, Gray Elves and their *urkāphan*, a Valdaan, the occasional Frost Giant, and an ATPG Alpha zealot..." I slammed my glass down, splashing half of my remaining margarita on the black lacquered table.

"Why is everyone trying to kill me?"

"Because you are an intrusion nexus."

"A what?"

"A focus, one that draws the attention of intrusions or attracts them outright. One that leads to any number of outcomes and the timelines that proceed from them." Hibara planted his cane on the floor between his knees and rested his hands on the pommel. "You know oracles and seers are the tools we use to alert us to impending events and intrusions."

"Good grief, don't tell me all this fuss is because of a *seer*. Half the time, they think their arthritis flare-ups are a sign from the Great Beyond."

"No, because *several* seers foretold your coming. I understand your skepticism as to any single seer's accuracy. However, know this. Every position of Eldridge's upper management is assigned an oracle. In my case,

Netsumi is not only my trusted friend, but as a *kitsune-kame*, she is also blessed with the sight."

Her whiskers twitched as she muttered, "Or cursed."

"As you might imagine, a seer's level in the corporation is commensurate with their aptitude. So, please understand that when *every* oracle in a direct line from my own Netsumi to the oracles tied to my superiors all had a unifying vision, we could not ignore it."

"Did Sofia Urdsen share this vision as well?"

"Yes, even at her ability, she had flashes of insight that made their way into her reports. They were disjointed images, offering little enlightenment."

"*That* I can believe." Though she did claim to see me in her Tarot... "All right, I'll bite," I grumbled. "What was this overarching vision?"

"The details vary wildly. Some end with the world entering a new age. Others end in blood, pain, and cataclysm—"

The import of the outer room's changing doomsday mural landed squarely on my neck, threatening a tension headache. Despite that, I couldn't stop an unintended scoff. "And this is supposed to change my opinion about the competency of seers?"

"—but you, Dr. Yeager, were the focal point in all of them."

I leaned against one arm of my overstuffed chair. "That's what you discussed with the other VPs at the Chamber of Ageless Waters in your reverse-time gibberish. Your supposed generosity to keep me ageless for Sindhu's sake was a ruse."

"Not entirely."

"Why go to such absurd lengths?"

"We of the Circle had tasked Dr. Petrakis to locate you. With his help, we brought you into the fold of Eldridge & S.Q.Amos." Hibara nursed his tea, rolling the crude earthen mug between flattened palms. "Each level of standing in the corporation affords its own level of protection against powers you cannot yet perceive."

The memory of Elrameshe's warning, "*You cannot yet identify the foe*," whispered in my ears.

"That is why your orientation had to be rushed," continued Hibara. "Signing the Oath was paramount. By doing so, not only did you make several obligations to the corporation, but the corporation extended its first protections to you as well. We had considered making you an assessor or adjuster as soon as your orientation was complete, but ultimately, we decided against it."

"Why didn't you? That would have afforded me a scribe, my Amelia, as well. And without all the skulduggery of Eldridge's precious secret society."

"Quite so, but the Circle concluded such a sudden and unwarranted promotion would attract even more unwanted attention to you—despite your notable bloodline." Hibara inhaled the last wisp of vapor rising from his cup. "It was I who proposed we make you one of the Circle. We hoped our ruse of waiting for Sindhu's cure would satisfy your curiosity for a time, and our motive would remain unquestioned. The actual reason for your acceptance into the Circle is the consciousness residing within you.

"You are not merely an intrusion nexus, Dr. Yeager. You are a *messenger*, and the consciousness you carry within is the *message*. One that must be protected until he can be delivered, as foretold."

I whooshed out a heavy sigh. "Oracles again."

Hibara gave his head the slightest hint of a tilt. "I am surprised by the depth of your cynicism, Dr. Yeager. Especially since you seem to place so much faith in one seer in particular."

"Surely," I punctuated with a smirk, "you don't mean Sofia." Hibara's stare induced a gulp of uncertainty in me. "No... don't say it. Not Sindhu."

"Elrameshe," he said, scarcely louder than a murmur.

Once I could breathe again, I whispered, "What do you know of Elrameshe?"

The ornate double doors leading to the Circle of Waters—or wherever Hibara desired them to teleport—shook mightily. Moments later, one of its great panels whipped aside, rocking in its track from the invisible hand that shoved it open. Behind the door opened the impenetrable curtain of blackness that defined the doorway's entrance in transition.

Netsumi inserted herself between Hibara's chair and the doorway.

Without warning, a lithe form wrapped in a filthy hooded leather jerkin dove headfirst out of the uncannily dark threshold. Landing into a roll, he clutched a rucksack under one arm. He left behind splotches of soil and blood on the carpet. The figure came to a stop on his feet. Eight ragged gashes scored the back of his jerkin and had nearly ripped through the strap of his rucksack. Blood seeped through the tears. Drawing a short sword from his belt in a flash, he pounced back at the door. His rucksack tumbled to the floor, dumping its contents.

"Get behind me, sorceress!" he cried.

Two arrows flew out of the silent darkness. One hit the floor where the visitor had crouched a moment before. The arrow's fletching, gold dotted with sapphire like eyes, quivered. I'd seen that hateful combination before, in a sorceress's headband.

The other streaked straight for my head. Left to my reflexes alone, I'd be flat on the floor with a wooden shaft sticking out of my eye socket. But my head somehow managed to jerk to one side of its own volition. Either Shadow had a hand in my dodge, or my upgraded paranormal quotient was paying off an unexpected dividend.

The second arrow pierced one of the binding spells hanging on the wall. Black ink seeped out of the hole, staining the arrow's shaft. It ran down the paper, scoring the vertical mural's oversized *kanji* ideographs with gouts of ink thick as blood.

Shadow's anger grew within me, judging by the burning sensation ridging the top of my scalp.

The leather-clad figure heaved the entirety of his meager weight against the door. From the ebony darkness issued a roar of an unearthly timbre. It sounded like it was inches behind the threshold's curtain of darkness. Somewhere beyond the beast's bellow, a voice faintly chanted. I hoped it was a spell to eliminate whatever made that hellish noise.

A rushing wind poured out of the dark opening, pitting its force against the leather-clad stranger. He cried out as he renewed his effort against the door. The creature's roar intensified, and then it and the whirlwind ceased with the sound of crashing boulders.

I dashed to the figure's side. Together, we trundled the door shut with a resounding *thunk*. His sopping wet hood fell away, revealing a ragged head of long auburn hair clogged with clots of mud. He planted his back against the door, bracing his legs.

"Barandir?" I exclaimed.

Loud as a log drum, the doors thrummed violently. Barandir bounced an inch off the doors before plowing his meager weight against them again. The doors replied with a scraping sound so large and thunderous, it could have been a front-loader.

"What is *that*?" I shouted.

"The *Turiathurin*." His gaze whipped around the room. "Wait— she was right behind me. Where is she?"

"Who?" asked Hibara, now standing.

"Elrameshe," he replied breathlessly. He grabbed the nearest handle and leaned with all his strength to open the door. It wouldn't budge. Thrashing like a drowning man, he pounded the door while screaming her name.

The thing behind the door continued to gouge against it, setting my nerves all a-jangle. With a crack of thunder, it stopped. On its heels followed a sudden rush of wind, rivaling that of an oncoming train chased by an F-3 tornado.

Silence—sudden and as unforgiving as a knife's edge.

Barandir almost toppled over as the door gave way, riding easily along its track. Beyond the doorway lay freshly cleaned office carpeting. He cried her name again into the expanse of the darkened hall.

Netsumi shuffled to the door, quietly shutting it again. "She has closed the portal from her side."

"Or she's dead," Barandir spat, glaring at Netsumi. "I was escorting her back to my portal to this world's nearest intersection of ley lines. We were taking our rest at a village when a *Kala-kwente* hunting party stumbled upon us."

"Hunting party?" Hibara tilted his head forward, steely peering over the rims of his glasses at the half-elf.

"The village was a well-hidden way station for those of my people hunted by the *Mori-kwente*, until granted sanctuary on Earth."

"You are sure your pursuers were High Elves, the *Kala-kwente*?" Hibara demanded in the harshest voice I'd ever heard him use.

"See?" I flung my arm to point at the open doors. "Shadow and I *told* you the High Elves were no good."

"What do you know of this?" Barandir approached, regarding me as though I had insulted him.

And here I thought elves couldn't stomp. "Your human half is showing, Spock."

"*Who?*"

"Never mind," I said with a dismissive shake of my head. "It was Elrameshe who first warned me of all this mess." I glanced at Petrakis. "When we escaped from Lick Observatory."

"What do you mean?" Barandir was practically nose-to-nose with me. "Warned you of what? The *urkāphan*? The *Turiathurin*?"

"Do you want to tell him, Hibara, or shall I?"

To my relief, regional Vice President Hibara seemed to regard my flippancy as amusing. He gestured with his hand, inviting me to continue. However, the corners of Netsumi's lips raised to bare her canines. Her whiskers twitched, signaling a desire for violence.

"I don't have the whole story," I said, stepping back from Barandir, "but someone here does."

The old head scar itched. Shadow knew I included him.

CHAPTER 51

Stalking the perimeter of the room, I reveled in the silence of a captive audience. If Hibara could play mind games like this, why couldn't I? If only I had his hypno-cane...

At any rate, it was better than tap dancing while I tried to figure out why Shadow and I were a *nexus*. All the leading players were present. Agatha Christie would be impressed.

"First things first. Barandir, what happened on the other side of the portal, in Middle Earth, *Tawar Cevan*, or whatever that place is called? You went there to learn what the shapeshifters said to me at Western Bay. Were you successful?"

"Yes. Their foul words were not much different than what they uttered in your own language. 'We are commanded to return you, the traitor's son, to the Great Cavern of the Five.' But there were critical differences in their translation I feel are important. I made some notes..." Barandir knelt to pick up his bag and its spilled contents. Separating a journal with a fore-edge depiction of a forest scene from the scattered disarray, he uncovered an oblong lacquered box. I nearly stumbled over myself when I recognized its patterns and corner braces of platinum. I snatched it up before he could return it to his torn rucksack.

"Where did you get this?" I demanded.

"That belongs to Elrameshe herself." Barandir remained stone-faced, but his voice betrayed that he was flummoxed. "I did not place that among my belongings. She carried it when we fled."

Rolling the box in my hands, I unsuccessfully tried to recall how Drs. Fleischer and Kovalenko opened their rune-covered boxes. Nothing shifted inside as I examined its exterior.

"What does it contain?"

"I do not know. The enchantress never opened it my presence. I perceived she didn't dare to do so. I advise you likewise, Yeager."

Whatever the box held, Shadow sorely desired its contents.

Continuing my perambulation around the room, I placed the box in Netsumi's hands. The pads at the end of her furred fingers were damp with perspiration.

"Please don't drop this," I said quietly. She nodded with astonishment in her feral amber eyes.

"So what was this difference in the shapeshifters' words?" asked Ventnor, impatient as always. Hibara rapped the heel of his cane on the floor sharply. The angle of Hibara's chin, pointed at Petrakis and Ventnor, was a rebuke as loud as a shouted command for silence. I got the feeling I was being tested—again.

"If the phrases from your report are accurate," began Barandir, "the closest translation is not 'We are commanded to return you, the traitor's son,' but more accurately as 'We are commanded to return the traitor's son *within* you.'

My scar burned with fear and rage in equal measure. With an accusing stare at Hibara, I said, "You're not at all surprised, are you?"

Turning the next room's corner pointed me in Barandir's direction. "A lot has happened while you've been off in *Tawar La-la-land*. You already know about Petrakis' and my little romp with the *urkāphan* shapeshifters in Washington. Since then, we determined it was an *urkāphan* inside Eldridge who poisoned Algernon. It was also him who tricked a Frost Giant to move my fiancée's cylinder next to one occupied by a Valdaan. He reconfigured her capsule somehow so that the Valdaan could steal her energy. Because of that, I was sucked into the loving embrace of the Void, nearly driving me insane. The cherry on top was getting ripped apart by the Valdaan itself.

"A few good things came out of that whole fracas, at least. Two particularly unsavory Frost Giants and the *urkāphan* were murdered by a *turiathurin*."

"The *Turiathurin*," said Barandir. "There is only one."

I halted a pace from him. "How do you know?"

"High Elf King *Bardor Dadwen* has only one High Sorceress, *Venameshe*, one of the Three Sisters. In kind, he has only one enforcer, the

Turiathurin, Guardian of Secrets."

"You've been holding back, Barandir," I said with a jibing grin. "Tell me, can this *Turiathurin* walk through walls?"

"No. It is as solid as you or I."

"Then it had help. If it's back in *Tawan Cevan* or *Band Cevan*, who knows who's behind it, giving the critter free rides between realities. At least, there's a small silver lining to that. Since there's only *one* giant, four —oops—*three*-fisted, eight-fingered cockroach, I guess that means you can cancel the security alert. It's no longer here in Eldridge for the time being."

"Indeed," echoed Hibara.

I focused my own frown of rebuke at him and Netsumi. "Shadow was right. The High and Gray Elves are up to their necks in this."

"Who is this Shadow?" asked Barandir. I think I stared at him for a long while before answering. For one who was as calm and resolute as granite under the worst stress, I feared he was on the verge of a nervous breakdown. Confusion ran rampant in his eyes.

"He and I are an intrusion nexus, or so I am told." I resumed my pacing, only to stop nose-to-nose with Director Ventnor. "And where were *you* the morning of March 27th, 1964?"

His face popped red in a single heartbeat. Petrakis repressed a snicker, placing a finger against his right nostril.

I returned his salute along with a wink. "I don't know about you, director... but Shadow and I were in the mountains near Anchorage that day. We were both killed. I from an avalanche caused by the Good Friday Earthquake, and Shadow by the *Turiathurin*. One of its claws had been hacked off as it crushed his beating heart."

Ventnor stifled a small gasp, from which he tried to divert attention with a fumbling hand over an ostentatious cough.

"Then that was indeed the same monster that pursued Elrameshe and me." Barandir's fists clenched at his sides. "It only had three of its hideous arms and a stump for its fourth."

"Three elven sorceresses were there as well. A High Elf dressed in blue, a Forest Elf in green, and a Gray Elf in red."

"The Three Sisters?" exclaimed Barandir.

I honestly considered he was headed for a straitjacket. I lowered the tension in my own voice for his sake. "I wouldn't know." Neither did Shadow, judging by my scar.

"Venameshe, Elrameshe, and Urdemeshe," Hibara explained. "Each

Elven kingdom has a High Sorceress—one of the Three Sisters."

"That's not right." I stopped in my tracks. "Elrameshe was not at Anchorage. A Forest Elf I didn't recognize, along with the other two, cast the spell that joined Shadow and me."

"And this occurred in 1964?" inquired Barandir slowly. He appeared to be looking deep within himself. "She would have been *Atsemeshe.*"

At the sound of her name, a fire bell clanged in my head.

"Atsemeshe?" I blurted out, recognizing the name Father had said on the phone all those years ago. The name, at whose mention, turned Mother into an automaton before we zoomed out of Fort Collins.

"Elrameshe's predecessor. Atsemeshe disappeared several years ago. Our kingdom could not be without a High Sorceress. After one year, our king declared Elrameshe as her successor, High Sorceress of the *Koire-kwente*, and thereby one of the Three Sisters."

My gut wrenched itself tight. "When did this happen? When did Atsemeshe disappear?"

"As you measure it, the year 1980."

I struggled to get the words out. "May 18th, 1980?"

"Precisely," Barandir tilted his head, scrutinizing me. "How could you know?"

My throat tightened up, and I wanted to cry. As did Shadow. "Atsemeshe died trying to save me and my parents. Just as she had always done—Anchorage, Lubbock, Los Angeles, Rapid City, Ft. Collins, Mt. St. Helens. Every time."

I blinked, trying to clear my eyes. It failed utterly. I took out my handkerchief to dab them. Throwing decorum to the wind, I also gave my nose a good, loud honk. "Lenoir taunted me that the bones next to my father's belonged to a female Elf. I think your Atsemeshe was buried under three feet of volcanic ash, along with my father."

Jamming the cloth into my back pocket, I cleared my throat. "Why were all Three Sisters present at our deaths?" I asked, the frog still in my throat.

"To save you and Shadow," said Ventnor.

"No," I snapped. "They were *already* there, with my parents and other Forest Elves."

"Other—?" interjected Barandir, but I couldn't let him sidetrack me again.

"They didn't just happen to stumble upon us. There was no time to call them—all the evidence of the scene indicated they were there the instant we died. They had already arrived, meeting in Anchorage for a reason other than to save me and Shadow."

The room replied with silence, my footsteps the only sound as I plodded past Ventnor again. I frowned at Petrakis, who flashed his damnable know-it-all smile, waiting to see if I could suss out the puzzle's answer.

"Such a meeting would never be allowed," grumbled Barandir. "The three kingdoms would sooner let their Ministers of the Right meet to exchange secrets of state."

"So it was a conspiracy." Which made sense. From the moment Elrameshe spotted me in the helicopter, she had been furtive. As I passed Netsumi, I eyed the box I had given her. My scar itched. "But if the kings' high sorceresses are so valuable, why let Elrameshe serve in Eldridge?"

"Half a century ago," said Hibara, "we established an exchange program with the *Koire-kwente*. On a yearly basis, a human mage and Forest Elf mage would live among the other people, learning their ways and magic. Elrameshe was a major participant, returning every few years. Though she pretended to be a minor mage."

"Then, you knew she was one of the Three Sisters and a spy?"

"Of course. The High and Gray Elves may consider humans little better than the primates from which we evolved. However, the sitting Regent of the *Koire-kwente*, like his people, regards us as kin. It was he who established the exchange program nearly a quarter of a century ago. Even though we both benefited, it is also a given we would spy upon one another. It is merely the way of both worlds, and permitted by the Human-Faerie Armistice. I will admit, however, I am baffled that the Three Sisters worked in cooperation."

My scar was burning. "What about this Regent? What happened to the Forest Elf king?"

"He was assassinated." Barandir still held his fists against his sides. His whole body trembled.

"Let me guess. By the *Turiathurin*."

"His body was torn apart, set upon by the beast while he sat on our kingdom's throne. The throne in our holiest of forests!" he spat. "Escorted and defended by the king's most trusted general, the royal consort and the young prince fled, escaping to *Cirbann Cevan*—your Earth—but to no avail. The monster tracked them down, and they suffered the same fate. First, the prince—we knew not where—then the royal consort near the mountain you call McKinley." With his right hand, he solemnly traced a line across his chest. "Their bodies are now at rest, standing in the Forest of the Revered, one of the few holy places in *Band Cevan* that still stands."

I raised an eyebrow at Hibara. "Why didn't Eldridge respond to such major intrusions?"

The Vice President turned his placid gaze toward the pair standing on the office threshold.

Ventnor coughed a pompous *harrumph* past his white walrus mustache. "Their deaths were foreseen, but Eldridge arrived too late to assist in any meaningful way. I was the adjuster assigned to escort the Regent back to their world."

"*You* were an adjuster?"

"Is that so surprising? Assessors and adjusters are often the first step on the path to management."

Note to self: memory wipe yourself, Yeager, at the first hint they want to promote you to either position.

"You escorted only the Regent?"

"My staff accompanied the remains of the queen consort and the prince." Ventnor held his chin high. He was not telling me something.

"What else? What did the Regent take with him back to *Band Cevan*? Was he wearing his steel armor? Was he wearing a headband of woven salamanders? Did he have a sword of wood that cut like steel, covered in black blood?" I pointed behind me in Netsumi's direction. "Did he bear this box back to his people? What was in that box?"

Ventnor's jaw clenched as he glanced at Hibara.

"Ventnor, you seemed startled when I described Shadow's death outside Anchorage." My scar felt like it could light a bonfire. I pointed an accusing finger at Hibara. "But *you* knew. You knew Shadow is this *prince* of the Forest Elves."

Hibara glanced at the floor, then back at me. As far as confessions went, it was good enough for me.

Barandir stumbled a step back. Contrasted against his austere countenance, his eyes betrayed his shock. "'Shadow must open the *lûth colca*,' Elrameshe said." His voice was barely a whisper.

"Open the what?" I said.

"The box. I did not understand her at the time, but Elrameshe said she had been tasked to return it to the one named Shadow. If what you say is true, Yeager—that you died with the prince, and he resides within you—this coffer will hold the answers you seek." With a hitch in his voice, he added, "If only Elrameshe..."

I relieved Netsumi of the glyph-covered box. Turning it every which way, I tried to read the sigils. My ears tingled with Shadow's words as he read them. Taking a deep breath, I repeated the syllables in a cautious, expectant voice.

The box lay inert in my hands.

"Doggonit!" I snapped. "Can we go somewhere else? This room is canceling out whatever magic unseals the box."

Netsumi gestured toward the rice paper tapestry pierced by the High Elf arrow, its ink still bleeding onto the floor. "That ward is broken. Need I remind you, Dr. Yeager, if you had attempted your spell while it was still in force, that would have been your third and final infraction."

The realization that Netsumi was absolutely correct made me gulp —I should be dead due to a moment's forgetfulness. I scolded Shadow, wondering if he realized the ward was rendered ineffective when he told me what to say. Somewhere between my ears, he shrugged his shoulders.

"The *lûth colca* were created by the Three Sisters," said Barandir. "Only they are able to open them."

I was about to contradict him, as Kovalenko and Fleischer had two of their own, but Ventnor beat me to the punch.

"Not quite." He stepped off the raised floor of Hibara's inner office. As he approached me, he removed his Hadrian Limited from his jacket's breast pocket. He dismissed me with a flit of his hand, and I took a half-step aside. "Hadrian, if you would be so kind as to assist?" He waved his pen once around the perimeter of the black wooden and metal box. As he did, I'm sure my eyebrows flicked upward when I glimpsed Hadrian's cap. It was enameled with the twisted one-eyed star, the same sigil on Kovalenko's earrings and embroidered into Fleischer's sash.

Ventnor closed his eyes and repeated the words I had spoken a few moments earlier.

The room resounded with a click, and the box shuddered open a crack. With smug satisfaction, Ventnor stepped back and placed Hadrian back in his pocket. Glancing sidelong in Barandir's direction, he said, "Generations ago, Atsemeshe, then Sister of the Forest, bestowed that privilege onto our Druidic order as well. One of the benefits of our exchange program."

"Well, sur-prise, sur-prise," I said, aping Gomer Pyle. "So, that's what gave you the ability to lay the Blue Watcher in the Aptitude Stones to rest."

"Smart boy," snipped Ventnor. "I was wise not to follow my first instincts regarding your employment."

"Which was?"

"To revive an old Druidic practice." His smile turned nasty. "Nail your intestines to a tree and chase you around the trunk, wielding a silver scythe until you tear all your guts out."

"Then I'm glad for both of us," I said, skewering him with my own scowling grin. "My Frost Giant friend wouldn't take kindly to wild party antics." I proffered the box to Hibara, who solemnly shook his head, then to Barandir, who looked like I showed him his own head.

Petrakis said, "No, my boy. The box was meant for you alone."

Sticking a pinkie under the exposed lip, I raised the lid a centimeter. No bolts of lightning, no migraine skewering my eyeballs together. So far, so good. I held my breath, bit down, and swung the onyx lid high.

Resting on satin the color of fresh spring moss lay four items: an amulet constructed of silver links forged into an egg-shaped spiral encasing three gems joined together; a small roll of parchment scarcely larger than my fist, tied with a ribbon and fixed with a wax seal; a signet ring of gold with a steel design of interlocking salamanders befitting that of M. C. Escher; and a headband of gold—not a complete circlet, but one that would flex to accommodate a variety of sizes. Wreathed with entwined salamanders slithering toward its forefront, its base rested in a circle of interwoven marble and wood.

"What are these things?" I asked of the room.

Barandir's whole body cringed in an expression of fear and awe. "The signet and crown of the *Koire-kwente*, last worn by King *Nen Cuithas*."

"Water that brings life," I echoed Shadow's translation of his father's name. "That makes sense, I've heard the name Cuithas before. And the others?"

"The scroll bears the seal of the king's signet. But the talisman is unknown to me."

"Not to me. At least not entirely. I think..." I squinted at the gems, glittering with life, caged in the silver spirals. "I've seen this before."

I placed the box on the conjuring table, resisted the urge to order another Mezcal paloma, and reached my hand over the amulet. Seeing no objections after a short pause, I grasped the item, holding it close for inspection. The gems' inner lattices glittered with life waiting to escape. I gasped with recognition—this was the amulet worn by the Green Sister, Atsemeshe. The one that floated by its chain in front of her, controlling the orb of energy that fused Shadow and me into one.

Could this be where the rest of Shadow lay encapsulated? Could this be his "silver castle?" I recalled Elrameshe's words before she disappeared from my first PQ assessment.

"The Gems of Binding?" I mused aloud.

The firm braided silver warmed in my palm. My fingertips tingled. A quick check revealed the dead skin over the last of the frostnip blisters had been replaced with new flesh—not even a scar. It wasn't long until I felt its pressure against my palm, magnetically drawn toward my heart. I relaxed my arm the slightest amount, allowing the amulet to guide it. My hand hovered inches from my heart. A crimp in my heart raced up my neck and down my arms. The dull ache where the Valdaan chewed through my ribs and tried to devour my heart vanished in a heartbeat.

I asked Shadow what the device was doing. He didn't reply in words, but left me with the impression the Sisters' magic healed in a way the Ageless Waters could not. I was compelled by his sentiment to allow the magic do its work. I let the device guide my arm further.

With the amulet grasped between my fingertips, it drew my hand rose above my head. Without warning, the device slipped from my tenuous hold and *thwacked* itself onto the top of my skull. It spun in place, resisting my fumbling attempt to pull it away, until the pattern of the silver rope found its resting place. I winced as it clung to every point of my burning scar, matching every groove of the remodeled bone.

A multicolored flash filled the room, and I doubled over from the sensation of a lightning bolt zooming from my brain down the full length of my Vagus nerve. My torso spasmed again, and the amulet fell from my head. It rolled on the floor, its silver oxidized to a patina of dark charcoal. The gems within had split apart, leaving lifeless pieces to rattle about in the rusted cage.

Shadow's voice boomed in my head, thrilling with enlightenment. *"I know."*

"What do you know?" I said between grunts and flashes of vertigo.

"If it's where I can find a large bottle of Dramamine, I'm all ears."

"I know who I am," Shadow thundered, intensely enough that I was compelled to echo him aloud. "I know *what* I am."

CHAPTER 52

A lifetime—maybe more—of images, sounds, smells, and sensations poured into my reeling brain. Music of towering woods and endless plains of tall grass. The balm of sweetest flowers and freshly turned loam. Rivers and lakes of the purest water.

Shattered by the sweat and cries of the Forest people as they labored under the lash of our supposed brethren. The proclamations by the *Hominus* mages of the *Consilium*—the Ultimate Law of *Terra Verum*—almost human, but with dragon's eyes. Their pronouncements in Latin of the unspeakable crimes of their fellow citizens, the High and Gray Elves. The evidence of their guilt laid bare, announced across throngs of *Hominus*. The augury of *Terra Verum*'s doom, shared by every seer of the *Consilium*. Portents of endless wars between the Elves and the *Hominus*, and the laying waste of every land in *Terra Verum*, if they or their creations were permitted to remain.

"Are these your memories, Shadow?"

"They belong to the other imprisoned with me, Michael. Karani Tur, the Red Watcher."

Him again? My vision cleared, returning me to Hibara's room.

"Who are you?" said Barandir, his voice barely a whisper, his eyes expectant.

Enervated to the point where I wanted to sleep for a month, I somehow managed to stand erect again. All I could do was to listen as Shadow spoke through me. "Decades past in *Tawar Cevan*, I was Anor Cuithas." I mustered enough energy to interject with a translation. "The Sun which brings Life."

"Cuithas?" Barandir whispered. His chestnut complexion blanched, and his knees quivered as though they demanded he drop to the floor and abase himself. Breathless silence held sway over the room.

"Scion of Nen Cuithas, *Tawar Aran* of the *Koire-kwente*, and *Nîdh Sirith*, his Queen Consort," Shadow and I pronounced in unison.

"*Tawar Aran.*" Though his voice was barely above an awed whisper, Barandir's pronouncement rang throughout the room. "Lord of the Forest, the slain King of the *Koire-kwente*."

The vision, followed by all this fuss and bluster, threatened to turn my stomach. "*Tawar Aran*—now I remember where I heard that title before. It was one of the phrases Dr. Fleischer called me before that stupid *Turia Feir*—or as Ventnor called it, the Blue Watcher—attacked us." I snapped my fingers. "That ties in with what the *urkāphan* assassins called me, too—the 'son of the traitor.' Is that why the *Turiathurin* killed him? How was the Forest Elf king a traitor?"

Despite being a bit theatrical, I put my arms akimbo as I faced Barandir again. "Since Shadow is this Anor Cuithas, who sounds like he's heir to the Forest Elves' throne, why did the Blue Watcher try to kill me? And for that matter, why did this so-called Red Watcher prevent Elrameshe from contacting Shadow? I think we could have avoided all this Eldridge cloak-and-dagger mishagas, not to mention half a dozen deaths, if there wasn't some blasted Elven roadblock every step of the way."

"So Elrameshe *did* contact you." Netsumi smiled at Hibara. Ten minutes ago, that would have worried me. Now, I didn't care one bit either way. I was close.

"Red Watcher?" Ventnor seemed genuinely surprised. If Eldridge's version of Mr. Monopoly wore a monocle, it would have popped out. "You know where he is?"

"In my head, apparently, just like Shadow. You know who that is?" I rattled my head, shaking a deduction or two loose. "Of course you do, Ventnor. Just like you knew the Blue Watcher."

"That is our name for him. When he lived, he was *Karani Tur*, a Gray Elf, now consigned to serve as one of two Watchers. *Turia Feir* was a High Elf, whose spirit was indentured to serve as the Blue Watcher."

I silently queried Shadow to fill in the blanks. He was just as puzzled as me.

"So why did one Watcher try to kill me while the other protected me and Shadow—"

"—*Prince* Anor Cuithas," corrected Barandir.

"They're both living rent-free in my head. I'll call them whatever I want," I snapped back. I glared at everyone. "What can I expect from this Watcher? Is he going to give me a big sloppy kiss or have his turn at tearing off my head?"

"Little is known of the Red Watcher," said Barandir. "Like his brethren, he is doomed to serve until his task is fulfilled."

"Which is...?"

"Only he knows."

"These colors..." I breathed deeply to collect my thoughts. "They match what I've seen two of the Three Sisters wear. What's the connection?"

Ventnor began with a pompous clearing of his throat. "Each species of Elven magic draws from the elementals bearing that color. High Elven magic is drawn from the latent powers of the skies. Sapphire is their gem of choice in their weirding. Forest Elves' ties to green should be obvious, even to *you*, I should think, Dr. Yeager." After another *ahem*, he prattled on, "They prefer emerald, though other minerals like jade figure prominently in their magic. The Gray Elves selected red. As a result, they favor ruby to focus their magic, but sometimes employ gems where impurities have tainted their pure color to red."

"Like red sapphire or rust emerald," said Petrakis.

"Precisely," said Ventnor.

"So, can someone tell me why these Elves became indentured servants?"

"It was one of the old Elvish ways." Barandir seemed upset and shifted his balance from one leg to the other. "There has been a generations-long enmity between the Gray Elves and the *Koire-kwente*."

"Maybe not so old where High Elves are concerned. You say you escaped a raiding party. What are these raids for? What do they do with their prisoners?"

"We never see them again."

"What did the *Koire-kwente* ever do to them to cause such enmity?"

Barandir remained silent. I repeated the question.

He finally replied, agony in his voice. "We do not know. We have no recollection, no record before the First Days."

"First Days?"

"Before, we did not exist. Then on First Day, we did."

My shoulders slumped. If there was one thing I trusted less than oracles, it was a creation myth. "Really—Adam and Eve?"

"No, our people *all* came to exist, untold millennia ago. Hundreds, thousands of *Koire-kwente*, young and old, just came to *be* in the blink of an eye. Dressed in wretched clothing and rags we did not recognize, they were all covered in sweat and filth. All in one great valley in our new world, *Tawar Cevan*."

I staggered with disbelief and consternation when an idea slammed into me. It was too mind-bending, too powerful to comprehend. "An entire people... *mindwiped*?"

"Not long after we came to be, so did the *Mori-kwente*. They appeared in our world, only to raid and steal our people, then vanish back to their world of *Band Cevan*. Much later, the *Kala-kwente* came as well."

"Like they walked through walls," I ruminated quietly.

"Yes," he moaned.

"The Blue Watcher sensed Shadow within you," added Ventnor. "He told me as much before I released him from the remains of the Aptitude Stones. I would agree—that enmity is still strong."

"Did he happen to say *why* he hated Shadow's guts? Other than this nebulous traitor crud."

"Not directly." Ventnor's grimace became sour. "I got the impression his task was to stop Anor Cuithas from completing what his father began."

"Which was?" Blank stares were the room's response. Even Shadow remained stupefied. "Is *that* the betrayal the *urkāphan* yammered on about?"

Something answered in their stead. The vision returned, walloping me right between the eyes.

CHAPTER 53

The great arena. In the largest city of *Terra Verum*. An enormous throng, hundreds of jeering *Hominus*. The *Consilium*'s decree for the banishment of both the High and Gray Elven races who presumed the power of gods, along with their abomination.

Despair and fear as whole nations are whisked from their hovels, their homes, their castles, and their lands in the blink of an eye by the mighty and irresistible magics of the *Consilium*. Throngs of Elven faces of every stripe: High and Gray Elves stripped of their lands, magics, and finery, exiled into the frozen and burning wastelands of *Band Cevan*; Forest elves swathed in clothing barely better than torn hides and soiled rags, banished to a separate world, *Tawar Cevan*, flourishing and favorable to their kind.

The first King and the first Green Sister of the *Koire-kwente*, their names lost to time. Selected by the *Consilium*, only those two were permitted to keep the haunting memories of *Terra Verum* and the horrific, blasphemous sins committed by the High and Gray Elves.

First Day in *Tawar Cevan*. Together, the two kept the secret. Together they guided the thousands of lost and bewildered *Koire-kwente* to build new lives in their new and beautiful world. Together, they passed the terrible secret on to their two successors, and so on, for generation after generation.

The tranquility of *Tawar Cevan* shattered when the *Mori-kwente* invade, armed with weapons and magic undreamt of. The fear of the people as loved ones are taken, never to return.

The faces of my father—no, Shadow's father, King Nen Cuithas—

and Atsemeshe the Green Sister, as they shoulder the burden of the *Koire-kwente*'s terrible secret on behalf of their generation and those to come.

The King, his mother, the Queen Consort Nîdh Sirith, and the Green Sister, all weary from generations of raids, skirmishes, and battles nearly plunging the worlds of *Band Cevan* and *Tawar Cevan* into war.

Until the day that doomed us all a second time. News from the Red and Blue Sisters that the old sins have risen again in *Band Cevan*. But amidst the horror, they also lay down a hope for the future. Plans are made. Work done in secret.

All culminating in the long-awaited arrival of Venameshe the Blue Sister and Urdemeshe the Red Sister. The Three Sisters together presenting to King Cuithas the power to enforce an everlasting peace between the three kingdoms and return home the lost *Koire-kwente*.

King Cuithas' hopes dashed on the eve of deliverance. An unknown force from the world of *Band Cevan* opening a portal in the royal hall. The king slain on his throne by the *Turiathurin* that tore through the hellish opening. Racing to the haven of *Cirbann Cevan*, the world of Humans, the world they call Earth. Unlike the *Consilium* of *Terra Verum*, this world's guardians are known to offer sanctuary. The royal family's pursuit by a squad of High and Gray Elves—*working together?*—sent directly from their hellish world to Earth. Ambushed along the slopes of a great mountain range in the northern Earth by the High. The destruction caused by angered bedrock, ensorcelled by the Gray. Running through the sacred shielding forests along the western face of this continent pursued by the High and their creatures of the sky and mountain. My father's most trusted general and my mother, running with me through the thickets. She, clutching the *lûth colca* close to her chest, while his sword slayed the last of our pursuers. Into the clearing where the High and the Gray had skillfully driven us. The clearing, where the beast lurked, waiting for us.

The *Turiathurin*, tearing out my own heart.

My body tensed, bracing against a hammering worse than when the Valdaan shattered my ribs, and the mother of all migraines poised to wrack my skull. They never came, thank God.

The waterfall of images and incessant pummeling of sensations parted.

I stood in an enormous room of silver, the walls dotted with scores of windows, their shutters flung open. No paintings graced the walls, no furniture had been placed except for a solitary silver throne in the center of the room. In the center of the nearest wall was a door of argent metal burnished to the point where it almost glowed. I called out for Shadow, but there was no response. After gathering my thoughts, I walked the perimeter of the room. Maybe I hoped duplicating my pacing in this place would make Shadow appear. Hell, I'd be happy if Hibara and the others appeared.

Pausing at every window, I realized each held a memory the amulet had dumped into my head, displayed like a museum diorama.

I broke into a sweat. I shouted as loud as I could. "Shadow—where are you? Is this your silver castle?" My voice echoed shrilly between the metal walls. "Watcher? ... *Shadow*!" I shrieked. My entire body twitched as naked fear overtook me.

Trapped! Alone? *Again*?

I gibbered their names over and over, each time more panicked than the last.

Would this place hold for me an eternal solitude, almost as sterile and abhorrent as the Void? My knees trembled. My attempts at courage wilted to gray dust. I wanted to curl up into a ball of tears.

A voice answered.

CHAPTER 54

On the silver throne sat Shadow become flesh.

Attired in lavish finery, his vestment was crafted with materials reminiscent of the dress his mother had worn when she stood over his corpse in Anchorage's forest clearing. Gone were the blood, scars, and wounds that desecrated his body in the forest deep. His smile was that of an old friend, guileless as a puppy.

"Anor Cuithas, I presume?"

A moment of thought crossed his face. Regaining his smile, he rose from his seat and approached. He embraced me as a long-lost brother. "Michael," he said with a tonality approaching reverence.

My arms returned the gesture, albeit awkwardly.

Holding me by the sides at arm's length, he said, "Strangely enough, I find I preferred it when you called me Shadow."

"Shadow it is."

From behind Shadow's throne arose a seething cloud of red mist. I goggled at the thing as it maneuvered around the great silver chair. Half my height, in the shape of an inverted teardrop, its vapors tumbled down to evaporate into nothingness. It gently bobbed as it approached. A febrile glow within weaved about in the vapors, beating like a heart.

"And who... or *what* are you?"

"I am *Tur Taurē*," it said, the walls echoing its reply. "The Watcher of forests and its people who live amongst the green of *Taurē Keman* and sometimes this world. The *Koire-kwente* call me *Karani Tur*. Your people know me as the Red Watcher."

My head was beginning to hurt. "Y'know, Shadow, I miss you

whispering in my ear to translate this gibberish."

"The Watcher speaks the tongue of the Gray Elves, the language spoken by those who attacked you in Washington. The *Taurē Keman* he speaks of is the land to which we had been exiled. What we call *Tawar Cevan*."

"Oh yeah, that helps a lot." I took a cautious step back. "Hold on... you said Gray? You've been stuck in here with the enemy all this time?" Another realization punched me in the gut. "A friggin' *Gray* Elf has been in my head all this time? How the heck do we get rid of him?"

"I am freed when my task is done," it replied.

"Which is...?"

"He is not permitted to say," said Shadow wistfully. "I have spent much of my time since Elrameshe freed me trying to pry that out of him."

I planted myself nose-to-nose with Shadow. "When were you going to tell me there's Gray Elf in my head?"

"Because it would cause you unnecessary strife, Michael."

"No *shinola*, Sherlock." It lacked punch, but I couldn't take the chance whatever I said here didn't spew out loud in Hibara's ultra-mag-icked parlor as well.

Shadow walked around the undulating red cloud. "He is a Watcher, unable to do anything, save for his indentured task."

"Again, with slavery? I think I understand why those *Hominus* from *Terra Verum* threw all you bums out."

The room shuddered, rocking to a point where even Californians would get nervous. The orb inside the mist burned with the color of blood set on fire. "You *dare* judge us when your kind practices the same abomination?"

"Abomination," I whispered to myself. Who knows what dance my eyebrows did. I reached for my scribe. "Amelia, please translate these words:" I rubbed my forehead, hoping it would help me remember my visions. I searched my memories for the Latin judgments handed down by the *Hominus* of the *Consilium* against the Elves. My prowess in Latin extends to little more than what I needed in the scientific world. Ask me to rattle off anything other than a bacteria's binomial nomenclature or "*Et tu Brute,*" and you'll be terribly disappointed. I supposed I could call up the Latin I had eideticized from Eldridge orientation, but that would be a slow process. Best if my scribe took care of it with her usual speed and panache.

"She is not there," said Shadow. "The pen you hold is nothing but a construct within your mind—as is this version of myself you see. The Watcher will allow no spirit but yours to enter this domain. Not Elrameshe, despite all her powers; not even your scribe, though her spirit be tied to yours."

"Then why are we here in your silver castle? It was destroyed just a few minutes ago. How did we meet in Anchorage? And why were you just a shadow then, Shadow?"

"*Hominus* is such a tiresome race," thrummed the Watcher as softly as he could, though the floor still vibrated with his every syllable.

"They are not the *Hominus, Karani Tur*. Humans are superior in many ways."

"Inferior in an uncomfortable number of ways, as well," Watcher boomed.

"Michael has proved sufficiently adept to keep all three of us alive—even you, *Karani Tur*."

Sinking an inch or two, the cloud sulked dark rust, bubbling like dry ice in water.

Shadow strolled over to a window not far from his throne. He beckoned me to join him. He swept his arm wide to include the entirety of the room. "These portals are how we were able to meet. These windows open to memories, most of them mine. Some are portals into *Karani Tur*'s memories, at least, the ones he is *permitted* to show me.

"But for the longest time, they were shuttered. All but this solitary window that opened to your world."

Peering through the window, I had a panoramic view of Hibara's office ceiling. The faces of everyone there ringed the diorama's field of vision. A potpourri of expressions and emotions stared back at me, from Petrakis' frightened concern to Ventnor's brassy sneer, Barandir's tight-lipped calm, Netsumi concentrating while applying a compress to my head, and Hibara's grim detachment.

"When I reach into this portal," said Shadow, "I see, hear, feel, *experience* everything in your life."

I stood in wonder for the longest time, until I suddenly gulped. I probably blushed bright enough to light a whole box of matches. "Everything?" I rasped.

"Everything." Shadow's grin was barely perceptible but had a definite lascivious edge to it.

I'm gonna have to do a ton of apologizing to Sindhu. Maybe some groveling, too.

"It wasn't until the day when you first encountered Elrameshe that I began to understand I was a consciousness separate from your own. She had sensed my presence—an easy enough task for her, since she and her Sisters created this sanctuary for my spirit. She tried to contact me, but *Karani Tur* stood in her way."

"She may have opened the silver castle's door, but she is not permitted entrance," said Watcher.

"But I could enter," I deduced. "You showed me where we died."

"Your presence, after Elrameshe had opened the door, was permitted," added Watcher.

Shadow led me to another window not far away. "This particular window opens to where we first met. It contains the memories of those involved in that fateful day when our lives ended, and the Three Sisters irrevocably intertwined our futures."

"With all those memories, why were you... a *shadow*, Shadow? When I first saw you, I thought you were a shapeshifter and almost knocked your block off."

"When we first came across each other, most of my mind and identity still resided in the amulet, held in Elrameshe's *lûth colca*. I had neither memories nor a sense of 'self' to project. I was a hollow spirit, colorless and waiting to be reunited with my mind and its memories.

"But we are getting ahead of ourselves. Though I had become self-aware, I could not access any memory—not even the memory of Anchorage. Not until Mr. Pellagati assailed this castle. *Karani Tur* defended me the only way he knew how. Pellagati's attack did not damage my sanctuary greatly, but he did manage to remove the shutters, the obstacles to my memories. I'm afraid he suffered a far worse injury."

"I'm not gonna shed any tears," I said.

"I brought you to this memory first to begin my healing. Ever since, I have wandered these portals, observing the memories they hold, reacquainting myself with the *Koire-kwente* who was Anor Cuithas. Relearning the history and the doom pronounced on our people by the *Consilium* of *Terra Verum*. Now, I have enough memories to present myself as more than a shadow. But even so, there are scores of windows I have not tried, so many portals I have yet to walk. I may know who and what I am, but I am not yet complete."

"Not to be an inhospitable host, but how long is that gonna take?"

Shadow shrugged as casually as a human. "That is anyone's guess. To be able to answer, I would need to know what I haven't learned yet. What was that phrase you used before? 'A necessary but insufficient condition.'"

"Yeah, not quite applicable here. But I get you."

He sighed heavily. "Then there's the prospect these windows, though numerous, might not contain all my memories. I might remain incomplete."

I ambled past nearby windows. "Is it too much to hope one of these contains my memories from before I died?"

"I understand how precious they would be to you, Michael." Shadow, walking beside me, squeezed my shoulder. "If I find any, I shall call you here again."

Past one portal, then another. They opened onto scenes I had not experienced when the amulet gobsmacked me. "I just realized something, Shadow. Every time we were attacked, more of this castle was damaged, more memories were made available to you—"

"Yes."

"—and my PQ level increased. I suppose my strength is actually yours, growing as you become more complete. I guess that means I'm a Mundane, after all." My emotions were a jumble. I didn't know if I should be sad, relieved, envious...

"That remains to be seen. There may be some of your memories in my silver castle that may prove otherwise. Besides, we both learned that training and time may improve wherever your true ability lies."

I continued walking, hoping to spot some portal's scene that synced up or jogged my memory, matching some vignette from the train wreck of visions.

"What are you looking for?" asked Watcher. He moved close, hovering near the closest window. Perhaps he thought I would jump through.

I stopped at the next window and pointed through the portal. "This."

Through the window, a diorama dripping with solemnity and significance splayed before us. Seemingly a dozen yards below us, an enormous amphitheater sat, nestled in the heart of a burgeoning city. The stadium's seats were filled with hundreds of *Hominus*. Thousands thronged the streets surrounding its outermost columns. The gathering was shielded from the sun by an acres-wide black tarpaulin, scored along its edges with myriad arcane symbols.

The burgeoning crowd watched the central square stage of stone with wide dragon-eyed intent. Seven *Hominus*, robed in black, stood before a semicircular arc of stone chairs bordered with onyx filigree. One figure in the group's center wore sleeves hemmed with white. It held one arm raised high, grasping a white scepter.

Two figures, one dressed in blue and the other in red, stood facing them from the center. Two waist-high granite columns laced with the same black stone rose in front of them. Rings of white energy firmly attached the defendants' hands to their stone pillory.

The Spanish Inquisition's *Auto-da-fé* could not be more imposing. I leaned toward the portal, careful not to cross any boundary, and squinted. Even so, I could not make out any further details.

"What draws you here?" inquired the Watcher.

"This was one of the images I saw after Atsemeshe's amulet glued itself to my head. Before this, what I saw was pastoral, peaceful. This was the first part of my vision when things started to go south. I have to assume it's important." Turning toward Shadow, I asked, "Which memory is this?"

"I do not believe it is one of mine. I have wandered through this memory many times, but I have not recognized any familiar face or vestment. Nor do I understand the language spoken by the central figure. So, I cannot tell whose memory it might be. The only thing I can tell you is, it is quite obvious he is pronouncing judgment upon the two prisoners."

"I think I can help in that department." I faced Watcher. "How do we get down there?"

CHAPTER 55

And just like that, Shadow and I were deposited on the enormous granite and marble square dais. We stood behind the two unlucky Elven stiffs, who themselves stood uneasy behind waist-high granite columns. With their wrists clad in white mystic energy against either side of their respective stones, their hands could not touch each other, let alone the parchment document affixed to their column's flat surface. Between them, an imposing mountain of a *Hominus* wielded an iron staff topped with a white crystal. At the rear of the platform sat the seven stone chairs, empty and waiting.

"Well, *that* was easy."

The guard scowling at his prisoners took no notice of us. Just like Shadow's memory in the forests of Anchorage, we were ephemeral shades, wisps of things unseen, that could observe but not take part in the events taking place around us. His attention was instead focused on seven empty granite and onyx thrones on the rear of the platform.

I whirled around to face the uncanny crowd of almost-humans. As they waited patiently, they stirred in their seats. A humming susurrus from scores of hushed voices hovered above the crowd.

"Notice that?" I said. "Time isn't frozen. I wonder why?" After my quick rubbernecking of the surroundings, I added, "Where's Watcher?"

"He cannot enter my memories."

"But you said some memories may not be yours. I'm inclined to agree since you recognize nobody here." I looked skyward toward the enormous canvas above our heads. "Watcher, could you join us, please?" With a pulse of air, like someone struck a drum as wide as the sky,

Watcher appeared next to the prisoner decked out in red.

"Glad you could join us," I said. Watcher remained silent, shedding vapor. "So whose memory is this? And where are the guys with the black robes?"

We waited, but no reply was given.

"Answer him, *Karani Tur*," commanded Shadow.

"I am not permitted an answer," the air thrummed with Watcher's voice. He almost sounded ashamed.

"What is happening here?" My eyes were drawn to the unforgiving stone columns. "Is it a trial? A whipping?"

"Ask me no more questions here. I am not permitted to answer," replied the ear-splitting broken record.

"Fat lot of good *you* are," I grumbled.

Every player in this living diorama was waiting for something or someone. I took the opportunity to familiarize myself with the surroundings. I didn't have far to go.

I was mildly surprised they were male elves—a High Elf dressed in blue and a Gray Elf clothed in red. Both scowled defiantly at their guard.

Though I didn't expect to recognize their faces, I did note their attire was strikingly similar and of the same material and colors as those worn by the High Elf sorceress and her sister Gray Elf in Anchorage.

I pointed to the two prisoner's faces. "Why is there no Forest Elf here?"

I nearly had a coronary when the guard slammed the butt of his staff on the ground three times, loud as cannon fire.

From behind each stone throne emerged a figure, robed in black, their floor-length robes fluttering in a lazy spring breeze. Each wore a covering shaped like a medieval sallet helmet, with a beaded curtain of silver draped over the face. Though I couldn't see any distinguishing features, they were obviously *Hominus*. "I take it this is the *Consilium*?"

"I believe so," said Shadow.

Their leader stepped forward. He uttered a short question in Latin. With my piecemeal grasp of the language, I translated, filling in the gaps as best I could. "Do the... accused... no, *guilty*, have anything to say before..."

The High Elf prisoner spoke before I could finish my ham-handed stumblings. His words rang out, filled with the purest spite. Shadow translated for me. "We, the Two Brothers, do not recognize the authority of the *Consilium* to dictate matters solely under the authority of Elven Law." He was interrupted by the strike of the guard's staff on the floor.

"Two Brothers?" I asked. "Are these guys sorcerers, like the Three Sisters?"

"Yes and no," Shadow whispered, even though no one else could hear us. "They were mighty wizards who preceded the Three Sisters."

I cocked my head toward the High Elf prisoner. There was something familiar in his voice. I was on the verge of recalling of whom it reminded me, when an out-of-the-blue inconsistency grabbed me. "Wait a minute, Shadow. How do you know these guys, the 'Two Brothers' as you called them? This had to be before your history in *Tawar Cevan*. Barandir indicated everything before First Day was erased from the Forest Elves' collective memory. How—?"

The Gray Elf spoke. As he spewed his vituperation at the *Consilium*, Shadow chimed in, "Unfortunately, I do not speak the Gray tongue."

"No need," I said. This time, I recognized the voice—albeit here, he spoke without all his usual bombast. Like a falling domino, the identity belonging to the High Elf defendant's voice came to me as well. "I'm willing to bet you essentially said the same thing as your High Elf conspirator."

I waited, but there was no response. "Didn't you, *Watcher*?"

Shadow's head jerked back as though he were slapped, and his whole body stiffened as he stared at the Gray Elf's defiant face.

"I am not permitted an answer," the Watcher boomed.

He didn't have to. He practically choked on his words.

The leader of the *Consilium* raised his right arm. The cuff of his sleeve hung heavy with bizarre sigils in milk quartz. I eyed some familiar symbols written among them with suspicion.

His hand gripped the base of a brilliantly white scepter. Projecting a voice practiced in passing judgment in a public setting, his pronouncements in Latin carried over the entire crowd. I set my mind to record his words in my memory. Repeating to myself those few words I recognized as anchor points to help me retain the body of his soliloquy, my train of concentration was broken by Shadow.

He parroted a sentence, then shrugged at me. "Unnecessary, Michael. I've listened to the *Regis*'s words so many times over the past three months, I could not help but commit it to memory. What his words mean, however, is tantalizingly beyond my reasoning. There are times I feel I am at a breakthrough and on the verge of understanding the language of the *Consilium*. Then my mind is overcome with a spasm, a wave of the most curious sensation, only to discover my thoughts are jumbled—whatever progress I had made, erased."

"I suspect that's because of your puffy red friend. But don't worry."

As I said, Latin is not my strong suit—my science background and eideticization of *Magic 101: Basic Latin for Spells* notwithstanding. However, it didn't take a master philologist of dead languages to deduce the meaning of words like *rapare, abominatio, damnatus*, and *intrusionem*. I understood why the *Regis*'s scepter shook with repressed rage. My own hackles were raised by phrases here and there, lifted straight out of the company Oath—like *Vita, Morte, et Sequitor.*

"Get us out of here," I said through gritted teeth to no one in particular.

A flash of red, and the three of us were back in Shadow's silver castle. Watcher hovered in front of the portal, his inner globe of crimson vaporizing mist furiously.

"What did you do, Red Watcher?" I stabbed my finger at him. "What crime did you and the Blue Watcher commit? What was so vile that the *Consilium* sentenced the both of you to serve imprisoned as Watchers for hundreds, maybe thousands of years? What did the High and Gray Elf races do, to deserve to be imprisoned in *Band Cevan*?

"In God's name, what did you *do*?"

"I am not permitted an answer," intoned the Watcher. "Only the king of the *Koire-kwente* and the Green Sister may learn that secret."

Shadow regarded Watcher with new eyes. His body angled away from his red companion, drawing his arms close.

I threw my hands up in disgust and walked toward the burnished metal door. "I've got work to do."

I flung it open, ignored the wall of red mist pouring down the doorway, and stepped through.

CHAPTER 56

My body gasped, greedily sucking in a lungful of air.

I found myself sitting in Hibara's overstuffed chair, sprawled out with my arms hanging over its sides. Around me stood a ring of concerned faces, just as I had seen them through the portal that allowed Shadow to experience my life with me.

Netsumi offered me a clay mug filled with water. I guzzled it, coughed half of it back out, and sipped the rest as quickly as I could manage. "So, how much of that did you hear?"

Petrakis blinked. With a rapid shake of his head, he replied, "My boy, you were out just scant seconds."

"Oh, *crud*." I patted my chest until I found my scribe. "Someone get me some paper while the Red Watcher's memory is fresh in my head." A storm of interrogation assailed me from every side. "No questions!" I barked, holding up my hand. "Just get me paper."

Ventnor produced a notepad from a jacket. I flipped past pages of his scribbles and Hadrian's perfect cursive until I found a blank sheet. I placed Amelia's tip on the paper.

"Amelia, please translate the following." Releasing her, she stood at the exact angle that I had held her. As quickly as possible before the memory faded, I tried my best to repeat what I had heard from the *Consilium*.

No sooner had I spoken a few words of the *Consilium*'s Latin, Barandir clapped his hands over his ears. Stumbling until his back slapped against the wall, he whimpered, "No—I may not hear the forbidden language." He closed his eyes and hummed a meandering tune softly to himself.

No one seemed surprised at Barandir's admission. Which only served to tick me off more. How much more did these guys expect me to discover on my own?

Stubbornly continuing, my attempts were littered with a few false starts and repeats. Shadow came to my rescue, filling in the gaps of my execrable Latin and equally poor powers of verbal recall.

"Allow me, Michael," whispered Shadow. "As I said, the *Regis*'s words are always with me."

My scribe jotted away as I concentrated on Shadow's recitation and parroted back his word-perfect Latin that I barely understood.

I ignored the distractions of Amelia's pirouettes and the words she wrote. Reading while listening and speaking would scramble my brains worse than rubbing my stomach and patting my head. I was more interested in Ventnor's and Hibara's solemnly nodding heads, and Petrakis' drawn face laden with shock and disgust.

The second I finished bucket-brigading Shadow's recitation, I asked him—mind to mind—how he, a Forest Elf, could utter the words of a language Barandir had declared unspeakable? All I got was another mental shrug of his shoulders.

I was tempted to tear the page out from Ventnor's notebook and eideticize it, hoarding to myself the precious knowledge Amelia had just disgorged. Such an action would be futile—any of my superiors could instantly access what she had written through their scribes or Central Records.

I read Amelia's English translation and wanted to puke.

"Netsumi," said Hibara. "Would you kindly escort Mr. Barandir outside? There is something we must discuss with Dr. Yeager."

Netsumi nodded, and one of her tails vanished with a flick and a whisper of wind. I looked behind me to see Ms. Emerald at the massive wooden double doors leading to the outer reception area.

Emerald smiled her polite smile and beckoned toward Barandir to accompany her. His expression tussled between embarrassment and frustration, while his stoicism struggled to tamp them both down. She opened the door, and into our room spilled a riotous cavalcade of angry voices and the sounds of physical altercation. Three humans huddled behind an overturned sofa, busying themselves with placing bets on a slug-fest between a troll and an ogre.

Taking a single step into the outer area, Emerald clapped her hands twice in rapid succession.

The room froze. Punches millimeters from connecting, knives and other weapons glinting as their edges dented each other, ogre versus troll, the suits cowering behind overturned chairs—all in the outer area stopped to gape at Ms. Emerald. There was fear in every pair of those eyes. The remains of torn red envelopes, pieces of shredded scrolls, and shreds of ribbons fluttered to the floor. Fists dropped to their owner's sides, knives were sheathed, and furniture was righted faster than you could say "Boo."

She strode into the room, and Barandir followed her without a word. With a grin that turned decidedly mischievous, Emerald closed the door.

My attention returned to Amelia's translation, reviewing every blistering accusation. By the time I reached the end, I was ready to spit nails. Shadow remained silent—due to shock or shame? I wasn't able to tell.

All eyes locked on me. I felt like a stray dog facing a pack of street mongrels. I didn't care. I bared my fangs.

"I saw how you two nodded as I dictated the *Regis*'s sentencing to Amelia. How long have you known of these crimes?"

I faced Petrakis. "How long did you know *Tawar Cevan*, the home of the Forest Elves, is a *prison* world, just like *Band Cevan* is for the High and Gray?"

His entire countenance changed into one of shock and disbelief. In a way, I was relieved—I would hate to think he was that deep in this mess.

Ventnor next enjoyed my glower. "How long did you know the *Koire-kwente*—the Forest Elves, Shadow's own people—were created as a *slave* race by the High and Gray Elves?" His mustachioed grimace telegraphed his disdain for the pipsqueak that dared speak to him in such a manner.

Get used to it, fat boy.

I turreted to Netsumi—not that I believed she had a hand in this, but the way this day was going, I couldn't afford to let her off the hook just yet. "How long did you know of the hundreds, the *thousands* of rapes and incests those two Elven mages—the so-called Two Brothers—forced upon their own peoples, all to serve some sick magically enhanced eugenics program to create the *Koire-kwente*?"

I ignored a gasp from Petrakis.

Finally, Hibara received what I hoped was my worst withering stare. "And what relation is this *Consilium* to Eldridge?"

That seemed to catch Hibara off guard—if you can call a slight narrowing of his eyes surprise. However, there was no shame or anger in his demeanor. More like he was still making his assessment of me.

"You didn't expect me to make that connection, did you?"

The cushions of Hibara's chair whispered a sigh as he sat. He motioned I do likewise. Coaxed by Netsumi with her all-too-familiar Gem Sisters' grin, I did so.

"I am intrigued, Dr. Yeager," said Hibara. "How did you come to this hypothesis?"

"The *Consilium*'s function was essentially the same as E&SQA—protect their world against intrusions, which is what they considered *Koire-kwente*. In addition to that, there were too many coincidences. Symbols on the robes of the *Consilium* are straight out of the Eldridge playbook. The judgment the *Regis* of the *Consilium* handed down, damning the High and Gray Elves to exile—parts of the Eldridge Oath of Service read like they were cribbed directly from his speech." I considered my empty glass. I could have used another belt, but losing myself in good hooch had to take a back seat until my mental chess game with Hibara was over. "So, is Eldridge in league with the *Consilium*?"

"Not an easy question to answer, Dr. Yeager," said Hibara. Silent as a ghost, Netsumi refreshed Hibara's mug of *matcha*. He held it close, breathing deep its wisps of scented steam. "As I stated before, Dr. Yeager, you—or more properly, you *with* Prince Anor Cuithas—form an intrusion nexus."

"Yeah, me and my Shadow." The air was too heady to even think of saying it as a jest.

"I had previously alluded that your nexus spawns several possible outcomes, several futures. Unfortunately, that is not the limit of the quandaries you represent. There are several realities other than our own, which may also be influenced. I do not know how to advise Prince Anor to steel himself—but as for yourself, Dr. Yeager, perhaps a strong cup of coffee is called for. You've had enough strong spirits for now."

Before I could object, Netsumi placed a delicate cup and saucer on the table, filled with the darkest espresso I'd ever seen. As I relished the distinctive notes of Hawaiian Moloka'i, she placed Elrameshe's box next to the saucer. "What do you expect me to do about this nexus? I've told you all I know. Now it's your turn."

Hibara handed his mug back to Netsumi. "For millennia, Eldridge has protected Earth against intrusions from aberrant creatures, alien worlds, other spirit planes, and other realities."

"This is not news." I tried to not let my impatience get the better of me.

"What is not widely disseminated, is that it was not always so. Long ago, parallel realities, parallel dimensions, and the versions of Earth that inhabited them were sacrosanct. Only in the past century was Earth opened to the parallel reality of *Tawar Cevan*.

"That previously inviolable boundary was first contravened by the *Consilium*, the magic-wielding *Hominus* from another Earth—the one they have the temerity to claim as *Terra Verum*, the 'Real Earth.' The memory you retrieved from the Red Watcher confirms our suspicions.

"While we have never had contact with this *Consilium*, it should come as no surprise that a world so similar to ours would likewise have an institution that serves a purpose similar to Eldridge's. What *did* surprise us was the method they chose to deal with the threat created in their own world. Whereas we place intrusions that cannot be otherwise resolved in storage locations like ILTS, they chose a more perilous method.

"Though I can understand their abhorrence of the crimes of the High and Gray Elves—the *Consilium*, in blind hubris, committed an even greater sin. They broke what never should have been broken. Either through ignorance or by egotistical presumption, they tore the æther between dimensions. And now all of Creation must bear the consequences of their foolishness." The muscles under Hibara's cheekbones bunched.

"And what was done once can be done again," I ruminated aloud. The memory of Elrameshe standing over the bodies of Shadow and me led me to the next logical step. "That's how the High and Gray Elves eventually began raiding the world of Forest Elves, and the Forest Elves could enter *our* reality. When did this all begin?"

"The exact age when the *Consilium* committed their original transgression is lost to ancient history. It may have been a century or millennia ago. *Koire-kwente*, being conceived as a slave race, were not permitted to read by their masters. They eventually created their own written language, but we can not even guess how much time passed before they converted their oral history traditions into a written record. We first became aware of the existence of Elves three-quarters of a century ago, soon after the conclusion of World War I."

"That recently?" I mused. "Did Eldridge consider them as intrusions?"

"No. They sought Eldridge out, always in sporadic small groups, always brought by a sorceress."

"Elrameshe's predecessor, Atsemeshe."

"Correct. Though we did not understand their language, we perceived they sought asylum. We elected not to commit them to ILTS but rather harbored them in Eldridge installations until they could return safely to their world—much like the amnesty we currently offer to the Frost Giants."

"Because they are hunted by the Gray Elves' *urkāphan* as well."

Hibara nodded. "While we did so, we had a team of linguists work on deciphering their language, led by Eldridge's top philologist."

"Who was that?"

"Tolkien, of course."

If I hadn't already finished my espresso, I might have sprayed it all over the table.

"Of course," I snarked. "Given Eldridge's love of secrecy, how on Earth could you allow him to write so many books about Elves and Dwarves and such?"

"We didn't," said Ventnor. "If you must know, we were forced to mindwipe Dr. Tolkien once we learned of his ill-advised pet project. Even so, he somehow managed to retain the knowledge of the various *-kwente* tongues. We assigned his case to an adjuster, who made Tolkien believe he had contrived the languages. The adjuster wisely corrupted his recall of several basic parts of the language. We couldn't have him accidentally casting *real* Elven spells in the Mundane world."

"If you need anything further," Hibara jumped in, "Ms. Mertens can assist you in finding his mission logs—later. For now, Dr. Yeager, please concentrate on the matter at hand."

"I guess my next question is, *why* were the Forest Elves banished to a separate world? Why were they exiled at all? They were not brought to justice in front of the *Hominus Consilium*."

"That remains hidden. Just as Eldridge has adjusters and the capability to perform individual mindwipes, the *Consilium* had something much stronger at its disposal. As you conjectured, they eradicated all memory from the Forest Elves of their previous lives on *Terra Verum*. They lived peaceful lives in *Tawar Cevan* generation to generation, king to king, until their paradise was invaded by the Gray Elves, and now, seemingly, the

High Elves as well."

"And so, the *Koire-kwente*, the Forest Elves, sought refuge on our Earth."

Hibara nodded. "When the *Consilium* had broken the first barrier, it was between neighboring realities. From *Terra Verum* to either *Band Cevan* or *Tawar Cevan* was but a single step. But it was enough. Because of their precedent, the boundaries between *all* neighboring realities were weakened. Eldridge soon discovered the aftereffects: ley lines appeared, their intersections opening portals that should never have existed; creatures beyond our wildest imagination stumbled into our world; it wasn't long before other realities—and the malevolent monstrosities that inhabited them—took notice of new worlds they could lay to waste.

"If that weren't bad enough, in their haste and foolishness, the *Consilium* sent the Elves to realities that themselves were separated by a single veil. It wasn't long until the Three Sisters learned the craft necessary to cross that boundary. With their newfound ability, the High and Gray Elves resumed their practice of enslaving their creation. Although this time, they captured their prey in raiding parties, dragging as many as they could back to *Band Cevan*."

"Where are these worlds, *Band Cevan* and *Tawar Cevan*? I mean, in relation to Earth?"

"*Tawar Cevan* is adjacent to our plane of existence. Thankfully, *Band Cevan* is not."

"And yet, all three races of Elf were present to bring me back to life and place Shadow in my head. Not to mention that the Red and Blue Watchers were permitted here. And let's not forget the little problem of the Gray's *urkāphan* and the High's *Turiathurin* having the license to kill in our little slice of heaven. Why is Earth suddenly the flippin' Grand Central Station of dimensions?"

"It seems the restriction of passing more than one barrier no longer hinders the Elves."

I rubbed my forehead, hoping to digest everything being thrown at me. "Wait a minute. Let's go back a little bit. Something doesn't add up. If the entire Elven races were mindwiped, how did the Three Sisters know to seek Eldridge out?"

"Therein lies part of the riddle. Atsemeshe, at the direction of Prince Anor's father, King Nen Cuithas, brought them directly to Eldridge in search of asylum. Perhaps Prince Anor would care to shed some light on this enigma?"

After a moment to ourselves, I replied, "Shadow's as much in the dark as you are. His memories are still not complete."

"Then perhaps it is time for you and Prince Anor Cuithas to take the next step." He nodded to Netsumi, who swiveled the black lacquered box to face her.

Daintily touching the wooden ends of the small scroll within with her furred paws, she placed it in my hands. I glanced between the royal seal, Hibara, and Netsumi, squinting my misgivings all the while. Turning the scroll over exposed rune writing on the bottom. It was entirely unfamiliar to me, but Shadow translated.

"For the eyes of Anor Cuithas," I read aloud.

I asked Shadow within, "*Are you all right with me reading this?*"

"*Proceed, but be silent.*" His reply was flat and hard as a cold steel ingot.

Sighing, I added, "Well, Elrameshe said to get this to Shadow. Here goes nothing."

I broke the seal, desiccated and crazed by the decades. The long, thin paper lay in my hands, delicate with age. As I coaxed the scroll to unwind, Shadow translated the text as it was revealed. We read, his voice whispering the language of the *Koire-kwente* in my ear, and yet I still understood. By the time we finished, his resolve had inched up my spine until my brain shivered.

"*Good God, Shadow. Do you want me to reveal any of this to Eldridge?*"

"*I trust you, Michael, to hold close those things meant to be between father and son.*"

"*You know I will.*"

The king's words I had just read echoed in my head. The strength of a father's love and pride in his son blazed like a torch in the dark. I compared it against the dutiful but loveless rearing my father provided. Envy struck my heart so strong, it made my chest ache. My cheeks burned, and I sniffed back wetness that my tear ducts were more than willing to dump into my sinuses. Through a voice that wobbled a little, I mumbled Uncle Billy-Bob's sage words and eideticized the entire scroll. I placed the blank roll of parchment back in its box.

Ventnor piped out a small gasp. I expected steam.

"*Matters between the king and his legacy, however, must be made plain,"* Shadow added. *"If Eldridge is ever to trust you—to trust us—the intrigues of King Nen must be laid bare. If anything, my people owe this to Earth for giving us safe harbor, and they will need our help."*

"Hold on, there, Shadow. Do you know what you're asking of me?"

Shadow was silent for quite a while. Everyone in Hibara's room shifted nervously as I struggled with my eyebrows. After a pause long enough for me to feel pinpricks of sweat, he said, *"Yes, I do realize what I am asking and what your superiors will then undoubtedly require of you. What you tell them is your decision. I only ask, regardless of your choice, that my father's revelations never reach the ears of Barandir and my people. There is too much at risk."*

"Don't talk to me about risk, Sunshine. I think I've already risked—and lost—more than my fair share here. And what did I get in return? My parents got enchanted decades ago to hide you away at the cost of my father's life and my mother's sanity. Not to mention she's held captive by the urkāphan, who want me dead. And let's not forget the Turiathurin who wants me torn apart. Two-thirds of the Elven nations want me out of the picture. And all that, on top of the only reason I'm hanging around Eldridge in the first place—Sindhu's locked in the deep freeze twenty-plus levels underground, with no one but me to change her back to human, and helping you puts her life on the line as well. How's that for risk?"

"There is one hope I can hold out for you. You might finally be rid of me and the Red Watcher."

"You think I haven't considered that? Well, there's one big problem in the way, buckaroo. Who's gonna be the new vessel? Whose body? Who are you going to kill—and that's even assuming the Three Witches will be in the mood to risk their own collective kiester a second time, casting a spell that could get them the High and Gray equivalent of a firing squad?"

"Yes, I know the situation... I believe your word is... sucks. But consider all that I have lost, all that my people have suffered, and what I fear they will ultimately lose."

I wanted to toss Shadow and everything else out the window, head straight to my favorite San Jose hole-in-the-wall, and lose myself in a bottle of crappy tequila. The only thing keeping me from going on a mission to drown myself in rotgut was an almost certain future as a mindwiped homeless drunk, cursing the gods under some nameless California bridge, leaving Sindhu forever sealed in a frozen prison I would never remember.

I crumpled into my seat, my head in my hands. Feet shuffled expectantly around me. A gentle hand touched my shoulder. I looked up, searching for the friendly face attached to that hand. I found Netsumi's eyes—feral, yet the kindest pair in the room. She replaced the espresso with a tall, sweating glass of ice water. I sipped, and man, did it feel wonderful.

By the time I downed the whole thing, I reached a decision. Or rather, I shuffled the decision into Hibara's lap. "Shadow has requested I share the contents of the scroll with you." Closing my eyes, called up the eideticized runes. I thrilled with a moment of revelation. I read and *understood* the runes. Shadow was quiet. He wasn't reading them aloud in my head as I had expected. Perhaps another benefit from good ol' Uncle Billy-Bob?

One good thing—it made the discreet omission of the Cuithas family's personal portions of the scroll loads easier.

"Like most kings, he tends to be formal and long-winded. I'll boil it down as best I can." All the better to keep management's noses out of Shadow's personal business.

"The communiqué begins with the usual 'if you're reading this, I must be dead' spiel. King Nen Cuithas was informed by Elrameshe that her counterparts of the Three Sisters sought refuge. Not in *Tawar Cevan*, but on Earth. The reason? Decreed by their lieges, the High and Gray sisters had been forced to create a terrible new magic.

"Though the scroll didn't give specifics, it says they smuggled this frightening knowledge out of their kingdoms and their world. They did promise their new magic was so powerful it would enable the High and Gray kings to seek horrible revenge upon the *Consilium*, the entire *Hominus* race, and ultimately conquer *Terra Verum*."

With a snort, Ventnor snipped, "What proof is there of such a thing?"

"Where do you think the *Turiathurin* came from? To use an engineering term, that monster is their 'proof of concept.' Imagine a whole army of those nightmares wreaking havoc upon their exiled home."

"Or our world," said Hibara, solemn as a monk. "They have already proven they can pierce the boundary from *Band Cevan* through *Tawar Cevan* to our Earth."

"What reason would they have?" scoffed Ventnor. "All the *urkāphan*, agents of the Gray, are dead. Their knowledge of Anor Cuithas is lost."

"Maybe so for the *urkāphan*," said Hibara, cutting him off. "Not so in the case of the *Turiathurin*." Hibara removed the cuff link from his left sleeve and exposed his forearm. Eight ragged slashes raked across his reedy arm. It was difficult to tell how deep the injury went, as all that were left were pink scars, thanks to his own membership in the Circle.

"I banished it at the end of our *disagreement*," he said, driving home the point by raising his cane. "I had hoped to some outer realm, but Mr. Barandir has confirmed it has somehow returned to *Tawar Cevan*."

"You were attacked by the *Turiathurin*?" Petrakis muttered, aghast. "Here, on this floor?"

He dismissed the others' concern with a simple shake of his head with closed eyes. "No. I was waylaid while returning from travels. The work to find new members for the School of Five Magics needed my assistance. Regardless of where the attack occurred, we must now assume the High and Gray Elves are aware that Yeager is alive and that Prince Cuithas exists."

"Oh, they know, all right," I grumbled loudly. "Lenoir pieced it together. They both have been sending forces to kill me. Every time they sent an agent through the two boundaries, it created a natural disaster here on Earth. Centered smack dab where they cross over."

"So where does Shadow fit in?" asked Petrakis.

"I think I know, based on everything we've discovered and what I've experienced. The Three Sisters had traveled to *Tawar Cevan* with their petition for asylum to King Nen Cuithas when the *Turiathurin* attacked. The Three Sisters transported the Queen Consort, Prince Anor, and the Regent to the nearest ley line intersection on Earth, near Anchorage. But the other Elves and the *Turiathurin* followed. Since they were from *Band Cevan*, not directly connected to Earth, their crossing caused an earthquake. You know the rest. Prince Anor was slain, and the Sisters transferred his spirit—soul, essence, whatchamacallit—into my head, raising us together as one living being. With the lifeless body of Prince Anor returned to *Tawar Cevan*, I think they hoped to fool the High and Gray Elves while Atsemeshe guided my parents to protect me and Shadow, until he could return and fight another day."

"What about this revenge spell? Where are the Three Sisters now?" drilled Ventnor.

"You'll have to ask them. I can only assume the High and Gray kings have neither the spell nor the Sisters yet. Otherwise, we'd be hip-deep in *turiathurin* crap by now."

"Does this mean you will take up Shadow's fight?" said Hibara. He scrutinized me again, probably digging once more at the urgent question of where my ultimate allegiance lay.

"Do I have a choice?" I snapped, rolling my eyes at the ceiling. "Even if I sit here and twiddle my thumbs, sooner or later, the *Turiathurin* will come for me, more *urkāphan* will decide to take a couple more pot-shots, or worst of all, downtown Sacramento and this building's gonna come down in the mother of all earthquakes, mud-slide, or tornado."

With everyone in it, including Sindhu.

Inside my head, I heard a whisper of gratitude. "*Thank you, Michael.*"

"It is settled then." Hibara rose from his seat, with his cane in one hand, and Netsumi assisting him by his free arm. They shuffled with slow, careful steps to the conjuring table. Netsumi muttered a phrase I couldn't quite make out. Something told me I didn't want to know.

The first time I entered this room, I had officially signed the Oath on a decorative tray, becoming a full employee of Eldridge & S.Q.Amos, Inc. On the conjuring table appeared that very same tray, holding another official-looking legal-sized parchment and a small oblong box bearing the Mont Blanc logo.

Hibara took out his own pen. I couldn't tell its make, but it looked handmade and would probably set me back more than a week's salary. He jotted out a few lines on the document, filling in the blanks scattered throughout, finishing with his signature at the bottom. From a small vest pocket, he produced a stone cylinder the size of a lipstick. He popped off the top half of the cylinder, exposing a freshly inked symbol. He stamped the document, leaving a small red circle inscribing three ginkgo leaves next to his signature.

Hibara approached me with Netsumi in tow as she carried the tray. She pressed the levers that dropped its hideaway legs and set the impromptu table in front of me. "Please read and sign," instructed Hibara.

Oh, crud.

"You want me to be an *adjuster*?!" I yelped, shoving the table back at Netsumi. Ventnor shook himself like he was on the receiving end of a bitch-slap. As for myself, all my misgivings spilled out.

"Oh, *nononono* you don't," I babbled, faster than Jerry Lewis. "I *can't* be an adjuster—I don't have the seniority. You don't know what you're asking. I'm going to be the worst—I don't even know half my

ATPG responsibilities as it is now. What about an assessor? I thought you had to be an assessor first. Besides, what am I supposed to do as an adjuster? I don't know the first thing about adjusting. Trust me, you don't want me throwing monkey wrenches into reality. You don't want me as an adjuster—*period*. Mainly because *I* don't want it." I thumped my chest. It wasn't nearly as imposing as I hoped it would be.

"You think we *want* to make you an adjuster?" trumpeted Ventnor, shouting me down. "We have no choice. You have Shadow."

"To accomplish your next assignment, it is a necessity. Please sign," repeated Hibara.

Netsumi opened the box, proffering the Mont Blanc contained inside to me. I ignored her, taking Amelia from my pocket. Petrakis' and Ventnor's eyes went wide, my mentor shaking his head in a mild scolding fashion.

Netsumi insisted, pushing the box forward over my hand. Her amber eyes were a command.

"You're not making me give up Amelia, are you?"

"No." Hibara's answer dripped ice and left no room for disobedience. "Sign."

I frowned my misgivings, placed Amelia on the tray, and extracted the Mont Blanc from its form-fitting case. Its heft and balance were immaculate, the type that promised hours of writing with ease.

I held my breath. Time came to a standstill. I saw my life flash before my eyes. Things would never be the same. Yada yada yada.

"I hope I'm doing the right thing, Sindhu." Was it a prayer?

I signed. There was that prick on my finger again, the one I feared might come despite Hibara's promise. A drop of blood slicked between my finger and the pen. I completed my signature in red.

A loud crack announced itself, which the tray amplified. A sonic boom directly above my head would have been less painful. Amelia lay broken in half on the tray, her ink well bleeding royal blue.

"You sonova—" I chomped my teeth together, clacking almost as loud as Amelia's death knell. I gripped the Mont Blanc in my fist hard enough to break its casing as well. "—*whore*!"

Petrakis and Ventnor paled whiter than hospital sheets. Netsumi growled, her fur bristling and her remaining three tails jumping ramrod straight.

"That was *Amelia*. You *killed* her!"

A furry hand pulled my head back by the hair, and an edge bit into my throat. "Unlike my counterparts, my knife is real."

Hibara stared me in the eye. "Let us reason together, Dr. Yeager. How does one kill something that cannot know death?"

We both took deep breaths. My shoulders unknotted. Once he observed that I had relented, he nodded at Netsumi. Silent as a silken breeze, her knife disappeared into a fold of the waistband cinching her kimono. I dabbed at my Adam's apple. No blood. Good—I'd hate to explain another suspiciously stained shirt to my dry cleaner.

Netsumi plucked the pen from my aching fingers, reverently placing it back in its box. Closing its lid, she returned it to me with a curt bow.

Hibara leaned in close to one ear. "Given your practice of giving your scribe a name, you might as well use the correct one. Her name is *Sindhu*."

My jaw dropped, as well as most of the blood from my face, I imagine. Swooning where I stood was definitely in the cards. I managed to whisper, "*What?*"

"She has been with you all this time, from the moment you signed the Oath. Except during those episodes where Sun Bin siphoned off her energy. I trust you will take extra special care of her now?"

"Fer crying out..." I sputtered. I tried recalling... *Sonovagun*, Hibara was right. I never used my scribe while I poked around ILTS or when the Valdaan was on the rampage. She spent almost the entire time in my desk drawer. "*Why*? Why didn't you tell me?"

Hibara watched and waited, implacable.

"Why couldn't *she* tell me?"

"She is bound by the rules of a scribe. She cannot recall her previous life."

"But why," I continued, holding back tears, "*why* make her a scribe? Why not keep her safe in the ILTS?"

"Remember the horror of the Void, Dr. Yeager? If the status chamber is not properly attuned to its occupant, it is torture. Her chamber was attuned to the human half of her body. We had hoped the Void might drive out the Euryale intrusion."

Glubbing out a few unintelligible syllables, my mind hugged itself, trying to find warmth. The memory of the Void still had the power to freeze my thinking process down to its core; still had the power to yank the bloody bandage off my darkest fears; still had the power to remind me what damnation feels like.

I shivered, nearly toppling again, imagining that Hell forced upon Sindhu.

Then, the totality of Hibara's intimation hit me. Of course, she wasn't just a human. I had seen her in the Void. As she *truly* was. "She's... not...?" I couldn't bring myself to finish the question.

Hibara stared at me. His eyes cut into my soul. "At first, we were not sure what she was. It wasn't until her image was caught on video that the three of us began to realize the truth. Her appearance to you and Drs. Petrakis and Hatahali, in her truest form, confirmed our suspicion."

Hibara's voice took on a gentle aspect, that of a bedside manner. "Dr. Yeager, I assume you are familiar with a being known as a *yakshini*."

Revelations that I had never pieced together before hit me with mind-numbing force. The lotus mandala that she favored in her art. The same design on the forehead of her spirit. Lenoir's third-degree taunt: *No record of your Sindhu Mehra in New Delhi—nor in all of India*. Their damned stupid company name: *They're Hindu spirits of nature and prosperity*.

I collapsed back into my chair, my world shaken to the point of collapse.

What have I been living with for so many years?

But I loved her.

I love her.

God help me, I *still* love her.

I don't know how, but I managed to find my voice. "Yes. She is a *yakshini*." I buried my face in my hands. "She's an *intrusion*."

"There is no longer doubt you are an intrusion nexus, Dr. Yeager. Evidently, the Elven races are not the only intrusions interested in you. We are still trying to understand how she has gone unnoticed all these years. Perhaps she is natural to our world."

He began pacing the room again, leaning hard on his cane. This time around, however, he restricted his circuits to the area rug, his hypnotic cane muffled. "During your training in company orientation, we became aware Ms. Mehra was in dire distress in her capsule. Having determined she was an intrusion, we examined her history, with special attention to her time with you at university. Though the being inhabiting her was not of this physical world, Netsumi did not sense any malice. I therefore extended her intrusion asylum, under the authority vested in my

Office by Eldridge & S.Q.Amos. I assigned her as a scribe, one of the few ways other than ILTS that we can constrain a rogue spirit. Assigned to you, she was designated as RPIN."

"So, you see, my friend," said Petrakis, "your life was *never* in jeopardy from Rule 4."

"Just as your new position affords you new perquisites paired with your responsibilities, the same is true for your scribe." Standing over me, Hibara tapped the box's Mont Blanc logo twice with his index finger. "Do not make me regret my decision, Dr. Yeager."

I searched his face through bleary eyes. "Why are you telling me this? What are you asking me to do?"

"Netsumi, please have Mr. Barandir join us."

The ponderous double doors swung open, revealing a picture-perfect outer waiting area—every chair righted and in its place; the reception desk ordered and polished; the carpet devoid of torn paper and red ribbon. The scent of fresh cleaner rolled into our room. With the exception of Barandir and the ever-pleasant Ms. Emerald, every other living creature had vamoosed. She held the door open, inviting Barandir back into Hibara's reception parlor. The poor Elf's face bore the blistered shock of a kid who just walked into their parents having sex.

"Mr. Barandir," began Hibara, "thank you for your patience. I wanted to thank you for your exemplary bravery in *Tawar Cevan*, and for bringing us the information contained in Elrameshe's box."

Resuming his detached demeanor, Barandir clasped his hands behind his muddied and bloodied jerkin. His eyes, however, remained on high alert, flicking from person to person in quick order. They came to rest on the burned-out amulet, and the unraveled scroll lying in the black lacquered *lûth colca*.

"When we are finished here," said Hibara, "please get yourself down to medical for a thorough check and take a personal day to attend to any additional physical needs. Starting the day after tomorrow, prepare your report on everything that transpired in *Tawar Cevan*, including any intelligence you may have gathered and recommendations for action. Have it on Dr. Petrakis' desk one week from today."

He leaned forward, turning his head at an inquiring angle. "Are we not going to assist Elrameshe?"

"I share your concern for the Forest Sister. However, one does not go rushing into a hostile situation unprepared." He held up a finger and dotted the air. "Which brings me to my next point. As the sole citizen of *Tawar Cevan* present, I require you to bear witness to an event of no small import. Before we proceed, you will be pleased to know Dr. Yeager has been promoted to Adjuster Second Class." Barandir regarded me with a gaze that hovered somewhere between confusion and awe. He really needed to get his emotions more under control—more than I and my eyebrows. "He will lead a sortie to *Tawar Cevan*, carrying out whatever plan your recommendations lead us to decide."

"I'll be *what*?" I spluttered.

Hibara ignored my outburst. "Mr. Barandir, you shall be Dr. Yeager's guide in *Tawar Cevan*. However, he and Prince Anor Cuithas will need additional protections you cannot provide." Hibara looked at me knowingly. Except he wasn't looking at *me*. "Neither can an adjuster. There is a special title and office that must be filled, and its responsibilities shouldered. Are you prepared?"

From within came Shadow's irrefutable whisper. *"Michael, there is something I need you to say and do."*

"Must I?" I mewled like a child.

"I heard you think it. Even though the Kala-kwente may send monsters hungering for your flesh, and Mori-kwente may send legions of assassins against you, your thoughts remained centered around Sindhu. She might be with you in spirit as your scribe now, but remember—I have lived your life with you. Every moment with her is locked in my heart as well. You don't require me to convince you that you need her, body and spirit, reunited…

"Do it for her, *Michael."*

"You fight dirty, Shadow."

"You forget. I am a prince. Royalty doesn't always play fair."

I heard my own snark in his voice. I couldn't resist a fatalistic chuckle.

My chest ached as I took a deep breath, imagining it might be my last taken as a free man. Shadow spoke a few sentences in his own runic tongue. I collected the ring from Elrameshe's box and put it on my right hand's ring finger. I was impressed but not surprised when it cinched to my size after sliding it on.

Shadow spoke, and I echoed his words aloud. I had no clue what he said, yet I knew their meaning the instant I uttered them. As I spoke, I also took the golden circlet from Elrameshe's ebony box, raising it before me.

The confusion in Barandir's eyes doubled. I suspect he was torn between the reflex to genuflect and the desire to slay the infidel who dared claim the royal signet. God save me from hero worship. I repeated Shadow's decree in English in his voice.

"I, Anor Cuithas, son of King Nen Cuithas and Queen Consort Nîdh Sirith, claim my birthright as King of the *Koire-kwente*. I shall accept the mantle in that fullness of time when the Forest Sister Elrameshe unlocks the Salamander Wreath and lays it upon my head."

"And you better be out of my head when that moment comes, Shadow," I groused deep inside.

The room remained silent as I sealed the crown in Elrameshe's box and handed the container to Barandir. I was the first to breathe again. "Now what?"

Netsumi and Emerald shuffled over to the sliding portal doors. Hibara uttered a phrase, and they slid open the doors, revealing a tiled corridor receding into darkness.

"Now," Hibara said without skipping a beat, "to prepare for your journey, you must learn everything an Adjuster Second Class needs to know. However, time is against you. Fortunately, we have an expert tutor."

A *clop-clop* of wooden shoes reverberated from the corridor. Out of the inky depth strode a mass of red covering a massive build and a ridiculous beak. No way on Earth I could mistake that mammoth man-bird for anyone but Caltrop.

"Tokyo's *Tengu*! You didn't tell me it would be Yeager." His beak creaked as he attempted his unnerving smile. "Now, Adjuster Second Class —drop and gimme twenty. No, make it thirty!"

Oh, crud.

THE END

<u>A request from the Author!</u>

I hope you enjoyed reading this work, as much as I did writing it. It would greatly help me if you file a rating or review on:

☑ Amazon
☑ Goodreads
☑ Your favorite bookstore's website
☑ All of the above!

Thanks!

GLOSSARY

Latin

Annulus Habilitas — Aptitude Ring
Lapidibus Habilitas — Aptitude Stones

Terra Verum — "True" Earth
Consilium — High Council of *Terra Verum*
Regis — leader of the *Consilium*
Hominus — inhabitants of *Terra Verum*

Forest and High Elvish

Kala-kwente — "those who live in light," High Elves
Koire-kwente — "those who live in the forest," Forest Elves
Mori-kwente — "those who live in darkness," Gray Elves

Band Cevan — "prison world"
Cirbann Cevan — Earth
Tawar Cevan — "forest world"

Turia Feir — "watcher of mortal men," Blue Watcher
Turia Taurē — "watcher of the forest," Red Watcher
Turiathurin — "guardian of secrets"

Lûth colca — "black box" used by the Three Sisters
Peradlon — "half outsider"

Gray Elvish

Lon Keman — Earth
Mbandō Keman — "prison world"
Taurē Keman — "forest world"
Phelek Lepan — "Great Cave of the Five"

Karani Tur — "Red Watcher"
Luin Tur — "Blue Watcher"
urkāphan — "horrible shape/veil," Gray Elf assassin

Japanese

fuan'na kimoi — "unnerving", "gross"

Mandarin

qíngrén — "lover"
tiánxīn — "sweetie"

www.ingramcontent.com/pod-product-compliance
Lightning Source LLC
Chambersburg PA
CBHW020639120726
47906CB00001B/35